The Order of the Scrolls Series

CURSEBREAKER

NANCY WENTZ

WHITAKER
HOUSE

Publisher's note:
This novel is a work of fiction. References to real events, organizations, or places are used in a fictional context. Any resemblances to actual persons, living or dead, are entirely coincidental.

Scripture quotations are taken from the King James Version of the Holy Bible.

CURSEBREAKER

First in the Order of the Scrolls Series

ISBN: 978-1-60374-080-7
Printed in the United States of America

Whitaker House
1030 Hunt Valley Circle
New Kensington, PA 15068
www.whitakerhouse.com

Library of Congress Cataloging-in-Publication Data

Wentz, Nancy, 1965–
Cursebreaker / by Nancy Wentz.
p. cm.
Summary: "Fictional story of a young boy in Depression-era Colorado discovering his prophetic gift and combating an Italian Mafia family with a generational curse of demonic possession"—Provided by publisher.
ISBN 978-1-60374-080-7 (trade pbk. : alk. paper)
1. Boys—Fiction. 2. Prophets—Fiction. 3. Demoniac possession—Fiction. 4. Mafia—Fiction. 5. Colorado—Fiction. 6. Depressions—1929—Colorado—Fiction. I. Title.
PS3623.E59C87 2008
813'.6—dc22
2008036116

1 2 3 4 5 6 7 8 9 10 12 ш 16 15 14 13 12 11 10 09

Dedication

To Mickey and Christian.
Soli Deo Gloria.

Prologue

Winter, 1565
Italy

A turbulent wind assaulted the night, moaning through the graveyard, enjoining dead leaves to swirl about his feet. He steadied his lantern, squinting at the tombstones that stretched before him. They rose like apparitions, enlivened by the shadows of barren trees caught in the light. Twigs clutched at his hooded cloak. He pulled at them impatiently.

Stealing upon a humble grave, laid amidst murderers, paupers, and the unbaptized, he knelt to decipher the etchings. Worn by time, the tombstone almost denied him the name of its dead. He pushed back his cowl and traced the engraving with his finger.

Frate Domenicano Salvatore Ansaldo
1471—1550
Dio ha la compassione sulla sua anima maledetta

Swinging a canvas bag from his shoulder, he extracted from it a shovel and a pickax. He tossed his cloak over the tombstone. The night air felt good against his flesh as he labored to exhume the grave.

He stopped once at a sound. His dark eyes scanned the eerie monuments leaning askew before him—silent witnesses watching without eyes, listening without ears, curious and apprehensive at his presence. Ignoring the uneasiness that stiffened the hair on his arms, he continued digging.

The shovel struck the coffin with a hollow thud. He fell to his knees, swept the dirt from the box, and grabbed the pickax, stabbing the corroded wood repeatedly until the lid lifted with no more resistance than a groan. The stench of mold permeated the air. He reached for the lantern, which reflected off the shaved crown of his head. Startled shadows leaped from the grave like souls before the judgment.

Death had paid the Dominican friar no homage. It had robbed him of his flesh and feasted on his bones. Fragments of the burial shroud remained adhered to their owner, as did gray hair to his skull. His gaping mouth, lacking several teeth, protested in silence the desecration of his grave.

Upon the corpse lay a wooden crucifix, the rosary entwining the fingers. The robber scanned the body, hesitantly patting the shroud. Finding nothing, the hope of discovery waned until he slipped his hands beneath the corpse. At his touch, the rib cage crumpled, rippling around his wrists as he delved, until his fingers grasped two scrolls. Shaking off the human remains, he placed the scrolls in the bag, climbed from the hole, and reburied the defiled dead.

He made haste to the monastery. In his cell, he barred the door and released his cowl to the floor. After lighting several candles to alleviate the darkness, he pulled the scrolls from the bag, gingerly spreading them across a wooden table. Though they had lain in the grave with corrupting flesh, he was amazed to find them unsullied, written upon with an odd shade of russet ink. He drew a candle closer. Choosing one, he read:

Et ait ei tibi dabo potestatem hanc universam et gloriam illorum quia mihi tradita sunt et cui volo do illa tu ergo si adoraveris coram me erunt tua omnia.

The pounding of his heart quickened. The legend was true—he had found the scrolls.

The Gregorian chant of distant choristers broke the early morning silence. He gasped—he had forgotten the Eucharist! He glanced at the painting on the stone wall, the fair Madonna enfolding the Christ Child in her arms, then looked back at the scroll. The reddish ink was smudged. He peered at it suspiciously. His eyes widened. *Blood.* It was written in blood.

Invitarme che cerca il potere e la fortuna nell'abbondanza. Invitarme che cerca i misteri del buio. Inviterà Lucifer.

Chills crept up his back. He crossed himself. Were not these words against the sacred Scripture? It was blasphemy. Heresy. Was he not risking his soul? Yet the words were so clear; did they not offer him the world? He glanced at the Madonna and Child again, then back at the scroll. The garnet rosary about his neck tapped against the table.

Chiunque invita Lucifer offrirà la sua anima, e ciò del secondo maschio nella sua casa per tutte le generazioni.

All the power of the world and the glory thereof was at his fingertips—his, Luccio Frattarelli—the abbot of the church of the Spirito Santo. With the heightening of his voice, the words fell from his lips:

La mia fedeltà, la mia anima, il mio corpo che do a Lucifer. Invito Lucifer a essere il mio padrone. Visito il suo demone potentemente, Il Governatore del Rotolo, vivere nel mio corpo.

Death took Luccio by surprise. The scroll slipped from his hands as he grasped at his heart. He tumbled backward over a chair, his sandaled feet kicking the floor in wild succession. A trembling cold seized his frame, congealing the blood in his veins. Then, struck with the conviction of his fate, his eyes opened in terror upon the Madonna and Child, and his breath ceased.

Moments passed as he lay there, his body not feeling the cold morning air. Then, a blistering gust swirled through the cell, scorching the wood, singeing the cowl, burning the painted images beyond recognition. The eyelids began to flutter, the eyebrows to twitch, the chest to rise and fall with regular breathing. The muscles in the arms and legs stretched as if released from bondage.

When the eyes opened, the life behind them was not that of Luccio Frattarelli.

One

Winter, 1931
Colorado, United States of America

A scream escaped the boy's lips. The startling pain across his left ear and cheek jerked his head to the side. His eyes snapped open. Looking around with the shocked confusion of broken sleep, he cringed to see the black pillar leaning over his bed.

"I ain't done nothin', Pa!"

"Get up."

He glanced out the window. A breath of air shook the broken pane, scraping the ice-frosted curtains against each other. Beyond them, the stars were bright against the sky.

"I ain't heard the rooster—"

Even as he spoke, he threw up his arms to shield his face. The hand came down hard against his head. It knocked his arms out of the way and found his throbbing ear once more.

"Get up, or I'll throw you down those stairs."

Shielding his ear, he strove to sit up. It wasn't fast enough. That hand seized him—

"No!"

—yanked him from his narrow bed—

"Not the stairs again!"

—and flung him toward the bedroom door. The blanket strangled his feet. He reeled across the floor, collided with the washstand, and fell on his back. Wresting away the blanket, he just escaped his father's boots as they stomped an inch from his fingers.

"Start the fire."

Coiled against the wall, he watched his father's rigid silhouette leave the room. He listened to the tread on the staircase, the steps through the kitchen below, and the slam of the back door. All was silent. Only then did he move. He stood on trembling legs, the warped floorboards creaking beneath his weight.

Testing the movement of his jaw, he cupped his ear and swallowed against the pain that traveled down his neck. His face felt hot.

"You all right?" a voice whispered from the darkness.

He looked at his two older brothers lying huddled together under a single blanket. The head of the oldest lifted, his youthful profile barely discernable.

"Yeah." The boy rubbed the bones of his chest through a tear in his long underwear.

"Stay clear of Pa." The profile sank back into the bed. "Today's the day Ma died."

The recollection shocked him. He felt sick to his stomach and wondered how long that pillar had stood over his bed.

Picking up his overalls from the floor, he maneuvered his feet into the threadbare pant legs. While securing the straps to the bib with safety pins, he slipped his naked feet into his boots, scrunching his toes against the cracked soles.

Not having heard the squeak of the back door, he went downstairs without fear, pulling a woolen coat across his shoulders. Finding a lantern burning in the kitchen, he took it and stepped outside.

The November chill seeped through his clothes. He looked at the moon, blew a warm stream of air from his mouth toward it, and watched the steam evaporate. The moon's glow beautified the farm to a shimmering, snowy landscape, but he saw no beauty there, only the skeleton of the plow, the empty corral, the sinister corner behind the chicken coop—a myriad of hiding places where his father might lurk. It was then his fear returned; somewhere in that darkness was his father.

He crept along the snow-covered path, afraid the sound of his boots would give him away. Placing the lantern by the door of the woodshed, he paused to wipe his bangs out of his eyes, his gaze traveling to the barn set against the open prairie, an expanse of blackness where nothing moved. A lantern burned within, emitting light between the loose-fitting boards. He heard the horse's neigh, the worried screech of a chicken, and the thud of an ax against wood. He had found his father.

Snatching an armload of wood, he ran back inside the house. As he hurried to build a fire in the kitchen stove, his mind raced to find places where he could hide. *The root cellar? No, too easy to be found. What about the barn down the road, or the lake? Yeah, the lake.* He could break through the ice. Maybe if he caught some fish, Pa wouldn't beat him that night.

No sooner had he decided where to run than the warmth of the fire encouraged him to linger. Daring to place an additional stick on the quivering flames, he dragged a chair from the table before the stove. He would run when he heard his father's step on the back porch, but for now, the glow of the crackling wood was too good to leave.

He fell asleep.

He did not hear the steps. He did not hear the door open. For a surreal moment, he hovered between dreaming and waking, feeling the brush of his mother's apron, the smell of bread. Then the door slammed. A rush of air stirred his hair like an icy hand. With a gasp, he spun around. Gazing up into the beardless face, an image flashed in his mind of the scarecrow suspended in the cornfield—that frayed figure no threat of storm could move. He feared its claw-like arms that stretched out for an embrace; he knew well the terror of that embrace. He bolted from the chair, knocking it over.

"Pick it up."

The words stopped him cold. Returning, he righted the chair, keeping his eyes averted and his hands ready to push it forward if his father made any abrupt movements.

"Sit down."

He teetered on his feet, debating whether to run out the back door or the front, when he noticed what was in his father's hands. In one dangled the downy body of a freshly killed chicken; in the other, the bloody cleaver.

He sat down.

"Remember your Ma?" His father tossed the chicken and the cleaver on the table.

"Yeah." The sight of the headless chicken set off a nervous spasm in his stomach.

"It's been three years. I reckoned you'd forgot."

An anxious moment of silence hung between them. Risking a glance, he found his father's unblinking gaze fixed on him. Yellow flames from the lantern quivered in his green eyes. When he spoke, his mouth revealed the bottom row of his stained teeth.

"She was a good woman. Kept this place nice. Didn't have much, but she made it stretch."

Removing his straw hat, he began to pace the floor. The sound of his boots scraping the wood sent a shudder down the boy's spine. He looked back at the chicken.

"I miss her cookin'. I miss her gettin' mad when I tracked in dirt. I miss watchin' her wash her hair and dryin' it front of the stove. She never fussed over nothin'—" he stopped his deliberate tread, "—except you. 'My baby's sick,' she'd say."

The hat slipped from his soiled fingers to the floor. He leaned close to the boy's ear.

"Then you got the fever."

His father's breath on his neck caused him to look around wildly. His shoulders flinched with expectation.

"She made me sell the cow to pay the doctor. I told her she already had two strong boys. Better to keep the cow. Then *she* got the fever."

The hand seized the boy's neck and squeezed.

"She died...and you got better."

With a jerk, his father spun him around, knocking the chair over. He lifted the boy close to his face.

"Why ain't it *you* rottin' in that graveyard?"

"I'm sorry, Pa." Tears stung the boy's eyes. His chin quivered.

"I should've drowned you in the river like a runt."

The fist rose like a pendulum.

"No! I'm sorry!"

It hailed on his head, cutting short his screams, blurring his vision with flashes of red. He felt his body being thrashed back and forth. The hand twisting his clothing nearly choked off his breath.

"Stop it, Pa!"

The beating stopped. Warmth trickled from his nose and mouth as he sagged in his father's grip. Through the spinning room, he saw his brothers in the doorway in their long underwear, their brown hair mussed.

The oldest stepped forward. "Let him go. It ain't his fault, and you know it."

"He killed her as true as I'm standin' here. He's got every bit of it comin'."

"It ain't his fault, and beatin' him ain't gonna bring her back. Nothin's bringin' her back. She's dead."

Staggering as if struck from behind, he pressed the boy backward against the table, his neck on the chicken's carcass.

"I know! I know, but she was everything...all I had... since we were kids...all I wanted." Anguish creased his tanned forehead. Sobs he could no longer control heaved in his chest until he laid his head on the boy's chest, wailing.

The boy dared not move. He shot his brothers a terrified plea with his eyes, but they, too, stood motionless.

"It ain't right that she died." He lifted his head, his face flushed, wet, the veins in his forehead and neck pulsating. "It ain't right that he lived."

He seized the cleaver and lifted it high.

The boys shrieked in unison, "No!"

Still caught in the trap of that great hand, the boy threw up his arms. Light glinted off the cleaver as it plummeted, its edge slicing across his uplifted palm. He felt no pain, just the keen sensation of his flesh opening, sending a streak of blood across his father's face.

The cleaver rose again. His brothers rushed forward. In a skirmishing blur of hands, he saw the cleaver pushed aside. His father reared back, shouting. Saliva dripped from his lips. One brother fell to the floor. The cleaver rose again. He closed his eyes. Screaming. A crack. A grunt.

He felt himself pulled to the floor by the hand that would not let go. Blood sprayed in every direction as he kicked and screamed, helpless until his brothers freed him and dragged him to the other side of the kitchen.

"Stop squirmin'!"

The oldest held his brother's wrist, forcing open his clenched fingers to inspect the gash while the other tried to soothe him. Too terrified to be calmed, he continued to scream, to struggle, even though his father lay motionless on the floor, the fire poker beside him.

Turning him away from the sight, they held him close until he settled into a quiet sob. The oldest then brought him to his feet. Grabbing a rag from the table, he wiped the tears that rolled down the boy's cheeks.

"Listen," he said, wrapping the rag around the bleeding

hand. “You need your wits. Run away. He’ll kill you next time. Go to town. Find Uncle Harald. Here’s your cap.”

Their father groaned. All stared at him for a silent moment, then rushed to the door.

“Run fast. Don’t tell nobody your name. Don’t let the sheriff catch you neither. He’ll bring you back or put you in the orphanage and work you till you drop dead.”

His brothers hugged him, then sent him out into the cold. He ran with one glance back, one final look at his brothers standing in the doorway. Into the darkness he ran, leaving a scattered trail of tears and blood behind.

Two

Denver, Colorado

Louie Fratelli always sat with his back to a wall—never against a window or a door. He had seen friends shot that way at the races or in barbershops; he had killed enemies that way in their homes.

Tonight, Tony Garda's back was to the door.

The bell rang above the door of Romano's Restaurant as two men entered along with the chill night air. The lit candles on each white tablecloth flickered in the breeze. Dusting the snow from their overcoats, the men sat at a window table that seemed prepared for them and waited.

Louie scanned the restaurant under his black eyebrows, observing that Tony and he were the only Italians. The rest were white men seated in pairs, speaking in low tones, wearing blue or gray suits with blue or gray fedoras. Although the kitchen conveyed the tempting aroma of sausage, pasta, and bread, no one had ordered food.

"You look like you've had a rough time," Louie said. "Where you been hiding?"

"Who says I've been hiding?" Tony flipped up the collar of his weatherworn jacket, concealing his neck as the brim of his hat concealed his face. His hunched shoulders twitched involuntarily.

"Heard you been eating at the soup kitchen. You can

always get a swell meal at Papa's. How's come you don't come around?"

"That's why you found me? To make sure I'm eating?"

Louie listened in vain for the clatter of dishes from the kitchen or the cooks shouting in Italian. One waiter maneuvered between the tables with a pot of coffee, quietly refilling cups. Occasionally, the men looked toward his table. Louie counted twelve. He took a final drag on his cigarette and crushed it the ashtray.

"All these suits and not a dame among them. It's screwy."

Tony slouched into the table, crossing his arms, peering back over his collar. Through the half-closed Venetian blinds, he saw a woman attempt to enter. A man in a bluish gray suit appeared and ushered her away.

"Who are they?"

"G-men. Maybe they fingered you for killing that Pompliano mug." The melted wax on the white candle between them threatened to douse the flame. With his thumbnail, Louie diverted the pool into the holder and the flame grew bright. "You can't beat a murder rap. You already got two strikes against you. You'll get pinched for life."

Uneasiness flashed in Tony's brown eyes. He rubbed his wan, unshaven face. One foot started tapping nervously.

"Are you packing a rod?" Louie asked.

The foot stopped tapping. "You think I'd pull a gun in a room full of cops? What kind of chump you figure me for?"

"One that don't wanna go down a third time."

Tony leaned back in his chair. Both feet started tapping. "What's the game? You setting me up?"

Louie slapped his round chest, looking hurt. "Would I squeal on a pal?"

"Maybe."

"What do you take me for? Ain't I always watched your back?"

"I don't like this. Something ain't right."

"Answer the question. Are you carrying?"

"Yeah."

"Swell. Let's beat it. You can lay dormy at the Fratelli Estate till the heat's off."

Louie brought his black fedora low over his eyes and buttoned the jacket of his pinstripe suit. They stood, and the twelve other men all stood simultaneously. Those near the windows closed the blinds. Ignoring this, Tony and Louie started toward the door when two of the men maneuvered in front of them.

"Leaving, boys?" one asked with a cheeky grin. "You haven't had your spaghetti."

"We're allergic to badges." Louie's fingers twitched as he unbuttoned his jacket.

"Maybe you'd like to eat downtown. I hear they're serving rigatoni at the jail."

"Why we gotta go downtown?" Tony demanded.

"Why do you think, sap? We're sending you up the river, where murderers belong."

"You got nothing," Louie said, edging away from Tony.

"Nothing but an indictment. You coming quiet-like, or you gonna give us trouble?"

Louie set his lips back against his teeth. He shoved the cop aside and took a large step backward. Reaching inside his jacket, he shouted, "Don't let them take you, Tony!"

By reflex, Tony's arm jerked toward his coat. He stopped himself instantly. Every cop drew his gun from the holster hidden inside his suit. With the synchronized sound of clicking hammers, a dozen guns appeared—all aimed at Tony.

He threw his arms above his head. "Don't shoot!"

Guns exploded from every direction. Bullets pierced his back, his chest, jerking him convulsively. He staggered toward Louie, who stepped back. When the last shot was fired, Tony fell to his hands and knees on the blood-splattered floor. He lifted his head painfully to see Louie's arms raised in complete surrender, his face set with cool determination.

"You...coward." Pink foam gurgled from his mouth, his throat. "You...crossed me."

Wheezing his final breath from the smoke-filled air, he slumped to his chest.

"Keep your hands up!"

Louie remained still. He watched as Tony's blood pooled on the floor and seeped toward him, encircling his shoes. Numerous hands patted him down, ransacking his pockets.

"Where's your gun, Louie?"

"What gun?"

"Since when does a Fratelli mug not carry a gun?"

"Since when does a Fratelli mug need a gun to get dinner?" He looked at the ceiling, submitting to the search. "I ain't done nothin'."

"You two didn't kill the nice young preacher? His wife's certain Louie the Lip plugged him. You're Louie the Lip, aren't you? Let's see the harelip just to make sure."

The cop spun Louie around while another pulled his arms down and handcuffed him.

"Yep." The cop grinned. "There it is."

Louie stiffened his upper lip, creasing his crooked nose. "No murder rap's gonna stick to me. Papa will have me out in five minutes."

"Quiet, you. You're scaring me."

"Shut up," Louie muttered. "Play the scene as you was told."

The cops pulled Louie from the restaurant through a growing crowd, all stretching their necks. Louie glanced over his shoulder for a last look at Tony's body before being shoved into a police wagon and taken away.

THREE

I'm sorry I killed her." The boy wiped his tears and runny nose with his coat sleeve, leaving a smear of dirt across his face. "I would've died instead of her. I would've died if I could."

Early in his escape, fear had given him speed to run, but as the adrenaline subsided, he soon tired, and the struggle to breathe began. With a strained walk, he ignored the tightness in his chest and plodded along the desolate, snow-packed road. He looked at his wounded hand clutched tightly to his chest. It was hot and stiff and it throbbed with each beat of his heart. The sleeve of his coat was soaked in blood.

The burgeoning sun on the horizon cast a pinkish hue upon the harvested fields. As he walked, the sun rose high, yet the scenery remained unchanged—rugged prairie interrupted only by an abandoned farm—until clouds formed over the mountains in the afternoon. By his eleventh hour of freedom, the sky grew overcast, intensifying the chill. The sun set with less ceremony behind the mountains, leaving him to shiver in the fluttering snow.

Hunched in his coat, glancing up occasionally to see where he was walking, he finally limped into town, only to find the streets empty and the stores closed. The journey was over, but as he haunted the sidewalks, seeking his uncle's house, he panicked, rambling around like a starving lost dog, looking in windows, searching the houses for one that was familiar. Fear of the sheriff kept him from asking for help; this fear made him anxious as hunger and loss of blood made him weak.

The wind picked up, falling and rising in pitch, quarrelling with itself while nudging him forward. The cold took him beyond the stinging ache of his extremities to an intense numbness, so that the simple process of moving took all his mindful effort. Likewise, he fought for every breath, coughing against the liquid in his lungs, gasping like a drowning man. He paused every few steps to catch his breath. This attack, instead of heightening his panic, turned it into sobering acceptance; he would never find his uncle's house, and he hadn't the strength to keep going. He sank against a tree, dropping his head back for his last gulps of air. He only wanted to sleep. He only wanted to die.

Barricaded from the wind, the snow rushed to cover him with an icy blanket. Sleep rose to him in waves; he accepted it and drifted toward an eternal slumber.

"Listen."

A faint presence breathed warmth into his ear. Seconds passed before his exhausted brain processed the voice. Nodding, he struggled to open his eyes. The snow was undisturbed and the allurement of sleep too strong. He closed his eyes again, eager to fall into that enveloping blackness.

"Listen!"

With a jolt, his eyes snapped open. He saw no one, but soft notes of singing reached his ears. Looking up, he found himself in a small churchyard. The stained glass windows glowed with light. The thought of a potbellied stove bright with coals brought him to his feet. Though his body yearned for warmth, it responded reluctantly, fighting his demands for movement. He fell twice as he staggered down the walk, catching himself at last on the handrail before the steps. Few as they were, he felt he could never make it. Somehow, he pressed his legs onward. When he arrived, he leaned against the door, exhausted.

He had never been inside a church before. The door seemed harshly closed against him. Standing there without the courage to open it, he listened to the singing. If he slid in quietly, maybe they'd let him sit beside the stove. Maybe they wouldn't kick him out.

He stirred his deadened arm enough to reach for the knob, forcing open his stiff fingers. The knob turned noiselessly and the door opened with less effort than he had expected. A breath of warmth welcomed him inside.

Just as I am, without one plea
But that Thy blood was shed for me,
And that Thou bidd'st me come to Thee,
O Lamb of God, I come! I come!

Holding books and singing, strangers—men, women, and children—stood with their backs to him. Not knowing what to expect, he removed his cloth cap, brushing his bangs from his eyes. No one turned to look at him. He was glad for that and slipped silently into the corner of the room, easing himself to the floor. His legs could hold him no longer. When the singing stopped, the congregation settled into the wooden pews, leaving an old man with white hair and silver spectacles standing at the front.

"Before I speak tonight," he said, "I want to thank you for your sympathy in the loss of our son-in-law, Fred, three days ago on Thanksgiving. It's been difficult for us, particularly for our daughter. We don't understand why this terrible thing has happened, especially to one of God's children, but we trust He will see us through."

The voice was calm and soothing, as was the warmth of the nearby stove that sent chills through the boy's body, awakening the nerves, tingling frozen flesh. His eyes closed.

When he awoke, he found himself facedown on the floor. Pushing himself up, he saw that everyone was still seated, and the old man was still speaking. He leaned his head against the wall, wondering how anyone could have so much to say, and closed his eyes.

"...and why is this? Because the world is full of sin. People who don't understand that can't understand why horrible things happen, like Fred's murder. Atrocities will always take place in this world, though most don't come to our attention quite so vividly, so violently. The world needs a Savior, and He has come. Jesus Christ was born that we might have everlasting *life*."

His eyes opened. Something in the way the man said *life* triggered a tingling sensation inside his chest, a tiny flash like the strike of a match.

"Jesus said, 'I am the Bread of *Life*.' 'I am the Way, the Truth, and the *Life*.' *Life* is important. We love *life*, and there's only one way to have everlasting *life*—and that's through Jesus Christ. He brings *life*. *Life* beyond this *life*."

The tingling inside his chest grew. He searched the room with his eyes, wondering where Jesus was sitting and what He looked like.

"This is a gift-giving time of year, and Jesus was given to us, but a gift must be received before it becomes a possession. Mankind rejects God's gift day after day—a magnificent gift that makes the difference between hell and heaven. Trust Him today. Confess you're a sinner. As we stand to sing the Doxology, come forward. Your only hope is in Jesus Christ, the Bread of *Life*."

The organist played, the people stood, and the boy found himself walking up the aisle. That tingling filled his chest.

"And a little child shall lead them." The old man extended his hand with a kind smile.

Praise God from whom all blessings flow;
Praise Him, all creatures here below;

Praise Him above, ye heavenly host;
Praise Father, Son, and Holy Ghost. Amen.

He was near the front when that tingling reached his head. The room grew dark and he stumbled.

The music stopped. Voices and trampling feet roared in his ears. Hands were touching him, turning him over, slapping his face. Someone was hurting his cut hand. He tried to open his eyes but saw only the blur of faces with flickers of light; then, everything went black.

Abruptly, the roar filled his ears again. Someone had picked him up. They were throwing him out and he knew why; he was bleeding on the floor. Pa hated it when he bled on the floor. He struggled. They didn't have to throw him out. He would leave by himself. He shouldn't have come inside. He was sorry.

A thought entered his mind that made his heart leap: Jesus wouldn't throw him out—not if He was *life*. If they threw him out, he would die in the snow. He didn't want to die anymore. He forced his eyes open to see the worried face of the old man peering into his own.

"Can I...see Jesus?"

The man looked stunned. He wondered if he had said something wrong, but he asked the question again.

"Can I...see Jesus...please?"

The man still looked stunned.

He tried to lift his head, to get away from the arms that held him. Maybe he could find Jesus on his own if they would just put him down and not throw him outside.

The arms held him tighter and rushed him toward the door. Someone pushed it open ahead of them and he was swept off into the cold. He felt snowflakes on his face; the tingling died in his chest.

Closing his eyes against the gray-white sky, he fell into the blackness that blocked out all sight and sound.

Four

"Good morning, Mr. Parnell. Guess who's in your office?"

Joshua Parnell paused as he took off his fedora. The knowing look on his secretary's face formed an instant knot in his stomach.

"Care to give me a hint?" Removing his overcoat, he hung it on the coatrack behind her desk and placed his hat on top of it.

"Think of a barracuda with a Ronald Colman mustache."

The knot in his stomach transformed into a full-fledged ball. "Angelo Carpinelli is in my office?"

"The one and only."

He sighed. "Bring me some coffee, please. Strong coffee."

Joshua stepped into the bathroom to wash his hands. Checking his reflection in the mirror, he rubbed at the red mark the hatband had left on his forehead and smoothed the strands of his light brown hair. *Not enough sleep last night*, he thought, lamenting his bloodshot eyes and pallor. He checked the polish of his shoes, straightened his tie, and wished he had worn his double-breasted suit instead of the brown tweed one. He shook his shoulders to loosen the tension.

"Here goes nothing," he said.

When he opened his office door, he found Angelo Carpinelli studying the traffic through the one narrow window in the room, his hands clasped behind his back to avoid any dust. When Carpinelli heard the door, he turned, his smile pressing the wrinkles toward his ears and spreading his dark, thin mustache. His black suit, tailored for the illusion of a large torso, could not disguise the delicate body hiding beneath the shoulder pads.

"Good morning." He offered his skeletal hand. "You look surprised."

"Only that you came without a couple of Papa Fratelli's thugs." Without smiling, Joshua returned the handshake firmly, intentionally lowering his eyebrows over his blue eyes. He could smell the tonic Carpinelli used to comb his graying hair into precise waves.

Before sitting in one of the two guest chairs, Carpinelli pulled a pressed handkerchief from his pocket and dusted the worn fabric. He had already stationed his derby and briefcase in the other chair.

Joshua felt embarrassed by the condition of his office—his ink-blotted desk, the stains on the gray carpet, the files stacked two feet high against three of the four walls. He sat in the chair behind his desk, grimacing at its squeak, while his secretary entered with two cups of coffee.

"I see you're still upset about the search warrant I quashed," Carpinelli said.

"You can't prevent me from getting a search warrant forever. I'll find the right judge."

"Ah, but I can. Indicting Louie Fratelli is such a misuse of your time."

"The court will decide after I present the evidence."

"What evidence? None exists."

"If you say so."

Carpinelli took one of the cups, inhaled its aroma, then placed it back on the desk as though it offended him. "I can prove Louie was elsewhere the night of the murder."

"I have an eyewitness who says differently."

"What you have is an unreliable witness, no murder

weapon, and no motive." Carpinelli leaned back and crossed his legs. His dark eyes traveled to the photograph perched on a mound of papers at the corner of the desk. "Your wife? Pretty. Blonde. I thought you favored brunettes."

Joshua felt his anger rise. He diverted it by gulping his coffee. Its bitterness almost made him choke, but he restrained himself to take another spiteful swallow.

"What do you want, Angelo?"

"Rest easy. The reason I came is separate from the case. My partners and I are impressed with your skills. We've watched your courtroom tactics and believe your ingenuity would make a resourceful addition to our firm."

"I'm honored."

"You should be. We're offering you a partnership. We'll triple your income with an up-front bonus of six months' salary. We understand you'll want to finalize your existing cases, so we would expect you in about three months." He glanced around the cluttered room. "We promise your office will be superior to this."

"How generous."

"Indeed. You're an intelligent young man, Joshua. Think of the political advantages. One day you could be *the* district attorney, instead of the *lowly* deputy district attorney."

"Let me get this straight." Joshua clenched his hands beneath his desk to keep from yelling. "You're offering a thirty-two-year-old man—who only has seven years' experience in law—a partnership based upon my ingenuity? It's not because I'm prosecuting your boss's grandson, is it?"

Carpinelli's face remained placid, his smile brazen. "Let me be clear. Mr. Fratelli is not my boss. He only secures the services of our establishment. The law office of Roma, Vitali, and Carpinelli is seeking your employment. Nothing more."

"Ever hear of the term *conflict of interest*?"

"Sanctimony will not improve your station."

"I'm not being sanctimonious. I prosecute those who break the law, and I'm prosecuting Louie Fratelli for first-degree murder. Now, if you look behind you, Angelo, you'll see the door."

"As you wish."

Joshua did not bother to stand. He watched Carpinelli come to his feet with dignified submission, retrieve his hat and briefcase, and leave the office; yet before closing the door, he said, "You're doing yourself a great disservice."

Joshua's adrenaline subsided. In its wake, he felt the sickening pressure to drop the case. He knew he did not have a prayer against the Fratelli family, least of all the kingpin's grandson. Something would transpire to prevent Louie from going to jail, of that he felt certain. Through Papa Fratelli's maneuverings, the state's sole witness might disappear, or the jury might be monetarily persuaded to agree upon a verdict of not guilty. More than likely, the case would not even make it to trial.

He opened his desk drawer and prepared himself a bicarbonate of soda.

Entering the bedroom with quiet steps, Pastor Edmund Elliott placed a steaming cup of tea on the nightstand beside his wife. The light of a nearby lamp shone on her white hair, brushed into a gentle bun. She sat on the edge of a brass bed, rubbing eucalyptus oil on the bare chest of the child lying before her.

Swallowed up in one of Edmund's shirts, the boy lay half beneath the blankets, battling to force the air from his lungs and gasp for another breath. Dark circles deepened the hollows beneath his green eyes as they wandered the ceiling without comprehension.

"How is he, Edith?"

"About the same, poor dear. Feverish. His eyes are open, but I don't think he knows I'm here. He doesn't respond to anything." With motherly tenderness, she stroked the thick brown hair from his forehead.

"I wish my hair still looked like that." Edmund looked at the swollen hand wrapped in homemade bandages. "How's his hand?"

"Infected. I soaked it in Epsom salts and cleaned it with spirits of turpentine."

He cringed. "And he let you?"

"He was unconscious. I found a sweet face under all that dirt and a skeleton under those rags. What did you do with them?"

"I burned them."

"Look at this." She carefully turned the boy onto his side and lifted the shirt to expose an array of welts across his back. "He's been whipped. He's covered with bruises and scars. I've never seen such a sight. What kind of animal would do this to a child?"

"The worst kind." He placed his hand on her shoulder and gave it a loving squeeze. "The doctor's on his way. I expect he'll want to put stitches in that hand."

"Then I hope he brings some ether. How old do you think he is?"

"He's sixty if he's a day."

"Silly, I mean the boy." She rolled him on his back and brought the blankets up to his chin.

"Nine or ten, I suppose. Want me to take over?"

"No, I don't mind. It's been a long time since I've stayed up with a sick child. Why don't you get some sleep?"

Shaking his head, he sat in the floral chair in the corner of the room. "I'll have my devotions in here. I wonder if he's ever had anyone pray for him before."

Edith smoothed his gaunt cheek with the back of her fingers. "Well, he has now."

"Remember, son. We don't eat until we've said grace," Edmund said, leading by folding his hands and bowing his head over the kitchen table. Edith brought a bowl of steaming corn and sat down beside him.

The boy stopped mid-chew. With a timid nod, he smeared the butter and biscuit crumbs across his mouth with the back of his hand and lowered his head.

"Dear Lord, we thank You for what we are about to receive, and ask that You bless the hands that prepared it. Amen."

Still wearing Edmund's shirt, the boy looked up through his bangs, though his eyes had never closed, waiting in silence for permission to chew.

"Go ahead, honey," Edith said, reaching over to wipe his face with her own napkin.

Edmund ate little by little, his attention more on the boy, watching him devour the meatloaf, baked potato, and biscuits that Edith had piled on his plate.

"Slow down," she laughed, pleased at his appetite. "No one's going to take it from you."

Unable to hide his own happiness, he smiled, food, teeth, and all, and shoved in another bite.

"Chew with your mouth closed," Edmund said.

"Table manners will come later," Edith answered for him. "Let's be thankful he's finally eating."

Edmund acquiesced with a nod, remembering the half-dead child lying on the bed, his fingers clutching the sheets as he fought for precious air. The thinness of his body had been painful to see, his ribs pronounced with each breath, the ligaments in his throat strained. Death had seemed a tangible entity, a smothering hand crushing the body to mine the soul. While the doctor had worked, the church had gathered and prayed in shifts until the third morning, when the labored wheezing had stopped. The silence actually had startled Edmund from his exhausted slumber in the floral chair. Gathering the Bible that lay open on his lap, he had leaned over the boy, expecting the still pallor of death, but found instead the peace of a sleeping child. That evening, the church had gathered to glorify God.

Now, the child was up, walking, eating, and presently leaning back in the kitchen chair, sleepy and content. Across the table, Edmund broke this serenity when he said, "Son, we've enjoyed your company these few days, but it's time you told us your name and where your home is."

The boy's shoulders sagged. He put the tip of his thumb in his mouth and bit it.

"Do I have to? If I go home, Pa will kill me. He done this with the cleaver." He extended his bandaged hand for both to see. "He was gonna kill me like he killed the chicken."

Edmund and Edith shared a look, their suspicions confirmed. She reached for the handkerchief in her apron pocket to dab her reddening eyes.

"Why would he want to kill you?"

"Because I gave Ma the fever and she died."

Pushing his plate away, Edmund crossed his arms on the table. "And did he give you those welts on your back?"

"He hits me with the razor strap. Once he throwed me in the well. My brothers fished me out."

He gnawed his thumb with determination, trying to read their expressions as they returned his stare with silence.

"You think I'm lyin'. I ain't."

"No, son." Edmund removed his glasses to rub the bridge of his nose. "We believe you. You mentioned your brothers. Do you have any other family?"

"I...uh...got an uncle."

"In town? What's his name?"

Misreading the hopeful look on Edmund's face, the boy visibly crumpled.

"You gonna send me to him?"

"Well, I—"

"What if he makes me go back?"

"I imagine he'll talk to your father—"

"Then I ain't sayin' who he is. And I ain't sayin' who I am."

"Calm down. We won't send you anywhere until we get to the bottom of this." Addressing Edith, he said, "Perhaps I should talk to the sheriff—"

"No! I ain't goin' to no orphanage!"

He pushed the chair away from the table so violently that it sent him reeling backward. Edmund and Edith stood as he scrambled across the floor like a frightened animal.

"They ain't workin' me till I'm dead!"

Weakness and terror labored against him as he tried to come to his feet, tripped on the shirt, and bounced against the wall. Edmund gathered his thrashing limbs and placed him back in the chair. Encircling him with her arms, Edith rocked him gently, shushing him with assurances that they would never send him to an orphanage.

"Can't I stay with you?" he cried, bolting upward. "I'll work hard. I'll do all the chores and I won't eat much. I'll try not to get sick and—and I can sleep outside on the porch and—and I'll be so good you won't have to beat me, and—and—and..."

"Shh, child, shh."

They shared a reciprocal look. Sitting in torturous silence, the boy, his face streaked with tears, searched their faces for any glimmer of hope.

"All right, son. You may stay with us for now. We will address this at another time."

He inhaled sharply. "You mean it?"

"Yes."

Relief in the form of uncertain laughter shook the boy's frame. Edith used her handkerchief to wipe his eyes and nose.

"We must call you something, dear," she said. "What shall it be?"

"Oliver Twist would be fitting," Edmund said with a wink.

"Do you like the name Luke?"

"How about Ichabod?" Edmund retorted playfully.

"Luke was my father's name. He was a godly man, a preacher."

"Thor?"

The boy nodded unevenly, still trembling.

Edmund clapped his hands. "Thor it is!"

"No," he giggled. "Luke. I want Luke."

Edmund feigned a hurt look. "But Thor was *my* father's name!"

"Thor is hardly a name to give a child in this day and age," Edith admonished.

The boy laughed again. It sounded like music to their ears.

Five

"Oh, boy." Joshua Parnell tried to swallow his anxiety as he entered the courtroom in his double-breasted suit.

He had arrived thirty minutes early, hoping for seclusion, time to organize his thoughts and papers, and time to quell his nervous stomach. He had not anticipated a crowd to hear Louie Fratelli's plea. Never in his career had he been involved in a trial that attracted so much public attention.

He maneuvered across the marble floor through the loitering mass. Sly glances were hurled at him. Fingers were pointed at him. He heard his name in the murmurings that resonated against the mahogany benches and into the high, ornate ceiling. He tried to ignore it until he reached the prosecution table and could occupy himself with the contents of his briefcase. The room felt cold. He wished he had a bicarbonate of soda.

Almost half an hour later, Angelo Carpinelli strolled in with Louie just as the bailiff announced the appearance of the judge. Next to Louie's bulking frame and swarthy complexion, Carpinelli appeared as pale and fragile as a paper doll.

"All rise. Division Six of the Tenth District Court of the City and County of Denver is now in session, the Honorable Clarence Whitfield presiding. Please be seated and come to order. Criminal case 31-1887, the People versus Louie Fratelli."

Judge Whitfield, somewhat breathless from the climb to the bench, settled in his chair like a sloth shrouded in a black robe. Despite his rotund size, his facial features were small. His wire-framed glasses were perched on his nose below his balding head and above his white, grizzled beard. He peered over the rims at Carpinelli.

"Does the defendant wish to enter a plea to the charge of murder?"

"Your Honor, I wish to make a motion for dismissal." Carpinelli stood, straightening his gray silk suit.

Joshua lifted his hands with confusion. "This is an arraignment. All the defendant needs to do is enter a plea of guilty or not guilty."

"I can hear arguments now, if both counsels are ready," Whitfield offered without the slightest inflection in his voice. "The defendant can enter a plea after I render a decision on the motion for dismissal."

"The defense is ready," Carpinelli said, clearly anticipating the decision.

"And you, Mr. Parnell?"

Digging through his briefcase and muttering under his breath, Joshua pulled out a handful of papers.

"Is the state ready or not?"

"Uh...ah...yes. I can give arguments." Out of the corner of his eye, he thought he saw Carpinelli smirk.

"Proceed at your own pace, Mr. Parnell. We do have all day, but kindly remember that it is Christmas Eve."

The crowd laughed.

Flipping papers between his agitated hands, Joshua said, "The state is here to show evidence that the Reverend Fred MacDonald was shot three times on November 26, 1931, on the corner of Seventeenth Street and Wazee Street at approximately two-thirty in the morning. He was taken to St. Joseph's Hospital, where he died at 9:37 that same morning. Mrs. Joan MacDonald, who was at the scene, identified Louie Fratelli as the perpetrator. We charge Mr. Fratelli with one count of murder in the first degree. The state seeks the penalty of death."

Looking at the judge, Joshua found his statement was accepted with little more than an unimpressed blink. He leafed through more papers.

"Your Honor, I hand you People's Exhibit 10, the coroner's report. Exhibit 11 is the deposition from the coroner showing that the trajectory of the bullets indicate the victim was shot at point-blank range. Exhibit 12 is photographs of the deceased, but the crux of our case is the eyewitness to the crime. Mrs. MacDonald's sworn statement is marked Exhibit 13, identifying Mr. Fratelli out of a police lineup as the man she saw murder her husband. There is also the victim's dying declaration, marked Exhibit 14."

"I'm glad you're prepared, counselor. Is that all?"

"Yes," Joshua said, feeling the color rise in his face.

With a touch of sarcasm curling his lips, Whitfield turned to Carpinelli. "Defense, what is your response to these accusations?"

"Your Honor," Carpinelli said, "the state has no doubt proven that a crime was committed. What the state has not proven is that Mr. Fratelli committed this crime. Mr. Parnell is relying upon the testimony of a hysterical woman who caught a glimpse of a man on a dark night. If you examine Mrs. MacDonald's statement, you'll notice that she saw a man with a mustache wearing a trench coat and a hat. I don't see how this shows probable cause to indict my client. Mr. Fratelli has two witnesses who will testify he was with them during the time of the shooting. Your Honor will refer to the Defense's Exhibits 15 and 16 showing their depositions.

"In addition, there is neither murder weapon nor motive. Moreover, the coroner's testimony indicated a .45 caliber gun killed the victim. Mr. Fratelli owns a licensed .32 caliber revolver. The lack of a murder weapon distances my client from the murder. Therefore, I request all charges be dismissed."

Joshua took a step forward. "We haven't found the murder weapon because we've been unable to obtain a search warrant of the suspect's residence—namely, the Fratelli Estate. I fully expect to overcome this obstacle."

"Objection. Whether the state can obtain a search warrant is irrelevant. I ask the statement be stricken from the record as it may bias a potential juror if a trial convenes."

Whitfield nodded. "Objection sustained. That portion of Mr. Parnell's statement will be stricken. The state is instructed not to make any further references regarding its inability to obtain a search warrant."

"May counsel approach?" Joshua asked.

"You may."

He walked to the bench in defiance of Carpinelli, who joined him. In a whisper, he said, "Why can't I make reference to—?"

"Because it implies that something incriminating would be found if a search warrant was obtained."

"Something would," Joshua retorted. "The murder weapon."

"That's why I'm not allowing it. It implies the defendant's guilt, not his innocence."

"It's my job to imply the defendant's guilt."

"And it's my job to ensure he receives a fair trial. Objection sustained. You lost this one."

"Thank you." With a simpering smile, Carpinelli turned to leave.

"Regardless," Joshua said, stopping him in mid stride, "the questions of motive, alibi, the reliability of the lineup, and the victim's own words should be addressed to and answered by the jury, not this court. The state can make its *prima facie* case against the defendant. If it doesn't succeed, then Your Honor can dismiss the case when the state rests."

"I couldn't agree with you more, Mr. Parnell."

Joshua's eyes widened with surprise. "You couldn't?"

Carpinelli's smugness vanished. "Judge—"

"The trial will proceed," Whitfield said for all to hear. "Return to your seats, gentlemen."

Louie sat straight up, his fleshy mouth gaping in bewilderment. Carpinelli subdued him with a hand on his shoulder.

Whitfield continued: "The trial date is set for February 11, 1932. In the interest of time and money, I will set bail after the defendant enters his plea—if there are no objections."

"None." Joshua bowed his head to hide his astonishment.

"No objections." Carpinelli's face was devoid of color. "My client enters a plea of not guilty."

"Bail is set at twenty-five thousand dollars. Court is adjourned."

Taken aback, Carpinelli stood for a few seconds to comprehend that the case was actually going to trial. When he caught Joshua looking at him, he turned, brought an equally aghast Louie to his feet, and left the courtroom in silence.

Outside, Joshua saw the *Denver Post* in the arms of a paperboy and read the headline: WILL MOB KILLING OF PREACHER GO UNPUNISHED?

He remembered at once that the Honorable Clarence Whitfield was up for reelection.

There was no reason to go home. There had been no reason for the past two months, and Joshua dreaded the quietude of his house more than ever on Christmas Eve. He returned to the office, hoping his secretary would still be there. She was not, so he secluded himself in the chair behind his desk, leaning his head against the cushion. He remained in that position for a considerable time, rubbing his eyes with the palms of his hands.

He couldn't blame his wife. Since he'd started working at the DA's office, he was rarely home. So why should she be home now? Still, he never thought she would leave him, especially for the produce man at the grocery store. She must have been dreadfully lonely.

A knock at the door startled him. Wiping the moisture from his eyes, he sat up, expecting the cleaning woman.

"Come in."

"Josh?"

He leaped to his feet as the door opened, recognizing the shapely silhouette that peered into the shadows. He'd remained in his dejected state for so long that he'd forgotten to turn on a light.

"Ah, just a second." Thrusting his arms into his jacket, he hurried around the desk, kicking the metal trash can across the room.

"Are you hurt?" the woman asked in response to his involuntary shout of pain.

"Yeah. I mean, no! Just a second."

Clutching his knee to his chest, he rubbed his shin as hard as he could, as quickly as he could, then straightened his tie and hurried to the door.

"Please come in."

Turning the light on, he moved back so Clara Crawford could enter.

"So, ah," he swallowed the pain, "what brings you here?"

"I wanted to spread some holiday cheer. I'm sorry for coming unannounced."

"Not at all. The pleasure is all the greater for being unexpected."

Her smile was fetching, the whiteness of her teeth offset by the red rouge on her lips. Her dark bobbed hair framed her porcelain complexion, enhancing the mesmerizing effect her large brown eyes always had on him. She wore a slim blue dress with a matching hat and a mink coat. A single gold brooch on her lapel glittered in the light. In her gloved hand was a small potted poinsettia. He took her coat and hat and laid them on a chair while she placed the poinsettia on the desk.

"I've never been to your office." She turned about, inspecting the cluttered room with a careful nod, saying nothing more.

"Oh, I fired the decorator. Another one is coming tomorrow."

He detected the fragrance of her perfume, Evening in Paris, a vivid reminder of their first meeting at a reception at the Governor's Mansion a month ago. He was lonesome and she was beautiful, receptive.

"Can I get you anything?"

"A glass of wine, perhaps?"

He hesitated, stone-faced, and she patted his arm apologetically.

"Oh, I know. Prohibition has put an end to all the fun."

"How about coffee?"

"That would be lovely."

He left for his secretary's office, returning later with two cups of coffee. He found Clara sitting in his chair, looking at the picture of his wife.

"Is this Gloria? I remember you said you were having difficulties. Did she come back?"

Unexpected tears welled in his eyes. He set the cups down, turning away to fight them back.

"No."

"I'm so sorry, Josh."

The words were heartfelt, and so was the touch of her hand when it rested on his. When he looked back, she was standing beside him.

"I have a confession." She gazed up at him through long, black lashes, then down as though deserving a scolding. "I came here hoping she didn't. Was it wrong for me to hope that?"

Words caught in his throat. He placed a cup in her hand.

"Here's your coffee."

She took a sip. Her nose crinkled beautifully at its bitterness.

Guilt pressed him. "I can't imagine *you* being lonely. Men usually fight for your attention."

"Apparently they have families to spend Christmas with."

"Don't you have any family?"

She shook her head, not daring to look up. "No. I never did."

He sighed. "Mine are buried in my backyard. Want to see?"

Stunned, she leaned away from him. "Is that why Gloria isn't coming back?"

He shook his head with a twisted smile. "No. I'm joking, trying to lighten the mood."

Again, she placed her hand on top of his. Her demure smile was a compelling force.

"We're abandoned souls alone on Christmas Eve. Perhaps we're meant to spend it together."

"That coffee's really bad, isn't it?"

She laughed. "Terrible."

"What do you say I buy you a great cup of coffee?"

"I'd love it."

He helped her with her coat, and they spent Christmas Eve together at a café. When he took her home on Christmas morning, the exhilaration of her company kept his spirits high. It wasn't until he stepped into his house that its emptiness struck him like a blow to the heart. Even Clara's beauty and companionship could not mend the wound caused by his wife's absence.

Six

On her self-appointed mission to fatten Luke, Edith Elliott was ecstatic when he gained a pound; only nineteen more to go and she would consider him reasonably healthy. Edmund Elliott's mission had already been achieved. He'd spent hours reading the Bible and talking about God to Luke, whose starved soul had embraced every word. On Christmas Eve, he'd accepted Jesus as his Lord and Savior.

It was during evening prayer time when Edmund, kneeling at the front pew of the church, heard Luke talking to himself. Initially, Edmund believed he was praying aloud. Upon listening, he realized that Luke was replying as though a voice was inquiring in his ear.

"Who are you talking to?" he whispered.

"Can God hear me if I answer in my head?"

"What do you mean, *answer*?"

Sudden awareness made Luke turn toward a brunette woman who sat three pews behind, her head cradled in her arms. Heavy sobs that she tried to restrain shook her shoulders.

"She's cryin' 'cause her husband left her and the babies. She's got no money."

"Yes, I know."

"God heard her prayer. He's sendin' her husband back."

"How do you know that?"

"He told me."

"Who told you?"

"God."

Edmund eyed him dubiously, wondering if he should warn him against lying.

The following day, the young woman called Edith, ecstatic that her husband had returned, fully repentant of his unfaithfulness. She passed this information on to Edmund, who meditated on it, kept silent, and waited.

That night at the church, Luke paused again in the midst of his prayer, turned, and sought someone out with his eyes. Edmund watched his piercing gaze settle upon one of the elders—a middle-aged man, a widower, and a faithful servant.

"What do you hear?" Edmund whispered.

"Tonight, he's getting his reward."

That night, Edmund lay in bed, staring at the ceiling. Realizing the uselessness of trying to sleep, he got up and studied his Bible. The morning found him on the telephone, calling the elder whom Luke had pointed out in the sanctuary. The telephone rang unanswered. He hurried to the man's house, but received no response when he knocked. He tried the doorknob and found it unlocked.

"Herb? Are you all right?"

The modest house felt hushed, chill. He searched the lower level, found nothing, then climbed the stairs.

"Herb?"

Silence. The bedroom stood empty, though the lights burned. He tried the bathroom door. Blocked. He forced it until it yielded and he could poke his head inside. With his suspicions confirmed, his heart fell when he found Herb's body on the floor. The doctor later determined that Herb had suffered a massive heart attack and died before he hit the ground.

When Edmund returned home, he told Edith the news, then drew Luke aside into the kitchen. Comforted by the warm stove, the freshly baked biscuits, and the open Bible between them, he began, "Remember the man you pointed to last night, son? Well, he passed away. He's in heaven now, enjoying his reward."

Luke's face filled with dread. "Did I kill him?"

"No, no, no." Edmund placed a comforting hand on his shoulder. "You had nothing to do with his death. It was his time and God took him home. Now then, do you know what it means to prophesy?"

Looking slightly frightened, Luke answered, "No."

"Last night, the Lord led me to several Scripture passages. In First Samuel, chapter three, God used a little boy named Samuel to declare His judgment on the house of Eli, the Jewish priest. He chose Samuel before he even knew the Lord, for it says in verse seven, '*Now Samuel did not yet know the LORD, neither was the word of the LORD yet revealed unto him.*' That means that before Samuel believed in God, God had already chosen him to be a prophet. Now, you may not see the similarities between you and Samuel, but the Lord is showing me that He has something planned for you."

"What?" Luke asked, his mouth slightly open, his eyes wide with wonder.

"I don't know, but I feel a pressing need to explain some things. Luke, to prophesy means to tell others exactly what God tells you, and sometimes to see future events. Some may call you a fortune-teller. Don't let them. You weren't born with some mystic power. This is a gift from God through the Holy Spirit, given to you only after you were saved. It should be used to communicate God's messages of love, wisdom, warning, and encouragement.

"It's a great honor to be used by God, and little Samuel was faithful and obeyed God in everything. So, if you want to glorify God like Samuel did, you must resist temptation. You must resist sin, because it will come between you and His will for you. Mind you, you will be tested, but don't be afraid, for it says in the book of Hebrews, chapter thirteen, verse five, that God '*will never leave thee, nor forsake thee.*'"

Edmund took a deep breath. He felt anxious, like he must speak quickly. Time was running out. His anxiety was increased by the blank expression on Luke's face.

"Do you understand?"

Biting his lower lip, Luke nodded, paused, then shook his head with less resolve. "You use lots of interesting words."

"Here," he sighed, his shoulders drooping, "let's try this. Don't trust in your own strength. Trust in God. Never doubt Him. He will always take care of you. And when some—"

A piercing shriek from Luke startled Edmund from his chair with a shout of his own and a painful wrench of his heart. Stifling a cry of horror with his hand, Luke recoiled against the farthest wall. Like a tortured creature, he pulled at his hair, kicking the floor, trying to push himself inside the unyielding wall. Edmund's anxiety turned to panic.

"What's wrong?"

"At the window! At the window!"

Edmund followed the direction of Luke's trembling arm. He hurried to the window and drew back the curtain, searching the tranquil street for anyone, a movement, a blur, anything. There was nothing, save the pall of an early cloudy evening. The church stood across the street, quiet in the snow.

When he turned around, Luke was gone.

Luke dashed out the front door without a coat or a hat, wearing only the clothes on his back, everything forgotten in the blind terror that possessed him. He ran as fast as he could down the street and veered into a neighbor's yard, along the side of the house, through the backyard, and into the alley. Ice and snow crunched beneath his feet. He slipped and fell but regained his feet so quickly that he barely felt the sting of ice on his hands. Clambering over a wooden fence, he dropped into a mound of snow.

The sight of his father's face looking through the kitchen window had sent a quake of fear through his body, which still trembled within. Beyond the frosted glass, while Pastor Elliott was speaking, his father had materialized like a phantom as dusty particles of gloom gathered to form soot on his tattered blue shirt and overalls. Their eyes had met in spontaneous recognition, then Luke had seen the cleaver—encrusted with bloody chicken feathers—clutched in his right hand; with his left, he had pointed to the back of the pastor's head.

Now, breathing hard in snowy seclusion, Luke clutched his chest and looked around to verify his security, then looked up. His father peered over the fence.

"You should have stayed in the house, boy."

Luke screamed. His father laughed—a terrifying thunder that split the air. A skeletal hand reached for him, the dirty, cracked nails budding into arced talons resembling flakes of shale. Luke twisted away. The claws caught the back of his shirt and ripped it open between his suspenders, just missing his skin.

He was running again before he was fully on his feet, stumbling, falling, arms flailing. The desire to survive drove him haphazardly between houses and turned him around obscure corners for no other reason than to ruin all chance of being followed. He ran for blocks before the buildings ended and the edge of town opened before him. Desolate fields rolled beyond his sight.

He stopped against a tree. A dry wheeze hissed from his lungs. His chest ached from the exertion of running, and his mouth was dry from gasping cold gulps of air. The back of his new shirt was in shreds.

With a fleeting look behind him, he stumbled inside a wooden shed and collapsed. Not daring to close his eyes, he glanced about, watching for movement outside while his ears listened for any sound. From the thin rays of light sifting through the vertical planking, he discerned the outlines of carpentry tools hanging from the walls.

Minutes crawled by. Nothing happened. It did not seem possible he could have outrun his father, or that he could escape from him by hiding. He had never outrun him on the farm.

"What do I do, God?"

"You learn the futility of praying...Prophet."

His head shot up.

"Pa!"

Green eyes without pupils, without irises, resembling coarse emeralds, glowed from beneath the straw hat, casting a lime haze throughout the shed. Like a scarecrow untroubled by erosion, the ashen neck and face began to decompose; cadaverous flesh stretched tight like leather, peeling back from an ulcerous mouth marked with jagged teeth. The air reeked of sulfur.

This time Luke could not escape the gnarled hand. It seized him, flinging him high into the wall. The impact knocked the tools from where they hung, and they toppled on him as he fell. He dropped to the ground, only to be yanked up and thrown violently against the other wall.

Pushing himself to his hands and knees, he tried to dodge that hand as it grasped his shirt for the third time, rending it, flinging him high against the door. It burst open at the shock. The earth spun as he tumbled in midair. He landed with a painful thud, sliding several feet on the ice before stopping.

Lying prone and hurt, he lacked the breath to scream when the hideous form materialized above him, grabbed him, and raised him high off the ground to meet its repulsive face. The stench emitted from its mouth made Luke gag.

"You cannot stop him, Prophet. You are a helpless lamb, and you will perish like the others. But take courage. You will never grow old. You will never fight a war. You will never bury a wife. Behold, Prophet, your martyrdom awaits."

The demon opened its mouth, the thin lips curling back over rotting teeth. Luke threw back his head and screamed, "Jesus!"

Thunder crashed directly overhead. The demon cowered. In a blinding flash of light, Luke saw a man in brilliant white with a billowing mass of red hair. With the swing of a sword, he seared off the demon's hands at the wrists. Luke tumbled to the ground.

Lightning flashed from the sword's tip. It jolted the demon off the ground, throwing it an immense distance. Electricity danced over its agonized body. It writhed in torment, its clothing steaming in the snow, until its contorted image faded into oblivion, leaving nothing behind except suffering shrieks.

Luke's legs buckled and he reeled to his knees. He felt dizzy. Looking at the man in white, his face masked by the brilliance of his clothes, Luke heard him say, "Run, Prophet."

In bewilderment, he came to his feet, his legs shaking. Wishing he could disbelieve everything he had just seen, he ran into the fields.

Seven

Thanks for coming tonight. It would've been dreadful to go alone."

"Yes, one doesn't dare be seen alone in public these days, does one?"

"Not at a party," she laughed. "You're so cute when you play hard to get."

Joshua Parnell was doubly troubled, first by the effect the ruts in the snowy road would have on his yellow Packard Phaeton, and second by the scent of Evening in Paris in Clara Crawford's hair. He felt the warmth of her coat as she snuggled close, and, though he could not see her distinctly, the sight of her when he picked her up at her downtown apartment was vibrant in his memory: the formfitting red silk gown that bared her flawless back, the lips and nails the color of blood, the diamond bracelets on each slender wrist, the peek at her ankles when he helped her into the car.

They had driven fifty miles north of the city. Following the directions Clara had brought, they had passed through a couple of small towns into farmland and, just when they thought they were lost, had discovered a line of luxurious cars—Cadillac limousines and Rolls Royces, some accompanied by chauffeurs—parked on the side of the snow-packed road. It led to a long two-story house adorned in lights. Shadows danced across the windows to the music that filled the air, while outside jovial guests threw snowballs at each other, unmindful of their tuxedos and evening gowns.

Half trusting Clara's assurance that he wouldn't be recognized, Joshua felt relieved, once inside, when he failed to see anyone he knew. The guests were wild—*too wild*, he thought. They seemed intoxicated, yet never in his life had he met so many joyous, careless people. This was a world unknown to him—a world of people seeking outrageous amusements, heedless of the cost—a world of total lasciviousness, and Clara threw him into it headfirst.

Hours flew by. It seemed they had just arrived when she drew him away from the crowd to the library at the back of the house. In its quietude, she wrapped her arms around his neck and pressed her crimson lips against his. Taking her petite frame into his arms, his wounded heart found solace in her caress, and he returned the kiss amorously.

"Why'd you do that?" he asked when she pulled away.

"Because you didn't." Her finger lightly tickled his earlobe. The sensation sent a shiver down his neck. "Will you do me a favor?"

"Anything."

"On the shelf over there is *The Great Gatsby*. Second shelf. Third book from the right. Would you fetch it for me, darling?"

"I'd be happy to." Desiring to please her, he found the book and pulled it from the shelf. "I'm more of an Ellery Queen man myself—"

With the movement, a narrow door opened in the paneling of the wall. She smiled and led him to it.

"Do you trust me?" she asked.

"I—I want to...."

Ducking, he followed her down a narrow staircase to a hidden speakeasy in the basement. The smell of perfume and cigarette smoke, and the sweet aroma of liquor, rose to meet him. He stopped.

Over the live jazz band, he shouted, "Clara, I can't be here!"

She took his hand, guiding him across the dance floor teeming with people on a colorful carpet of confetti and balloons. Against the shifting crowd, he endeavored to pull away.

"I'm a public official!"

Pressing against him, she said in his ear, "Look at it this way. No one can accuse you without self-incrimination. Isn't that what you lawyers say?"

Reluctantly, he allowed her to drag him to a square table in the back. A waiter placed a bottle of champagne and two champagne flutes before them. Joshua stood, determined to leave, when Clara drew near once more. Hugging him close, she stroked the nape of his neck with her nails and kissed his ear.

"If there's anything you'd like to do tonight, *anything*, let me know."

Beneath the tablecloth, he felt her ankle rub against his shin as she crossed her legs. With a sharp breath, he poured and gulped a glass of champagne to her cry of glee. She instantly refilled it. They finished two bottles and started on a third when, at midnight, he bid 1931 a hearty farewell and sang his greetings to 1932 with the tottering throng of drunken guests. She rewarded his gaiety with a prolonged kiss.

"Let's go start the New Year right," she whispered.

"Help me, Josh," Clara laughed, wavering on her feet. "I can't walk straight."

He happily placed his arm around her waist as they stumbled from the house to the car. With much laughter and some fumbling, he found the keys, and they were off, the Packard's tires pluming snow behind them as the headlight beams bounced ahead. He fixed his eyes on her rather than the road, joining her slightly slurred voice in a discordant harmony of "You and the Night and the Music."

"I don't know what to make of you," he said when the song ended.

"What do you mean?"

"You're different from anyone I've ever known. You do exactly what you want. You're not tied to anything or anyone."

She nestled into the seat, looking cozy in her fur. "Hmm, I wouldn't say that."

"What responsibilities do you have, besides being beautiful?"

She looked at him with dreamy, half-closed eyes. "My only responsibility is taking care of you, and I love my job."

"I'd like to take care of you, too."

He wrapped his arm around her as she curled up next to his side.

"I think you're going too fast," she said.

"Me or the car?"

He took his eyes from the road to look at her lovely face. Suddenly, her expression turned to terror. She screamed.

His head shot forward in time to see a body double into the hood of the Packard. The car jolted with the sickening thud of metal against flesh. Blood spattered across the windshield. With his heart in his throat, Joshua slammed his feet on the brake and clutch. Clara flew into the dash.

He struggled with the steering wheel as the car fishtailed across the snow, the body still sprawled on the hood. Gliding over a patch of ice, the car spun around twice—hurling the body into the darkness—before the Packard slammed into a snow bank.

Everything was quiet. Dreadfully quiet. With his heart beating wildly against his chest, he looked at Clara.

"Are you hurt?"

She was slumped in the seat, a knot forming on her forehead. He touched her to verify she was breathing, then turned his attention outside. Cautiously, he opened the door and got out to examine the car. Streaks of blood glistened across the yellow paint, dripping off the dented hood and grill. He turned and vomited. If he was drunk before, he was sober now.

Holding his stomach, he staggered down the road with halting steps. In the dusky light, he followed a trail of crimson drops into a ravine. He tried to descend it, but the slick soles of his shoes caused him to lose his balance and he fell, sliding several feet to the bottom. He rolled directly into the body. It lay crumpled in a heap, its face opposite his own. He recoiled with a shout of fright. The body didn't move. Gaining courage, he came forward to search the motionless face. His hand flew to his mouth.

The young boy lay sprawled in the snow, his tattered clothing drenched in blood.

"No, no, no." Joshua beat his fist against his leg. "Please. Not a kid."

Reaching for the boy's throat, he unbuttoned the collar of his shirt to feel for a pulse. Yes, it was there. His hope revived. Perhaps the boy could be saved—only...he would have to admit to hitting the boy...under the influence of alcohol... during Prohibition. He was a public official. The scandal would end his career. It meant prison.

The boy moaned. His hand lifted, grasping for something that wasn't there, only to fall limp. Strands of his hair stuck to a wound that flowed freely with blood, running a path down the side of his face.

Joshua looked up and down the ravine. No one was around. Guests leaving the party would have to come down this road. Clara would soon regain consciousness. He had to act fast.

With his head spinning, he picked up the boy. Against the

slickness of his shoes, he struggled up the ravine to the car. Wrapping the boy in a blanket from the trunk, he laid him across the backseat, then got behind the wheel again. With shaky, blood-covered hands, he started the car.

After a few nerve-racking minutes spent releasing the car from the snow bank, he drove at a hurried pace, but not as recklessly as before. Miles passed while his eyes combed the fields until he found what he was looking for: railroad tracks.

In the shadow of a dead tree, he parked the car and removed the boy, whose teeth were chattering uncontrollably. He cried out softly; Joshua clenched his jaw against the sound. He carried him to the railroad tracks, knelt, and positioned him so that in the end there would be nothing left of the child but scattered remains.

He stood, looked in both directions, and wondered when the next train would come. Without looking at the boy, without pausing to reconsider, he hastened to cower in the car's shadow, twenty feet from his victim.

Long minutes passed. He debated whether to drive away, trusting in what he hoped was inevitable, or to wait in order to confirm the result. A glance into the car confirmed that Clara remained unconscious.

Far in the distance, the doleful sound of a train whistle broke the silence of the night. His head shot up. Moments later, a light appeared. It closed in quickly; he heard the rush of iron against iron, the straining of engines pulling a heavy burden.

Joshua's breath clouded the air. His heart beat faster as the distance between the boy and the train decreased. His eyes shot from one to the other, the span growing shorter, his chance of being convicted growing slimmer.

One hundred fifty feet...one hundred feet...eighty...

With a tremulous shudder, his heart seemed to stop beating.

What am I doing? I'm committing murder!

An unearthly horror overwhelmed him. An impression seized his soul that he stood before an angry God with an unseen multitude of witnesses to condemn him.

Sixty feet...fifty...

He was closer than half the space between the boy and the train. Wasting this opportunity could be politically fatal to him, but he could not deliberately kill a child...could he?

Horror pressed hard upon his heart. No, he could not.

He charged. Racing on foot against the train, its whistle howling in his ears, he dove and caught the boy beneath his arms. The child's foot caught the rail, and he slipped from Joshua's grasp. Joshua snatched frantically at the boy's shirt and, with a diving motion, leaped clear of the tracks, feeling the heat of the locomotive on his heels. He landed hard on his chest, the jolt sending shock waves through his body. He rolled down a slight incline. The boy rolled farther away. The train, deprived of its prey, surged by, its whistle uninterrupted.

Joshua remained prostrate, struggling to take in air while the train passed, listening to its fading noise, wondering if the conductor saw the incident. Another sound reached his ears—a gasp that turned into a shuddering moan.

Crawling on his hands and knees, he groped through the shadow of the incline until he felt a shirt. His hands fumbled upward until he found a face. The boy did not react to the touch. His breath sounded raspy and troubled, each gasp ending in a rattling grunt of pain.

Joshua slid his arms beneath the child once more and carried him back to the Packard. Wrapping the shivering boy back in the blanket, he laid him carefully in the backseat, then regained the driver's seat, muttering, "What have I done? What have I done?"

Eight

An hour passed before they were back in Denver. Joshua was careful to drive the speed limit, avoid the major roads, and keep to the back alleys of the industrial area. Somehow, the brick warehouses, stories high in their claustrophobic proximity, offered him shelter. If he remained in their gloom, illuminated solely by the Packard's headlights, perhaps his guilt would remain hidden as well.

Clara groaned. Joshua did nothing to help her as she straightened herself in the seat. He sat like a stone behind the wheel, unable to look at her.

"What happened?" She pushed her hair from her face, rubbing her forehead. "Ouch."

"Are you all right?"

"I think so. What happened?"

"You don't remember?"

She thought for a moment, and then her eyes widened in horror. "We hit someone!"

The muscles of his jaw tightened.

"Josh!" She dug her nails into his arm. "You didn't leave him out there, did you?"

He motioned with his head to the rear. Spinning around, she looked at the backseat and threw her hands up to stifle a scream.

"Is he—is he—?"

"He's alive."

"He's so—so—" She reached out to touch the boy, withdrawing her hand instantly. "Who is he?"

"I don't know. Just some kid."

"Drive faster. We have to get to a hospital."

"Clara, I can't take him to the hospital. Try to understand. I can't."

"You have to! He's bleeding! He'll die!"

He said nothing. She grew silent with understanding. Her eyes darted around frantically.

"Bring him to my apartment, then. We'll—we'll think of something."

"Thank you," he whispered, almost inaudibly. "Do you know a doctor we can trust?"

"His parents will be looking for him. What do we say if the police ask questions?"

"No reason why they should. No one saw the accident."

"But your car—isn't it damaged?"

"Someone hit it while we were at the party. We came out and found it that way. Can you remember that?" His hands quivered on the steering wheel. He held it tighter.

She nodded. "Are you all right?"

With barely a shake of his head, he stared straight ahead. "No. I almost killed a kid." He swore with passion. "I almost murdered a kid."

Joshua backed the car into the alley, sheltering it in the shadows of an overhanging fire escape beside Clara's apartment building. He retrieved the boy from the backseat while she hurried around the corner, her high heels clicking on the wet pavement.

"It's clear, Josh. Wait. I can see his arm."

"How's this?"

"It still looks like a dead body. Just hurry up."

Under the night's cover of darkness, they hurried to the building entrance. She placed the key in the lock and opened the street door. He breathed easier when they made it inside and the light extinguished their shadows. Avoiding the elevator, they rushed up the stairs to her apartment. She unlocked her door and stood back to allow Joshua to carry the shrouded form inside. She locked the door behind them.

"Wait here. I'll get some towels."

The room was dark, and she neglected to turn on the lamp. He heard her steps retreating, caught a sliver of light as she opened a door, just enough to slip in, and promptly closed it behind her. A surge of panic seized him at her disappearance. He stood there, waiting anxiously for her return, feeling the weight of the limp boy hanging in his arms.

As his eyes adjusted, he could make out black forms of furniture, pictures on the walls, and a large mirror on his right that reflected a red neon sign through the window on his left. The Venetian blinds were partly drawn, casting striped beams of light diagonally across the carpet.

"Josh?"

A light came on. With a glance, he took in the spacious living room, adorned with white and black art deco furnishings. A painting of Clara, a glamorous contrast of light and shadow, devoid of color, hung above the fireplace.

She returned with a quilt and several towels, some of which she spread over the white embroidered sofa. He laid the boy on them and drew back the blanket.

In the revealing light, she gasped to see the wounded features. The boy's skin was bluish, his lips purple, and he shivered in his wet clothes. She placed the quilt over him and folded a towel under his head. Leaning over the sofa, she smoothed his brown hair away from his eyes and found the ragged gash across his forehead. His hair was matted with blood. The pain she caused induced him to stir.

"What are we going to do?" Joshua asked, watching her helplessly.

She pressed him into a chair with a hand on his chest. Pouring a glass of scotch from the nearby tray, she fitted it into his clenched hand and said something in his ear that he did not hear. He nodded anyway and noticed that she retreated to the bedroom. He fixed his eyes on the boy on the sofa, on the blood drying on his face, on his struggling gasps for air.

Gulping his scotch, Joshua dropped the glass on the carpet and pressed his palms hard against his ears—he could still hear the boy breathe. He squeezed his eyes shut—the grisly image became clearer. He remained in that desperate position, wishing the boy would die, wanting the boy to die, praying the boy would die. He couldn't listen to that breathing anymore; he couldn't look at that young face.

He cursed himself. "I should've left you there. It would all be over." Then he cursed the boy. "Die already! Die and get it over with!"

The bedroom door opened. Removing his hands from his ears, he wiped away the sweat that had beaded on his upper lip. Certain to close the door behind her, Clara returned, having exchanged the evening gown for a simple gray dress. Glancing nervously at her watch, she drew a breath from the cigarette in her hand.

He reached out for her. "What are we going to do?"

She came to him hesitantly, almost with a measure of guilt. Wrapping his arms around her waist, he rested his cheek against her abdomen. She patted him on the head, released herself from his grasp, and said nothing. As she turned away, a knock sounded at the door.

He jumped. "Who's that?"

She hastened to the door. He stood and blurted, "Clara, don't—!"

With her hand on the knob, she said, "I'm sorry, Josh," and threw open the door.

There stood Angelo Carpinelli. Joshua's heart sank.

"May we come in?"

Behind him stood another man. They noticed the boy at the same time. The second man hurried to him, a black bag in his hand.

Joshua watched Clara close the door. She remained at a distance, intensely avoiding his gaze.

"Don't blame her," Carpinelli said, understanding his thoughts. "She had no choice." To Clara, he said, "Tell the boys to come out."

Eager to leave the room, she opened the bedroom door and motioned with her hand. Two men in dark suits walked out. One carried a camera. Joshua understood everything now. He sank into the chair.

"How is he, Dr. Ameche?" Carpinelli asked.

The doctor, an older, nondescript Italian, lifted the boy's eyelids. His eyes, green and dull, had practically rolled back into his head. The doctor flashed a small light into the blood-shot eyes; the pupils constricted.

"There doesn't seem to be any brain damage." Removing scissors from the bag, he cut the shirt and the suspenders from the boy's body. Upon exposing the badly bruised ribs, he asked, "Is there a warm room I can take him, somewhere quiet?"

"Not yet." Carpinelli motioned to the young man with the camera. "Dominic, photograph everything. Get clear shots of his face and the wounds—the more graphic the better. When you're done, there's a yellow Packard in the alley. Photograph the damage."

Dr. Ameche frowned when forced to give the photographer

room. Dominic took several pictures, replacing the burnt-out bulb after every dazzling flash. Each pop of the bulb made Joshua jump. He stared at his hands.

Once Dominic finished, Carpinelli ordered, "Benny, take the child into the other room."

Clara led the way while Benny roughly lifted the boy. His head fell back and a fresh stream of blood ran from his mouth.

"Careful, you dolt!" the doctor shouted.

With a humph, Benny ignored the remonstrance and carried the boy into a second bedroom. A spotted trail of blood followed them. Joshua perceived it as his own lifeblood draining away.

A smile twitched on Carpinelli's lips. "Dr. Ameche is an excellent physician. When I heard of the accident, I brought no one less than the Fratellis' family doctor."

Gathering the bloodied towels from the sofa, Carpinelli cast them on the floor. He sat across from Joshua to study him with distinct enjoyment.

"Are you prepared to discuss the dismissal of all charges against Louie Fratelli?"

"You came right to the point." Joshua lifted his head, clearing his throat.

Carpinelli kicked one of the bloody towels to Joshua's feet. "Say the word and this can all go away."

Joshua sighed. "You don't leave me much choice."

"No, I don't. I admit this isn't the way we'd planned it, but it's a delightful twist."

"Was Clara in on it the whole time?"

"As I said, she had no choice."

The door to the bedroom opened and Dr. Ameche stepped out, his frown deepening into a smoldering scowl.

"The child is in deep shock. I insist he be taken to a hospital."

Carpinelli turned to face him. "What is his condition?"

"He has five fractured ribs and a severe concussion. He's lost a tremendous amount of blood. To make matters worse, he's suffering from an exacerbation of bronchial paroxysms."

"Which means?"

"He's having an acute asthma attack."

"Is that all?"

Dr. Ameche glowered. "Isn't that enough?"

"Will he live?"

"He'll be dead by sunrise. I've given him morphine to alleviate the pain. I can do nothing more here. At the hospital, I could—"

"Thank you, doctor."

"I must insist—"

"I said *thank you*, doctor."

Carpinelli turned back around, and the doctor, doing everything in his power to suppress his anger, returned to the bedroom.

"What is your decision, Joshua? I can make it as though this boy was never born."

Joshua shrugged, beaten. "I can't drop the charges. It'd look too suspicious. I suggest we arrange a mistrial."

"A nugatory trial." Carpinelli sat back thoughtfully. "What do you recommend?"

"A prejudicial error, a deadlocked jury, anything, but it must be in the natural course of events. I'll do something prejudicial. You object and ask for a mistrial. I won't challenge it. Understand?"

"Fully. See that *you* understand."

Joshua stood and took his car keys from his pocket.

"Leaving so soon?"

"As hard as it is to leave you, yes, I must go."

When Joshua opened the door, the young man with the camera stood on the other side, blocking his exit. For the first time, he stood face-to-face with Dominic Fratelli and looked into the dark eyes of a murderer. Joshua shrank back at the cold expression of deadly indifference, a startling dichotomy as it came from a handsome face, one Joshua would have expected to see on the silver screen. Dominic stood there with his black hair perfectly combed, his shoulders squared, and the butt of a gun peeking out from his tailored pinstripe suit. Joshua turned to Carpinelli with silent beseeching.

"Did you get the pictures, Dominic?" Carpinelli asked.

"Yes, sir."

"Then Mr. Parnell may go."

Dominic stepped aside, an aloof smile on his lips. Joshua knew he would have killed him as easily as he'd released him. He left the apartment without looking back, and heard Carpinelli say, "Sleep well, Joshua—if you can."

NINE

Grateful for the solitude of a few short moments, Dominic Fratelli reclined on the embroidered sofa in Clara's living room. He folded his hands behind his head, stretched out his long legs, and permitted her portrait above the fireplace to mesmerize him. After immersing himself in her eyes, he let his gaze follow the graceful lines of her heart-shaped face, posed partly in shadow to accentuate her cheekbones, before his eyes rested on the slight smile of her lips.

"Yo, Dom. Want a donut?"

Dominic cringed. Benny's voice stung his nerves like shattered glass. Bringing his brows low over his brown eyes, he glared at Benny, who had emerged from the kitchen with a plate of jelly donuts.

"Keep your voice down. You'll wake Clara."

"Who cares?" Benny plopped in an adjacent chair, contentedly scrutinizing the donuts. "You're too dizzy for this dame. She would roll you ten times over if she wasn't so busy giving you the air."

Dominic did not answer. He straightened the creases of his pressed trousers while observing Benny's wrinkled suit and the oily sheen that glinted on his balding head.

"You know," Benny continued, "I ain't never seen a guy strike out with a prostitute before. She's the first dame who ain't dropped at your feet in a heap."

Dominic came forward, rubbing his jaw with his large hand. "You're about three seconds away from serious injury."

"Don't get in a sweat. I'm just saying, one guy to another, she's bad news."

"I'll worry about that."

"It's your funeral." Seizing the plumpest donut, Benny stuffed half of it in his mouth, not stopping to chew as he said, "When you think we'll blow this nursery? It's been three days. Nobody's gonna snatch this kid."

"Did it occur to you to take a bath this morning?"

"No. Why?" Benny squeezed the remainder of the donut in his mouth, smearing jelly across his lips. "I wish that kid would pop off already."

"We're here until he dies. Deal with it."

"He's behind schedule."

"How inconsiderate of him."

"Hey," Benny said, exposing the contents of his mouth, "how about putting him out of his misery? I could snap his neck real quick. He wouldn't feel nothing."

Dominic shook his head with incredulity. "You're all heart, Benny."

"Well, I'm getting cabin fever. I gotta get out of here. If I don't, I'll burst."

Wiping the powdered sugar from his hands onto his black pants, Benny tossed the plate onto the coffee table. Standing, he pulled a set of keys from his pocket, jingling them as he paced. A silver four-leaf clover dangled from the chain.

"I'm in no hurry." Leaning back, Dominic gazed once more at Clara's painting.

"Say, ain't she the dame that was in that movie with that one guy?"

Dominic merely said, "Yes."

Benny snorted, still pacing. "They don't make silent movies no more, or ain't you heard? She's yesterday's news."

"Not in my paper. By the way, your pants are unzipped."

Looking down, Benny's face flushed. Turning aside, he fixed his zipper, muttering, "Chump."

Dominic's ear caught the soft click of Clara unlocking her bedroom door. He stood, donned his suit jacket, and checked his thick hair with a brush of his fingers. A smile crossed his face as he watched her door open just enough for a lovely brown eye to peek out. Seeing him, she froze, blinked, and finally opened the door with resignation.

"Good morning," he said.

"Good morning." Forcing a smile, she hurried toward the boy's bedroom.

While her face was averted, he scanned her shapely figure, starting at the blue chiffon dress, moving on to her silk stockings, and pausing on her ankles. His gaze returned to her face when he said, "Clara."

She stopped. He gave her a grin he knew was both boyish and charming.

"I wondered if I might take you out this evening. There's a new Cagney picture out."

Her eyebrows arched skeptically. "I thought we couldn't leave the apartment."

"Benny can watch the kid."

"Think again, pal," Benny called out, his mouth overflowing with jelly filling.

She fought back a laugh. "Thanks, but we'd better not go against Mr. Carpinelli's orders." Turning, she entered the second bedroom and closed the door.

With a content smile, Dominic inhaled the aroma of her perfume.

"You got it bad, pal," Benny said. "That dame's turned you into mush."

The sweet yet pungent odor of laudanum made Clara crinkle her nose as she entered the darkened room. "Good morning, Abigail," she whispered. "Can I get you some coffee?"

"No, thanks," said the plump nurse.

Seated beside the bed in a sanitized white uniform, her dusky figure was outlined by the sun's endeavors to shine through the drawn shades, haloing the woman's hennaed hair with an unnatural orange hue. Her chubby hands soaked a small towel in a basin of water beneath the window, then wrung it out.

"How is he?" Clara asked.

"Restless. I can't bring his fever down."

Sitting on the edge of the bed, Clara watched the insensible boy toss and turn in heated unrest. His skin glistened with sweat. Stitching mended the gash on his forehead, tender sutures set upon purplish bruising that slipped down into one swollen eye. Piles of bandages lay at the foot of the bed, replaced by fresh ones that hid the contusions on his ribs.

"It breaks my heart to watch him suffer," Abigail said, inspecting the bottles of isopropyl alcohol and antiseptic powder on the nightstand. "Dr. Ameche said it's a miracle he's lasted this long."

"Yes, it is." Clara looked into the boy's battered face. In a softer tone, she said to him, "I'm so sorry. I wish this hadn't happened," and stroked his cheek with the back of her fingers.

He cried out at the touch, recoiling as though burned. She jerked her hand away, giving Abigail an uncertain look when his eyes snapped open. Bloodshot and wild, his vexed green irises searched the room until fixing on Clara's face. He sat straight up in one movement. She shrank back with a surprised gasp.

"Woman"—his voice was youthful yet authoritative—"your lips drip as the honeycomb and your mouth is smoother than oil, but your end will be bitter as wormwood. Your feet go down to death. Your steps take hold on hell."

Horrified, she struggled to move away, but a greater force held her there.

"But the Lord is merciful," he continued. "He sees the wickedness forced upon you. If you seek His righteousness, He will deliver you from destruction as He delivered Rahab."

He grew silent, witnessing every word pierce her soul. Then his eyes rolled back into his head, and he fell limp onto the pillow. He lay still as if touched by death.

Suddenly released, Clara staggered away. Abigail jabbed her fingers into the soft flesh of his throat, searching for a pulse and sighing when she felt one.

Without removing her eyes from his ashen face, Clara backed up against the door, felt for the knob with her hand, and opened it behind her. Backing out, she closed it, shutting out the sight of his battered body.

His words echoed in her head. Fear stirred within her such as she had never known—fear of death, of judgment. While she destroyed men's lives—though coerced by Papa Fratelli—she was destroying her own. She had never realized it before.

She covered her face with her hands in mortification, shaking. Images of men flashed before her—men she had brought to their downfalls. With each one, she shuddered. A faint moan escaped her lips when Joshua Parnell's face materialized.

Ten

Pastor? Mrs. Elliott?" Luke's throat felt dry, his voice hoarse.

He opened his eyes. Thinking he was lying in his bed in the Elliotts' home, he rolled over to go back to sleep when his eyes snapped open again. Sitting up, he looked around doubtfully. The room was different. The bed was different. His heartbeat quickened.

"Pastor? Mrs. Elliott?"

A snore reverberated next to him like a rumble of thunder. It startled him, and he almost jumped out of the bed. Studying the shadows, he discerned a figure slumped in a chair. It adjusted itself with satisfaction and continued snoring. He scrutinized it, his imagination running wild, until other sensations started vying for his attention: hunger and a deep ache that invited him to look at his wrapped ribs. But first, he had to hide from the monster.

Gingerly, he pushed the blankets off and climbed out of the bed. His weak legs betrayed him, and he crumpled to the floor. To his horror, the monster stirred. Expecting it to leap up and trample him in its rush, he pinched his eyes closed and pressed himself against the carpet. Nothing moved or made a sound. It wasn't until the snoring resumed that Luke regained his feet.

His knees trembled. Covering himself with a blanket, he grasped the furniture like a toddler and stretched his arm toward the door. With a glance back at the monster, he escaped into the next room. Feeling his way along the wall through the darkness, he came upon another door that moved with little effort against his hand. He felt the carpet change to cool linoleum under his bare feet and knew that he had found a kitchen. Stroking his hand against the wall, he found the light switch.

The brilliance of the light blinded him. Squinting, he staggered toward the icebox with pangs of hunger cinching his stomach, threw open the door, and grabbed the first thing he saw: a bottle of milk. Gulping it as it streamed from both sides of his mouth, he emptied the bottle, set it aside, and lunged at an apple. He had barely taken a bite when something moved in his peripheral vision.

The icebox door jerked away from him. His head shot up. He reeled back, gaping wildly at the gun aimed point-blank at his head. Seeing only a steel barrel inches from his forehead, a sudden burst of laughter brought his eyes up. A young man loomed over him, laughing. Luke felt caught between embarrassment and panic, with milk dripping from his chin and his mouth full of apple.

"Sorry, thought you were Benny." The man, endeavoring to control his amusement, pointed the gun at the floor. "By now, I thought you'd be dea—um...I mean...How do you feel?"

Luke chewed, swallowed, and asked, "Where am I?"

"Tell you what. Tomorrow, I'll introduce you to someone who'll answer all your questions. His name is Mr. Carpinelli."

"Who are you?"

"I'm Dominic. How do you feel?"

"My head hurts and my chest does, too. Did I fall down?"

"You lost a showdown with a Packard. What's your name?"

With hesitation, he answered, "Luke."

"Luke what?"

As he stared at the young man who held the gun loosely in his hand, Luke realized that he was being studied, as well. He shifted nervously.

"Do you remember your last name?"

"Yeah."

"Care to share it with me?"

"You a policeman? You ain't sending me back home or to the orphanage, are you?"

Dominic considered him for a moment before understanding crossed his face. "No, I'm not a policeman."

With that assurance, Luke looked in the icebox. He swallowed against the gurgling of milk in his stomach.

"You're starved. Let's see what we can find." Dominic peered into the icebox. "We had steak for dinner. I can make a sandwich out of the leftovers. Let's get you to the table."

As he was helped into a chair, Luke asked, "If you ain't a policeman, are you a bad man?"

Dominic cast him a narrowed glance.

"Only policemen and bad men carry guns."

"I'm...a bodyguard."

"What's a bodyguard?"

"A man who protects people. I protect my father from men who would like to hurt him and his business. I need a gun to do this."

Watching Dominic cut the cold beef into slices, Luke salivated, mesmerized as they were placed on the bread with tomatoes, cheese, and lettuce.

"Why do they wanna hurt your Pa?"

"Because he's rich and powerful."

"You protectin' him now?"

"No, I'm protecting you."

Luke's eyes shot to Dominic's face. "Bad men wanna hurt me?"

"Well, they would like to take you someplace that's not safe."

"How come? What'd I do?"

"Ask Mr. Carpinelli tomorrow. In the meantime," Dominic placed the sandwich before him, "eat before you fade away."

Seizing the sandwich, Luke ripped off a mouthful with his teeth and nearly swallowed it whole. Watching him force it down with some difficulty, Dominic poured him a glass of water.

"Chew it. You'll make yourself sick eating like that."

Accepting the water with a thankful nod, Luke drank it and proceeded to chew his food. Halfway through the sandwich, his bites became smaller, his chewing slower, and he fought the yearning to close his eyes.

"You'd better go back to bed," Dominic said. "You're going to slide right off that chair."

"Nuh-uh. I don't wanna. There's a monster in there."

"Really?" Dominic grinned. "What does this monster look like?"

"Like a big turtle with orange hair."

A woman's scream pierced the air. Spinning out of the chair, the gun instantly in his hand, Dominic opened the kitchen door just enough to peer into the next room. A slight smile touched his lips. Lowering the gun, he pushed through the door and out of Luke's sight.

"The child!" a woman cried. "He's gone!"

Dragging himself from the table, Luke shuffled across the floor. Pushing the door open slightly, as Dominic had done, he peered through the opening. He saw a woman in white pulling her flaming red hair with excitement; a fat man, half-awake, swaying on his feet; and a young woman in a purple robe emerging from another room.

"Calm down," Dominic said. "He's here. Luke, come out, please."

Securing the blanket around his shoulders, Luke pushed the door open. Coming to stand beside Dominic, he looked at the adults surrounding him, who stared back as if he was a curiosity on display.

Noticing Dominic watching her, the young woman drew the robe around her and smoothed her mussed hair. Dominic replaced his gun in the holster under his arm, looking embarrassed that she had caught him.

"Oh, thank goodness." The woman in white walked toward Luke with arms outstretched. "How did you get up without me hearing you? It's back to bed with you."

Bending down, Dominic whispered in his ear, "There's your monster."

Blushing, Luke allowed her to take him into the bedroom where he crawled into bed, too weary to care who the strangers were, and drifted off immediately.

"I can't believe he's alive, let alone walking around," Clara said after Abigail had ushered Luke away. "Is he all right?"

"He seems to be," Dominic said. "He was hungry. That's a good sign."

"Should we call Dr. Ameche?"

"I will in the morning."

Saying good night, she returned to her room and locked the door with the flick of a key.

"What'd you tell that kid?" Benny demanded, his face flushed with agitation.

Dominic looked at him. "What's wrong with you?"

"I dreamed I got scratched by a cat. A cat with green eyes." He jerked his shirttail out of his pants, lifting it high to wipe his sweat-streaked face. "That's bad luck."

"Kill the light." Dominic stretched out on the sofa and closed his eyes.

"It ain't normal, him being up like that." Benny switched off the floor lamp and the room went dark. "Dr. Ameche said he should be dead."

"You don't intend to help him on his way, do you?"

Benny said nothing.

"That wasn't a rhetorical question."

"I got no plans made."

"Don't make any. *Capisci*?"

Rolling over, Dominic announced an end to the conversation. He heard Benny fidget in the chair and mutter, "It ain't normal. He ought to be dead."

Eleven

The invasion of light scattered Luke's dreams into fleeting images. An exchange of voices murmured above his head, tossing words curiously back and forth like a whispering game. He moaned and turned his head on the pillow. The talking stopped. Luke started to fall back to sleep when the whispering game resumed.

He felt the displaced pressure of someone resting on his bed. Hot breath exhaled on his face. Envisioning his father looming over him, his eyes snapped open. A face hovered directly over his own—a shriveled face with dark, bulging eyes, a hooked nose, pinched lips, and a thin mustache. Luke shrieked, and the face withdrew in fright.

The little man promptly recoiled to the foot of the bed. Beside him stood Dominic, his arms crossed over his chest and one hand casually covering his mouth, trying not to laugh.

"I don't think Mr. Carpinelli intended to scare you," Dominic said. "He's the gentleman I told you about."

Luke took a deep breath and rubbed his eyes with his fists until vibrant patterns danced in his vision. His startled heart pounded soundly against his chest; he hated waking up scared.

Carpinelli came forward tentatively. "I'm astounded at your quick recovery, son. How do you feel?"

"Okay, I guess." Luke leaned against the headboard, drawing the blankets under his arms.

"Would you like something sweet? Some chocolate, perhaps?" His courage renewed, Carpinelli pulled a chocolate bar from his jacket pocket with flourish.

Seeing the candy wrapped in glittering gold foil, Luke sat forward. "For me? All this?"

"Of course. Haven't you had chocolate before?"

"Once. Thank you, sir." Accepting it, Luke unwrapped it carefully so as not to tear the precious foil. He broke off one piece of chocolate precisely on the grooved indentation and offered it to Carpinelli. "Want some?"

"No, thank you. It's all yours."

Seeing the chocolate, Benny left the corner of the room where he had sulked to stand by Dominic. When he reached for the candy in Luke's hand, Dominic elbowed him sharply in the ribs.

"What?" Benny pulled his hand back, his face reddening. "He offered."

Carpinelli gave him a harsh glare as he sat on the bed. When he looked at Luke, his countenance changed to compassion with drastic suddenness.

"I hear your name is Luke," he said. "What's your last name?"

Luke chewed the first piece in slow savoring bites and watched Carpinelli casually scrutinize him. The benign smile on Carpinelli's face remained fixed.

"Well, can you tell me where you live? I want to contact your parents. I'm sure they're worried."

"They ain't worried. My Ma's dead and my Pa's glad to be rid of me."

"Really." Carpinelli stroked his chin with his index finger and thumb. "You ran away?"

"Yes, sir."

"I ran away when I was young, too. Would you like to tell me about it?"

"My Pa's rough on me." Luke shrugged and unfolded a dog-eared corner of the foil. "I didn't wanna take it no more."

"He beats you?"

"I don't wanna talk about it."

"Right. Let's try something else. Why don't you tell me the last thing you remember before last night?"

Swallowing the candy, Luke broke off another piece with meticulous accuracy. "I don't remember a whole lot. I was walkin' in a field somewhere. It was dark. Some bright lights came at me real fast. I don't remember nothin' after that, till I woke up last night."

"Let me fill in the gaps for you," Carpinelli said. "The bright lights were the headlights of a car right before it hit you. The man driving the car was drunk. He tried to hide you because he was afraid to go to jail. So, for your protection, we took you away. That's why Dominic and Benny are here to guard you. Do you understand?"

Luke didn't know what to say, nor whether he believed Carpinelli; he knew he didn't like his mustache. He looked at Dominic and Benny to see if they agreed with the story and found Benny staring at the chocolate bar.

"Now," Carpinelli said, "is there anything I can get you?"

After a moment's thought, Luke brightened with an idea. "Yeah, can I have a Bible?"

The mouths of all three men dropped open.

"You want...a Bible?" Dominic stammered.

Not understanding their bewilderment, Luke said, "Yeah. Do you read yours in the morning or before you go to sleep?"

"Uh..."

Standing abruptly, Carpinelli turned away. "Benny, get the boy a Bible."

"What! Why me? Send Dominic."

"Get the boy a Bible," he hissed through his teeth, his face flushing a deep red. "Is that too difficult?"

Benny growled in his throat. "Just where am I gonna get one?"

"A bookstore, a church, anywhere. Just don't steal it." Carpinelli headed for the door, eager to leave the room. Over his shoulder, he said, "I'll check on you again, Luke. Let Dominic know if you want anything else."

"Why does God's Word frighten you? Is it because you exchanged its truth for a lie?"

Carpinelli came to a dead stop. Luke set the chocolate aside. His expression grew intense, and his green eyes became startling pools of vivid color in his pallid face.

"The path you've chosen is slippery. It leads to everlasting torment. The hand of the Lord withholds you from destruction, but only for a season. Listen to this warning. It will be your last."

If a bullet had struck Carpinelli, he could not have been more stunned. "Leave us," he said without moving.

Exchanging looks of bewilderment, Dominic and Benny left the room without a word. After they closed the door, Carpinelli turned and asked in a low voice, "How do you know these things?"

"The Holy Spirit speaks to my heart."

"And do you understand everything He says?"

"No, but I want to obey."

The corner of Carpinelli's mustache twitched. "What else do you know?"

"I know that you, a prophet of the Lord, rejected His Word. You abandoned the faith and counted salvation as nothing. Because of this, God gave you up to your sinful lusts."

A sharp intake of air snatched away Carpinelli's breath, forcing him to swallow with difficulty. With a voice he didn't seem to trust, he said, "Astonishing. God replaced me with a child. You've no idea what a brilliant move that was...or how humiliating. No wonder the Ruler of the Scroll despises you.

He fears you. Do you realize he's tried to kill you three times? He simply laughed at me."

Carpinelli shook his head. His gaze drifted out the window. "I had barely graduated from law school when I received the gift of prophecy. I didn't ask for it. I didn't want it, but I obeyed God and gave His message to the demon. That's when it laughed. I expected persecution or torture—even death—but not ridicule. It said God had tried to destroy it for centuries and failed. It called me a fool and asked why I followed a God who couldn't even restrain one of His fallen angels. Then it offered me something I'd never had. Power."

A light glinted in Carpinelli's eyes as he looked back at Luke. "It kept its word. I control people's lives. I control yours. One word from me and Benny would put a bullet in your head without blinking. Do you know why I don't? Because I *choose* not to."

"Wrong," Luke said. "You don't because you still fear God. Miserable wretch. To appease your pride, you exchanged a few years of gratification for an eternity of anguish. You're no different from the prophet Balaam who loved the wages of unrighteousness. It would be better if you had never known the righteousness of Christ, for it will be worse for you in the end."

The gleam in Carpinelli's eyes expired. "Shut up. I won't hear it."

"You will hear it. Have you forgotten that the Lord will judge you? Yes, you have the power to choose. Choose you this day whom you will serve."

As soon as he finished speaking, Luke suddenly pinched his eyes closed; his hands covered his ears.

"What's wrong?" Carpinelli stepped forward.

The sounds of anguished cries and clamors for mercy pierced Luke's ears. A swell of heat rushed at him, carrying a myriad of screams as if someone had opened the door to a torture chamber. A horrid stench stung his nose. Then, as if the door had been closed, the screams stopped. The screeching pain in his ears subsided, leaving a dull ache in their place. He uncovered his ears and opened his eyes. With a terrified gasp, he threw himself against the headboard.

"What do you see?" Carpinelli paled with realization. "*Who* do you see?"

A hellish creature stood over Luke's bed, extending a tenacious arm toward him; its spindly fingers, five points of radiating heat, almost touched him. Luke fell back against the mattress, recoiling as they neared his face. A dense haze swarmed around the demon like wisps of yellow sulfur. Luke buried his face in the blankets to keep from gagging, feeling the demon's hot, sulfuric breath on his neck.

"I am not here for you, Prophet."

Luke lifted his head, hardly daring to breathe. The demon withdrew. Clothed in a filthy robe, once a royal blue, the massive fiend loomed over an apprehensive Carpinelli, waiting like a vulture waits for death. Luke pushed himself up.

"The Lord still protects him!"

"As you said, but only for a season. It is time for the harvest."

Looking desperately at Carpinelli, Luke pleaded, "Once you walked in the light. Once you ate from the table of God. Don't reject the Holy Spirit. Come back."

"Why?" Carpinelli demanded. "So I can be weak? Why should I rely on God when the demon gave me the power to rely on myself? Do you think me a fool?"

"You can't see what I see!"

"I know. I can't see it, but I know. It's Death." Sadness turned the corners of Carpinelli's mouth downward, his mustache twitching in an uncontrollable spasm. "I've made my choice."

In triumph, the demon threw its evil head back with a shout. “The dog returns to its vomit!”

Carpinelli left the room without another word, not seeing the maleficent spirit who vied for his soul, the spirit in whose grasp he would be led into eternity.

Luke wept bitterly.

TWELVE

My word, man. What's happened to you?"

The concern in Andy Ballantine's voice was the first solace Joshua had felt in almost a week. Shamefaced, he stood before his legal adversary and occasional friend. Painfully aware of his disheveled, unshaven appearance and the curiosity of Andy's secretary as she eyed him over her stenography, Joshua allowed Andy to take him by the arm into his office.

Andy placed him in a high-back leather chair, shut the door, and sat on the corner of his mahogany desk. "Are you sick? You look like you haven't eaten in days."

Joshua glanced vaguely at the bookshelves, lined from floor to ceiling with law books, and at the richly polished furniture and brass fixtures. No stain marred the carpet, nor was dust allowed to gather on the windowsills. The slight smell of furniture oil hung in the air.

"Yes, I'm sick," he said finally, wondering if he was doing the right thing. "You have no idea how sick. I wish I was dead."

Over the next hour, he confessed everything about his failed marriage, the Louie Fratelli trial, the boy he almost murdered, Clara Crawford's betrayal, and Angelo Carpinelli's threats. He kept his eyes averted, unable to endure the contempt he feared he'd find in Andy's face.

When he finished, Andy asked, "Have you told this to anyone else?"

"No."

At last, he found the courage to look at Andy, impeccably dressed in a double-breasted suit, his flaxen hair cut short, his broad face stern, contemplative. He carried no expression of disgust or scorn. He simply listened with his hands folded before him.

"What do I do?" Joshua's raspy voice trembled to the point of breaking.

"Go home. Eat. Sleep. Bathe. I'll make some calls and see what I can do."

"No. You must tell me. I don't know which way is up anymore."

Andy began to pace the room. "You won't like it."

"What's to like about any of this?"

"I see three things that must be done. First, you must get rid of the car."

Joshua winced. "My car? It's brand new."

"It's evidence. Wash off the blood, if you haven't already, and park it on the street. During the night it will be stolen."

"By whom?"

"By Herbert Hoover. Second, we must find and destroy the negatives and photographs taken of the victim and the car."

Joshua breathed out disparagingly. "They could be anywhere."

"Third, we must recover the victim, preferably alive."

With that, Joshua threw up his hands. "You want the impossible."

"You'd be surprised how impossibilities become advantages in the right hands."

"I'm sorry." Joshua shook his head intermittently. "But for all we know, that boy is already dead." He squeezed his eyes shut. "There was so much blood—"

"Tormenting yourself won't help," Andy snapped. "I'll also need the girl's address, Clara—what was her name?"

"Crawford."

Andy stopped pacing. "Wasn't she an actress in the silent movies? Brunette? Pretty?"

"Very pretty. I'm not stupid enough to get framed by an ugly woman."

Andy laughed. "Just stupid enough to fall for a Fratelli moll. I'll need the layout of her apartment—the doors, windows, what room they put the victim in, et cetera."

"I'm sorry. It's—it's all a blank. I can't remember any of it. All I remember is the blood. And what if the boy's not there anymore?"

"It's a starting place."

"How much time do you think we have?"

"As long as Louie's trial lasts. I'd prolong it if I were you."

Joshua sighed. He ran the fingers of his trembling hands through his unkempt hair, then attempted a smile.

"What do I owe you, Andy, besides my life?"

"A fifty-dollar retainer."

"How long we been locked in safety deposit?" Benny grumbled. Sitting forward on the sofa, he pulled a queen of hearts from the cards in his hand and dropped it onto the coffee table. He took one last drag from his cigarette, blowing the smoke into the cloud haloed around his head, and crushed it in the ashtray.

"Three weeks." With a satisfied smile, Dominic glanced at the painting of Clara on the wall. He picked up the queen and laid down his hand. "Gin."

With a one-syllable expletive, Benny tossed his cards on the table. "Ain't you sick of it?"

"Not in the least."

"Ain't you sick of the food?"

Dominic cocked an inquisitive eyebrow. "What did you have in mind?"

Benny frowned. "A kid baked in a calzone."

"You'd still be hungry. How about Romano's?"

"Swell."

Dominic reached into his pocket for a coin. "We'll toss to see who goes for it. Call it."

"Tails."

Tossing a dime in the air, Dominic caught it and declared, "Heads. I go. Hand over some dough."

"You goin' someplace?"

With a start, Dominic spun around. His hand instinctively moved toward his gun. Finding Luke standing on the other side of the sofa, he shook his head and said, "Make some noise when you enter a room. It's not wise to sneak up on armed men."

"Spooky kid." Benny dragged out a crumpled ten-dollar bill, wadded around a rabbit's foot, from his pants pocket. "Always sneaking in and out of rooms like some ghoul. Ought to nail him to the floor so he'll stop creeping around."

"Are you all right?" Dominic asked, noticing the pallor of Luke's face and the haunted look in his eyes.

"You goin' someplace?" Luke repeated.

"Perhaps you should lie down. You look like you're about to keel over."

Luke shook his head. "Don't go."

"Why not?"

"Because you won't come back."

"Oh, I'll be back." Seeing Clara emerge from her room, Dominic stood, buttoning the collar of his shirt and straightening his tie. "Do you think I'd leave this gorgeous woman alone with you?"

"You'll get killed."

He turned on Luke with raised eyebrows. "And you know this how?"

"Maybe he's got a crystal ball." Standing, Benny proudly lifted the lint-flecked rabbit's foot. "What if I go, fortune-teller? Will I get whacked? I got my rabbit's foot with me."

Luke studied him and then said, "No, you won't die."

"This is absurd," Dominic said. "*I'm* going."

"Dom," Clara interjected, coming forward to touch his arm, "maybe you shouldn't go."

This sudden interest in his welfare encouraged him to move close to her. "Would you care if something happened to me, Clara?"

"Can it," Benny said. "I'm itching to get out anyway."

Dominic turned around with surprise. "You believe him?"

"I'm calling his bluff." Sticking the rabbit's foot in his pocket, Benny reached for his hat.

"Um, Benny, before you go…." Dominic waved his hand toward Benny's trousers.

His balding head flushed bright red. He turned away, zipped up his pants, and left the apartment.

"Romano's is only four blocks away. It shouldn't take Benny two hours."

Speaking primarily to himself and without breaking stride as he paced the floor, Dominic studied the face of his pocket watch. Gathering its gold chain, he placed it back inside his pocket and pulled the revolver from his shoulder holster to verify that it was loaded. He turned on his heel, then stopped short, scarcely in time to keep from running Luke down. He promptly aimed the gun away from Luke's head.

"What did I say about sneaking up on me?"

Luke said in a singsong voice, "I know where Benny is."

Stepping around him to renew his pacing, Dominic placed the gun back in his holster and extracted the pocket watch again. Trying to match his stride step for step, Luke trailed after him.

"Don't you wanna know?"

Dominic smirked. "All right, pal, spill it. What have you done with him?"

"Nothin'. He got shot. He's tryin' to get back. Three other men got shot, too, all brothers, but they ain't gonna make it back. They're dead."

Dominic stopped and stared hard at him, blinking twice. "Don't try to be funny."

"If you'd gone, you'd be dead, too."

"Luke, what were you doing before you came in here?"

"Readin' my Bible."

"Go back to your room and read your Bible."

"But I—"

"Scram."

"Sometime," Luke said, walking backward, "would you help me read it?"

"Uh...I'll uh...think about it."

Grinning, Luke ran and jumped on his bed. Happily surprised at the unexpected bounce, he hopped to his feet, testing the mattress's springs. "Hey, Dom! Look at this!"

From the corner of his eye, Dominic noticed the kitchen door swing open. Pressing her shoulder against it, Clara entered with a tray in her hands bearing two short glasses, a bottle of scotch, and a steaming cup of hot chocolate.

"Here, let me help you," he offered.

"Thanks."

Relieved of the tray, she took the hot chocolate to Luke's room, attempting to smile.

"Watch this, Miss Clara." Luke grinned at her unabashedly and jumped with renewed effort until his fingers brushed the ceiling. Laughing with his achievement, he dropped to the mattress on his bottom. "Did you see that?"

"Yes, I did. You must be feeling better. Want some hot chocolate?"

"Thanks." Accepting the cup, he placed it on his knee, dunking the melting marshmallows with his finger.

"I think that's the first time I've seen you play."

"Play?" He looked up, licking the marshmallow off his finger.

"You know, like other boys your age."

"My Pa says playin's for city kids. Me and my brothers just work. Miss Clara, would you read the Bible with me? My Ma taught me to read, but sometimes the words are hard."

"Um...maybe some other time." She backed out of the room. "I need to talk to Dom."

Ignoring his hopeful expression, she hurried to sit beside Dominic on the sofa.

"No sign of Benny yet?" she asked while he poured the scotch.

"No, nothing." Taking a sip, he held the liquor in his mouth momentarily before swallowing. "I like it."

"You should. It's your father's."

"Here's how." He downed the remaining scotch and returned the glass to the tray. Pulling a gold cigarette case from the pocket of his suit jacket, he asked, "Did you hear what Luke said to me?"

"No."

"He claims that Benny was shot and three men, all brothers, were killed tonight. He still thinks that if I had gone, I would've been killed, too. Cigarette?"

She accepted one absently. After lighting her cigarette with a gold lighter that he pulled from the same pocket, he lit one for himself.

"Do you believe him?" she asked.

"No, but Angelo puts stock in it. Luke said some strange things to him the other day. Angelo was changed afterward and not for the better."

"Do you remember what he said?"

"He asked Angelo why he exchanged God's truth for a lie. Whatever else he said, Angelo took it seriously. What struck me as odd were the words Luke used. They weren't the words of an illiterate child."

"Do you think he really knows the future, or is he just nuts?" she asked, looking over her shoulder at Luke, who was licking the last remnants of chocolate from the inside of the cup.

"I suspect he's been groomed. He also took a bad blow to the head. He's probably a little balmy."

As Dominic refilled his glass, he noticed that she had not touched her scotch. She grew silent, thoughtful. It struck him that she looked scared.

"Clara, don't take what he says to heart. He's just a kid with a creepy imagination."

"Benny's back!" Luke shouted unexpectedly.

The announcement made Clara jump. Dominic opened his mouth with a prepared reprimand when a loud thud sounded against the apartment door. Motioning Clara to remain quiet, he pulled his gun and cautiously approached the door. He perceived heavy breathing with grunts of pain on the other side.

"Dom," a voice panted. "Let me in."

"Benny?"

He unlocked the door and opened it. Losing his leaning post, Benny reeled into Dominic's arms. Clara sprang up and quickly closed the door.

"I caught one in the arm," Benny breathed through his clamped teeth while Dominic half carried him to the nearest chair.

Seeing his left sleeve saturated with blood, Dominic

removed his coat to inspect the free-flowing wound. "The bullet passed through," he said. "Clara, hand me that bottle and call Angelo. Tell him to get Dr. Ameche over here."

Luke came forward quietly. At his entrance, Benny struggled to get to his feet.

"I'm gonna kill you, you little punk! You said nothing would happen to me!"

Luke shook his head. "Nuh-uh. I said you wouldn't die."

"You little creep! Then how come Dom would of died?"

"Because he ain't fat like you."

"You piece of garbage!"

"Sit down!" Dominic shoved Benny back into the chair as he lurched toward Luke. "Drink and tell me what happened."

Benny took a long swig of the scotch that Dominic had put in front of his face and wiped his mouth with the back of his hand.

"Somebody knocked off the Pompliano brothers at the restaurant. All three of them rubbed out in front of me. I got plugged in the arm. I spent the last hour ducking the cops."

"Who pulled the hit? One of our boys?"

"Got me." Benny glared at Luke. "It's his fault. He lied. I'm gonna pop that kid. When Carpinelli's done with him, I'm gonna gut him like a fish!"

"He had nothing to do with it."

"He knew it was gonna happen! He knew I'd get shot and said nothing! I told you! Wait. Wait!" Benny dug frantically in his pocket. "Where's my rabbit's foot? Where's my four-leaf clover?"

"You're a superstitious idiot. Luke," Dominic said over his shoulder, "go to your room."

As Luke obeyed, Benny screamed after him, "You're dead, kid! You're dead! I'm gonna bleed you white!"

THIRTEEN

Voices shouted from the living room: Carpinelli demanding answers from Dominic, Dr. Ameche repeatedly telling Benny to sit still, and Benny growling curses against Luke, interspersed with barks of pain. Gathering the blankets into crumpled mounds, Luke sat on the bed behind the closed door. Tears brimmed in his eyes.

"Why do I have to stay here, Lord? Why can't I go home with Pastor and Mrs. Elliott? I don't understand what You want me to do. I don't understand these pictures in my head. I don't understand the words You put in my mouth. Please, let me go home!"

A loud bang sounded against the door. Someone struggled violently with the doorknob.

"I'm gonna snap his neck!" Benny yelled.

Carpinelli shouted something unintelligible and someone pulled Benny from the door.

"Oh, God! They're gonna kill me!" Luke buried his face in the blankets, his hands clenched together, his eyes closed. "I'm nobody! I'm just a kid! I wanna go home!"

Abruptly, he sensed a change in the room. It felt cool. He opened his eyes to find that the light had gone out. A wind had risen, swirling shadows around the room, tugging at the iridescent robe of the man standing before the window. In the swaying light, Luke could just discern his noble features through the thick red hair that tousled around his head. The vibrant robe was inlaid with gold, and around his waist was a golden band. In his left hand he held an ornamented silver shield, and in his right was a flaming sword.

Luke's mouth dropped open.

"Do not be afraid, child," the man said. "Before you were born, the Lord ordained you as a prophet. You will go where He sends you. You will say what He tells you. You are to declare destruction to the abominable ruler who holds dominion over this city, for he has turned it into a way station for the dragon and his kingdom. This ruler must answer for the depravity he has thrust upon the innocent. Behold, Prophet, the abomination against the children of God."

The angel stretched his right arm toward the open space of the room. Luke followed the motion as the wall opened into visions of centuries past: Men, women, and children in peasant garb run in terror through an ancient city. Armored soldiers pursue them on foot and on horseback, impaling Christians with their swords, leaving the mortally wounded on the streets beside the dead.

Before his eyes passed decades of bloodshed and slaughter, eager persecutions against Christians, false witnesses dragging them before tribunals with promises of merciful deaths for those who would renounce their faith, innocents accused of heresy and beheaded, boiled in oil, or roasted alive as torches to brighten the streets at night. Annihilation spreads to all quarters of the earth. Thousands are slain, and innumerable followers of Christ are martyred, plagued at every turn by a domineering evil disguised in the bodies of rulers. Passing from father to son, king to prince, ruler to heir, this evil extends through the ages while the blood of Christians stains the roads and the rivers flow as crimson streams.

"Stop! Make it stop!" Luke screamed. "I don't wanna see no more!"

He shook his head vehemently. Violent chills rose from

his spirit, draining the warmth from his body. Looming over the butchered martyrs, an oppressive evil darkened the vision. Luke felt the presence weigh on him and burden his soul, pressing his heart with hopelessness.

"Prophet," the angel said, "these are the works of the abominable power raised from hell, seven devils sent in succession to torment the redeemed. *You* will end this. *You* are chosen."

Groans came from Luke's throat. He could not blink. "Why me? Why me?"

The air reeked of sulfur. The glowing red eyes of a demon dominated the vision. It was unlike the others he had faced. The long face, tarnished by corruption, was darkly handsome, as if retaining some previous beauty. A sharp, angular jaw held firm below well-defined cheekbones and an aquiline nose. The flesh possessed the pallor of death. Black hair clung to its scalp beyond its high forehead.

"Behold Aeneas, the devil of the sixth curse. Prophet," the angel pointed his sword at Luke, "you are chosen."

Luke screamed. Hands grabbed him. He fought in wild terror, yet he saw only the murdered Christians, heard only their screams harmonizing in timbre with his own. The hands held him down with greater force, restraining his arms and legs. Something stabbed him in the arm. He writhed against the steel-gripped hands and threw his head back and forth to bite them until a haze came over his eyes. The vision faded and the clutching hands turned into numb pressure. He tried to fight but could no longer move. Warm blackness swallowed him into nothingness.

No longer thrashing or biting like a rabid animal, Luke lay quiet, supine, the red marks on his wrists and ankles displaying the pressure Dominic and Carpinelli had used to hold him down.

Few things unnerved Dominic. He was neither a spiritual nor a superstitious man, but he felt an ethereal foreboding he could not identify. Carpinelli, too, seemed to sense something; his gaze traveled the room as though searching for some ghostly presence.

"Children who suffer trauma sometimes experience nightmares," Dr. Ameche said while taking Luke's pulse. He spoke reassuringly, even while his furrowed brow belied his own diagnosis. "The sedative will make him sleep through the night."

"I'll make him sleep with the *angels*."

Dominic heard a familiar click. He spun around to find Benny standing in the doorway, his gun aimed at Luke. Before he could react, Benny's outstretched arm jerked upward. The gun exploded with a shot. It jolted him off his feet. Struck by an invisible force, he flew back into the wall with a thud, sliding down until he lay sprawled on the floor. Blood oozed from his nose. The gun lay smoking a few inches from his wrenched hand.

Few things angered Dominic, but a bullet hole in the wall a foot above Luke's head ignited his wrath. Without a word, he picked up Benny's gun and placed it in the waistband of his pants. Then he pulled Benny over his broad shoulder. His composure as he carried Benny out of the apartment defused the panic, releasing Clara and Dr. Ameche from their fright so both could tend to Luke. Carpinelli, however, remained fossilized, reminding Dominic that the attorney rarely saw the violent aspect of the business.

Despite his poise, Dominic seethed with rage. Within a minute, he stood on the dark, wet pavement outside. A car drove by, showering them with a mist from the street that brought Benny out of his dazed state. He wiggled uncomfortably.

"What's this? The bum's rush? Let me down!"

Dominic said nothing, thinking only of the bruises he had left on Luke's wrist and ankle. He walked around the brick building and into the trash-strewn alley, setting Benny down on his feet. The shadows befriended him, veiling his dark violence. Scattered above, dimly lit windows watched with bored eyes, half closed by blinds, while the red neon sign across the street flashed a silent alarm to passersby. A streetlight fifty feet away refused to acknowledge the scene, showing a circumference of ten feet around its base and no more, but the snow on the cobblestones had no choice but to accept the blood.

Benny crumpled facedown in the alley, gasping, coughing fine sprays of blood from his mouth. Dominic stepped back, breathless, wiping the sweat from his face. His knuckles stung, but his head was clear.

"Be glad your gun backfired," he said, resting his hands on his knees and glancing over his shoulder. "If you'd killed him, I'd be dumping you in the South Platt River right now."

"It didn't...backfire." Benny gasped, clutching his stomach. He lifted his head from the snow, spitting blood and saliva. "Something hit me...threw me back."

"You're all wet." Dominic reached for his wallet. "You'd better lie dormant. Do you need some cash?"

Benny sneered at him as he struggled to stand.

"Keep your dough. Give me my rod." He reached out and yanked his gun from Dominic's waistband. "I ain't blowing town. Got it? You can tell that to Mr. Carpinelli *and* Papa Fratelli. And next time I spot that kid, I'll crack his head open like an egg."

"And I'll hang you on a meat hook. *Capisci*?"

Benny shoved him aside. Dominic watched him hurry away into the dark, yelling back, "He's gonna bring this family down! Mark my words!"

Inside Luke's darkened bedroom, a glow fell on his sleeping form. Standing guard at the window, shield poised and sword drawn, the angel watched him with vigilant determination.

FOURTEEN

The aroma of freshly brewed coffee reached Dominic as he wiped the remnants of shaving cream from his face with a towel. He paused, looked at his pocket watch, and lifted his eyebrows with mild wonder. After patting his face and neck with cologne, he checked his appearance in the bathroom mirror, tightened his tie, and secured the revolver in his holster.

When he walked into the kitchen, he found Clara at the table in her purple robe. Her hair was tousled around her head, uncombed, as if she had withstood a tempestuous wind. A cup of coffee waited before her.

"You're up early," he said.

When he sat beside her, he found her eyes staring off into nowhere. He had never seen her so disheveled, so wild. He rather liked it. He touched her arm. She jumped. Upon seeing him, she drew her robe around her with one hand and tried to smooth her hair with the other.

"I'm sorry, Dom. I didn't hear you come in. Would you like some coffee or just me?"

"I'll just take you."

"What?"

He laughed. "Are you all right?"

"No, I had a miserable night." She gave up trying to manage her hair and rested her chin on both palms. "I couldn't stop thinking about last night. Do you think Benny's okay?"

"It's not the first time he's been shot. It won't be the last."

She sat quietly for a moment and then asked, "What do you think about Luke's predictions coming true?"

"I don't believe he can see the future, if that's what you mean."

She nodded her head slightly, allowing her gaze to wander off.

"Can I tell you something? Before Luke recovered, back when we thought he would die, he said something disturbing to me. I told myself he was hallucinating, but he was dead-on."

"What did he say?"

"He looked me straight in the eye and told me every terrible thing I've done." She shook her head and looked at him. "How is that possible?"

"It's not."

"But you told me what he said to Angelo and how it affected him. Then, last night, he said the Pompliano brothers would be killed, and they were. He said you would've died if you had gone instead of Benny. With all my heart, I believe you would have."

"Clara," he said, taking her hand gently, "do you trust me?"

She searched his intense dark eyes with desperate hope. "Yes."

"Then do as I say. Take some sleeping powder and go back to bed."

He brought her to her feet, wrapped his arm around her, and led her to her bedroom. Complying like an obedient child, she took the sleeping powder, lay on the bed, and accepted the quilt he stretched over her.

"Try to sleep, Clara. We'll talk later."

Dominic closed her bedroom door and walked directly into Luke's room. He entered without knocking and found Luke standing beside the window in his new blue and white striped pajamas. Leaning on the sill with his arms, his chin resting on his hands, he watched the traffic below. His hair looked tangled from a night of unrest.

"Good morning," Dominic said in a strong voice.

Luke swung around with a startled gasp. Dominic frowned and came forward. He stood intentionally close to Luke, folded his arms, and leaned against the wall, observing how Luke inched away to keep a wary distance between them.

"You gave us quite a scare last night. Did you have a bad dream?"

"Somethin' like that."

"Want to talk about it?"

"I wanna forget it."

"Well," Dominic said, "there's something I want to talk about. How did you know the Pompliano brothers would be murdered last night and that Benny would be shot?"

Luke shifted his gaze outside the window with a sigh. "I just knew."

"You'll have to do better than that."

Luke shrugged indifferently. A movement outside caught his attention—a group of boys romping through the snow with schoolbooks in their arms. He watched them run down the street laughing, his shoulders sinking with an air of acquiescence.

Observing this, a sudden thought occurred to Dominic. He asked, "Who took care of you when you ran away from home?"

Luke cast him a distrustful glance. "These old people."

"What old people?"

"A preacher and his wife. They were real nice to me. I miss them."

"Did this preacher and his wife know you were a runaway?"

"Yeah."

"Did they try to send you home?"

"I wouldn't tell them who I was, but they didn't care. They let me eat as much as I wanted and they taught me things."

Dominic cocked his eyebrow. "Like what?"

"Like the Bible and Jesus. They said God gave me a gift."

"You don't say. Does this gift allow you to tell people their futures or their pasts?"

Luke looked up at him. "Sometimes. How'd you know?"

"I've been around the block a few times."

Luke peered down into the street again, looking toward both ends of the block, then back at Dominic with confusion.

"So, that's their racket." Dominic smirked knowingly. "Take in a stray kid, feed him, and teach him the tricks of the trade. How much did they rake in off your *gift*?"

"Huh?"

"I know a con man when I see one, and you, my friend, are one of the best."

Luke stared at him, stupefied.

Dominic grinned. "Oh, this is beautiful. They even suckered you. Do you know what a con man is?"

"No."

"A con man deceives people to gain something in return, usually money."

Furrowing his eyebrows into a wounded line, Luke exclaimed, "I ain't a con man."

Dominic burst out laughing. "Your face is your fortune! You're a natural. Tell me, how did you pull off last night's escapade with Benny? I never saw him as an easy mark."

"What's an easy mark?"

"A sucker. A chump. Someone a con man thrives on."

"I ain't a con man," Luke repeated fervently.

"You tell fortunes. I've never met a fortune-teller who wasn't a con artist."

"I ain't a fortune-teller neither!"

"Then what are you?"

"I'm a prophet!"

Dominic paused for a full second before bursting out with laughter again. Luke flushed a deep red.

"A prophet! You *are* good! I like you, kid. I like you."

Clara kicked off the quilt. She felt unbearably hot, breathless. Prickly needles of pain traveled across her body in swells, causing her to thrash about on the bed and pull at her hair, the same way she'd thrashed in the dream where she'd found herself dangling from her hair in a great subterranean catacomb of the eternal dead.

Black caverns spotted with fiery pits extended beyond her sight, glowing with molten lava. These boiling lakes of mire, hideous with the stench of sulfur, teemed with arms and human faces, their skin black as pitch, their gulping mouths gasping for air like fish grapple for food. Flocks of carnivorous birds flittered among these pits, landing on heads to gouge their scorched beaks into the faces as they surfaced.

From every direction, the strained discord of groaning reached her; she couldn't escape the sound of voices crying for mercy. Below her flowed a river simmering with fire, filled with men and women struggling against each other as the current drew them downward. With no hope of rescue, they fixed on Clara as an escape, lunging for her dangling feet. She screamed as they dragged her closer to the fiery river, kicking at them until they lost their grip or until the current pulled them away.

A blistered face burst from the river beneath her. A scream tore from her throat as powerful, burning hands clamped onto her legs. Despite her efforts to break free, a man climbed up her body until his face was on the same level as hers. Fire dripped from oozing wounds on his body and seared her flesh.

He cursed her; through the worms that crawled from his mouth and nostrils, he cursed her. Then she recognized him: Joshua Parnell.

With one hand grasping her struggling body, he pulled at her hair with the other, ripping it out by handfuls, until they plunged together into the molten tide. Swallowed in the stewing river, she felt the heat peel her flesh away from her bones.

Joshua grabbed her head and held it down under the agonizing current. Fighting and clawing to escape him, she kicked hard against his stomach, which forced him away and brought her head to the surface. With a desperate gasp, she saw him again just a few feet away. Uttering a rancorous curse, he swam toward her. At that moment, she recognized that this was her future...*for eternity.* She could not even die to escape it.

Something brushed against her face. Startled, she looked up. A scarlet rope dangled from the top of a precipice where Luke stood, holding it fast. Dressed in white, he glowed like the purest of lights in the depth of hell's darkness.

"Rahab," he shouted, "grab the rope!"

She seized it. With amazing strength, he pulled her from the fiery stream, away from Joshua, who strove to grab her feet as she was drawn upward. When she reached the top, Luke helped her climb onto the ridge. She collapsed at his feet, charred and depleted of strength.

"Choose, Rahab, between an eternity of this," he pointed to the souls wallowing in torment below, "or an eternity with Him."

She followed the movement of Luke's hand as he pointed toward a cavern. Inside the brilliant light that illuminated it, the source of Luke's radiance, stood the clear outline of a Man. Luke stepped toward Him. She crawled after him, begging him to wait, when a hand suddenly grabbed her ankle. With a shriek of panic, she spun around to see Joshua clinging to the precipice, a hellish sneer on his worm-eaten face. He dragged her back toward the burning torment, back to the perpetual agony beneath her. Screaming in terror, she fell....

"Please," Clara whimpered through her tears as she burst into Luke's room. "Help me."

Luke and Dominic spun around to look at her. Dominic reached out for her. "What's wrong?"

She evaded his grasp to fall on her knees before Luke. Perspiration fastened her robe to her skin. "You were there. In my dream. I saw you."

"Do you know who the Man was that you saw?" Luke asked.

"No."

"He's Jesus Christ, the Son of God. He can save you from going to hell."

Dominic took a menacing step forward. "Don't pull this stuff on her. Understand me?"

A single glance from Luke stopped him. The authority in his face caused Dominic to retract his step and be silent. Luke turned back to Clara.

"The Bible says that everyone's a sinner and that we're all gonna die. But God loved us so much that He sent Jesus to die on the cross for our sins. After He died, God brought Him back to life again. If we believe in Jesus, we'll spend forever with Him in heaven."

"If I believe in Him, I won't go to hell?"

"No. The Bible says anybody who calls on the name of the Lord will be saved."

"Even me?" Fresh tears poured from her eyes. "I've done terrible things."

"It don't matter. God will forgive you. You wanna accept Him as Lord and Savior?"

"Yes." She nodded fervently. "What do I do?"

Slipping to his knees beside her, Luke sought her hands and held them tight. He squeezed his eyes shut.

"Pray this. Dear Lord Jesus..."

Softly, her articulation echoed his. "Dear Lord Jesus..."

"Please come into my heart. I believe You are the Son of God. I believe You died on the cross and came back to life again. I believe only You can save me. Please forgive me for my sins and help me live a good life. Please be my Lord and Savior. Thank You, Jesus. Amen."

When she finished the prayer, she dropped her head with exhaustion onto Luke's shoulder.

"Thank you," she whispered.

Dominic shook his head slightly, watching the scene. With no hint of a smile, he said, "I'll hand it to you, kid. You're the best I've ever seen. You even had me going for a minute."

Luke turned toward him angrily and Clara slipped from his arms to the floor.

"Clara!" Dominic dropped to his knees and lifted her limp body into his arms.

Her eyes opened briefly before rolling back into her head. In a sudden spasm of violence, she flailed awkwardly. Luke backed away to avoid her thrashing arms and legs, which struck Dominic several times as he struggled to restrain her. He came clumsily to his feet, attempting to lift her to the bed, when she broke away. Swinging her arms, she hit him across the face with an unearthly power. He stumbled backward, tripped over the corner of the bed, and fell. Landing flat on his back, he gaped at her wildly. When he regained his feet, he reached for her once more.

"Don't touch her!" Luke shouted. At Clara, he yelled, "Leave her!"

With a maddening scream of torment, she threw back her head, spinning herself around in a circle before a final shudder seized her and she collapsed. Dominic hurried to her side. He took her lifeless face into his hands and brushed away her hair.

"Clara!" He glared threateningly at Luke. "What did you do to her?"

Luke smelled sulfur. Before his eyes, an ethereal outline materialized above Clara's inert body, strangely beautiful, its slender figure shrouded in scarlet. Its eyes seemed like sapphires in its deathly, ashen skin. Unkempt black hair fell in tangled wisps across its emaciated shoulders.

"How dare you send me from her," the demon said in a defiant hiss, its husky voice echoing as if in a stone chamber. "I own her, Prophet."

"Not anymore," Luke said.

"Not anymore *what*?" Dominic snapped as he moved Clara to the bed.

"Who are you?" Luke demanded.

Dominic scowled at him. "What do you mean, who am I?"

"I am the spirit of prostitution. This woman has been mine since she was thirteen."

"Get out of here! Go back to the pit! You can't have her!"

The demon leered hatefully at him, curling its lips back over its teeth.

Dominic stared incredulously at Luke. "Who on earth are you talking to? And what's that awful smell?"

Luke scowled back at the demon. "She's bought with the blood of the Lamb. You don't own her anymore."

Without warning, the demon pounced. Like a tiger, it clawed for his throat as a scream of multiple octaves tore from its throat. Before it could touch him, a flash of light separated them, repelling it backward. An angel stood between them, his garments illuminating the room with an incandescent glow. He lifted his great sword. With divine accuracy, he threw it into the heart of the demon. The propelling force of the sword drove it from the room and from Luke's sight into the vastness of eternity. A shriek filled his ears, then faded with the smell of sulfur.

Clara opened her eyes. Dominic breathed a sigh of relief and sat beside her on the bed.

"Darling, are you all right?"

She smiled weakly and patted his arm before stretching out her hand to Luke. When he stepped toward her, Dominic grabbed him by the arm and dragged him roughly to the side.

"What was all that about?" he whispered angrily.

"You wouldn't believe me if I told you," Luke snapped back.

Dominic shook him with one brisk jerk. "Try me."

"She believes in Jesus now, so I told the demon it had to go."

"You're nuts." Dominic shoved him away with exasperation. "You're right, I don't believe you. I don't even understand you. Just tell me—is she all right?"

Luke nodded.

After a few moments of silence, Dominic chuckled, looked at Luke with renewed amusement, and said, "You *are* good."

FIFTEEN

Joshua was filled with dread when he saw the large envelope on his office desk, his name boldly printed across the front. It lacked a return address, but he felt certain it came from Carpinelli. He regarded it until the mystery became too much and he opened it. It was—as he'd feared—the photographs. A typed note was attached: *Be sure your sin will find you out.*

Nausea churned in his stomach as he perused the black-and-white pictures of his dented, bloody car parked in the alley by Clara's building. The next picture startled him so much he had to choke down the bile that rose in his throat; he was sitting in the chair in her apartment, staring at the blood on his hands. He couldn't remember it being taken.

With dismay hanging on every nerve, he turned to the next picture. With barely a glance, he slammed them all face-down and caught his breath. He had forgotten the boy's fair features—but he had not forgotten the blood.

Carpinelli had planned it well. The photos were delivered on the first day of the Louie Fratelli trial. Now, he would have to plead his case with their images burned into his memory.

"Your Honor, the state calls Dr. Henry Kelsall as its first witness," Joshua announced.

Judge Clarence Whitfield did not bother to look at Joshua

or the witness when he approached the stand to be sworn in. He seemed preoccupied with a cuticle on his thumb.

Joshua strolled across the marble floor before the jury, a compilation of older, conservative men whom the prosecution had chosen, and younger, unchurched men of the defense's preference. He avoided looking at Carpinelli and Louie, knowing both would be wearing smug expressions. He did not look at the crowd at all.

"Dr. Kelsall," Joshua said to the aged doctor who still laid claim to his dark hair, "when and where did you first meet the deceased, the Reverend Fred MacDonald?"

"At St. Joseph's Hospital on November 26, 1931," Kelsall said softly.

"What time was it?"

"About two or two-thirty in the morning."

"And what was the occasion?"

"The hospital called to say a man had been shot." Kelsall shook his fleshy head with regret. "I hurried over and found the young Reverend MacDonald. He was in shock. His wife was there, poor woman. The nurse and I tended his wounds and gave him stimulants. We worked all night trying to improve his shocked condition with injections of salt solution and adrenaline."

"Exactly where had the victim been shot?"

"In three places." Kelsall pointed to his upper right arm. "One bullet went in about here, shattered the bone, and was projected into his chest cavity. A second bullet went through his thigh, and the third entered under the sixth rib, passing through the splenic area, that is, the diaphragm, lungs, and kidneys."

"Did you recover any bullets from the body?" Joshua asked.

"Yes, sir."

"Where?"

"At the morgue."

Joshua smiled faintly. "From what part of the body did you recover the bullets?"

Kelsall blushed behind his spectacles. "From his back, below the shoulder joint."

Joshua took a bullet from the evidence table and handed it to the witness. "I hand you Exhibit 15 and ask you to state to the court what it is."

"That's the bullet we took from his back."

"A .45 caliber bullet, to be precise." Joshua retrieved the evidence and laid it back on the table. "Your Honor, I ask that Exhibit 15 be admitted into evidence."

Whitfield glanced up briefly from his cuticle.

Turning back to the witness, Joshua said, "Did Reverend MacDonald recover?"

"No," Kelsall said. "His condition deteriorated. He died about nine-thirty a.m."

"Did Reverend MacDonald say anything before he died?"

"He asked for his Bible, but his wife couldn't find it."

"Did he make any other statements?" Joshua asked.

Carpinelli stood and said, "I object to any statements Reverend MacDonald made at that time. I understand the state has a dying declaration. Since the statement cannot be corroborated, this question may bias the jury."

"Your Honor," Joshua said, "the dying declaration shows the deceased clearly identifying the defendant as the shooter."

Carpinelli leaned over the table, shaking his head with annoyance. "Nevertheless, the deceased didn't sign it. How do we know this is the actual statement?"

Whitfield did not even look up. He moved on to another cuticle and asked, "Doctor, was Reverend MacDonald in a condition to sign this statement at the time it was dictated, or at any point afterward?"

"No," Kelsall said. "He was too weak."

"I'm not objecting to his inability to sign it," Carpinelli said. "I object because it cannot be corroborated. Furthermore, it is irrelevant."

"Irrelevant?" Joshua's eyes opened wide with disbelief. "How can the murder victim's dying statement possibly be irrelevant?"

Carpinelli cast a cold, deadly stare at him. This time, Whitfield looked up.

"I'll take a short recess to weigh this decision," he said. "Court will reinstate in ten minutes."

The gavel sounded.

Carpinelli's face went white with fury. He took Joshua by the arm and dragged him off to the side.

"What do you think you're doing?" he demanded. "I should think the photos you received would have quelled any delusions you might have of winning this case."

Joshua jerked his arm away. "Yes, and to think I was afraid you'd forgotten me."

"Then why are you retaliating against my objections?"

"The judge would be suspicious if I didn't. This has to look realistic."

Carpinelli's mustache twisted with agitation.

"Listen," Joshua said, "besides the dying declaration, the only thing that places Louie at the scene of the crime is the testimony of MacDonald's wife. She only saw him briefly at the crime scene, and then again at the police lineup. Tell me you can't shoot down her testimony. Besides, I've no motive to argue. You know this."

Carpinelli smoothed his fingers over his mustache to stop the twitching. "You better be right."

The door to the judge's chamber opened and Whitfield took his place behind the bench again, this time with a fingernail file. Joshua and Carpinelli took their seats.

“The court will sustain the defense’s objection, based on the probability that the jury might be prejudiced,” Whitfield said. “The state’s argument will be stricken from the record and the dying declaration will be removed as evidence. Is there anything further, Mr. Parnell?”

“No.” Joshua felt disappointed, but not surprised.

Whitfield turned to the defense. “Mr. Carpinelli, proceed with the cross-examination.”

“I have no questions, Your Honor.”

“Then, due to the time, the court will reconvene tomorrow at 9:00 a.m. Court adjourned.”

The ring of the telephone broke the silence in Angelo Carpinelli’s den. Setting aside the documents before him, he reached across his desk to answer it.

“Yes?”

“It’s me,” a man said on the other end. “Two PIs are scoping the girl’s apartment from the building across the street. They’re wise to everything. They’re waiting for a chance to snatch the kid.”

Carpinelli nodded knowingly. “I anticipated this. Has a plan been made?”

“Nothing solid, but they’re prepared.”

“All right. I need you to do something....”

Sixteen

Clara noticed movement in Luke's darkened bedroom. She set down her magazine beside Dominic and left the sofa, quietly approaching his room. When she peeked in, she found him curled in a fetal position on the bed. When Luke saw her, he sat up at once. The light from the window shone on his striped pajamas. Sitting down beside him, she smoothed the hair from his forehead and saw in his face that he was relieved to see her.

"What's wrong, honey? Can't you sleep?"

"I had a bad dream," he whispered, as if the sound of his voice would reawaken the nightmare. "I dreamed about my Pa, that he sent me to my room 'cause he didn't wanna look at me. He said I made him sick."

He lowered his head. She watched his thin fingers toy with the folds in the blanket.

"He sent my brothers outside, then he came upstairs." He looked up at her, his eyes wide with confusion. "How come he came upstairs if he didn't wanna look at me?"

"I don't know," she said softly.

He gazed at the blankets again. "I counted his footsteps. Sixteen. Then he walked five steps to my room. He opened the door real quiet like. He didn't say nothin'. He just looked at me 'cause he knew there weren't nowhere for me to go. Then he beat me somethin' awful. It hurt, but I didn't scream or nothin'. That made him madder, so he throwed me down the stairs."

"Oh, honey, it was just a bad dream."

"Nuh-uh." He shook his head. "It happened. Once, when he throwed me down the stairs, I didn't wake up for hours. That's what my brothers said. I don't remember. I wish I'd stop dreamin' about it."

Wrapping her arms around him, she held him close and stroked his hair, which smelled of shampoo.

"Where was your mother when this was happening?"

"Dead. I killed her. That's why he does it."

"Why do you say that?"

"Because I gave her the fever and she died."

She held him closer. "Luke, believe me. You didn't kill her. I'm so sorry you went through that. You know that Dom and I would never hurt you."

"I know. Only my Pa can hurt me. He can 'cause I killed my Ma."

Wanting to refute this belief a second time, she could see him yawning and decided to wait until morning. "Try to sleep. Lie down and I'll tuck you in."

"Can I have another hug? My Ma used to hug me. I miss it."

"Honey, you can have as many hugs as you want."

She squeezed his small frame, brushed the mass of soft hair away from his forehead, and kissed it. While tucking him in, she had an inspiration. She dug her hands under the blankets, found his feet, and tickled them mercilessly. He barely moved, enduring the torture with high-pitched squeals of laughter. When she stopped, he asked for another hug, and she had to tuck him in again. This happened three times. Finally, she said good night and tucked him in so tightly that he couldn't move.

In the living room, she found Dominic watching her with new appreciation in his eyes.

"Is he seeing monsters again?" he asked, smiling.

She sat next to him and shook her head slightly. "His monsters are real."

Luke rolled from his stomach to his back with a drowsy moan and briefly opened his eyes. In the darkness of the room, broken only by the dim light from the window, he saw the glow of a tiny orange light floating above his head. It grew bright for a second, then faded to its former dimness. He looked at it dreamily and closed his eyes.

A creak sounded near his bed. A puff of warm smoke billowed in his face. Luke inhaled it and started to cough. Suddenly, he felt a hand on his mouth—a fat, foul-smelling hand that stifled his coughs and pressed his lips painfully against his teeth. His eyes opened wide.

The tiny orange light—the smoldering end of a cigarette—grew bright again, illuminating Benny's sullen face behind it. Luke screamed out a sharp, muffled shriek.

"Make one more peep and I'll snap your neck."

Luke's terrified eyes darted toward the door; his hope of seeing Dominic fell when he saw the door shut tightly. He looked back at Benny. The high shadows made by the burning cigarette stretched Benny's eyebrows into triangular arches and his scowl into a gruesome grin, a jack-o'-lantern come to life.

Benny took the cigarette from his mouth and blew the smoke into Luke's face again. Luke held his breath and pinched his eyes closed against its burning sting.

"Dirty little punk. I ought to ice you right now, but I got a beef to settle first."

The need for oxygen forced Luke to breathe in the polluted air. He immediately started to cough. Fearing Benny would blow more smoke in his eyes, Luke squinted through his lower lashes and watched him crush the cigarette on the nightstand with a twist of his fingers. Orange ash burst in a final flash of life, leaving only a wisp of smoke curling up from its crumpled stub. Benny reached into his pocket and withdrew his gun.

Luke screamed again and jerked his head from side to side, fighting to be free as his feet kicked at the blankets. He grabbed Benny's wrist with both hands and dug his nails into the taut tendons. Benny stifled the cry by pushing Luke deep into the pillow and jabbing the muzzle of the gun into his temple. His lips barely moved as he said, "Stop the dance, or I'll pump one into your head."

Breathing hard against the heavy hand, Luke stopped struggling. Uttering a satisfied grunt, Benny brought his face down close to Luke's. "I got questions, see? So, keep your beak closed till I say you can answer. And don't yell for Dominic, 'cause he can't hear nothing right now. And if his dame comes through that door, the last thing she'll see is your brains splattered all over this bed. Got it?"

Luke nodded and Benny hesitantly removed his hand.

"You warned Dominic that he'd get shot that night the Pompliano brothers got hit. Why didn't you warn me?"

"I only do what God tells me," Luke said, rubbing the nasty taste of Benny's hand from his lips with the back of his hand, "and He didn't tell me to warn you."

Benny uttered a string of curse words. "Don't give me that business. I don't believe it. You're some kind of Gypsy, a fortune-teller or something. These things I know about, and if you knew I'd get shot, you know other things, too. I want to know my future, so spill it, or this is yours." He lifted the gun so that it glinted in the light of the window.

Luke glared back, setting his jaw in firm defiance. "God ain't said to tell you nothin', and I ain't tellin' you nothin' on my own."

Benny shook his head with dwindling patience. "One thing I can't stand is a canary that won't sing." He slapped Luke hard across the mouth with the back of his hand. The blow snapped Luke's head to the side. "You must rate yourself a pretty tough boy, but if you don't start squawking, I'll bounce you off these walls. If that don't work, I'll send you through that window, and I don't care if it ain't open."

"Go ahead and try," Luke taunted, turning his head back to glare at Benny. "See how far you get."

Grabbing Luke by his pajamas, Benny jerked him off the bed and brought him close to his face. "Listen, you—!"

The sudden brilliance of lightning pierced the darkness of the room. A horrendous clap of thunder simultaneously shook the building. Benny recoiled in fright and dropped Luke back on the bed.

"What the—?" He surrendered his hands high into the air. "I didn't touch him!"

Landing on his back, Luke sat up quickly when the lightning receded. Then he froze. He saw movement in every recess of the room—a mass of hissing cats slinking toward the bed, their golden eyes glowing.

Dropping his arms, Benny followed Luke's gaze, seeing nothing.

"What's wrong?" he demanded.

Luke's eyes flashed at the ceiling. With a terrified shout, he pressed himself against the headboard.

"You're in one of them trances! Whad'ya see?"

Above them crept dozens of stalking felines, suspended by their feet, held by some unnatural force. The ceiling moved like a blanket of fur, caterwauling with eagerness. They began to drop with heavy thumps, landing on the bed, running over Luke's lap, leaping over one another in their zeal to attack Benny. One draped itself around his neck. In the vision, he shouted in terror as he kicked and pulled at them. Blood streaked his face and hands, saturating his torn clothing as the cats ravaged him with their sharp, vicious teeth.

Not seeing any of this but perceiving the horror manifested on Luke's face, Benny grabbed him by the shoulders and shook him violently.

"Come out of it!" He struck Luke across the face again with the back of his hand. "Whad'ya see?"

"A dead man."

Dominic's voice shattered the macabre vision like the smashing of glass. The light switched on and his strong arm slipped under Benny's arm. He swung Benny into a half nelson and yanked him from the room. Before Benny could react, Dominic spun him around and plunged his fist three times deep into his belly. Benny doubled over, grunting loudly with each punch. With his head hanging down, he did not see Dominic's fist as it slammed into the side of his head, sending him to the floor.

Dominic's cheeks were flushed with rage, his hair tousled around his head. Both hands were clenched into fists. Blood trickled from the swollen purple bruise on his temple. The fine red drops spattered across his shoulder stood in stark contrast to his white shirt. He threw a glance over his shoulder toward Luke.

"You okay?"

"Yeah," Luke said, slipping off the bed and to his feet.

With grim intent, Dominic watched Benny haul himself to his feet, his red face wet with perspiration. Gasping large gulps of air, Benny eyed Dominic's menacing stance before the door, debating whether or not he could take him.

"I got business here, Dom. It don't involve you."

"If you wanted him, you should've killed me."

"You think I'm stupid enough to whack Papa's favorite son?"

Benny staggered forward to force his way back into Luke's

room. Dominic pulled his gun from the holster beneath his arm, flipped it with smooth proficiency, and raked its handle hard across Benny's forehead. His skin split open; blood splattered across his face. With a shout, Benny reeled back, his arms flailing wildly as he fell.

"Now you know what it feels like to be pistol-whipped," Dominic said, tenderly touching his own wound with the tips of his fingers.

Clutching his bleeding head with one hand, Benny shouted several expletives. He stopped suddenly when he realized he was still holding his gun. He looked up. Seeing Luke leaning against the door frame beside Dominic, Benny came to his knees. He lifted his gun.

Dominic aimed his revolver directly at Benny's chest. Benny hesitated, then lowered his gun. He braced his hand against the wall to help himself stand.

"Just let me ask the kid a question. I want to know what he saw."

Luke swallowed uneasily. Glancing at Dominic, he put a hand to the growing lump on his face.

"Come on! Give! What did you see?"

"I saw you in torment," Luke said softly, "...in hell."

Benny couldn't seem to move at first, then aimed his gun at Luke. Dominic pushed Luke aside, and suddenly Benny was looking into the barrel of Dominic's revolver. It stopped him cold.

"Get out, unless you want another mouth where your nose is," Dominic said.

Benny's eyes darted with indecision between the gun and Luke, who peered around Dominic's back.

Dominic pulled back the hammer.

Finally, Benny backed away, maneuvering around the furniture until he reached the door.

"Someday," he said, pointing his finger at Luke, "that kid's gonna make swell trunk music."

Not daring to turn his back on Dominic, Benny opened the door behind him and stepped out. He did not bother to close it.

Dominic listened to Benny's footsteps as he descended the stairs and waited for the slam of the front door of the building before he closed and locked the apartment door. Replacing his gun in its holster, he returned to inspect Luke's swollen cheek.

"You okay? You're not going to cry or anything?"

Luke straightened his posture and set his shoulders back. "I've had worse."

"I'll bet you have." A thoughtful smile crossed Dominic's face. "You'll have a beautiful shiner in the morning."

Luke pointed to Dominic's injured head. "You'll have a beautiful shiner, too."

Dominic's smile turned into an embittered frown. "He knocked me cold. I didn't even hear him pick the lock. Come on." He placed a gentle hand on Luke's shoulder. "Let's clean ourselves up so you can go back to bed."

"I don't wanna go back to bed. Every time I wake up, somebody's in my face."

"Would you feel safer if I slept in the chair next to your bed?"

"Yeah," Luke nodded as they walked toward the bathroom. "What'd Benny mean when he said I was gonna make swell trunk music?"

"Don't worry about it."

"Yeah, but what's it mean?"

"It's an unpleasant way to dispose of a dead body," Dominic said flatly. "Leave it at that."

Nodding with solemn understanding, Luke said, "So, they hide the body in a trunk. What's the music part about?"

"If I told you, you wouldn't sleep for a week, and while we're on the subject of dead bodies, I suggest you work on your prophetic timing. Telling someone he's going to be tormented in hell, especially when he has a gun in his hand, isn't wise. Got it?"

Luke nodded sheepishly. "Got it."

SEVENTEEN

"Good to see you, Andy," Joshua said, welcoming Andy Ballantine into his office with a handshake. He motioned toward a chair. "Sit down. Care for some coffee?"

"No, thanks," Andy said with a vague smirk. "I've heard about your secretary's coffee." He placed his briefcase on the floor and sat down. "Are you on your way to the courthouse?"

"Yes. Why? What's happened?" Joshua sat across from him in the chair with a feeling of dread churning in his stomach.

"Well, it's not so much what's happened as what *hasn't* happened. We've searched Angelo's office and house. There are no pictures or negatives of the victim—not even a hint as to where he might've hid them."

Joshua dropped his gaze to the floor in disappointment. "I expected as much. He's not foolish enough to leave them lying around." He looked back at Andy with a sigh of resignation. "What next?"

"We're still watching the girl's apartment, waiting for an opportunity to get the boy. An interesting incident transpired last night, however. One of Papa Fratelli's men, Benny Rosario, was seen slapping the boy. Papa's son, Dominic, threw him out."

"Poor kid can't get a break. Is he okay?"

"Apparently. It confirmed one thing for us. Only one man is guarding him now."

"One man?" Joshua asked. "Couldn't we take him by surprise?"

"You're obviously not familiar with Dominic Fratelli. Whereas Louie is a brainless killer, Dominic is a cunning assassin. He's ruthless, *and* he's on the social register."

"Swell. We're up against a dapper killer. Does he place engraved apologies on the bodies he leaves behind?"

Andy grinned. "I bet the police wish he did. They might solve a few more murders. But if Dominic shot our men, the police would definitely get involved, which would bring your name to the surface. They'd want to know why a child was being held captive in that apartment and everything would come out. It's best to wait for an opportunity. When it comes, we won't be slow to act on it. Incidentally, how is the trial going?"

Joshua forced a frustrated laugh. "It's not easy letting a murderer go free while trying to convict him before the court. I wish it was over."

"It's only just begun." Andy stood. "Well, if there's nothing else—"

"Actually, there is. You might want to sit down again."

Andy sat as Joshua reached for his briefcase and extracted a large envelope.

"Here. Take these. I can't bear to look at them."

Andy accepted the envelope, opened it, and was caught off guard by the graphic photographs inside. He looked away, took a couple of deep breaths, and then studied them closely.

"How did you get these? They're copies, I presume?"

"Yes," Joshua said, "a little forget-me-not from Angelo."

Andy chuckled and pulled several photos from the bunch. "Here. Destroy these."

"What are you laughing at?" Joshua snapped with irritation. "That boy almost died."

He snatched them from Andy's hand. Flipping through them, he saw that the pictures were of himself and his car. None was of the boy.

"I'm sorry." Andy's face reddened. "It's not the pictures. It's just that I remember you saying you couldn't remember what the girl's apartment looked like. Well, when Angelo, our shrewd colleague, gave you these pictures, he also gave you the layout of the apartment."

Joshua showed the first signs of a smile in two months.

"Your Honor," Joshua said, addressing the court, "the state calls Mrs. Joan MacDonald to the stand."

For the first time, Judge Whitfield was attentive. He watched the attractive woman come forward with interest. A blonde in her early twenties, she was the tragic model of premature widowhood. She wore a black dress and a veiled hat, and she clutched a small Bible in her gloved hands. Carpinelli barely glanced at her as the bailiff swore her in.

"Mrs. MacDonald, what was your relation to Fred MacDonald?" Joshua asked.

"I was his wife," she answered softly.

"What was his occupation?"

"He was the pastor of Clear Creek Chapel here in Denver."

"Mrs. MacDonald, can you tell me where you were on the twenty-sixth of November, 1931?"

"Yes. Fred and I were spending Thanksgiving with my parents in Loveland. We got a late start home and arrived in Denver around midnight."

"And are your parents here today?" Joshua asked.

"Yes." She pointed to an elderly couple sitting behind the prosecution table. Joshua glanced at them with vague interest.

"Mrs. MacDonald, explain to the court what happened that night."

She took a deep breath and braced herself against the chair. "We were driving through the intersection of Seventeenth and Wazee, not far from Union Station, when another car ran the stop sign and crashed into us. Neither of us was hurt, so Fred was about to get out to look at the damage when two men from the other car jumped out. They were yelling and stumbling like they were drunk, so Fred decided to stay inside. We locked our doors. One tried to force the door open on my side. When he couldn't, he became upset and shook the car."

"Can you identify this man?" Joshua asked.

"No. It was too dark."

"Then what happened?"

"Louie Fratelli came to Fred's side of the car and demanded that he roll the window down."

"I move that the word *demanded* be stricken," Carpinelli said with a distinct frown. "The witness must tell the court exactly what the suspect said."

She bit her bottom lip and glanced at her parents for direction.

"Motion sustained. Please answer the question, Mrs. MacDonald." Whitfield peered down from his bench, his eyes moving from her legs to her face.

"He took the Lord's name in vain and said, 'Roll the window down.'"

"Which man said this?" Joshua asked.

"He said it." She pointed directly at Louie. Out of the corner of Joshua's eye, he saw Louie slink down in his chair.

"Please go on," Joshua said.

"Mr. Fratelli looked closely at Fred and asked what his name was. Fred wouldn't tell him. He said he wanted to look at Fred's license, but that was only an excuse to get the window down."

"I ask that her conclusion be stricken," Carpinelli said, scarcely glancing up from his notes.

Whitfield nodded in agreement. His eyes traveled back to her legs. "Yes, it will be stricken. Please continue."

"Fred pulled a piece of paper out of his wallet. I don't know what it was, but it wasn't his license. He rolled the window down just enough to slip it through the opening. Mr. Fratelli grabbed it and tried to get his fingers through the window, but Fred rolled it up in time. Then Mr. Fratelli cursed and said he couldn't see it in the dark, so Fred suggested he read it in the beam of the headlights. He did this, and, while he was standing in front of the car, Fred put it in reverse and backed down the road to get away."

She hesitated, unconsciously squeezing the Bible in her hands. The crowd sat in quiet zeal, watching her gaze wander the floor with pensive recollection and the frown on her pretty face intensify as she relived her husband's murder.

"Mr. Fratelli ran and jumped on the hood of the car. He busted the headlight and pulled the horn wire loose. Then, he swung around on the running board on Fred's side and shattered the window in the door with his fist, hitting Fred right in the face. Glass flew everywhere. Fred started bleeding. He swerved the car around to get away, but the engine died. That's when Mr. Fratelli put his hand inside the door and opened it. Fred braced himself against the seat to kick him off and yelled at me to go for help."

Tears streamed down her face. She dabbed at them with her gloved hands. Joshua pulled his handkerchief from his breast pocket and offered it to her. Smiling gratefully, she accepted it.

With a shaky breath, she continued, "When I got out, the other man grabbed me. I never saw his face. I screamed. He put his hand over my mouth, dragged me to his car, and forced me into the backseat. I got out on the other side and ran back to our car, when he"—she pointed an accusing finger at Louie—"shot my husband three times."

Louie dropped his eyes.

"Somehow...somehow I got back into our car. Fred wasn't moving. When I touched him, he fell across...fell across my lap."

Joshua allowed the widow a few moments to compose herself while he glanced at the jury, knowing her attractiveness wouldn't hurt her testimony. The twelve men regarded her somberly, some shaking their heads.

"They ran back to their car and drove away," she finally said. "I pulled myself from under Fred and ran up the street, screaming. Two men came out to help me. They put Fred in their truck and took us to the hospital."

"Mrs. MacDonald," Joshua asked, "have you identified the perpetrator as Louie Fratelli?"

She nodded vehemently. "Yes."

"For the record, will you point him out one last time?"

"He's sitting next to that man there," she said, clearly indicating Louie and Carpinelli.

Following her gesture, Joshua froze. His heart jumped inside his chest, threatening to leap into his mouth. Sitting behind the defense table was the boy—the boy he had almost killed—dressed in a dark blue suit with a cap in his lap and his hair perfectly combed. The bruising on his cheek and the purplish black eye caused his pallid complexion to have an unearthly, translucent hue, like one near death.

As if sensing that he was being watched, the boy's head turned directly toward Joshua and their eyes met. He caught his breath. A sharp pang of guilt seized his chest. The straightforward gaze of the boy's green eyes hollowed out a part of Joshua's soul with the terror of standing condemned before a revengeful ghost, horrifying in its ethereal presence yet placid in its innocence and timeless youth. That unwavering gaze said as clearly as any words could utter: *See what you've done to me?*

He knows! Joshua thought. *They've told him who I am! He knows I almost killed him! He knows I tried to kill him! Stop looking at me like that! Oh, I'm going to be sick! Why doesn't he say something if he knows? Why doesn't he—?*

"Are you still with us, Mr. Parnell?"

Whitfield's voice felt like a blow jump-starting his heart. He became aware that his lingering silence had brought the attention of the entire courtroom upon him. Shaking himself free of his reverie, he forced himself to turn away.

"Ah...let the record show that the witness identified the defendant as the murderer," he said. "You may examine."

A fleeting look at Carpinelli showed his undisguised pleasure. Joshua almost staggered to the prosecution table. His hands were trembling and wet. He hid them under the table.

Carpinelli stood before Joan MacDonald with an air of pious indifference. He glanced at her coldly before looking away, preferring to gaze at the distant walls of the courtroom.

"Mrs. MacDonald, you said you saw two men, but you could identify only one. Were there street lamps nearby?"

"No. It was dark," she answered.

"Then how is it you identified the perpetrator?"

"I saw his face in the headlight when he bent down to read the paper Fred gave him."

"And what exactly did you see?" he asked.

"I saw Louie Fratelli."

"What you saw is a man you *believed* to be Louie Fratelli. Isn't that correct?"

"No, I saw him quite clearly."

"Please give the court a detailed description of the man you saw."

"I saw a heavyset man wearing a black Chesterfield coat

and a fedora," she said. "He was Italian and had a thin mustache, just like he's wearing now."

"I ask that her last words be stricken," Carpinelli said.

"Objection sustained," Whitfield said, his gaze still lingering on Joan's calves.

"When was the next time you claim to have seen the defendant?"

"Three days after Fred was murdered," she said. "I picked him out of a police lineup."

Carpinelli leaned against the witness box, close to the young woman's face, forcing her to move back uncomfortably.

"Let me understand this. Three whole days passed since the murder, and yet you claim you could identify a man out of a police lineup—a man whom you had seen only briefly in the undiscriminating beam of a headlight on a dark night?"

Her pretty face darkened in anger. "I would know my husband's murderer if it had been three whole years."

"Tell me, Mrs. MacDonald, the other men in the lineup, what color were they?"

"They were white."

"Not Italian?"

Her eyes narrowed. "I couldn't be certain."

"Did any of the other men have mustaches?"

"Some."

"I see," he said, intentionally pausing for dramatic effect. "Is there any chance you were mistaken when you picked Mr. Fratelli out of the police lineup?"

"No."

"No?" he asked with feigned incredulity. "Had you ever seen the defendant before the night of November 26, 1931?"

She clenched her teeth and forced out a quiet, "No."

"Did you notice any irregularities in the appearance of the perpetrator when you saw him in the beam of the headlights?"

"What do you mean?"

"Did you notice any abnormalities in his appearance?"

"Not that I remember," she said with hesitation.

"Not that you remember. I see. You did not notice whether the perpetrator had a harelip, did you?"

"He had a mustache."

"That's not what I asked. Did the perpetrator have a harelip?"

"I don't remember."

"Judge, may the court recognize that Louie Fratelli was born with the obvious birth defect of a harelip"—every eye in the courtroom turned to look at Louie, who sank deeper in his chair—"but Mrs. MacDonald never made mention of it to the court or to the police in her description of the man who murdered her husband. Mrs. MacDonald, do you know why the perpetrator wanted to know your husband's identity?"

"No."

"Did your husband have any enemies?"

Her eyes opened wide in astonishment. "Certainly not."

He turned his back on her. "I see. So, as far as you know, Mr. Fratelli did not know your husband and, therefore, had no reason to murder him. Isn't that correct?"

"I don't know why he did it. I just know that he did."

Carpinelli took a deep breath, smiled, and turned toward Joan. "Let's get back to the crime, shall we? When did you get out of the car to run for help?"

"When Mr. Fratelli was struggling with Fred."

"How far did you run?"

"Just a few feet before the other man grabbed me. He pulled me to his car and threw me into the backseat."

"Did you notice what kind of car it was?"

"It was a 1928 Studebaker."

Carpinelli looked startled, confused. "How can you be

certain? It was dark. You were frightened. You were being chased by a faceless perpetrator."

"Because my parents own the same type of car. I recognized it right after the crash."

"Well, in your haste to notice the year and make of the car, did you happen to see the license plate number?"

"There wasn't time."

"You mean to tell me that there was enough time for you to determine the year and make of the automobile but not enough time to read the license plate?"

"I didn't even see the license plate," she retorted.

"What kind of car was your husband driving?"

"A 1927 Ford Model T—um, I mean a Model A."

"You're able to give the year and make of the perpetrator's car, but you can't even remember the model of your own car?"

When she opened her mouth to protest, he cut her off with a condescending wave of his hand. "Never mind. That's all I have."

"You may step down, Mrs. MacDonald," Whitfield said, and watched her do so while he addressed the court. "Gentlemen, I would like to adjourn for the day and reconvene Monday morning at 9:00 a.m. Court adjourned."

Nearly in tears, Joan reached for her parents, who stood to meet her with their arms outstretched.

Pleased with himself, Carpinelli turned around in his chair and smiled at Luke, immediately noticing his black eye. When he looked at Dominic, who sat at Luke's left, to demand an explanation, he saw the white bandage across his temple and the black eye directly beside it.

"What happened to you two?" he asked.

"Benny," Dominic simply said.

"Where is he now?"

"I don't know. I threw him out."

"You should've done more than that," Carpinelli scolded. "I'm glad you were able to bring Luke here on such short notice. Take him back to the girl's apartment now. His presence has accomplished what I intended."

With a wry glance, Carpinelli eyed his opponent across the room. Joshua was staring into his open briefcase as though he was considering losing his lunch inside it.

"Luke! Luke!"

Luke's head shot up. Joy brightened his eyes at the sight of the elderly couple embracing Joan MacDonald. Their faces beamed with excitement. Their arms opened wide.

"Pastor! Mrs. Elliott!"

Carpinelli and Joshua spun around to see the boy rush toward the old couple until Dominic yanked him back. He thrust Luke into Carpinelli's arms and said, "Get him out of here, fast."

Carpinelli dragged Luke from the courtroom, kicking and screaming out the Elliotts' names.

Dominic pressed toward the Elliotts as they attempted to follow the struggling boy through the crowd. His hand seized Edmund's shoulder and brought him to an abrupt halt. Edmund turned with surprise to find a concealed gun jabbing him in the ribs.

"Find another kid for your fortune-telling racket," Dominic said into his ear. "This one's no longer yours."

Dominic put his gun back into his suit and disappeared into the throng, leaving the Elliotts standing there, stunned.

None of this was lost on Joshua.

Eighteen

I don't wanna go upstairs," Luke grumbled. "I wanna go back to Pastor and Mrs. Elliott."

He twisted his shoulders away from Dominic's prodding hand as it forced him through the doorway of Clara's apartment building. Reluctantly entering the lobby, Luke stopped at the base of the staircase.

"I already told you. I can't let you do that," Dominic said, nudging him forward. "Don't make this harder than it has to be."

Luke spun around and swatted Dominic's hand away with exasperation. "Stop pushin' me! I don't wanna go!"

"You have two options"—Dominic crossed his arms and blocked the door as Luke studied his chances of reaching the exit—"and running out that door isn't one of them. You can walk up those stairs, or I can carry you up those stairs. Now, which will it be?"

Luke set his face in a defiant pout. He crossed his arms, glared beneath his furrowed brow, and stood his ground.

Suppressing a laugh, Dominic feigned irritation and shook his head. "So, you've chosen to be carried."

Before Luke could reconsider, Dominic picked him up with one arm and ascended the stairs. Luke didn't utter a word. He didn't fight. He kept his arms stubbornly crossed and his expression sour until Dominic set him against the wall next to the apartment door.

"Stay put." Dominic pulled the latchkey from his pocket but hesitated before sliding it into the keyhole. Luke's sulking countenance, downcast eyes, and pouting bottom lip made him feel like a rogue. Flipping the key over in his hand, he sighed apologetically. "Look, I don't call the shots. I'm sorry it has to be this way, but until I'm told differently, this is where we stay."

Driving his hands deep into his pockets, Luke scowled at the floor while the toe of his shoe burrowed into the carpet.

"It's not all that bad. You have new clothes. You eat well. You're not scratching at death's door anymore. I know you're bored and you miss your friends, but you've probably never had it this good. Am I right?"

Luke's foot kept digging until it bored a permanent impression in the carpet.

"Beats living with your father, doesn't it?"

"I don't know." Luke shrugged his shoulders, refusing to look up. "I get beat up here, too."

"It's that mug of yours. It turns some people into suckers and others into brutes. I promise you this: if Benny lays a hand on you again, he'll be the one making beautiful trunk music. Now, wipe that pout off your face and I'll teach you how to play cards. Okay?"

With a playful shove, Dominic jostled Luke off balance. Luke grinned, righting himself. "Yeah. Okay."

Feeling slightly less like a heel, Dominic inserted the key into the lock. He had barely turned it, feeling the latch give way to his pressure, when a voice warned, "She's not alone, friend."

The voice was close. Its tone sent shivers of dread through Dominic. He spun around, catching a glimpse of a man standing in a nearby doorway, his figure silhouetted by a dim light, his face concealed by his fedora. From inside the apartment, Clara screamed, "Dom! It's a trap!"

Dominic swung around, pushing Luke behind him as the door flew open.

"Hands up, Fratelli!" A burly man in a brown suit loomed in the entrance, but Dominic primarily saw the revolver pointed at his chest. With a thrust of his arm, he knocked it aside as it exploded with a shot. The blast rang in his ears, and the bullet splintered the staircase railing. Bolting forward, he drove against the man with all his might, throwing his fist square across his jaw. Arms flailing, the man tumbled backward with a shout, landing on his back beside the coffee table.

Dominic reached for his gun. A dark blue blur rushed toward him. Before he could turn, a second man jumped from behind the door, arms open wide, tackling him from the side. The force sent them both reeling. Unable to keep his balance, Dominic fell hard on his stomach, his hand pinned beneath his chest and his gun useless against his palm.

"Get off your duff and help me!" the man yelled, pressing all of his weight on Dominic to keep him down. His voice wavered with fear. The man in brown rolled to his knees. Sweat streamed down his reddened face. Dominic was struggling fiercely for an inch of leverage, just enough to free his arm, when the man in brown lifted his beefy fist and brought it down brutally on his wounded temple.

Flashes of light and pain burst through his head with the first two blows. He heard the words 'Lights out!' just before the third blow pounded him into a sea of blackness. He drifted in that abyss for what felt like hours, pressed into its murky bog by a cumbersome pressure, until the weight lifted. Sifting through the muffled words that resonated in his ears, he realized that only seconds had passed.

One man said, "That was a cinch."

"Says you. He didn't belt *you* in the mouth."

"Tie him up. I'll grab the kid."

"Where's his gun?"

"I didn't see one."

Through the fog, Dominic heard the sounds of a brief struggle and of Luke shouting, "Let me go!" One man yelped with pain. Then he heard Luke's light feet running down the stairs with heavier feet in pursuit. Pain pounded through his head, a sharp rhythm coinciding with each beat of his heart.

Opening his eyes, he saw a blurry image of the sofa. Clara stood frightened against the wall. The man in brown stood over him, legs spread wide, the gun in his hand pointing at Dominic's head. He raised himself to his hands and knees.

"Plant yourself in that chair," the man said, jerking the gun sideways, "and no one else will get hurt. All we want is the kid."

Dominic's vision became clearer. Greatly exaggerating his efforts to stand, he intentionally fell on his knees before regaining his feet.

"I never figured you'd have a glass jaw, Fratelli."

"Dom!" Clara reached out to help him, but Dominic stretched out his left hand to keep her away, stumbled forward, and drove his right fist with all his might into the man's sternum.

With a grunt, he doubled over. Reeling back, Dominic hit him hard in the face with his left fist, spinning him halfway around and sending him tottering to the floor. Fumbling against surprise and pain, the man came to his knees, lifting his gun as he turned. Dominic drew his revolver, pulled back the hammer, and aimed the barrel an inch from the man's face.

"Always check for a gun," he said.

Dominic noticed that the man's terrified eyes were blue just before he pulled the trigger. Clara's scream rivaled the explosion. Blood splattered the carpet, the wall, and Dominic's suit and hands. The force of the shot propelled the body backward to the floor. Dominic calmly wiped his bloody hands on his ruined suit and replaced the revolver in its holster. Turning, he walked to the door and looked around; the man in the shadows was gone. Returning to the dead body, he knelt beside it and ransacked its pockets. No wallet. No identification.

Clara stood braced against the wall, mouth slightly open, eyes wide with horror.

Dominic rose to his feet and took her gently by the arms. "Did they hurt you?"

She seemed not to hear him; her stare was fixed on the bloody corpse. The nose and mouth were obliterated, replaced with a gaping hole of mutilated flesh. Only the blue eyes remained.

"Clara, look at me." He cupped her jaw in his hand, directing her face toward his. "Did they hurt you?"

She shook her head absently, her fingernails sinking into his arms.

"Call Angelo. Tell him what happened. Pack some things for you and Luke and go to the Fratelli Estate. Do you understand?"

He drew her to the telephone, trying to secure her attention by placing the receiver in her hand and turning her away from the body.

"Did you hear what I said?"

She peered up at him. Unable to speak, she simply nodded.

"I'm going after Luke. I'll meet you at the estate. Lock the door behind me."

Stepping unceremoniously over the corpse, he left the apartment. Once outside, he searched up and down the street, catching the bobbing sight of the man in blue running at full speed three blocks away. He turned a corner and disappeared from view. Luke was nowhere to be seen.

Dominic ran. Dashing into the street, he dodged two streetcars and scarcely avoided being struck by a dairy truck.

Reaching the other sidewalk, he pressed through the pedestrians, ignoring their surprise at seeing a young man with bloodstained clothes charging down the pavement. In moments, he approached the same street where the man had turned and saw him running in the distance. Block after block he chased him, gaining on him, sidestepping people and cutting between cars in traffic, disregarding angry shouts and screeching brakes. By the time he reached Union Station, only a half block separated them, but still he had not seen Luke.

The man turned into a narrow alley between two brick warehouses. Gauging his distance, Dominic slowed to a walk, his heart beating firmly against his chest. The roar of a freight train clattered nearby, its doleful whistle warning of danger.

He felt hot. Loosening his tie, he took a quick look around. Seeing no one, he drew his revolver. It was warm. With his back against the wall, he glanced around the corner. The man in the blue suit, breathing hard from his run, tottered down the alley, his own gun poised in preparation. He paused, taking deep breaths as he searched inside the wooden crates and garbage cans that lined the alley.

"I know you're here, kid," he said between gasps. "Come on out. I want to take you home. You want to go home, don't you?"

Dominic watched him approach a low-level staircase leading down to the basement entrance of a building. Propping himself against the wrought iron railing, he leaned over and looked below, panting.

"There you are. Come on up. I won't hurt you. Honest."

Dominic aimed his gun.

"I said get up here. Don't make me come down there and get you."

Receiving no response, the man was turning to descend the stairs when Dominic pulled the trigger. The blast of gunfire ricocheted off the buildings. The man jerked backward wildly. His hat flew off his head. Somehow, he managed to stay on his feet. Lurching forward, he stumbled two steps and clutched the railing. Blood spread across his chest.

He raised his gun and his head at the same time, straining to behold his killer, before another shot exploded in the air, dropping him dead on his face in the wet cobblestone alley.

Glancing around for witnesses and seeing none, Dominic entered the alley. His steps echoed off the brick walls. With his foot, he shoved the body onto its back, bending over to feel the pockets. No wallet. No identification.

Standing, he looked down the stairs to see Luke crouched in a damp corner.

"It's all right. Come on up."

Luke did not move. His hands clutched at his chest as he coughed and gasped for air.

"What's wrong?"

Between each wheezing breath, Luke whispered, "Can't... breathe...."

Returning his gun to its holster, Dominic hurried down the stairs to kneel before him. Seeing the bluish color of Luke's lips and the paleness of his skin, he loosened Luke's tie and undid the top buttons of his shirt.

"You ran too fast, that's all. Take slow, deep breaths."

Shaking his head with erratic movements, Luke tried to speak. The only sound that came from his lips was the wheeze from deep within his lungs. Giving up, he dropped his head back against the wall. His eyelids fluttered closed.

"Don't do this, Luke." Dominic tapped his cold cheeks. "Come on, pal. Stay with me."

Reaching under Luke's legs and back, Dominic cradled him in his arms and laid his small head upon his shoulder.

"Don't worry. You'll be okay. Just breathe."

Dominic took the stairs two at a time. Careful to divert Luke's head away from the corpse, he carried him into the street toward Union Station, where he hailed a cab. In the distance, he heard police sirens.

NINETEEN

Thank you for seeing us on such short notice," Edmund Elliott said, removing his hat and extending his withered hand. "This is my wife, Edith, and you know our daughter, Joan."

"Yes, yes. Please come in," Joshua replied, returning the gentleman's handshake and observing that he was dressed in a gray suit, somewhat dated yet pressed and spotless. He smiled at the elderly woman, adorned in a floral turquoise dress, the hem only inches above her ankles, and gently shook her frail hand. For Joan, still dressed in mourning, he softened his smile and patted her on the forearm.

"Please sit down."

He pulled a third chair from the reception area into his office. Hurrying around his desk, he took his seat, ignoring the squeak, and clasped his hands together tightly to hide his impatience.

"What can I do for you, Reverend?"

"First, we wanted to thank you," Edmund said. "Fred's death was a terrible shock, and it's a great comfort to know you're doing everything you can to bring Louie Fratelli to justice."

Joshua cringed inwardly, muttered a half-articulate response, and brushed the gratitude off with a wave of his hand.

"Second," Edmund continued, "we were wondering if you noticed a boy in the courtroom today, sitting behind the defense table."

"I believe so." To keep his eyes from bulging with anticipation, Joshua furrowed his eyebrows and cleared his throat. "A good-looking lad about ten, wearing a dark blue suit, thin, brown hair, bruised eye?" He could have bitten through his tongue. *So much for being casual.*

"Yes, that's the one. You're very observant."

"Not really. I heard you call out to him and saw him being carried away. Is he your grandson?"

"No, but we consider ourselves his guardians, and we'd like to have him back."

"Are you his legal guardians?" Joshua put his elbows on the desk, folded his hands again, and tried keep his fingers from wiggling.

"No. You see, he's a runaway. His father beat him, so we took him in. The last time we saw him was on New Year's Eve. We had no idea what had become of him until today."

"Mr. Parnell," Edith implored in a gentle voice, "you saw how glad he was to see us. He was happy in our home. We hoped you could help us."

"Unfortunately, if you aren't his legal guardians, I've no grounds to return him to you. However, if we can notify his parents, I might be able to do something. What's the boy's name?"

Edmund smiled sheepishly. "It gets a little tricky here. We don't know his name."

"I see. How long did you say he stayed with you?"

"I know this sounds odd, but Luke never told us his name."

Joshua cocked his eyebrow. "Luke?"

"That's the name we gave him," Edmund said. "He was so afraid he'd be returned to his father that he refused to tell us anything, so we gave him a name. It was better than calling him 'Boy.' We hoped that in time he would feel comfortable enough to tell us."

"So, you don't know his name, where he's from, or who his parents are?"

"Correct."

"In essence, he could disappear off the face of the earth and no one would know. No one would care."

"We would know," Edith corrected him. "We would care."

Joshua barely heard her; he did not even look at her.

"Perhaps you didn't notice," Edmund said, "but as Luke was carried off, a young man approached us. He pointed a gun at me—right there in the courtroom—and said Luke was no longer ours. Do you know who this man was?"

"You don't know how sorry I am to tell you this, Reverend, but that was Dominic Fratelli, one of Louie's relatives." Joshua watched their faces drop with dismay and felt his own stomach churn.

"How did Luke get mixed up with them?" Edith asked. "He's a good boy."

"It probably wasn't his fault." Unable to meet her fretful gaze, Joshua glanced down and bit his lip. "Believe me, *nothing* would please me more than to return him to you, but it's impossible. The Fratellis are an organized crime family. Their power in this city is too great."

"Does that mean Louie won't be convicted for murdering Fred?" Joan asked, tears forming in her eyes.

Joshua couldn't meet her gaze either. "Mrs. MacDonald, the chance is slim. You are the only witness, and the defense has questioned your testimony. I've no motive to argue and no murder weapon to produce. Louie has both an alibi and the best defense attorney in the state."

After several moments of silence, Edmund interjected, "I may have a motive."

Joshua looked up at him.

"It's possible the Fratellis had a personal vendetta against Fred, and they may be holding Luke as a form of collateral. Perhaps that's why Dominic knows who I am."

His wife and daughter looked at him with surprise. Joshua's throat tightened while his stomach seized into a knot.

"Wha—wha—what do you mean, 'collateral'?" he stammered. "Collateral for what?"

Before Edmund could answer, the door bolted open. Andy Ballantine burst inside, his red face perspiring, his tie wrenched into a knot beneath his unbuttoned collar. He had almost spoken until he had seen that Joshua was not alone. After a quick study of Andy's expression, Joshua stood.

"An urgent situation has come up, Reverend. I must defer our conversation to a later time. Will you give my secretary a number where I can reach you, please?"

The Elliott family came to their feet, cordially hiding their disappointment, and retired from the room as Andy slumped into one of the vacated chairs. Joshua locked the door behind them, turned, and demanded, "What's wrong?"

"Two of my men are missing," Andy said breathlessly. "I fear they're dead."

Joshua walked around his desk and sank into his chair. "How? Why?"

"Dominic took the boy out of the apartment today. There wasn't time to tell you." Andy ran his fingers through his short blond hair, leaving portions of it standing straight on end. "We had to act fast. They were followed to the courthouse."

"Yes, I saw them."

"I sent two men to the girl's apartment to wait for their return. Later, a passerby reported hearing gunfire and the police found blood on the carpet. My men have been missing ever since."

"Wonderful," Joshua groaned. "Now the police are involved. How long before they trace this back to us?"

"With any luck, never. They've disappeared—Dominic, the girl, the kid. They don't want the police involved any more than we do. Papa Fratelli won't let his favorite son go up for murder, so it's not hard to guess where they're hiding. Are you familiar with the Fratelli Estate? It's a fortress, an empire. It's so far removed from the law that it might as well be a foreign country. If he's there, you'll never see that boy unless Papa Fratelli wants you to."

"I'm lost." A strangling sensation constricted Joshua's throat as though Andy had tied a weight around his neck and thrown him into a river.

"I've done all I can." Andy threw his hands up in frustration. "These men were young. They had wives, children."

"I'm sorry." Joshua pulled at the imaginary weight around his throat with his fingers.

"So am I. You'll have to sabotage your case against Louie and pray Angelo doesn't take you down afterward. It's all you can do."

For a full minute, they sat in silence until Joshua's stomach demanded he prepare it a bicarbonate of soda. He opened his desk drawer to pull out the baking soda.

"You won't believe this," he said, rummaging through the drawer. "Remember the people you saw in here? They're the victim's in-laws, the Elliotts. But they're also something else."

With a shrug of his shoulders, Andy asked, "What? Gunrunners?"

"Hardly. They are the boy's self-appointed guardians."

Andy blinked a couple of times. He sat up straight. "The boy you ran over?"

"No, the boy I keep hidden in my pocket. Of course, the boy I ran over. Who else?"

"Well, it's a little coincidental, isn't it?"

"It's more than coincidental." After measuring the precise dosage of baking soda, Joshua stirred it into a glass of water and took a drink. "All they know about him is that he's a battered runaway and they want him back. They call him Luke because he's afraid to tell them his real name."

"Where do these people come from?"

"Loveland."

"Not much up there except farmland."

"And a little farm boy who turned my life upside down." Joshua took another drink.

A shrewd smirk turned Andy's mouth into a sneer. He leaned forward and rested his elbows on his knees.

"Is that the same little farm boy who jumped in front of your car and begged you to bash his head open?"

Joshua's hand flew to his mouth to keep the drink from spewing across the desk. Swallowing it with one hard gulp, he glared at Andy. "I didn't deserve that."

"Neither did he."

"Whose side are you on?"

"Yours," Andy said, "but his life's been turned upside down, too. One minute he's playing dominoes with Grandma and Grandpa; the next he's learning Italian. You have an obligation to get him out of there."

"Just what do you think I've been trying to do the last few weeks? Should I place a call to J. Edgar Hoover next?"

Andy's blue eyes narrowed into slits. "How bad do the Elliotts want him back?"

"Why?"

"We could backdate guardianship papers and retrieve him *legally*."

"That's fraud!" Joshua exclaimed. "That's illegal!"

"So is the consumption of alcohol, reckless endangerment, vehicular assault, tampering with evidence, and leaving the scene of a crime—or need I remind you, Deputy District Attorney?"

Joshua sat back, stunned into silence.

"Somehow, we've got to get that boy," Andy said, standing. He smoothed the unruly strands of his hair with a stroke of his palms. "I'll check with the police to see whether anyone reported a runaway fitting his description. You saw him today. What does he look like? I can't go by those photos you gave me. His face must be disfigured after taking a bite out of your car."

"No, it's not," Joshua snapped. "His face is just fine. He's a good-looking kid, maybe nine or ten years old, brown hair, green eyes, probably Anglo-Saxon or Scandinavian. He's thin. I'll bet he doesn't weigh fifty pounds. I don't know what good this will do."

"Leave that to me. I suggest you reconsider offering the old folks the guardianship papers. If you don't, perhaps I can find his *real* family, this mysterious kindred who so terrorized him that he was loath to reveal his own name. Perhaps with the right incentive, *they'll* help us get him back. Maybe they miss knocking him silly around the house."

"Enough!" Joshua shouted, jumping to his feet. "I'm not the bad guy here! I didn't mean to hit him, and I can't go back in time to change it!"

Bracing himself against the desk with both hands flat, Joshua closed his eyes to control his breathing. In a quieter tone, he said, "I'll speak to the Elliotts. They're honest people. They may not go for this."

"If they want him badly enough, they will." Andy stepped toward the door. "Explain to them the danger he's in. Ask if they want him brought up as a paid assassin frequenting prostitutes and running liquor on back roads. Tell them the life expectancy of a gangster is short. He'll be lucky to see his twenty-first birthday. You get the picture."

Joshua opened his eyes to the distinct feeling that the weight around his neck had finally reached the muddy bottom of the river, drawing his doomed body behind it.

TWENTY

From the third-story landing at the Fratelli Estate, Clara surveyed the wide-open marble hall, noting that nothing had changed since her last visit. Every sculpture, every masterful painting, every inlaid piece of Baroque furniture was in its place. The Tiffany chandeliers were burning, gaslights that illuminated the heavily papered walls with a yellow glow and lightly brightened the stairway of polished golden oak that ascended to the fourth story of the mansion. Nothing was amiss.

Having unpacked the few items that she had brought from her apartment, Clara descended the stairs, deciding to wait for Dominic and Luke by the massive fireplace in the hall. She paused on the first landing of the grand staircase, the stained-glass window behind her.

"You have never looked more beautiful, *bella mia*. The light through the stained glass reveals the red in your hair."

The voice sent shivers of fear through Clara. At the sound of Papa Fratelli's voice, she started and looked down to find him at the base of the stairs, one hand on the railing. He stood in perfect darkness—not the décor around him but he himself. The late afternoon sun filled the entrance hall, yet he refracted it, an impenetrable shadow ascending the stairs. Though he walked through the arched light from the stained-glass window, he did not emerge from the gloom until he stood before her.

Clara took a step back, wondering whether to run past him or further up the stairs. In the end, she simply stood there, terrified, although nothing in his demeanor provoked it. He was, in fact, smiling in a fatherly manner, his hands clasped thoughtfully behind his back.

"I frightened you. I am sorry."

"Hello, Papa," she said, forcing herself to smile. "I didn't know you were there."

Struck with his overpowering presence, she gazed into his swarthy face, a handsome one resembling Dominic's, though older and framed by soft, silver hair. He stood tall, distinguished, and well-dressed in a tailored black suit and smelled pleasantly of tobacco and cologne. Despite his smile, she perceived ruthlessness in his dark eyes—a perpetual expression inclined toward wanton butchery. While that look had always disturbed her, it now terrified her; she had seen the same malicious indifference in Dominic when he had killed the man in her apartment.

Turning from Papa Fratelli's malevolent eyes toward the front door, which stood adjacent to the staircase, she said, "Dom and Luke should be here soon, don't you think?"

A floorboard creaked behind her. She felt his breath upon her neck, the warmth of his hand on the small of her back. She did not need to look at him to know the craving in his eyes. She wanted to recoil; she did not dare.

"I am pleased you are here, *bella mia*." He spoke the words close to her ear. "This old house lacks in feminine warmth, and I have thought of you often."

Closing her eyes, a moan escaped her just before the doorbell rang.

"Dom!" she cried out.

The butler arrived, dressed in formal black attire, and had barely opened the cumbersome oak door when Clara heard Dominic say, "Get Dr. Ameche over here now."

His voice sent a flood of relief through Clara as Papa Fratelli stepped back, removing his hand. Bearing Luke in his arms, Dominic brushed past the butler. The sound of his steps echoed on the marble floor, resounding against the high-coffered ceilings of the entrance hall. With a nod, the butler closed the door and disappeared quietly.

"Dom! What happened?"

Looking up and to the right, he found her leaning over the banister. Though shivering from the February chill, having sacrificed his jacket to wrap around Luke, his face lit up with a smile.

"You look beautiful with the sun coming through the stained glass," he said. "I never knew there was red in your hair."

"Dominic?"

They both glanced up to see Carpinelli descending the staircase. His mustache twitched with agitated spasms. Hastening downward, he peered into Luke's ashen face. The boy's eyes were lost in a vacant stare as he concentrated solely on forcing the air from his lungs and gasping for another breath.

Seeing the blood on Dominic's clothing, Carpinelli demanded, "What happened? Was he shot?"

"No. He's having an asthma attack."

Carpinelli sighed with relief. A bead of sweat trickled down his cheek. He pulled a handkerchief from his pocket to dab his face.

"Where's Papa?" Dominic asked. "I thought I saw him standing there."

Clara turned around to see that, indeed, Papa Fratelli was gone.

Immediately forgetting the question, Dominic demanded of Carpinelli, "Did you take care of the body?"

"Yes, the boys did when they picked up Clara."

"They'll find another one in an alley off Fifteenth and Delgany."

"Did you recognize either of them?"

"No. Hired muscle. Clara, how did they get inside your apartment?"

"They picked the lock after you left for the courthouse," she answered apologetically. "I never even heard them."

"Let's get Luke upstairs." With an outstretched hand, Carpinelli directed him toward the staircase. "I have a room prepared."

Clara could see that something in Carpinelli's demeanor made Dominic hesitate; he had grown too calm too quickly. His mustache had stopped twitching.

Dominic narrowed his eyes with suspicion. A sudden blaze of anger seemed to ignite within him. "Why aren't you surprised by this?"

"What? Oh. I received a tip." Avoiding Dominic's gaze, Carpinelli brushed Luke's hair away from his forehead with feigned compassion. "I think we should get him into bed."

"You were wise to this and you didn't tell me?"

"Wasn't someone there to warn you?"

"A split second before the goon tried to shoot me, but I hardly consider that a warning. He could've killed me or Clara, and who knows what would've happened to Luke? How would you've explained *that* to Papa?"

"I needed to send a message to Joshua Parnell. Besides, I knew you could handle it."

"Don't patronize me." Dominic breathed the words through his teeth in a low voice. "If Clara had been hurt, you would be dead at my feet this very moment."

"Now, now. Let's not be hasty in our judgments," Carpinelli said with an uneasy smile. His mustache resumed its twitching. "You underestimate your talents. It transpired exactly as I had expected. Now, let's get the boy upstairs."

Carpinelli hurried up the stairs past Clara. Dominic lingered to glare at the back of his head.

"So, this is where you're hiding."

Clara's hand flew to her mouth with an involuntary gasp. For a terrified instant, she thought Papa Fratelli had entered the room; when she saw Dominic peering beyond the door, she released her breath with a sigh.

"It's dark in here." Entering, he closed the door behind him and approached her.

She had purposely kept the lights off, desiring seclusion. Sitting on the red velvet window seat with her legs drawn up beneath her, she had occupied her troubled mind by staring out the window into the night's darkness. A fire burned in the hearth, straining to illuminate the shelves of ancient books, the antique furnishings, and the polished hardwood floor; it shunned the deep recesses of the room, abandoning the corners to cool darkness.

He sat beside her on the window seat. The glow of the fire lit one side of his handsome face, the firelight reflecting in his eyes. She tried to lighten her expression with a smile, but the dismal thoughts that pervaded her mind drew the smile into a frown. Her fingers played absently with one of her rings.

"What's wrong?" he asked.

"Nothing, really. How's Luke?"

"Dr. Ameche gave him some ether and laudanum. He'll be incoherent for several hours. Is that what's bothering you?"

She averted her eyes. "I can't stop thinking about that man dying in my apartment today."

"I'm sorry you had to see that," he said, his voice softening. "Death is rarely a pleasant thing to watch."

"But did you have to kill him? He just wanted to take Luke back to Josh. He said he wouldn't hurt anyone."

"He shot at me, Clara." Dominic raised his eyebrows with disbelief. "He tried to kill me. Had he succeeded, do you think he would've left you as a witness? I had to take him out."

"You're right. He did shoot at you." She adjusted herself uncomfortably on the seat. "But what about the man who chased Luke? Did you take him out, too?"

"I don't ask you to understand the business I'm in," he said, selecting his words carefully, "only to accept its rules. I've never killed anyone unless it was necessary. As for Luke, are you certain nothing would've happened to him? If Joshua is so desperate to get him, where does that desperation end? Would he feel safe only if Luke was dead? It's not a chance I care to take. Besides, I like having the *bambino* around."

"Yes, you're right," she said, nodding her head like a chastised child. "But how many men have you killed?"

"Don't ask questions if you're not prepared to hear the answers."

The warning in his voice brought her head up. She searched his eyes, seeking remorse. Finding none, she looked away in disappointment, asking, "Is this what you want to do for the rest of your life?"

"I don't have a choice. I was born into it. If I left, my life wouldn't be worth the air we breathe. They'd spot me like a lead dime."

Suddenly, she grabbed his hand and squeezed it tight. It felt warm, strong. "But what if we left together, Dom? You and I. We could take Luke and disappear."

Encouraged by this outcry, he moved closer and cradled her slender neck in his hand. "We don't have to run away to be together, baby."

"No," disappointment once again made her look away, "but do we have to stay *here*?"

"Is that such a bad thing?"

"It's—it's not my home."

With a slight smile and a fetching tilt of his head, he said, "It could be."

"I'm afraid of your father." Her eyes flashed up at him, imploring his understanding. "He's made me do terrible things."

"Those days are over. The past doesn't matter to me." He moved closer until their faces were only inches apart, his gaze alternating between her lips and her eyes.

The pleasant smell of his cologne reached her as she lifted her face toward his and closed her eyes. She had scarcely felt the brush of his mouth on hers when a vigorous knock on the door broke the spell. It opened before they could respond. Carpinelli stuck his head inside. Dominic released her and came unhappily to his feet. She shifted nervously in the window seat.

"Oh, pardon me." In the uneven glow of the fire, Carpinelli looked embarrassed. "I was looking for your father, Dominic. Do you know—?"

"*Upstairs*," Dominic growled through his teeth.

Muttering an awkward "Thanks," Carpinelli quickly closed the door.

TWENTY-ONE

"Awaken, Prophet. I have not waited this long to watch you sleep."

Sifting through the levels of unconsciousness, the voice invaded Luke's sleep like a trespasser, pushing aside the curtains of a drugged slumber to confront an uncomfortable light.

With weak movements, Luke tried to pull what felt like cotton from his mouth. His hands found nothing there, yet the substance seemed to fill his throat and lungs, allowing only slight amounts of air to filter through. He forced his eyes open, resisting their desire to remain closed, and realized he was struggling with an asthma attack.

"Look at me, Prophet. Tell me what the Lord of Hosts has sent you to say."

The derisive voice sounded close. Searching for its source with his groggy eyes, Luke found himself lying in a four-poster bed in an unfamiliar room, his back propped with silken pillows, his body nestled between goose-down quilts. The room was vast, elaborate, decorated with rich Victorian furnishings, and he was alone in it.

"Dom?" he whispered, forcing the name from his hoarse throat.

An oppressive blanket of sulfur seemed to draw over his face, stifling him, extracting what little oxygen remained in his lungs. He gasped for air and clutched his chest as a demon materialized beside the bed. An ungracious smile turned the corners of the demon's mouth while the gaze of its glowing red eyes was embedded in Luke's soul. Hints of splendor lingered in the long, corpse-like face, the brusque jaw, the aquiline nose. Its black hair, pulled back tightly over its prominent forehead, gleamed with an indigo sheen, its hue similar to the shroud draped over the demon's ethereal form.

"Do you know me, Prophet?"

Luke groaned with terror in short, mournful whimpers. A chill rose from his spirit, a foreboding sense of hopelessness. He tried to push the quilts off; they felt like lead and wouldn't budge. He dug his heels into the mattress and pressed deeper into the pillows as the demon's face drew nearer to his own and his vision was filled with the embodiment of evil.

"I do not come as an angel of light to deceive you. You see me as I am, and now that I see you, I wonder that I feared you at all."

With one claw-like hand, the demon pulled down the quilts, exposing Luke in his blue striped pajamas. Horror surged through him as the demon took his left arm in its hot hand, pushed the sleeve away, and scrutinized its thinness. He was powerless to stop it, and the terrified groans in his throat increased in intensity. He feared the demon would snap his arm in two like dry kindling.

"I have beheld you since Bartholomew was summoned to protect you. He guards all the prophets while they walk with God. He has been diligent in his task with you."

The demon spread Luke's hand open to study its width and slender fingers.

"Why has God placed this burden upon you? Does He expect *this* tiny hand to bring me down? You are fragile. You struggle for your very breath. Why doesn't He heal you? Have you not asked Him this?"

Gently laying Luke's arm on the bed, the demon delved its

burning gaze deep into Luke's eyes. Luke felt violated, like his inmost thoughts and fears had been plundered and laid bare.

"It is unjust, Prophet. You are too young to die. God has thrown you into this blindly. He calls it faith. I call it foolishness."

A coughing fit took hold of Luke's chest. The demon waited patiently as Luke gasped frantically to relieve the rattling of his lungs. When the spasm passed, he slumped against the pillows, depleted of strength and desperate for air. The demon shook its head with contrite pity.

"You have suffered since birth. Have you not asked God why? If you are more valuable to Him than many sparrows, why did He allow your father to hurt you? Was He watching the sparrows fall when you were beaten into unconsciousness? Was He counting the hairs on your head while you starved in your father's house?"

Goose bumps rose up along Luke's body. Swallowing, he tried to restrain the torrent of tears that filled his eyes. He turned his face away.

"It is because He is the Lord of the weak. He does not want you to be healthy and sound, because then you would no longer need Him." The demon offered its massive hand for his acceptance. "Luke, do not be deceived. God holds your life in His hands, but then so do I. He *can* heal you but *will* not. I *will* heal you *if* you allow me to open your eyes to the truth. Take my hand. You will never be ill again. No one will hurt you again. I will bring your brothers to you. Would anything please you more?"

The demon extended its hand again. Its image blurred as Luke tried to blink away the tears.

"I see the hope in your heart, Luke. I see your spirit and flesh struggle. I will heal you, give you peace, and the visions that torment you will fade away. I do not ask you to turn from God, only to realize that you cannot accomplish His will. He will not blame you because you are only a child. Luke, you are tired. Are you ready to rest?"

The struggle to breathe became unbearable, the sulfuric reek stifling. Luke's shoulders quivered with his pronounced gasps for air, yet it was nothing compared to the grief in his heart at the thought of his brothers. He knew he would never see them again if he did not accept the demon's offer. He knew it with as much certainty as anything that had been revealed to him in previous visions. Tears streamed down his face. He looked at the ceiling, his lips forming the words, *Jesus, where are You?*

Abruptly, the demon's hand moved suffocatingly close to his face, threatening to clamp down on his mouth and nose. It shuddered as though restraining its fury and desire to crush Luke's head with one squeeze of its mighty grip.

"You would be wiser to pray to me, Prophet. Bartholomew cannot interfere this time."

The demon's voice boomed in Luke's ears. His glowing eyes ignited with renewed flame. Trembling, Luke closed his eyes, inhaling the sulfur from the leathery palm above his face. He feared it would be his last breath.

"What will it be, Prophet? Shall I kill you or restore you? Pray to me and you will keep your life."

Luke kept his eyes closed and shook his head with as much vigor as he could muster.

"Fool. Then I will force you."

Luke felt the immense hand thrust itself upon his chest. The long fingers enveloped it, squeezing his frail ribs. Luke's eyes snapped open. A blaze of fire seemed to ignite within him. It burned through his lungs and into his throat. Tears poured from his eyes. He opened his mouth to cry out, but no sound was emitted. The speed of this assault cut off his breath, but within seconds, his lungs expanded with precious oxygen. He could breathe! But the agony of the fire—he screamed.

The room was spinning. The demon's face rotated above his head like a pinwheel. Even his own screams swung around his head in crying twists of sound. His body convulsed in frantic thrashings until the hand released him and the pain decreased into a throbbing, burning sensation.

Almost instantly, murky shadows enveloped the demon's face and weakened Luke's screams into hollow shrieks. The last thing he heard was, "To whom shall you pray now, Prophet?"

Carpinelli climbed the grand staircase to the second floor, using gradual steps to conserve his energy. Lately, he seemed to tire easily. He had not slept well in weeks—not since Luke's identity had been revealed to him. He had even lost weight, which was something he did not relish. Now, his tailored suits needed to be modified. Perhaps he should adopt Joshua Parnell's renowned habit of consuming gallons of bicarbonate of soda....

He stopped. A scream caught his attention, an agonizing shriek coming from the floor above. He quickened his pace to the third floor and followed the weakening cries down the hall to Luke's room. Once he reached the door and his hand touched the knob, the cries stopped.

He threw open the door and looked straight at the bed. He did not see Luke, though he discerned a slight mound beneath the rumpled quilts. Approaching it uncertainly, he drew back the quilts. Beneath them lay Luke, his skin as pale as the sheets, his pajama top ripped to shreds. Deep scratches ravaged his chest. Carpinelli heard no sound of hampered breathing.

He touched Luke's throat to feel for a pulse and was astonished when he felt one pounding against his fingertips. Removing the remains of the pajama top and tossing them on the floor, he gathered Luke from his contorted position, laid him decently on the bed, and drew the quilts up to his chin. Carpinelli then combed the room with his eyes.

"I know you're here, Aeneas. Show yourself."

The dark angel appeared on the other side of the bed, ominous, enraged. The horrifying sight did not awe Carpinelli, nor did the sulfuric odor repel him. He was angry.

"What did you do to him?"

"What does it matter to you what I did to him?"

"Well, you don't have to torture him."

"Torture him? I *healed* him."

Carpinelli yanked the quilts off to expose Luke's chest. "Is that what you call *healing*?"

"Do you challenge me? Or do you seek to redeem yourself back into God's good grace?"

Dropping his gaze regretfully on Luke, Carpinelli sighed. "Neither. Both. I don't know. What will you do with him?"

"He will choose his fate...*as did you*."

Carpinelli winced. Feeling the sting of those words, he said, "There's no victory in the corruption of a child. Why not kill him and send him straight to God?"

"Fool, there is *great* victory in the corruption of a child! As for killing him, do you think I have not tried?" The demon regarded Luke with a malicious glare. "The Lord of Hosts insults me with this child prophet. Therefore, I will destroy what He holds dearest. I will erode his innocence. I will use his naiveté against him. He will not even know that the one he was sent to destroy has beguiled him. In the end, I will watch him in eternal torment"—his glowing eyes met Carpinelli's own withered ones—"by your side."

"You can't tempt him like the others," Carpinelli said, ignoring the sinking sensation in the pit of his soul. "He's too innocent, too young. If you lure him into an immoral lifestyle, he'll recoil."

The demon arched a heavy eyebrow. "Not if I introduce it gradually. Not if the most important influence in his life acquaints him with these desires as he grows. Not if I occupy the position most relevant in his life."

"You mean his father?" Carpinelli asked with puzzlement.

"No. With one whose influence is already established."

"Dominic?"

"Yes." The demon nodded. "Dominic."

TWENTY-TWO

In the soft glow of a nearby lamp, Clara sat before the vanity in her room. Staring into the mirror, she looked not at herself but beyond her reflection—at the dimness behind her, the canopied bed, the wardrobe, and the lace-curtained windows. Against her better judgment, she was falling in love with Dominic. Ever since he'd come to stay at her apartment with Luke, she had fought it by avoiding him; yet the more she had remained aloof, the more he had pursued.

All she had ever wanted was security, and she could easily delude herself into thinking she could find it with him at the Fratelli Estate. When Papa Fratelli had found her living among the women of Market Street—a shoeless child of twelve, dressed in only a petticoat—she thought she had found security in his provisions, only to find herself a prey to his demands and a predator to men. Now, under Dominic's protection, she thought she could be happy...except for two things. First, Dominic was as dangerous as his father; second, since finding Christ, she was learning the true meaning of security.

She opened the drawer of the vanity and removed Luke's Bible, which she had packed along with his clothes. Although she had little opportunity to read it and did not fully understand all she read, the Psalms in particular were like a balm to her spirit, which had been broken by a life marked with quiet desperation. She opened the book to Psalm 46 and read the first three verses aloud.

"God is our refuge and strength, a very present help in trouble. Therefore will not we fear, though the earth be removed, and though the mountains be carried into the midst of the sea; though the waters thereof roar and be troubled, though the mountains shake with the swelling thereof."

A movement in the mirror caught her eye. Spinning around, she screamed when she saw Papa Fratelli standing there. She looked at the door. It was closed, locked.

"I sensed the change in you, *bella mia*. I now understand the cause. How much of that have you read?"

"How did you get in here?" she demanded, clutching the Bible close to her chest.

"Have you read that '*the wages of sin is death; but the gift of God is eternal life*'? That '*God sent not his Son into the world to condemn the world; but that the world through him might be saved*'?"

He stepped forward into the light. She started, expecting the advances of a depraved miscreant; what she found was the gentle air of wisdom, of graciousness. The concern in his voice equaled the sincerity in his face; it took her aback.

"I—I know that Jesus died for my sins...and that if I believe in Him, I won't go to hell."

"True, but are you worthy of that gift? For it is written, '*Be ye holy; for I am holy.*' Are you holy, *bella mia*? We both know what you are and what you have done. Does not your shame rise before you? Do you not blush to read His Word? Does the blood on your hands not burn when you touch those sacred pages?"

She sat speechless. He continued, "God said, '*I will have mercy on whom I will have mercy.*' There is no mercy for me. No redemption for me. I am one of the '*vessels of wrath fitted to destruction.*' How, then, can you believe that He could have mercy on *you*, after all you have done? Are you righteous, *bella mia*? Because only the righteous shall inherit the kingdom of God."

"Don't take my hope from me!" she cried, standing, holding the Bible even tighter. "It's all I have!"

He pulled a pressed handkerchief from his pocket and dabbed at her tears like a father. Gathering her into his arms, he rocked her gently, hushing her violent sobs.

"Come, child. Do not put your faith in '*things hoped for*,' in '*things not seen*.' We both know what you are...and what you must do."

Joshua tried to keep his attention fixed on the Louie Fratelli case file lying open on his office desk. He had repeatedly forced himself to read it, to concentrate on his notes, only to have his thoughts wander off before he had read even two sentences. The words blurred before his eyes, and, before he realized it, he was staring at the shaft of sunlight beaming through the window, illuminating dust particles that swirled in the air. Shaking himself from his reverie, he looked back at the file again. He was getting a headache.

"Good morning, Mr. Parnell. I hope I'm not too early."

The voice brought Joshua's head up with a start. A broad smile crossed his face. "No, of course not, Reverend."

Walking around the desk, he greeted Edmund Elliott with a handshake, then removed a stack of files from one of the chairs before his desk and plopped them onto the floor.

"Please, sit down. I'm glad you came."

"Certainly," Edmund said, sinking into the chair with the deliberate slowness of age. "I appreciate the invitation."

Joshua returned to his chair, sat down, then stood up again. "Care for some coffee?"

"No, thanks," Edmund said, waving off the suggestion with polite refusal.

Joshua sat back down, feeling nervous. "I'd like to discuss your theory about the Fratellis' vendetta against your family, and how the boy—I mean, Luke—plays into it. He weighs on my mind. In fact, I've thought of nothing else this whole weekend."

"Yes. Luke weighs on our hearts, as well. He's always in our prayers."

"Uh...yes...I'm sure he is. Anyway, I've considered the prospect of placing him under your guardianship"—Edmund's face brightened—"but I'm running up against a couple of obstacles. Foremost, we must locate his parents. If they are found to be unfit, or if they can't be found at all, he'll become a ward of the court, which may look favorably upon appointing you as guardian. You said he came from abusive circumstances, and, while I don't want to return him to a dangerous atmosphere, we must exhaust all possibilities of finding his family. If there's any information you can give me, it would be appreciated."

Edmund rubbed his chin thoughtfully. "Well, from his clothing and mannerisms, we suspect he came from a poor farm. He mentioned that his mother was dead and that he had brothers. He also said he had an uncle in town, but I never learned his name. Aside from that, Luke was very secretive."

"That will give us somewhere to start, only...." The words faltered on Joshua's lips. He shook his head with a sigh and watched Edmund's expression cloud with anxiety.

"Only...what?" he prompted.

Joshua took a despairing breath. "Only, I'm concerned for his welfare. It's unfortunate that he fell into the Fratellis' hands."

Edmund's face grew pale. "They wouldn't hurt him, would they?"

"Physically? I hope not. Mentally? Most certainly. Warp his values and integrity? Definitely. Destroy his chances for a decent life as a moral, upstanding citizen? Without a doubt. These people are criminals. They'll bring him up in their way of life. He'll learn to use a gun and learn to kill. He'll be taught the business and follow the rules—or pay with his life. This is what discourages me. They'll fill him with every depravity that you and your wife would protect him from. The longer this boy stays in their hands, the less chance you have of redeeming him."

Joshua hung his head, shaking it deliberately, sorrowfully. After several moments of this drama, he lifted his eyes to see that Edmund's countenance had fallen. His faded blue eyes did not blink. They stared at nothing.

Did I paint a black enough picture? Come on, old man. Take the bait.

But Edmund did something unexpected. He folded his hands, bowed his head, and prayed. Speechless, Joshua watched as Edmund's lips moved with prompt petition—"*Blessed is he whose transgression is forgiven, whose sin is covered,*"—until, at last, he lifted his head, breathing a sigh of relinquishment.

"Mr. Parnell, I've committed Luke into the Lord's hands. I can ask for no better protection, and, as Luke has already been redeemed, the Lord will deliver him from these men. I believe this with all my heart."

Joshua merely stared at him. It took some time to regain the use of his tongue. Wondering how he would break the news of his failure to Andy, he forced a pained smile. "I'm prepared to hear your theory of the case, if you're prepared to give it."

"By all means." Edmund resettled himself in the chair. "Last night, you said you didn't have a motive for Fred's murder. I believe I can help. A few months ago, Fred met a man named Tony Garda."

"Tony Garda?" Joshua sat up with sudden interest. "The man the police shot when they arrested Louie?"

"Yes. The day before Fred died, he confided in me something that he had never told Joan, fearing for her safety. One night, he discovered a man, Tony, lying drunk in the gutter on Larimer Street. Fred helped him to a flophouse and took care of him. Over the next few weeks, Tony started attending church and accepted Jesus as his Savior, but he couldn't break off his relationship with the Mafia. He was scared. Then a rival gang shot him. It wasn't a serious wound, so he recuperated at a place called the Fratelli Estate. He told Fred about some strange things he found in that mansion—things he couldn't understand."

"Such as?"

"Such as a dungeon and a skeleton."

Joshua cocked an eyebrow. "Really, now."

"And a book."

"Let's get back to this skeleton. Was it in the dungeon or a closet?"

Edmund frowned. "I know this sounds fantastic, but Fred wasn't one to create stories."

"I'm sorry." Feeling like a chastised child, Joshua gestured apologetically with his hand. "Please go on. What is this book you mentioned?"

At the request, Edmund pulled a small, worn book from his suit pocket. "It's quite rare. It's dated 1756. London."

Accepting it, Joshua carefully opened the cracked leather binding and exposed the fragile brown pages to the air. It smelled of dust. "*Italian Fables of the Sixteenth Century*. How did you get this?"

"Fred left it with me for safekeeping. He said Tony had given it to him."

"And this has relevance to Fred's murder?"

"In some way. I couldn't begin to explain how. There's a

fable marked with a ribbon called *The Order of the Scrolls*. A Dominican monk wrote it. It's intriguing."

"And you say Tony got this from the Fratelli Estate?" Joshua asked.

"Apparently from this dungeon."

"When did he give it to Fred?"

"Thanksgiving Day—the day Louie shot Fred."

"Tony was also shot in Louie's presence," Joshua said with a thoughtful pause, "which possibly explains something." Glancing down at the file that minutes before couldn't retain his attention, he sifted through several sheets of paper, licking his thumb to aid the process. "Your daughter witnessed another assailant at the scene." He scanned each sheet as he spoke. "The police assumed it was Tony. I'm not so sure. I remember reading something in the police report when Tony was killed. Here it is."

Edmund left the chair to peer over Joshua's shoulder and started to read the section he indicated.

"When Louie was arrested, he didn't have a gun on him. Gangsters always carry their guns. Why didn't Louie have his?" Before Edmund could respond, Joshua answered, "Because he *knew* he and Tony would be arrested. Louie *knew* Tony would draw his gun, giving the police justification to shoot him, but he didn't want that possibility for himself. Also, look at Tony's final statement: 'You coward. You crossed me.' It was a setup."

"But if Louie wanted Tony dead, why didn't he just kill Tony himself?"

"Because then Tony could be the scapegoat for the unknown assailant who grabbed Joan when she ran for help. If he really wanted to leave the Mafia, as you said, he was expendable. I suspect the unknown assailant, the only other witness to the crime, is still out there."

Both men grew silent. Edmund returned to his chair.

"So," Joshua said at length, crossing his arms over his chest, "how does Luke fit into your theory?"

"I haven't quite figured that out. I thought they might be holding Luke as collateral, but there are flaws in this theory. First, how could they tie him to us? We're not related, and Fred never met him. Second, they've never contacted us, which also excludes their threatening to hurt him if Joan testified. In fact, Dominic Fratelli made it clear that we're to have no contact with Luke, so I can't fathom why they're keeping him. There must be a connection somewhere. I don't even know how he fell into their hands."

"Uh...Yes...It w-would be...ah...g-good to know that...." Pressing his hands together, Joshua brought them to his lips. He took a deep breath. "Aside from this, you believe the connection between Fred, Tony, and Louie centers on this book found at the Fratelli Estate. Is that correct?"

"Sir," Edmund raised his hands in humble subservience, "you're the attorney. You tell me."

"It's intriguing. Unfortunately, it's also circumstantial."

"Perhaps, but it's also too coincidental to be simply intriguing. There's something under the surface. Would you humor me and read the fable?"

"Yes, Reverend." Joshua smiled. "I'll read it. It's the least I can do."

TWENTY-THREE

Never before had Jack Novak seen such an impoverished farm. Snow camouflaged its barrenness, but nothing could enhance the slanting two-story house with white paint splintering from its deteriorating sides, or the barn patched with miscellaneous pieces of wood where neglect and decay had worn through.

At a glance, he thought it was abandoned. It seemed improbable that a farmer would allow his plow to rust in the snow and his wagon to rot under soggy hay left there since harvest. He almost drove by until he caught a glimpse of a man beside a horse, bending over the animal's lifted hoof, prying at something.

Pulling his Model A Ford off the dirt road, he parked it in front of the house and got out. The frigid air chilled him. He pressed his fedora down over his light brown hair and grabbed his briefcase from the floor. He closed the door and faced his own reflection in the window of his car. Tall and pale, his slender frame clad in a black suit, he looked rather daunting, a little like an undertaker. How poignant.

"Good morning," he said without a smile, approaching the farmer with an outstretched hand. "Neils Warner?"

Intent on removing a stone from the horse's withered hoof, the farmer hadn't noticed him. Upon hearing the greeting, he lifted his head with a start of surprise and released the horse's hoof in a single movement.

"You from the bank?" he demanded. "I got no money to pay you."

"No, sir. My name is Jack Novak. I'm a private detective. Are you Neils Warner?"

"Yeah…so long as you ain't from the bank."

With this assurance, Warner wiped the dirt from his callused hand on his pant leg and returned the handshake. Novak scrutinized him. He wasn't old, perhaps thirty-five, yet the creases that wrinkled the tanned skin around his eyes and drooped his frowning mouth aged him twenty years, as did the strands of gray hair peeking out from under the broken straw hat. A coat, with buttons and elbows removed by time, hung loosely on his lean frame.

From the corner of his eye, Novak noticed two teenaged boys, dressed in little more than rags, standing near the house. They hesitated in their chore of chopping wood, watching their father and Novak with apprehensive eyes. Neither wore a coat; both looked an unhealthy shade of pallid blue, like bloodless ghosts doomed to haunt an icy prairie. Novak did a double take to make sure they weren't inventions of his imagination.

"I'm here on behalf of a gentleman who has an interest in your family." Novak gestured toward the house. "Can we talk inside?"

"Ain't here good enough?"

"What I have to say you may want to hear sitting down."

Warner's green eyes widened. He turned toward the house, indicating with a nod that Novak should follow. The boys dropped their axes and ran inside behind them, slipping into the shadows as Warner and Novak sat down at the kitchen table.

The morning sky was overcast, making the room as dim as early evening. Warner grabbed a lantern and lit it with the strike of a match. With this flickering illumination, Novak saw the boys as tormented specters, haunting the room with their silent presence, gaunt features, and inherited frowns. In the timelessness of their attractive faces, both ghosts bore the fragility of time-ravaged youth, robbed vitality, and hunger left unfulfilled. The severity of their green eyes unnerved Novak. He removed his hat and looked away.

The house was neither filthy nor clean, but it lacked every article of comfort that would make a house a home. He saw no sign of a woman's touch, no pictures or curtains or rugs, no evidence of indoor plumbing or electricity. He saw only four shabby chairs, the table, and a wood-burning stove. The heat emanating from it was insufficient to warm him, much less the house.

"What you have to say ain't good, is it?" Warner said, bringing Novak's attention back.

"I'm afraid not."

"It's about my boy?"

"I'm afraid so."

Warner nodded and breathed a slight sigh. Neither of the boys moved, nor seemed to breathe. Novak leaned forward.

"Three months ago, a young boy was found on the side of a road near Loveland, the victim of a hit-and-run accident. This boy fits the description of your son, who was reported to the sheriff as a runaway. Unfortunately, it's taken me this long to put the two together. I apologize for asking, but I need positive identification to prove he was your son."

"*Was?* He's dead?"

"I'm sorry. Yes, he was found dead."

One of the boys gasped; Novak forced himself not to look and see which one. Warner merely blinked; the impact of those words had not yet struck him.

"Where do I have to go?" he asked.

"Nowhere. His body was interred in a cemetery at the

expense of the gentleman I represent, but I have some photographs...."

Novak opened the briefcase and extracted a large envelope. Warner held out his leathery hand with frank acceptance.

"I must warn you. These photographs are unpleasant. I don't think your sons should see them."

Having completely forgetten their presence, Warner motioned over his shoulder with a brusque wave of his hand. "Get outside."

With reluctant yet silent obedience, the boys left the kitchen from the back door. Novak was relieved to see them go; they gave him the creeps.

He released the envelope into Warner's control; the man opened it without emotion. Regardless of what Warner expected to see—perhaps the boy lying tranquilly in a coffin—he was not prepared for the graphic sight of his son's violently assaulted body. He jolted back in his chair as if he had received a blow. His tanned skin blanched; his eyes turned red, watery. With each appalling photo, he collapsed a little more. Long minutes passed. His lips moved with irrational mumbling as the sight of his broken, dead child burned itself into his mind and heart.

"Is this your son?"

"Yes," Warner breathed despairingly.

Novak withdrew a document from the briefcase. Unfolding it, he placed it on the table. "I understand his name was Erik Warner. Was that his full name?"

"Erik Anton Warner."

The name emerged from Warner's lips without mindful effort. Novak wrote it on the document and placed it intentionally upside down on the table. He extended his pen.

"What's this?" Warner accepted these items uncertainly.

Novak smiled to himself when he realized Warner could

not read. He turned the paper around for him. "The certificate of death," he lied, pointing to the line where he wanted a signature.

Warner hesitated over it, seemingly unwilling to admit his lack of education. He scribbled an attempt at a signature and returned the paper and pen to Novak. After watching him fold the document and replace it in his briefcase, Warner suddenly came alive with questions.

"Who's this man that buried my boy?"

"He's a respected citizen who wishes to remain anonymous. He was saddened when he heard about the boy found dead in the snow. Since no one claimed the body, he paid for the burial and hired me to find the next of kin."

Warner's bloodshot eyes blinked several times. "It'll take some doin', but I'll pay him back."

"There's no need." Another envelope appeared from the briefcase, and Novak pressed it into Warner's hands. "In fact, he sent a gift for the family."

Warner shuddered with repulsion. "I won't take money for my boy's death."

"It's not for his death. It's for the needs of your two living sons."

Warner brushed the envelope aside, forcing Novak to lay it on the table.

"Did they find who killed him?"

"No, sir. A passerby found him half buried in the snow. Frozen."

Warner swallowed. His voice grew weaker as he struggled to maintain control. "Where's he buried?"

"Loveland Burial Park."

A tear ran down his tired cheek. "Does he have a tombstone?"

"Yes. It says, 'Unknown boy, asleep in the arms of Jesus.'"

With that, Warner laid his head on his arms on top of the

photos. "Someday...it'll read 'Erik Warner.' Someday...I'll bury him beside his mother."

Quietly closing the briefcase, Novak stood. "I'm sorry for your loss."

"I wanted him dead," Warner said without lifting his head. Novak paused. "He killed my Jenny and I wanted him dead... but not like that. My brother told the sheriff that he ran away, not me. I should've looked for him. He was still my boy...."

Novak felt a twinge of unexpected guilt. He hurried out the back door, wanting to leave the poverty and depression of that farm, when the sight of the wraithlike boys stopped him cold. They stood before his car, blocking his escape. He did not know what to do or say; he felt stunned by their sorrowful demeanors and their startling green eyes, the only color in their ashen faces.

At length, he asked, "What are your names?"

"Charlie," the oldest said softly.

The younger brother whispered, "Nate."

"What happened to Erik, sir?" Charlie asked, his voice breaking in his throat.

Another wave of guilt flooded Novak. Looking at his shoes, he rubbed the back of his neck uneasily. He could lie as long as he did not look directly into their faces.

"He was hit by a car. He's dead."

Novak glanced up to witness his lies stab the boys like fatal daggers. Charlie's shoulders sagged like those of an old man. A tear ran quickly down his dirt-streaked face. Nate simply bowed his head.

"It's my fault." Charlie looked despondently at his brother. "I made him run off. I told him never to come back. I...I killed him." He did not wait for a reply to his confession. He turned and dragged himself into the field.

Nate watched him go, then looked up at Novak one last time. In his young eyes, Novak saw death and despair in all their immensity. He looked back at his shoes. Nate followed his brother into the distance where Charlie sank, heedless of the snow, beneath a barren tree.

Novak muttered a string of obscenities under his breath. He turned toward his car when he heard a broken cry from inside the house.

"Oh, God, forgive me! I've killed my son! I've killed my son!"

TWENTY-FOUR

"Wake up, pal. You've been asleep for twelve hours. You're sleeping your life away."

These words and the hand on his shoulder roused Luke from slumber. His weary eyes opened to find Dominic bending over him with a smile. He glanced around the unfamiliar bedroom. "Where am I?"

Dominic ruffled his already tangled hair. "You're at my father's house. It's Saturday morning. How's your asthma?"

"Okay, I guess." Still trying to wake up, Luke sat up and rubbed his eyes.

"Good. Get up. Breakfast is almost ready. Your own private bathroom is right through there. You'll feel better after a shower."

Following Dominic's extended hand, Luke pushed back the blankets and slipped out of bed. Abruptly, Dominic grabbed his arm and spun him around.

"What happened to your chest?"

Luke looked down at the tender, raw scratches and touched them with his fingers. "I had another bad dream."

Dominic drew his eyebrows together into a worried line. "What are these dreams about that make you so self-destructive?"

With a reluctant shrug, Luke wiggled out of his grasp. "I don't wanna think about them."

"I'm not letting you off that easy." Taking Luke's hands,

Dominic scrutinized his fingernails, which were short, clean, and unbroken. "What happens in these dreams?"

"Different things. They're always bad and scary. Don't make me, Dom. Please."

"If they continue, you'll have to tell me so we can find a way to make them stop. *Capisci*?"

"These kinds of dreams ain't gonna stop." Luke pulled his hands away and lumbered toward the bathroom. "I see them when I'm awake."

Dominic stared after him, dumbfounded. Glancing down, he saw the wadded pajama top on the floor, flecked with tiny specks of blood. He took it and held it up, seeing at once that the material was sliced through as with a razor.

He looked back at Luke, his frown deepening, and thought, *Who did this to you?*

Dominic rushed from Clara's empty room, leaving the door wide open. His footsteps resounded on the grand staircase. When he reached the entrance hall, he yelled for the butler. He heard the man shuffling forward before he saw him enter from a hallway in the back of the mansion.

"Where is Clara?" Dominic shouted.

"I'm sure I don't know, sir," the butler replied with wide, startled eyes.

"Where's my father?"

"In the library, sir."

Dominic stormed to the room. He wrenched the doorknob but found it locked. Swearing, he stepped back and, with one thrust of his foot, kicked in the door. It flailed on its hinges, sending the broken lock and fragments of wood flying.

"Papa! Where are you?"

He searched the room in vain. Finding no one, he tossed

aside one of the plush chairs before the fireplace; it had been moved from its proper place and was in his way. Thinking the butler had lied, he turned to leave when he felt the hardwood floor move beneath his feet with a peculiar squeak. He stopped and looked down. In the space where the chair usually sat, he detected that the whole section moved, a neat square of three feet by three feet. With his foot, he tested the floorboards. Once again, they moved. He had found a trapdoor.

There was no handle or fingerhold that he could use to open it easily. Slipping his fingers into the tiny crevice, he lifted the edge of one side a little so that he could get a better grasp. After several attempts, he finally gained enough leverage to lift it. Dank air came from the opening, which terminated in darkness far below. Astounded, he leaned back to regard it.

Dominic stood, went to the door, and called for the butler to bring a flashlight. His request was granted without question, and Dominic returned to the trapdoor alone.

The red sandstone staircase, comprised of slabs left over from the mansion's foundation, wobbled beneath his weight. Each step was marked with grime from repetitive use. After descending a distance of at least two stories, he discovered that the stairs ended at the mouth of a narrow stone passage. The temperature had cooled considerably. Spider webs adorned the walls and ceiling, their owners fleeing the probing light.

Dominic ventured through the brief passage to a heavy wooden door, Gothic in structure. Time and moisture marked its vertical planking with age, yet it remained stalwart, bound with wrought iron hardware. As he examined it with the beam of the flashlight, he tried to open its latch but found it tightly bolted. He applied his shoulder to it. It moved under the pressure with a complaining groan but refused to give way. He took a step backward and slammed his shoulder into the door. It burst open, pitching him into the room.

By the glow of a dozen candles, he found his father sitting

in a chair at a roughly hewn table, both of which were distinctly medieval. Shadows from the flames wavered upon his face, exaggerating his brooding expression. The sight of his favorite son barging in uninvited did not seem to surprise him.

Discovering the dungeon-like stronghold took Dominic aback. The walls of the room dripped with moisture. The smell of mold permeated the air until it was almost unfit to breathe. The room was sparsely decorated. A bookcase lined with ancient volumes stood against the far wall. Papers were strewn on the table, which Papa Fratelli had turned facedown at the intrusion. In the shadowy recess of the room, Dominic noticed a short, narrow door, locked fast with a rectangular bolt. He felt as though he had stumbled into a sixteenth-century edifice.

"What is this place?" he demanded. Though briefly distracted from his immediate concerns, all of Dominic's hostility returned. "Why didn't you tell me about it?"

"It is my sanctuary," Papa Fratelli said calmly. "Now that you have discovered it, be gone."

"Not until I get some answers. Where's Clara? She's not in her room, and her bed hasn't been slept in."

"What is that to you?"

"What concerns her concerns me. Where is she?"

"I sent her to entertain an associate," Papa Fratelli responded, folding his arms across his chest and lifting one curious eyebrow.

Dominic took a threatening step forward. "Who? Where? Bring her back now!"

"Why does this astound you? She has done it before. Many times."

"Why didn't you tell me?"

"Because she is mine, and I will do with her as I please." Scrutinizing Dominic's anger carefully, he said, "My son, never in your life have you raised your voice to me. Why do you do so now?"

Dominic's eyes smoldered with rage. "Because I told her those days were over! Because she's going to be my wife!"

Had he thrown ice water into Papa Fratelli's face, he could not have shocked his father more. After several moments of amazed gaping, he stood and walked around the table, smiling, his arms outstretched to embrace his child in full Italian style.

"Dominic, my son, had you only told me."

Dominic remained still while his father held him. Animosity, mistrust, and confusion raged within him.

"When did you decide this?" Papa Fratelli released him and took a step back.

"I've...I've always felt this way about her."

He slapped Dominic heartily on the back. It made him jump. "You have asked her, then?"

Immediately, he felt foolish. He looked at his feet. "No, not yet."

Footsteps sounded from the passage. Before the intruder could be questioned, Carpinelli stepped inside, his expression full of wonder. Observing Dominic's unexpected presence, he froze, his eyes going from the elder Fratelli to the younger.

Dominic found himself being led toward the door and maneuvered into the passageway.

"Congratulations, my son. You have chosen a beautiful bride. I will announce the engagement tomorrow night at your birthday party, so it would behoove you to ask the girl soon."

"But where is she?" Dominic demanded.

Without an answer, Papa Fratelli smiled and closed the door in Dominic's astonished face.

"You look happy enough," Carpinelli said, frowning as he poked his thumb at the door and toward Dominic, who had been recently evicted. "What did Dominic say to you?"

Across Papa Fratelli's swarthy face spread a diabolical smile, accentuated by the flittering candlelight in the dungeon. He set his cunning eyes on Carpinelli, whose very skin crawled at the permeating evil.

"It seems I have a bride, Angelo. How considerate of my son to arrange this."

"You don't mean Clara, do you? That trollop?"

"That trollop is exceptionally beautiful." Returning to the chair, Papa Fratelli folded his hands neatly across his chest with pride. "My son has good taste."

"I should think you'd have more vital things on your mind than women."

"The curse must be carried on, and she will give me handsome sons."

"How did Dominic find his way down here? You didn't show it to him, did you?"

"He found it on his own."

Carpinelli raised his eyebrows. "And you don't find this at all disturbing?"

"What can he do with the knowledge now? After tomorrow night, it will not make any difference."

TWENTY-FIVE

Please, don't," Clara begged. "Don't touch me." She turned her face away from the reek of tobacco as the man leaned close to kiss her.

The bristles of his white beard brushing against her chin and the caress of his effeminate, manicured hands on her arms made her cringe with revulsion. In the dim light of the smoky drawing room, Clara watched him back away with uncertainty. He leaned against the couch, a smoldering cigar in one hand. Somewhere in the shadowy room, a phonograph warbled "All of Me."

"I don't understand. Didn't Papa tell you...?" Almost with embarrassment, he failed to finish the question and moved to take her in his arms once again.

"Yes, but"—she pushed him off—"I can't do this anymore."

She quickly stood and donned the fur coat she had draped across a nearby chair.

"This won't do." He stuck the chewed cigar between his flat, lusterless teeth. "If Papa won't come through on his part, I won't come through on mine."

Fear instantly replaced her repulsion. She stepped toward him with an entreating hand. "No, please don't call him. Give me ten minutes. Just ten minutes."

"This won't do at all." Ignoring her, he stood and reached for the brass candlestick telephone on the end table.

"Don't you understand?" she cried with rising hysteria. "He'll kill me!"

"No, *you* don't understand." With his back to her, he brought the earpiece to his ear. "I asked for you specifically."

Seized with terror, she made a dash for the door.

"Give me Papa Fratelli," he said into the mouthpiece. "This is—Hey!"

He dropped the telephone and took hold of her by the waist as she ran by. Swirling her around, he threw her headlong onto the sofa. She bounced slightly against its cushions, her hair falling into her face.

"You're not leaving until this is settled." He took the telephone from the floor. "Papa, this is—"

Regaining her feet, she grabbed a nearby marble statuette. "God, forgive me," she said as she swung her arm high and brought the statuette down on the back of his skull.

No shout or groan of pain sounded from his thick lips. With the cigar still in his mouth, he simply wilted on the table, crushing it with his enormous weight.

The statuette broke in two. Dropping it, Clara lingered over his inert body long enough to hear Papa Fratelli's inquiring voice on the telephone. Then, she ran. Swinging open the door to the drawing room, she hurried into the darkness of the mansion. Before her loomed a vast black room. She rushed forward, knocking over unseen obstacles to find the front door, which she came across almost immediately. Opening it, she ran out into the dark street.

Winter's predawn chill greeted her with a slap of frigid air. It permeated her fur and black satin gown. The tingle of falling snow lighted upon her face. Looking around, she recognized at once the quiet neighborhood of Millionaire's Row, a community of mansions financed by Papa Fratelli's unscrupulous connections. She would find no help there.

"God, help me," she prayed.

With a frightened glance over her shoulder, she ran across the dim street to the next block. Then horror struck her heart. A thin layer of snow had accumulated on the ground, betraying her footprints and path. It did not matter how fast or how far she ran. They would find her. She had to get off the street. She had to get out of that neighborhood.

Hoping to find a taxi or the trolley, she ran from street to street toward downtown, throwing fleeting looks behind her and holding up her gown to keep from tripping on its hem. Gradually, the mansions yielded to rows of apartment buildings and businesses, lifeless storefronts that offered no hope. Somewhere, not far off, a church bell struck two o'clock in despondent tones.

With each foot pinched in a wet high heel, she half-ran, half-limped into the entryway of a store. Stopping to lean against its doorframe, she clutched her chest to ease the pain of exertion and looked about frantically. A light burned in a rooming house across the street, but she saw no movement behind it.

He's going to find me. He's going to kill me. I'm going to die... alone....

She whirled against the door and tried desperately to twist open its icy knob. Locked. She rapped her frozen knuckles against the door and peered inside the window. Everything remained motionless, black. Looking back at the light in the rooming house, she wondered if someone would look out if she screamed.

Before she could initiate the plan, a sound—the crunching of snow beneath the tires of a slow-moving car, the furtive creeping of one who searched for something or someone—made her blood run cold. The sound of Papa Fratelli's car—it was unmistakable. Dread filled her body.

No! Dear God, please! No!

The glimmer of headlights illuminated the darkened

street. She pressed deep into the shadow on the opposite side of the doorway as Papa Fratelli's Phantom Rolls Royce drove by. One man sat in the front seat behind the elongated engine, another in the back. In its high black polish, she saw herself cowering in the doorway.

The car did not stop. This heightened her anxiety. She knew better than to think Papa Fratelli had not seen her. In his eerie manner of knowing everything, he had found her. He was simply toying with her now. He would be back.

Watching the car turn the corner, knowing she had a few seconds at most, she dashed to the next building. It, too, was locked. Peering through the door's windowpane, she banged on the wooden frame with both fists. The inviting aroma of baking bread tugged at her stomach, and, in the back of the bakery, a light burned. Tears brimmed in her eyes.

"Help me! Please! Someone, please!"

Hearing movement inside, she pounded furiously on the door with renewed hope when two car doors slammed behind her. She did not turn around. There was no need. In the reflection of the window, she saw the Phantom idling behind her. Two men walked toward her in trench coats and fedoras, their black silhouettes outlined in the headlights of the car.

A cry of terror escaped her lips, a scream of ferocity that tore from her throat and pealed through the street. In desperation, she brought her fists against the door again, missed the wooden frame, and smashed them through the window. The shattering of glass rang through the air. She screamed and brought her arms back through the jagged glass to find her hands and forearms covered in blood.

A hand grabbed her from behind, whirling her around. Papa Fratelli's enraged face was inches from her own. His chauffeur stood nearby, watching.

"Since you are not to be trusted, *bella mia*, my son must find another."

He seized her throat with one hand, cutting off her screams. She pried at the unrelenting grip, her nails digging deep into his skin. A violent shudder ran through her body, the culmination of all her fears. She knew he was killing her; she knew she was dying. She stopped struggling and accepted the painful crushing of her throat, praying that she would soon lose consciousness. As she crumpled, she saw his hate-distorted face transform into the viciousness of a mad animal, and the smoldering, dark eyes erupt into two glowing coals of fire. She smeared her hands across his jaw to push that horrid face away. Suddenly, he threw her to the ground. Her head struck the concrete. Pain roared through her skull as a trickle of air found its way down her throat.

"Her blood is on me—the blood of the redeemed." Cursing profusely, Papa Fratelli yanked a handkerchief from his pocket to wipe his face. "Put her in the car. Take me home, then finish the job."

"Sure, boss."

Two arms lifted her. She was unable to hold her head up; it dropped back, dangling like her limp arms. The sharp ache inside it turned into a dull throb.

"Brother, what a waste," she heard the chauffeur say in a voice that grew distant. "You just don't find class-act dames like this lyin' around, and here he throws one away."

Her vision faded to black.

A cigarette smoldered between Dominic's lips. He sat sprawled on the cushioned chair in Luke's room, his shirt collar open, his tie discarded. The room was dark, except for the flickering orange light of the fire. Its warmth lulled him. His head felt woozy, heavy. He tried to focus his eyes on his pocket watch. At last, after rubbing them, he read the time: two in the morning.

He brought a whiskey bottle to his mouth and finished the light brown liquid in several gulps. Through the smoke-filled air, he looked at Luke, who lay sleeping in his bed, snuggled comfortably beneath the quilts. Dominic stretched out his leg and gave the mattress a jolt.

"You awake?"

Luke's eyes remained closed.

"You sleep like the dead."

He brought the bottle to his lips again. Finding it empty, he cursed and flung it into the fireplace. It shattered, spraying tiny fragments upon the hearthstone that glistened in the firelight. Luke did not stir.

Retrieving another bottle from his pant pocket, Dominic opened it, tossing the lid across the room.

"He shouldn't have done it. He shouldn't have sent her. And *you*," he pointed a shaky finger at Luke, "you have no idea what's in store for you, but *I* do. You'll pass out drunk for the first time at age twelve. At thirteen, you'll knock over a store and spend your first night in jail. You'll know your first woman at fifteen...."

He sank deep into the chair, brought the bottle to his lips, and drank.

"You'll shoot your first man at sixteen, and you'll watch him die while he begs you for his life. Before you're twenty, you'll lie rotting in your grave, filled with holes from some punk's tommy gun....Why I'm still alive, I'll never know."

Wiping the liquor from his mouth with the back of his hand, he studied Luke's youthful profile.

"If you stay here, Papa will warp your soul into his own image...like he did mine." He swore. "He'll tarnish your innocence...."

He took another drink and tried to focus his eyes. Luke's image had grown fuzzy.

"I'd sooner end your life....One bullet in the heart....You won't feel a thing...you'll be in heaven...and I can go to hell with Benny."

This sobering thought made him laugh. He dropped the bottle. Whiskey saturated his pants as the bottle toppled to the floor. He cursed and found he was too drunk to stand. Accepting the comfort of the chair, he closed his eyes, whispering, "Sorry, Luke...I'll have to kill you in the morning."

"Dominic Fratelli, this night your soul is required of you."

The bellowing voice made Dominic jump. He had only been asleep in the chair a few moments before the brightness of the sun shone directly into his eyes. Arrows of pain ricocheted through his head; a sudden nausea rose in his stomach. He threw up his hands to block out the glare.

"Ahhh! Turn off that light!"

No one obeyed the command, so he came to his feet to escape the overwhelming glow—one arm draped over his eyes, the other outstretched as a guide—when a hand, landing squarely in the center of his chest, shoved him back into the chair.

"Wha—!"

He tried to peer beyond the brilliance streaming through his upraised hands. He thought he discerned a silhouette.

"Fool, get that light out of my eyes!"

The radiance diminished enough that Dominic could look at the person without shading his eyes. What he saw was unexpected. A giant stood over him, dressed in white. Except for the red hair, the features were barely distinguishable in the brightness; Dominic detected the outline of a square jaw, powerful arms, and a chest that was twice the width of his own. Without thinking, he reached for his gun as he stood.

"Who the—!"

This time, he was not shoved back into the chair. He sat willingly as the giant drew a sword the length of his mighty arm and positioned its point directly beneath Dominic's chin. All bravado forsook him when he felt the razor-sharp edge touch his throat.

"Dominic Fratelli, you will be held accountable for your wickedness. You will be judged for the blood you have spilt. Will you also tempt the Lord's wrath by threatening the life of His prophet?"

Dominic's mouth fell open. Gooseflesh crawled in swift progression over his body. He felt certain that his heart had stopped.

"I was sent to slay you, but the Lord heard the prayers of His prophet. Your life is prolonged. Take heed, for the prophet is in your hands. And be not deceived: his death is your death."

The flat end of the sword smacked Dominic under the chin and shut his mouth. He threw his head back against the chair, squeezed his eyes closed, and waited to be pierced through. An eternity passed as he sat there streaming with sweat, waiting for death.

"You can look now. He's gone."

Luke's voice was a welcome sound after the thunderous utterance. Hardly daring to open his eyes, Dominic squinted through his lashes. Only the firelight illuminated the room. Turning toward the bed, he found Luke sitting there, his green eyes shining from the orange glow.

Sweat plastered Dominic's shirt to his chest. When he tried to speak, his parched tongue stuck to the roof of his mouth. He searched for the whiskey bottle, found it under the chair, and brought it to his lips when, out of nowhere, Luke handed him a glass of water. He did not even see Luke stand up to get it, but there it was before him.

Allowing Luke to remove the bottle from his hand in exchange for the water, Dominic closed his eyes and drank. It coursed down his throat like a refreshing stream and revitalized his tongue. When he emptied the glass, he opened his eyes and looked at Luke. His voice, when he spoke, sounded like a strained whisper.

"So, it's true. You are a prophet."

Luke nodded.

"Who was that? Was that God?"

Luke shook his head.

"An angel?"

Luke nodded.

Shooting to the edge of his seat, Dominic shouted, "Say something! Will you?"

When Luke opened his mouth to reply, Dominic silenced him with a wave of his hand. He got to his feet and paced the floor erratically, clutching his head between his hands.

"I'm drunk. Yeah, I'm loaded. I'm hallucinating."

Luke silently watched Dominic pace the room, contriving different scenarios aloud, until he stopped suddenly before him with desperate eyes. He grabbed Luke by the arms and lifted him up, bringing his face close to his own.

"Tell me it wasn't real! Tell me I'm hallucinating!"

Luke touched Dominic beneath his chin and brought his hand forward. When Dominic saw his own blood glistening on Luke's fingers, he threw Luke onto the bed and ran to the bathroom to gape at himself in the mirror. Yes, he was bleeding. Not much, just enough to trickle down his throat. He flushed his chin with cold water, dried it tenderly with a towel, and inspected the mark across his neck. The insignificance of the scratch did not diminish his anxiety. When Luke spoke beside him, he nearly jumped out of his skin.

"He was gonna kill you, you know."

His terror was now complete. He expected death from an enemy's gun. Death from a being who could walk through walls was something entirely different. His vision blurred....

"Dom? Dom, wake up."

Opening his eyes, Dominic found himself staring at the ceiling with Luke on his knees beside him, applying a wet washcloth to his face.

"What happened?"

"You passed out."

His pride wounded, Dominic grabbed the side of the bathtub to pull himself into a sitting position.

"You don't look so good."

"I'll be all right. Give me some air." He rested his forehead against his arm, fearing he might be sick. "Was that your guardian angel?"

"Somethin' like that," Luke said.

"Does he hang around a lot?"

"Yeah, mostly when somebody wants to hurt me."

The words stung. "I would never hurt you, Luke. Do me a favor, though. Next time he's around, let me know so I can leave the room."

Luke erupted into a delighted squeal of laughter.

Raising his head enough to peer over his arm, Dominic asked, "How old are you?"

"Eleven and a half."

"I had you pegged at ten." He shook his head ruefully. "A prophet. You of all people. Pray tell, what happens now, Elijah?"

Luke's face brightened with surprise. "You know about Elijah?"

"I'm not ignorant." Grabbing the washcloth from Luke's hand, he rubbed his face vigorously with it. "Am I supposed to be born again now or something?"

"No. You have to ask Jesus into your heart first."

"Oh, brother." Dominic buried his head back in his arm, shaking his head miserably. "I'm not ready for this. I'm going to bed."

Coming to his feet proved to be more difficult than he had expected. The floor seemed to move of its own accord, so Luke helped him to his room, where he collapsed on the bed. With a weary hand, he waved Luke off.

"Thanks. You're a good angel—I mean, a good prophet—I mean—get out of here. I'll deal with you in the morning."

When Luke turned to leave the room, Dominic called after him, arresting his steps.

"If you tell *anyone* that I blacked out in there, I swear I'll break your scrawny neck, angel or no. Got it?"

A smile spread across Luke's face. He quietly closed the door.

TWENTY-SIX

Sleeping in his bed that night did not appeal to Joshua. It felt empty, lonely, so he chose the sofa and lay there under a quilt in his pale blue flannel pajamas, watching the blaze from the fireplace reflect off the walls and furniture.

The solitude of the night exaggerated every sound in the oversized house. Every time he closed his eyes, a creak would cause them to snap open again. The clock struck two before he gave up sleeping and switched on a light.

He stoked the fire, made some coffee, and sifted through the contents of his briefcase, coming across the book of fables. It surprised him. He had forgotten about it, and now, looking at its worn leather binding, he felt impelled to read it. Nestling back beneath the quilt, he opened the book at the faded purple ribbon.

The Order of the Scrolls

> ***O ye! Unhappy soul whom misfortune hath brought this letter, take heed. Let this story reveal to thee the evil unleashed. 'Tis more than legend. Yea, 'tis truth I write and truth I take to my grave as I lift mine eyes to the glory of eternity and relinquish my life to the pall of death. The powers of hell exceed my attempts to withhold this evil and I fear it shall soon be released. Vain is my hope that I may prevent it. I write in secrecy for I am watched.***

Know then that in the days of yore, after the death and resurrection of our Lord Jesus Christ, that Caiaphas, the high priest of Jerusalem, was deposed by Vitellius, governor of Syria, for the unrest that arose within Israel. Greatly ashamed, Caiaphas escaped into Rome. His heart hardened in pride, he cast from him the Law of Moses to seek refuge with the Herodians. And it came to pass that a sorceress bewitched him. He took her as his wife and she bore him two sons.

In that day, the persecution of the Church was great. Caiaphas, now a great sorcerer, did besiege the Church on each side. Unclean spirits possessed him to take a poor Christian youth and kill him secretly. In his blood, Caiaphas wrote the first cursed scroll and thereby released the demon Larkin through the power of the devil. This scroll enabled the demon to choose which of the sons of Caiaphas he would indwell. He chose the second son because he was of beautiful countenance. The demon slew the boy to possess his body and rose to power throughout Rome, tormenting Christians to their deaths. In due time, he took a heathen wife who bore him two sons. Upon the youngest son reaching five and twenty, he slew him to possess his body, thus enabling the curse to thrive through two generations.

The Lord rose up the prophet Dimitrius who, through the power of the Holy Ghost, wrote the scroll of judgment that condemned the demon back into the pit and destroyed the cursed scroll with hell-fire. Unbeknownst to Dimitrius, the demon wrote a second scroll in Christian blood that empowered the demon Melchior.

The demon Melchior fell by the word of the Lord written in the scroll of judgment by the prophet Elam in the Year of our Lord 635. The third demon Deodatus fell by the word of the Lord written in the scroll of judgment by the prophet Josiah in the Year of our Lord 1086. The fourth demon Seumuis, who tempted the prophet Caleb, who trusted not in the strength of God, was brought down by the prophet Darius in the Year of our Lord 1232. The fifth demon Alaric tempted three prophets of the Lord through the weaknesses of their flesh, until the prophet Jonathan brought him down by the word of the Lord written in the scroll of judgment in the Year of our Lord 1312. The sixth demon Aeneas was brought down by the prophet Ferdinand in the Year of our Lord 1510, yet he failed to destroy the cursed scroll by hellfire as the other prophets had done.

This scroll and the scroll of judgment came into the hands of a humble Dominican monk of the church of the Spirito Santo in Naples. I, Salvatore Ansaldo, am he who writes these words for the benefit of those who follow. 'Tis ordered that upon my death, these two scrolls, as they cannot be destroyed except by hellfire, be buried with my bones. 'Tis my hope to end The Order of the Scrolls before the sixth scroll can unleash the evil of Aeneas anew and prevent the writing of the seventh scroll.

O! That they would rot with my body! Bitter is the knowledge that they shall not. Holy and Mighty God, I have served Thee. To Thee I lift up my spirit. Let Thy will be done.

Joshua closed the book, feeling even less at ease in his lonely house than before.

"Mr. Parnell?"

The voice, accompanied by a simultaneous rap of knuckles against the open door, brought Joshua's attention away from the law book lying open on his office desk. He looked up to find Edmund peering inside the doorway, an apologetic yet eager expression on his soft, wrinkled face. Joshua stood with a smile.

"Hello, Reverend. Come in."

Edmund came forward with two large books and a journal under his arm. He set them on a chair before shaking Joshua's outstretched hand.

"I'm sorry I didn't call first. I came straight from the library. Am I intruding?"

"Not at all. Have a seat." Joshua sat and leaned forward on his elbows. "You know, I read that old book you gave me. It gave me the willies."

"What I've come to tell you won't ease them. Do you have a few minutes?"

"For you, Reverend, always," Joshua said sincerely. While the preacher was naïve and somewhat backward for his day, Joshua enjoyed his company. There was something refreshing about his country manner—something steadfast, believable.

"If you don't mind humoring an old man, I have a few questions to ask. First, do you believe in God?"

Joshua's smile waned. He felt snookered. "I suppose."

"Do you believe in the Bible?"

"I've never given it much thought."

"Angels? Demons?"

He scratched his forehead with embarrassment. "I fail to see what—"

Edmund held up an apologetic hand. "I'm not going to

preach. Your answers have told me how you'll accept the information I've gathered. If you don't believe in God and the Bible, you won't believe what I have to say."

"Forgive my ignorance. I'm not familiar with theology. What I know is the law."

"Well, are you familiar with the fall of Lucifer from heaven? The Bible tells us he tried to usurp the throne of God. There was war in heaven, and he and a third of the angels fell. These angels are what we now call demons. Lucifer is known as the devil, or Satan."

Edmund waited for a response, but Joshua said nothing. He blinked a couple of times.

"The Bible says in Ephesians chapter six, verse twelve, that '*we wrestle not against flesh and blood, but against principalities, against powers, against the rulers of the darkness of this world, against spiritual wickedness in high places.*' This means that even though we can't see it, there is a war going on all around us—a struggle of angels and demons over the bounty of souls."

"Reverend," Joshua squirmed in his chair, "I'm curious to know how this relates to Fred's murder. That's where my interest lies."

"And mine, as well. Fred was the victim of a curse that has ruled governments and murdered thousands, yet almost no one knows about it. In the story you read, the Dominican monk was writing about this curse. If you'll indulge me, I'll explain."

While loosening his tie, Edmund opened the journal on the desk, turned to a selected page, and scanned the words with his finger.

"I found him in an old encyclopedia: Dominican Friar Salvatore Ansaldo. He was born in Naples, Italy, in 1471, was a grand inquisitor of the Spanish Inquisition, and was a well-known preacher of indulgences. Later, he was converted by the Protestant Reformation and denounced the Roman Catholic

Church. He went into seclusion, spending his last years as a historian. It's believed that he went mad, creating stories about demon possession. In 1550, he was charged with heresy and hanged. He was buried in unholy ground with two scrolls. A legend developed that claimed those scrolls held the secrets of wealth and power. Later, the friar's grave was robbed."

Edmund looked up, hoping for a response. Joshua couldn't think of one, so Edmund plopped one of the heavy books down on the desk and opened it at a bookmark.

"I checked out *The History of the State of Colorado*. I've spent a considerable amount of time researching Antonio, or *Papa*, Fratelli's heritage."

Leaning back in his chair, Joshua let out a sigh. "I could've saved you the trouble. I have a complete dossier on him."

"On his criminal activities, maybe. Not on his heritage or what it means."

"I don't understand you."

"Papa Fratelli came to America in 1870 with his father, Vito Frattarelli, his mother, and an older brother. Vito changed their last name to Fratelli to hide the life of crime he had led in Italy. He was a powerful and dangerous man, what they called a *mafioso*. He invested in the railroad, increased his fortune, and came to Denver when it was little more than a cow town. The founders ignored the brothels, saloons, and gaming houses that Vito built because he helped finance artesian wells to provide the city with water. He also financed the streetcar lines and built a hospital and an orphanage. No one cared that the indigent children he took off the streets became hoodlums and prostitutes."

"They still don't care," Joshua added dryly.

"Vito died in 1885, and his oldest son soon after. They're buried at Riverside Cemetery in an elaborate mausoleum. I've been there. These people lead brief lives. Their women always die young. Did you know any of this?"

Raising his eyebrows to try to appear interested, Joshua said, “Can’t say that I did.”

“Then you probably didn’t know that in Italy, the Frattarellis were a prominent banking family. They go back to the sixteenth century, and they’ve used their wealth to influence politics.”

Joshua shook his head. “Look, Reverend. This has been a nice history lesson and all, but how does it apply to Fred’s murder?”

A light gleamed in Edmund’s eyes. “Tony Garda stumbled onto something in the Fratelli mansion—something he wasn’t meant to see—a dungeon, a skeleton, and the book of fables I gave you. He told Fred about them, and now both are dead.”

“Uh....” Joshua hemmed, pausing for a pregnant moment. “Can you back up? I think I missed something.”

Edmund inched forward on his chair. “One of Papa Fratelli’s ancestors robbed the grave of the Dominican friar. He found the cursed scroll, read it, and brought the sixth demon, Aeneas, up from hell. The curse has been over this family for nearly four hundred years. The blood they leave in their wake is evidence of this. The fear that Tony and Fred would come to this conclusion is why they were murdered. There’s your motive.”

Joshua’s eyes felt dry. His brain felt dry. Clearing his throat, he said, “Are you suggesting that Papa Fratelli is the sixth demon, Aeneas, raised from hell?”

Relief spread across Edmund’s face. “Yes. You understand.”

“Am I to infer that *you* are the prophet who’s supposed to send him back to hell?”

“Me?” Edmund leaned back with genuine surprise.

“Why not? You’re a man of God. The book says God raises up prophets to bring the demons down. Why not you?”

Edmund's smile grew strained. "You're being facetious. I'm not a prophet."

"Well, then, you'd better tell God to get busy and send that prophet, because none of this will help me convict Louie Fratelli of murder. I need an eyewitness or a smoking gun, not a centuries-old curse that no one in his right mind will believe."

Edmund sat quietly, not looking at anything, staring off into space.

"I'm sorry." Joshua cringed with guilt. "I don't mean to ridicule your beliefs, but I can't go into the courtroom with an indictment of spectral evidence. Does that make sense? Reverend?"

"What?" Edmund looked back at him, roused from his thoughts. "No—ah, yes. It makes perfect sense." He stood, collecting his books.

"I hope I haven't offended you."

"No. I understand your position, and my time wasn't wasted. The Lord has opened my eyes to something...incredible. I never would have believed it." He extended his hand. "Good day, Mr. Parnell."

Joshua returned the handshake hesitantly. "Well, what is it, if I may ask?"

"The prophet has been sent. If I told you who he was, you wouldn't believe me. Good day, sir."

TWENTY-SEVEN

MURDER/SUICIDE SHOCKS FARMING COMMUNITY

Police are trying to unravel a mysterious murder/suicide that occurred yesterday in a small farming community twenty miles north of the town of Loveland. Harald Warner discovered his brother, Neils Warner, 36, lying in a pool of blood on the kitchen floor of his farmhouse, dead from what appeared to be a self-inflicted gunshot wound to the head. A .22 rifle was found by his side. Behind the house were the bodies of Warner's sons, Charles, 15, and Nathan, 13, shot in the head execution style at point-blank range.

Police suspect that Warner, in a fit of despair or madness, lost control and killed his sons and himself. Sheriff Knutson of Loveland said, "A guilty conscience might be the reason." Money and photographs believed to depict the dead body of Warner's youngest son, Erik, 11, were strewn about Warner's body. Police have not ruled out blackmail.

Harald Warner informed the police that his brother had been depressed since Erik was reported missing in November 1931. The father had claimed that Erik ran away after a family argument. "We fear Erik's disappearance might be a cover-up for murder," Knutson said.

Police intend to excavate the earth on Warner's

> farm to determine if the boy is buried there. Until police can locate the body, the cause of his death or disappearance may remain a mystery.

Joshua lowered the morning newspaper to his office desk as the words registered within his brain. A creeping fear spread through his body. With a quavering voice, he asked the operator to connect him to Andy Ballantine's office, only to learn that Andy had not yet come in. Leaving a harried message with the secretary, Joshua slammed the telephone down merely to snatch it up again with a second thought. This time he requested Andy's home. There was no answer.

The fruitless endeavors to reach his attorney aggravated Joshua's every nerve and muscle until he thought he might explode. He slammed the telephone down again, just as Andy entered his office without knocking.

"I've been trying to reach you," Joshua snarled.

"No doubt to thank me and treat me to a celebration." An air of smugness surrounded Andy as he made himself comfortable in a chair.

Josuha snapped, "Have you seen the paper today?"

"No. I've been busy covering your unwieldy tail. The detective I sent to find the boy's family contacted me this morning. Are you interested in his findings?"

Joshua said nothing. He found it difficult enough to fix his feverish eyes upon Andy without formulating an answer to a stupid question.

With the pleasure of keeping Joshua in suspense, Andy waited with a grin before he reached into his suit jacket and produced a folded document. "Here. You may thank me now. I'm thinking dinner at the Brown Palace."

Joshua accepted the document and unfolded it flat against the desk. He read the words, "RELINQUISHMENT OF GUARDIANSHIP. I, Neils Warner, do hereby—"

With a thump, he dropped his head on his desk. He felt sick. "No. Oh, no," he moaned, crushing the paper into a crumpled wad. "What have we done?"

"What are you doing?" Andy snatched the document away and tried to smooth out the wrinkles. "Do you know what it took to get this? Do you know how much money I gave that farmer to get his signature? Five hundred dollars!"

Joshua groaned.

"Look at me! What's wrong with you?"

Without lifting his head, Joshua pushed the newspaper across the desk.

Andy grabbed it, mumbling something derogatory as he began to read. Then he grew silent; Joshua heard only the shuffling of the newspaper. Finally, after folding the paper and laying it carefully on the desk, Andy said, "Don't worry. There's no evidence to trace this back to us."

Joshua lifted his head in disbelief. "Is that all you care about?"

"It's what *you* should care about." Andy adjusted himself uneasily in the chair. He crossed his legs to appear nonchalant, but his naturally fair face had grown flushed.

"Are you made of stone, man? What about Neils Warner? What about those boys? They're dead! They're dead because of us!"

"*We'll* be dead if you don't shut up," Andy said, his voice straining as he sat forward.

"You paid him off! You paid cash for his son like you were buying a lousy stick of gum!"

"That's not exactly what happened."

"Then what? I thought you would—"

"You thought I would *what*, Josh? That I would ask this man to give his son over to a complete stranger? *'Pardon me, sir. I understand you have three sons. How much for the youngest?'* Is that what you thought?"

"You told him the boy was dead then, didn't you?"

"I told him no such thing."

"Don't argue semantics with me, you shark. You instructed the detective to tell him that his son was dead, didn't you?"

"You're forgetting something, Josh. That man beat his son. You told me so yourself."

"That's irrelevant. Regardless of how his father treated him, there's no excuse for what you did. You even gave him those appalling pictures. Can you imagine how that poor man felt when he saw them?"

"Yes, but why was Erik in those pictures in the first place?" Andy retorted. "Neils Warner and his sons are dead because *you* got drunk with a gun moll and ran over Erik. None of this would've happened if *you* hadn't initiated it. Or have you forgotten?"

Shaking with fury, Joshua jumped to his feet. "*I* haven't forgotten any of it! *I've* been paying for it every minute of every day, but *you* are the reason Erik no longer has a family! You may as well have handed the gun to his father and told him to blow his brains out!"

His stomach churned violently. Bracing his hands against the desk, he took long, deep breaths. With a sudden thought, he looked at Warner's scrawled signature at the bottom of the relinquishment document. He glanced up.

"How did you get him to sign this if he thought his son was dead?"

"He thought he was signing the death certificate." Andy looked away, his fervor muted. "Apparently, he couldn't read."

"Apparently, my foot. You counted on it. Did it occur to you that he might want to see his son's grave—a grave that doesn't exist? How did you get around that?"

"It matters little now."

"Answer the question!" Joshua shouted, slamming his hand on the desk.

"I purchased a grave site at the Loveland Burial Park," Andy admitted in a quieter tone. "Erik has a quaint tombstone with a lamb perched on top and an epitaph that reads, 'Unknown boy, asleep in the arms of Jesus.' It's touching. You really should visit it, considering you nearly buried the boy there yourself. I covered more than just the bases, Josh. I covered your—"

"I no longer want you to cover anything of mine! You're fired!"

Andy nodded sharply and stood, his ruddy face glowing with sweat. "I'll bill you."

"Ha! Bill me for what?" Joshua chuckled with incredulity. "Your incompetence?"

Andy's eyes smoldered.

"I hired you to do three things," Joshua continued. "Destroy all evidence of the accident, get the original pictures and negatives, and get that boy away from Papa Fratelli. You never got the pictures or negatives. Instead, you clued in Angelo, and he retaliated by bringing Erik to the courthouse. You also never got Erik. Instead, you underestimated Dominic Fratelli and got two of your men killed. Now you're responsible for the deaths of the Warner family. It's a wonder you succeeded in stealing my car without telling the police about it. You've failed in everything and only made matters worse for me. Now, get out of here before you manage to let me win the Louie Fratelli case."

Andy narrowed his seething gaze. Looking down at the Relinquishment of Guardianship, he picked it up, wadded it into a ball, and tossed it back on the desk.

"This is moot now that Erik is an orphan," he said. He turned toward the door, opened it, and looked over his shoulder with a sarcastic leer. "Now he's a ward of the court. Wouldn't it be ironic if Papa Fratelli adopted him?"

TWENTY-EIGHT

Dom, wake up. Wake up!"

"Uhhh." Without opening his eyes, Dominic pushed away the pestering hand that tugged at his arm. "Quit it, Luke."

"No, you gotta wake up!"

He barely opened one eye—enough to see the early light of dawn, enough to feel the enormous pounding in his head from a terrific hangover. Finding the pillow, he dragged it over his face.

"Uhhh. Go away."

Luke was quiet long enough to make Dominic think he had gone away when Dominic felt a displacement on the mattress and a bouncing that threatened the stability of his stomach.

"Stop jumping on the bed or I swear I'll shoot you!"

"Not until you get up."

"What's so da—" Dominic stopped himself from swearing. "What's so important that I have to get up now?"

Luke stopped jumping. He simply said, "Clara."

Dominic pushed the pillow aside. He looked at Luke, who towered over him, fully dressed and ready for the day, his hair still damp from a recent shower.

"What did you say?"

Quick as a cat, Luke hopped off the bed and ran out of the room.

"Hey! Where are you going?" Dominic shouted before clutching his aching head between his hands. Literally rolling out of bed, he lugged himself after Luke, tucking in his shirttails as he went. He was still dressed in his clothes from the previous night, and he had an awful taste in his mouth.

When he reached the stairs, he saw Luke bounding down them. He followed at a slower pace. By the time he reached the front entrance, Luke had run out the door and left it open, allowing the frigid morning air to waft through the room.

Dominic used his hands to block out the morning glare and to keep the listless snow from falling in his eyes. Peeking out behind them, he saw the Phantom Rolls Royce idling in the driveway and Luke standing on the running board, looking into the backseat. Luke glanced over his shoulder to make sure Dominic was following and ushered him forward with an impatient wave.

"Hurry up, Dom!"

Forcing himself to traverse the fifty-foot trek, he stood beside the car at last, his shoulders drooping. "Okay. I'm here. What is it?"

Luke pointed inside. Dominic followed the motion. Leaning his hands against the car to squint through the window, he saw nothing at first except the black leather interior. Then he straightened. He grabbed the door handle. It was locked.

"See, I told you," Luke said.

Hurrying around the car with Luke running behind him, he tried the other door, only to find it locked as well. He took his gun from its holster under his arm. "Stand back."

Luke took two steps back and covered his ears with his hands. Aiming the barrel at a deliberate angle toward the door handle, Dominic pulled the trigger. The explosion caused Luke to jump. The bullet punctured the handle, bursting the lock. Returning the gun to its holster, Dominic opened the door and caught Clara, who fell into his arms.

Limp, silent, she dangled backward, her hands almost

touching the ground. Her eyes were closed, her full lips slightly parted, slightly blue. In a moment of disbelief, Dominic stared at her and at her blood, which was smeared on the interior of the car.

"Clara?"

He knelt, tenderly gathering her from the car until she drooped in one of his arms and her legs rested upon his uplifted knee. Dried tears streaked the ghostlike pallor of her face. Deep purple bruising marred her slender throat.

"Clara!"

She felt cold. The fur coat hung off her bare shoulders, exposing her blood-streaked skin to the falling snow. He placed his ear to her chest, then glanced up at Luke.

"She's alive."

"Yeah, but her number's up."

Dominic snapped his head toward the voice to find Papa Fratelli's chauffeur, Mario—lanky, gaunt, his dark face pitted with pockmarks—leaving the mansion. He held a cup of coffee in one hand, a cannoli in the other.

"I got orders to finish the job. Ain't never knocked off a dame before. I was hoping she'd keel over on her own. Dumping a frail in a ditch, especially a swell looker, ain't my kind of racket."

"Who told you to finish the job?" Dominic felt his angered pulse pounding against his temples. He stood, cradling her against his chest.

"Papa. Who else moves the muscle around here?"

"I do. Who did this to her?"

"Papa." Mario took a sip of coffee. "He would've finished it except she bled on his glad rags, so I get the chore of cleaning out the backseat."

Dominic took a threatening step forward. "You're lying."

"If I'm lying, I'm dying. I watched him throttle her with my own peepers. She must've crossed him. Ain't never seen him this steamed up. Give her here, Dom. I got some ugly business to finish."

"Touch her and you're a dead man."

Looking hurt, the chauffeur raised his cannoli helplessly. "What's your beef with me?"

Dominic stormed toward the mansion. Luke hurried ahead to open the door for him. Upon stepping foot into the entrance hall, they both froze. In the distance, both Papa Fratelli and Carpinelli emerged from the library, speaking in hushed tones. When they saw Clara in Dominic's arms, they checked both their steps and their discussion. An awkward silence prevailed.

Perceiving the hatred and betrayal in Dominic's flushed face, Papa Fratelli took several steps forward, his extended hands imploring understanding. "Dominic, my son. Come to me and we shall talk."

Without a word, Dominic turned, taking the stairs two at a time up to the third floor with Luke running behind. In Clara's room, he laid her on the bed and ordered Luke to bring warm wet towels from the bathroom. Removing her fur coat, Dominic covered her with the blankets.

"She okay?" Luke asked as he brought the towels.

"I don't know. She's unconscious. Bring me some dry towels, too. Luke—wait." Dominic did not turn to look at him; he focused his burning eyes on Clara's face. "Give it to me straight. Did Papa do this?"

"Yeah. He hurt her real bad."

"Why didn't you tell me this would happen?"

"Because I didn't know. I only know things when God tells me."

"Why did Papa do it?"

"You gotta ask him that."

"You tried to kill her?" Carpinelli asked, aghast. "Why? And today of all days."

"Because the honor of the Fratelli name is worth killing for," Papa Fratelli said simply.

"You couldn't wait one day? *One day?*"

Carpinelli could not sit still, nor could he keep his confounded mustache from twitching. He paced the dungeon, breathing the dank air deeply if only to quiet his pounding heart. Papa Fratelli sat behind his medieval table, feigning composure, pretending to be interested in the ancient papers before him.

"I rely upon the obedience of my people in order to govern this family," he said. "Those who do not obey are dealt with. You of all people should know that."

"But you've just alienated Dominic. We need him."

"Stop your pacing," Papa Fratelli snapped. "It aggravates me to no end." He inhaled with sharp, abrupt surprise. He grabbed his chest, his body contorting in agony as a staggering pain flung him headlong across the table. The howl of a tormented dog escaped his grimacing mouth. With a swipe of his arm, he sent the papers flying.

"Dear God, please take care of Miss Clara. She's hurt real bad. Please heal her...."

"What—what's wrong?" Carpinelli asked. He took a step back as a surge of divine force drove Papa Fratelli to his knees. The veins in his neck bulged, throbbing up into his brilliant red face.

"And bless Pastor and Mrs. Elliott, and Charlie and Nate and Pa, and Dominic, too. He's real scared about Miss Clara...."

"I will not have this in my house!" Papa Fratelli screamed. "Kill him!"

Terrified, Carpinelli took another step back. "Wh—Who?"

The horrible howling filled the room again. Spittle

stretched between Papa Fratelli's lips. He pulled his gray hair in a frenzy. "The Prophet! Kill him!"

Carpinelli's face turned chalky white. He raised his hands and shook them fervently along with his head. "No. I can't. I won't kill God's anointed."

Papa Fratelli came to his feet and bolted forward in a single movement. He struck Carpinelli fiercely across the face with the back of his hand. The blow knocked him off balance and threw him into the wall. "Do it!" A sluggish drop of saliva dribbled from Papa Fratelli's mouth.

"Don't make me," Carpinelli pleaded. He braced his back against the wall and cupped his swelling lip. "I'm already facing judgment. I don't want his blood on my hands."

"Go! Or you will find yourself in judgment sooner than you think!" Papa Fratelli's unearthly cry of anguish shook the room, sifting dirt through the cracks of stone above their heads. The table and chair rattled. Several books tumbled from the bookcase to the floor.

Carpinelli stumbled out the door from sheer terror, feeling his way with outstretched arms through the dark passage. When his feet struck the stairs, he stumbled up them and through the trapdoor. Bursting through the library door with cobwebs streaming from his clothes, he startled the horror-struck servants huddled in the entrance hall. They scattered like frightened rats as he blundered past them toward the grand staircase. Fearing his legs would falter, he pulled himself upward with the handrail.

Death awaited him at the top; if he did not obey, death assuredly awaited him at the bottom.

On the third floor, he paused to catch his breath and loosen his tie. Steadying himself with a hand on the wall, he crept down the hall. At Clara's room, he stopped just beyond the open door to peek inside. He saw her lying unconscious on the bed, and Luke—his replacement—kneeling faithfully and humbly before his God.

"And Lord, I really don't understand what's happening, so please help me to do what's right, to do Your will...."

Jealousy seized Carpinelli. His mouth pressed into a flat, bloodless line. He stepped inside, lifting his hands toward Luke's thin neck. It would take little effort to break it.

From the bowels of the mansion, he heard the command: "Kill him! Kill him now!"

"And Lord, please—"

His hand clamped down on Luke's mouth and nose, stifling his prayer. Fixing Luke's writhing body against his own, Carpinelli wrapped his arm around Luke's shoulders and tried to wrench his head one way and his shoulders the other. A high-pitched scream sounded in Luke's throat. He arched his back, clawing at the hands while his feet kicked the floor in a violent cadence. Carpinelli gritted his teeth and twisted harder.

Two arms wrapped around Carpinelli from behind. Stalwart hands fell upon his wrists, wresting his grip from Luke's thrashing body with ease.

Gasping, Luke dropped to the floor, looking with bewilderment at his would-be murderer while those powerful hands grabbed the back of Carpinelli's shirt collar and threw him face-first into the wall. Carpinelli squeezed his eyes shut just as his nose smashed into it with a distinct, painful crack. A brilliant array of colors flashed before his tearing eyes. Those forceful hands pinned him there as blood oozed down his face.

"Fool!" Dominic's furious voice exclaimed in his ear. "Did you think I'd stand by and watch you kill him?"

"I didn't see you!" Carpinelli muttered awkwardly, his face crushed against the wall, his hands struggling against the young mobster's strength. "My nose! You broke my nose!"

"Then you're as blind as you are stupid. Did Papa send you to kill Luke? And Clara? Answer before I put a bullet through your brainless skull!"

"Just—just Luke."

"Why?"

"Because he can't. You broke my nose."

"What do you mean, 'he can't'?"

"Luke is protected," Carpinelli muttered. Dominic's meditative silence upon hearing this made Carpinelli ask, "Can I sit down? You broke my nose."

Dominic's answer to the request was a violent thrust against Carpinelli's back. "If he's protected, what made you think *you* could kill him?"

"Nothing," Carpinelli groaned, "but Papa said he'd kill me if I didn't. He probably still will."

"Not if I kill you first. Why does he want Luke dead?"

Carpinelli slumped feebly against the wall, giving up the fight. The blood running down the back of his throat made him feel nauseated. Suddenly, he felt a gun shoved into his ear and heard the click of the hammer being pulled back.

"I can blow a hole through your head right here, right now."

"You won't believe me."

Dominic growled under his breath. "Try me."

"Because Luke is a prophet of God, and your father is in league with Satan." Warm blood ran into his mouth. He tried to spit it out. "Please. Let me sit down."

The pressure on his head lessened abruptly. Before he could take advantage of it, Dominic yanked him from the blood-spattered wall and threw him into the hallway. Tripping from the force of the thrust, Carpinelli fell on his hands and knees.

"Get out before I gun you down like a dog."

Carpinelli lifted his throbbing head in time to see Dominic

slam the bedroom door shut. Through the halls of the mansion, a demonic cry of blasphemy rose from the lowest level. Carpinelli heard his name bellowed. He wasted no time. He came to his feet, rushed down the stairs at a speed belying his age, and burst out the front door.

TWENTY-NINE

After Dr. Ameche dismissed him from Clara's room, Dominic waited in the hall outside her door with his hands in his pockets. His dark, mulling eyes surveyed the hallway warily, then rested on Luke, who sat across from him on the floor, his back against the wall and his arms resting on his uplifted knees.

"Listen," Dominic said in a low voice. "We're getting out of here tonight."

Luke looked up with surprise. "Really? How?"

"During the party, I want you to stay with Clara. Don't leave her for any reason. I'll send up some food. Later, when the guests are drunk, I'll come for you."

"Where we goin'?"

"Away." Dominic glanced nervously down the hallway again. "First off, I want some straight answers about this prophecy racket of yours. Initially, I thought you were a con artist. When I realized you believed it yourself, I decided you were a nut. After last night," he touched his wounded chin, "I have to believe you're a prophet. Even Angelo says so. Therefore, you're not here by accident, so give it to me square. Why are you here?"

Luke leaned back against the wall. He grew silent. He folded his hands and started fiddling with his thumbs.

"Don't give me the air, kid. Tell me why you're here."

The dueling thumbs fought a brief war. "I can't. It's a secret."

Dominic's eyes narrowed. "That's just swell. I've saved your sorry neck more times than I can count, and you're keeping secrets from me. Spill it before I shake it out of you. You know something about my father. Is that why he wants you dead?"

"Yeah."

"All right. Give it to me."

"Nuh-uh."

Straightening to his full height, Dominic took his hands out of his pockets. "You're pushing it. If it's about my father, I should know."

"You don't wanna know." Luke met his gaze straight on. "You wouldn't understand anyhow."

"I already know the worst about him. What can you, a tight-lipped brat, tell me that I couldn't understand?"

"Okay!" Luke shouted from his own mounting frustration. "Your father's a demon! He ain't even human! There! I said it!"

Dominic threw up his hands. "Argh! You rotten little punk. I can't get anything out of you."

"I ain't a rotten little punk." Hurt clouded Luke's eyes as he crossed his arms over his chest. "You just won't believe me. You don't wanna believe I'm a prophet. You don't wanna believe an angel cut you last night. You don't wanna believe your father's a demon. You don't wanna believe in God, but if I hadn't prayed for you last night, that angel would've taken you to meet Him. You sure would've believed then, only it would've been too late. So, I saved your sorry neck, too."

"Listen," Dominic pointed his finger at Luke, who returned the antagonistic gesture with a sulking glare, "you believe in voices you hear in your head and nightmares you see when you're awake. These things don't make sense to me, and part of me still believes you're off your rocker. I stand on reason. It's not reasonable that my father is a demon. What would that make me? Half demon? I can't believe in things I can't see, things I can't feel."

"What about the angel you *saw*?" Luke snapped. "Didn't you *feel* it when he cut your chin?"

"Look, wise guy—" Dominic took a menacing step forward.

Luke threw his arms up to protect his head from the blow he expected. Dominic froze. Seeing Luke recoiled against the wall and the frightened look in his wounded eyes made him feel like a callused heel.

"This isn't getting us anywhere," he said in a gentler tone.

Realizing he wasn't going to be beaten, Luke tentatively relaxed his arms, though his eyes retained a wary mistrust as Dominic moved beside him.

"I'm sorry." He ruffled Luke's hair. "I didn't mean to lay it on you that hard. It's just that some of the stuff you feed me is a little difficult to swallow."

Luke shrugged. "It's okay."

Dominic sank against the wall to sit next to him. "No, it's not okay. I just need time to sort things out. What's more important is that we get out of here without having our throats slit in the process." He shook his head with quiet dismay. "I wish tonight was over."

"He shouldn't have done it," Dominic said under his breath. "He shouldn't have hurt them."

Sitting with his elbows on his knees and his chin resting on his left palm, Dominic dangled his pocket watch in his right hand, propelling the slender timepiece by its chain like a golden pendulum over his shoes. His wide-open eyes stared at nothing.

"He shouldn't have done it."

Luke lay beside him on the antique settee, curled into a ball and sleeping soundly under Dominic's jacket. Dominic sat on the other end waiting for Clara to awaken, waiting for the bleak light of an overcast day to surrender to night, waiting for his birthday party to begin so they could attempt their escape.

"He shouldn't have done it."

He lifted his gaze to Clara, who lay motionless in bed. Dr. Ameche had washed away all the traces of blood and exchanged the ruined gown for her purple silk robe. The gauze wrapped around her forearms and hands, and the darkening bruises so prominent against her porcelain throat, incited Dominic's fury anew. He came to his feet with a rush and paced the room like a captive animal. Sliding his watch into his pocket, he drew his revolver from its holster, confirmed that it was loaded, and returned it.

Luke sighed in his sleep. With a sideways glance, Dominic watched him roll onto his stomach, losing the jacket to the floor in the process. Dominic picked it up and draped it over him once more.

"Dom?"

Hearing Clara's strained voice, he spun around to find her eyes open, her bandaged arm stretched toward him. He quickly approached the bed. Descending on one knee, he took her hand gingerly into his own. "How do you feel, baby?"

"Papa—" He came close to hear her throaty whisper. "He—he tried to kill me." Tears moistened her brown eyes. "Tried to strangle me."

"I know." A wave of guilt washed over him. He dropped his gaze to the delicate hand clutching his.

"I thought I'd never see you again. I thought I was dead." Panicked sobs racked her slender body. "He—he sent me to this man. He wanted me to...I couldn't—Dom, I couldn't!"

"I know." He brought her fingers to his lips, pressing them in a kiss to divert his boiling hostility. "I know everything."

"I can't stay here! He'll kill me!"

She tried to sit up, kicking her feet to release the weight of the blankets. As gently as possible, he laid her back against the pillows.

"Calm down," he said, wiping her tears with his finger as he coddled her cheek in his hand. "We're getting out of here tonight."

Hope brightened her face, lessening her agitation.

"Everything is planned. Stay in here during the party. Don't leave for any reason. I'll come for you and Luke at the first opportunity."

Her anxious fingers clasped his hand. "Where are we going?"

"Anywhere you want, baby."

"I don't care," she said ardently. "As long as I'm with you."

For fear of hurting her, he suppressed the longing to take her in his arms and forced himself to be satisfied with another kiss on her hand. "Perhaps," he said, "we can find a justice of the peace along the way."

Surprise dazzled her misty eyes. "You want…to marry *me*?"

"Since the day we met."

"I never knew. I thought—" She dropped her gaze, fighting the flushing of her cheeks.

"You thought I wanted one thing from you, like every other louse. Clara, I want to spend the rest of my life with you, however short that might be."

She smiled through her tearful astonishment. "So do I."

Those three words sent a flood of relief through his heart. Sitting on the bed, he tenderly wrapped his arms around her as she nuzzled her head against his shoulder. They sat in silence, holding each other for a long while as he softly rubbed her back. The prominence of her ribcage against his hands concerned him; she had lost weight.

"Dom, would you do something for me?"

"Anything you want, baby."

"Remember the pictures you took of Luke the night of the accident? The ones Angelo used to blackmail Joshua Parnell?"

"Yes."

"Do you know where they are?"

"Yes."

"Can you get them?"

He pulled away to look into her eyes. "Why?"

"I want to give them to Joshua. I want to stop the blackmailing."

A pang of jealousy knitted his eyebrows together. "He means that much to you?"

"No, it's not that." Her hand squeezed his earnestly. "It's just that I destroyed his life. I couldn't live with myself if we ran off and I did nothing to fix it."

"You didn't destroy his life, Clara. You didn't hit Luke with a car. He did."

"But I caused it. If I hadn't set him up, he wouldn't have hit Luke."

"You didn't set him up, either. Papa did, and if he hadn't chosen you, it would've been another girl. Joshua was destined to hit Luke. Even so, I've no sympathy for him. He cared more about going to jail than he did about Luke dying. Moreover, he had only one thing on his mind with you that night."

"Nevertheless, I feel guilty. Please, Dom. Do this for me?"

He stood, one hand stroking his jaw. "I don't know. They're not easily accessible. It would be tricky."

"Where are they?"

"In the wall safe in the library, and, as I discovered, Papa can be in the library even if you don't see him."

"What about tonight while he's at the party?" she asked.

"No. It's not feasible. If I left, he'd look for me. He doesn't trust me any more than I trust him."

"But what if you distract him while *I* get the pictures?"

He frowned. "What?"

"I'll go down the back stairs and sneak into the library. Just tell me where the safe is hidden and what the combination is."

His frown deepened. "Neither you nor Luke is to leave this room. Is that clear?"

"Please, Dom," she entreated. "I don't want this on my conscience."

"And I don't want your death on mine. The answer is no. Joshua will have to play the cards he's dealt."

"But nothing will go wrong if we plan it right."

"A million things could go wrong. Get the idea out of your head, woman. It's not going to happen."

"But, Dom—"

"Clara," he snapped, "there are two people I value enough to risk my life for, and Joshua isn't one of them. You and Luke are the only ones who matter to me. I'll do everything in my power to protect you, but don't test my capabilities. My father is an evil man. Already today, he's tried to murder you both. As luck would have it, I was there to save you. I can't call on that luck every time. If you don't do as I say, you impair my ability to protect you. *Capisci*?"

"He tried to murder Luke?" Her eyes widened with fear.

Shaking his head, he lifted his hand to ward off further questions. "I won't take chances with either of you, and I don't want to hear any more about Joshua."

Silence hung between them as he stepped toward the window to watch the snow fall in a listless flurry. The setting sun, darkening the late afternoon to an ashen dreariness, dampened his mood further. He desperately wanted to see the sun, to see its brightness against a blue sky, to feel its warmth, but he felt only the cold seeping through the window, an invisible mist enshrouding his spirit with the heaviness of doom.

He dug his hands deep into his pockets, wrapped his fingers around the pocket watch, and held it tightly.

Thirty

From his bedroom high on the third floor, Dominic detected the sound of music reverberating in the banquet hall below. As he tightened the white bow tie around his neck and checked the tailcoat of his black tuxedo in the mirror, a thought occurred to him: this would be the last time he would see his family and friends—or so he hoped.

From that night on, he, Clara, and Luke would be running for their very lives, forever looking over their shoulders. Never would a night pass when he could sleep without the fear that their throats would be cut by morning. Knowing this, he made a plan. Papa Fratelli would expect them to run south to Mexico, or perhaps Argentina; therefore, they would beat it north toward Canada. They would drive straight through without stopping to rest. They would find some small town, change their names and appearances, and live discreetly. If Papa Fratelli ever found them, it would mean instantaneous death for Clara and Luke; his death, however, would be a prolonged, torturous affair.

This thought produced a churning dread deep within his stomach. He had seen his father torture; he had seen his father kill. Never had he felt such a keen apprehension, such a fear of the future or death. Until now, he had believed in neither God nor Satan; death was a shadow that sometimes drew near, but he had never feared it—until now.

Since learning of Luke's identity and finding Papa Fratelli

in the eerie depths of the mansion, he had realized that a mystery surrounded his family. With further dismay, he had realized his entire life had been manipulated by the masterful puppetry of his father. With clever grooming, his father had raised him as a cavalier agnostic, a hedonist. He felt deceived. He felt robbed.

He felt the gun beneath his arm. Its hard presence gave him reassurance. It was the only solid thing he had left to hold on to.

Stirring himself from his thoughts, he crept down the back staircase with his suitcase to his awaiting Deusenburg, which was parked near the kitchen. He placed the suitcase in the backseat, returned to the kitchen, and ordered the servants to deliver two meals to Clara's room.

Cheers filled the air when he entered the banquet hall, an elongated room decorated in Victorian splendor—high walls paneled with golden oak and a ceiling carved with intricate figures. An Italian fresco adorned the upper part of an entire wall and watched over the tables, which were surrounded by ornately carved chairs and covered with a bounty of food. Dozens of guests surrounded Dominic in a propelling throng of silk gowns and marcelled hair, tuxedos and concealed weapons. He glanced at his father over the gathering horde of celebrants, offering an apologetic nod for being late. Papa Fratelli returned it with a smile, a thoughtful one of expectancy that made Dominic feel like he had been knifed and kissed at the same time.

At once, two women attached themselves to his arms, while a third pressed a white rose against her painted lips and placed it in his lapel. After satisfying each with a meaningless kiss, he peeled them off to join the friends he intended to leave forever.

Someone thrust a drink into his hands. Toasts were raised in his honor. Stories and jokes were told in drunken slurs.

Giggling couples hastened upstairs in search of unoccupied rooms, while a minor squabble resulted in broken furniture and a slight amount of blood. A dance orchestra, a band of nine men in striped white and blue jackets, played a fox-trot for several young women who danced before an audience of men, all content to sip gin and watch.

Two hours had passed in this manner when Dominic pulled his pocket watch from his vest. *Quarter after ten.* Replacing it, he was considering the inebriated state of the crowd and scanning the room for his father when he heard voices yell out from across the room.

"Benny the Creep! Where you been hiding?"

"We heard you got your fortune told. Figured you were in hell!"

The gibes and laughter made Dominic swing around. His eyes searched the crowd.

"I hear there's a kid around someplace, Benny. Ain't you afraid of kids no more?"

"Run out of babies to beat up, or did you come to finish the job?"

The sarcasm continued as Benny wove his way through the crowd, scowling at the hecklers. When he saw Dominic, contempt spread across his wide face. Dominic's blood began to boil. Curbing his desire to bolt forward and unload his gun into Benny's chest, he stood still, making Benny cover the distance between them. Much of the noise grew quiet once they stood a foot apart.

"You didn't expect to see me, did you?" Benny asked, his fleshy lips sneering.

"Fools die for want of wisdom," Dominic answered.

Benny's lips moved silently for a moment, trying to create a retort for an insult he could not understand. He finally just said, "Well, you ain't giving me the bum's rush, see? *Papa* invited me."

"What does he want with you?" Dominic asked, turning his head away from the reminder of Benny's chronic bad breath.

"Says he's got a job. What's it to you?"

"What job?" A disturbing sensation crept up Dominic's spine.

"If he'd wanted you wise to it, he would've told you. Says if I pull this off, I'm back in the family and hitting on all eights. So back off, or I'll show you how I take the heat." Benny opened his jacket wide to expose the gun inside.

Dominic narrowed his eyes, unimpressed. "You'll never be back in the family. You've lost all credibility. No stand-up guy hurts a sick kid."

To Dominic's surprise, the enthralled audience responded with an explosion of catcalls.

"Waste the lousy bum!"

"Burn the creep!"

"Pants him!"

When Benny grabbed his belt tightly, his face reddening with mortification, the multitude erupted in laughter. Missiles of food soared toward his back and stomach. A carefully aimed hors d'oeuvre knocked his hat from his head.

Dominic smiled with grim approval until a voice shouted into the crowd, "Yo, Benny! I snagged your pal! He's got the lowdown on when you're gonna swing with the devil!"

The clamor of the party fell when all heads turned toward Mario, Papa Fratelli's chauffeur, who dragged a writhing, unwilling Luke by his neck into the banquet hall. Dominic's heart fell at the sight. When Luke saw Benny, the apprehension on his face changed to fear. This fear turned into bewilderment when half a dozen young women suddenly swept him from Mario's grip and swarmed around him like he was a diamond on display.

"What a sweetheart," one mewed coolly. "Let's have a closer look. Why, you're just the cat's pajamas."

Two came to their knees, mussing Luke's hair and stroking him like a pet. "Look at those emerald eyes! He's gonna be a heartbreaker."

"He looks so sad and thin." Another coddled his surprised face in her bejeweled hands. "What's wrong, sweetie? Want mama to find you something to eat?"

His eyes widened with alarm. He stumbled and twisted around. Avoiding the grasp of one, he fell into the arms of another.

"If only you were older, honey..." one whispered in his ear. "Think you could grow ten years overnight?"

Luke gaped in panic at the made-up faces, drowning in the glitz of jewelry and silk, painted nails and perfume, until Dominic laughingly said, "That's enough, ladies. Let's keep him virtuous. Come on, Valentino."

Dominic's delivering hand reached into the crowd of pouting women and extracted a disheveled Luke. With his handkerchief, he rubbed at the lipstick on Luke's cheeks and forehead.

"What'd they do that for?" Luke asked softly, his face blushing.

"They think you're adorable. Women kiss everything they think is adorable. If it makes you feel better, every guy in this room would've given his gun to trade places with you."

"Except Benny!" Mario shouted suddenly. "His idea of love is a big piece of cake!"

Dominic shot Mario a dangerous glare as the gang seized upon his taunt. Yelling crude insults mixed with laughter, they shoved pieces of moist birthday cake into Benny's grimacing face. He swung back, his mouth sputtering obscene words while they smeared his neck and clothes with white and red frosting. Fraught with rage, he reached into his coat and drew his gun. This brandishing action sent the crowd stumbling backward, but Benny wallowed in his achievement for only a second. In one sweeping movement, every man in the room drew his gun; Benny's triumph evaporated with a series of clicks as they pulled back the hammers.

Sensing a reprisal, Dominic reached for Luke to pull him out of the way. He turned, but Benny spun around before he could grab him. Dominic barely saw the scorn on his face before the black blur of a gun struck him hard across his wounded temple. A stunning blow of pain darkened his vision at once. The impact of the floor jolted his body. Fighting the impending darkness, he tried to lift himself from the floor, to peer through the mist and focus on the struggle he could barely detect. He heard Luke cry out. Women gasped. Someone uttered a curse.

He shook his head. Pain shot behind his eyes in vibrant colors. A whirl of nausea forced him back on the floor, and his ears were filled with a roaring flood of sound. He lay there, his eyes wide open, his vision fixed on what he thought was a chair, until the swirling in his head subsided and the mist before his eyes cleared. Pushing himself up again, he saw Benny's thick arm wrapped around Luke's neck. Luke's thrashing feet dangled off the floor.

In the stillness of the room, a movement caught Dominic's eye. Bearing a look of approval, Papa Fratelli entered the doorway with Joe, Dominic's older brother, beside him—stout, dumpy, surly, yet bearing a full head of black hair. When Joe noticed Dominic sprawled on the floor, he took a step forward, his hand reaching for the gun inside his tuxedo, when his father laid a firm hand on his arm, stopping him short.

Enjoying his returned control, Benny turned around, swinging Luke with him, meeting the stunned faces in the room with the gleam of foolish pride. In doing so, he turned his back on Dominic, who quietly rose to his feet, ignoring the ringing in his head.

Benny jabbed Luke in the head with the muzzle of his gun. "See? I ain't taking no flak from the likes of you! Kill me and you kill him!"

Dominic stepped behind Benny and pressed the barrel of his gun against the base of his skull. He pulled back the hammer. Benny froze.

"That's the second time you've pistol-whipped me," Dominic said, exhaling his hot breath against Benny's ear. "I didn't like it the first time. Let the kid go. I don't want to spoil his shirt."

Benny squeezed Luke tighter, forcing a pained cry from Luke's throat.

"Have you forgotten?" Dominic asked, patting Benny's fat, sweaty cheek. "He's God's prophet. If you kill him, he'll go straight to heaven. When I kill you, you'll go straight to hell." Wiping the sweat from his hand onto Benny's shoulder, he uttered in a low voice, "What's wrong, Ben? Feeling hot? Are the flames licking at your feet already?"

Visibly, audibly, Benny swallowed. His glance at Papa Fratelli received a nod of approval. Squeezing his eyes shut, he tightened his finger on the trigger of his gun. "Time to die, fortune-teller," he hissed in Luke's ear.

Dominic raised his arm. With all his strength, he drove the butt of his revolver down on Benny's head. Blood pulsed down Benny's face. A woman screamed. Like a lump of dead weight, Benny dropped into a crumpled heap. Using his foot, Dominic shoved Benny's body off Luke and helped the boy to his feet. He motioned to two men nearby.

"Take this garbage to the dump."

While they obeyed the command by dragging Benny's heavy, food-caked body out of the banquet hall, Dominic looked at his father across the room. Papa Fratelli's expression soured into a mirthless frown. He whispered something in Joe's ear and left the room. The dance orchestra roared back to life, revitalizing the party as if the scene was provided for amusement alone. Servants hurried forward with ready mops and pails, swabbing the area clean of food and blood, a familiar task to them.

"You're bleedin'."

Luke's voice took Dominic's attention away from the surreal scene. Pulling the handkerchief from his pocket, he pressed it against his temple. He tried to forget the pounding in his head; he had no time for it. Bending down, he grabbed Benny's gun. "Did Mario force you down here?"

"Yeah. He wanted to play a joke on Benny."

"Some joke. It almost got you killed. Was Clara all right when you left her?"

"Nuh-uh." Luke shook his head with a frown. "Mario pushed her on the floor when she tried to stop him from grabbing me. He said he'd come back for her tonight after midnight."

"That son of a—" Dominic cut the curse short. He took a deep breath to control the flame of anger that burst inside him and placed Benny's gun in the waistband of his pants. "Get upstairs and stay there. I have some business to discuss with Mario."

THIRTY-ONE

Dominic hardly noticed the snow fluttering around him. He lingered a few feet outside the kitchen entrance, his breath mingling with the smoke from his cigarette, his eyes surveying the grounds of the estate. Its silent, snowcapped landscape illuminated against the white sky made him feel exposed. He brought the cigarette to his lips, stepped back into the shadow of the mansion, and adjusted his grip on the revolver in his hand.

In his peripheral vision, he saw three dark figures exit the mansion. He did not have to turn his head to discern who they were. Mario walked a couple of steps in front of two other men, saw Dominic, and hurried over to stand beside him.

"What's the gag, Dom? Why call the dogs on me?" He jerked his head uneasily at the men behind him.

Dominic's solemn gaze remained on the scenery. "I wanted to speak with you."

"Out here?" Mario crossed his arms and stomped his feet. "Ain't it warmer inside?"

Dominic took another draw on the cigarette, vaguely aware of its orange glow. "Did Papa give orders to bring Luke downstairs?"

"Yeah. He said he wanted the party to get rough, you know, stir up some action."

"Did he say why?"

"Papa doesn't say why. He just says do."

"I won't tolerate anyone harming that kid," Dominic said, flicking a speck of ash from the lapel of his tuxedo.

"You're stacking the deck against me. That ain't the way it was."

"Then correct me."

"Papa meant it as a joke. Everybody knows Benny's off-track with that superstition racket."

"Your joke almost got Luke killed. It was poor judgment."

"Hey," Mario laughed nervously. "It was Papa's joke, not mine. Uh...by the way, how's your head?"

Glancing over his shoulder at the men behind him, Mario shuffled his feet in the snow. After inhaling the final draw of his cigarette, Dominic flicked the butt into the snow. Mario followed the movement with his head.

"You're an empty suit," Dominic said, turning to face Mario for the first time. He stepped closer, noting the fear in Mario's eyes and hearing the chattering of his teeth. "As if it weren't enough to risk Luke's life, you also bruised my woman. That alone warrants a death sentence."

"I never laid a glove on her!" Mario's eyes widened with genuine terror. "On the level! That kid's lying if he said different!"

Dominic lifted the gun. Mario took a step back, throwing his hands up in defense. Immediately, the men came forward to seize his arms.

"There's one thing I know." Dominic aimed the barrel point-blank at Mario's chest. "That kid doesn't lie."

Two shots burst from the revolver. Mario's body jerked with each. Simultaneous explosions of blood, bone, and flesh splattered from his back. He dropped backward without a cry of pain, his face frozen in fear. The men released his arms, allowing him to plop softly into the snow.

Dominic returned the revolver to its holster. Dusting the snowflakes from his tuxedo, he stepped over Mario's feet and walked toward the mansion, saying over his shoulder, "Bury him."

Returning inside, Dominic took two steps up the back staircase—and stopped. He hesitated, his foot on the third step and his hand on the rail. The sounds of the party were all around him: music, laughter, the clanking of dishes. Harried servants dashed from the kitchen to the banquet hall with fresh food and back again with dirty plates. An intoxicated guest stumbled among them, searching for a quiet corner in which to curl up.

Dominic took another step and stopped. Luke and Clara were upstairs. Now was the perfect time to bring them down and get away, but a nagging sensation held him back. The scratch on his chin tingled strangely.

He tried to take another step, but could not bring himself to ascend the staircase. Something wasn't right; he could feel it. At last, he turned around and hastened through the passage. Maneuvering through several guests, he took one step inside the banquet hall and stopped dead in his tracks.

"Not again," he growled. "I can't leave that kid alone for one minute."

Luke stood on top of a table, looking alone, scared. A lively crowd surrounded him, throwing questions and voicing their frustrations at his silence. Diffidence creased his brow into a worried line. He bit his lower lip while searching their faces with his big, unblinking eyes.

Dominic stormed forward, his jaw clenched tightly. He muscled his way through the gathering, throwing people out of his way, ignoring their drunken protests and the congratulatory birthday slaps on his back until he reached the table.

With a reproach on his lips for Luke's disobedience, he stopped short when he saw Joe holding Luke's wrist tightly.

Relieved to see Dominic, Luke quickly said, "I tried to go upstairs. Honest. He said if I didn't tell him his fortune, he was gonna make me swallow my teeth."

Dominic scowled at his brother. "Let him go, Joey."

"Nix." Joe's full mouth twisted into an inebriated grin. "We want our fortunes told."

"You don't know what you're asking," Dominic warned with a shake of his head. "Did Papa put you up to this?"

"We're just having fun. Help me out. Make him read our palms. Have a séance. Levitate a chair. Something like that."

"He's not a pet monkey. He doesn't do tricks. Let him go."

"Why? Is it past his bedtime?" Joe smirked at Luke, his eyes narrowing into a leer. "Come on, fortune-teller. We heard you called the Pompliano hit. Own up to it."

"I ain't a fortune-teller," Luke snapped back. "Stop callin' me that."

"You see the future, don't you?"

Luke said nothing. The hand that held his wrist squeezed tighter. Wincing, he finally said, "Sometimes."

"Sometimes. Then you're either a fortune-teller or a liar."

"I ain't no liar!"

"But you know the future?"

"Yeah!"

An appeased smile crossed Joe's face. "If you know the future but you're not a fortune-teller, then what on earth are you?"

"Here it comes," Dominic muttered.

"I'm a prophet! God tells me what's gonna happen!"

Grinning with pure antagonism, Joe kneeled, jerked Luke's wrist so that he almost lost his balance, and beseeched, "Oh, Great Prophet! What words have you from...*God*?"

Boisterous laughter ensued as the heckler bowed his head

like one in the presence of greatness. Luke's youthfulness and the battered quality of his waiflike appearance only enhanced the spoof. Dominic surveyed the crowd of drunken gangsters, an unruly group with an arsenal in arm's reach. He thought of Benny—and of Luke's tactless method of doling out doom—and his uneasiness grew. He had to get Luke off that table before he shortened his life expectancy. He tried to pry Joe's hand from Luke's arm.

"Joey, if you don't—"

"Child of the devil, you ask for the Lord's word. Prepare to hear it. '*The fool hath said in his heart, There is no God.*' You, Joseph Fratelli, are that fool."

Dominic froze. The authority in Luke's childlike voice sent goose bumps along his arms.

Joe's head shot up with a start. "What?"

"You don't believe in God or His Son," Luke continued, "and neither do you believe in the judgment that will follow the violent end to your life. The enemy will come in disguise and strike you six times. The dead will heap upon you before your soul descends into eternity. This is the word from the Lord."

Joe released Luke's wrist as though it burned him. He came to his feet. No one laughed. The importunate questions stopped. The audience stood in astonishment.

"Kid thinks he's cute," Joe mumbled. "He won't think so when I pop him on the button."

Bringing his arm back, he swung at Luke's head. Dominic caught his fist in midair before it made contact. He shoved Joe backward.

"Not wise, Joey," he said through his teeth. "You've no idea who you're dealing with."

"*You, Dominic Fratelli,*" Luke said, the severity of his striking eyes startling Dominic into chastised silence, "heir to the curse, repent of your wickedness and pray to God that your murderous heart may be forgiven. Accept Christ and enter into His kingdom, or suffer the punishment of your ancestors. This is the word from the Lord."

Luke then turned toward the crowd, raised his slender arms, and shouted, "You generation of vipers, how will you escape hell? Leave, for your enemy is upon you, your sins will be judged, and hell's greatness will be increased this night! Turn to Christ, and though you die, yet shall you live! This is the word from the Lord!"

Silence fell on the room. Some turned to look at their fellow guests with uncertainty. Dominic pulled his gun out and held it loose by his side. A man standing nearby nudged him with his elbow, saying, "I don't get it."

Tightening his hold on the revolver, Dominic waited. At first, the audience remained in shock; then, a woman giggled. Another joined her. Amusement overcame confusion, and soon the room thundered with laughter and applause.

"Fair act for a scrawny kid," Dominic heard someone say. "He should try his bit in vaudeville."

Dominic felt the tension lift from his shoulders. He returned his gun to its holster. Content with the entertainment, the crowd dispersed. The dance orchestra played once again. Guests started to dance. Bottles of alcohol were emptied, and demands for more were met when several young men entered the banquet hall wearing white waiter jackets over black pants. Each pushed a cloth-draped cart stacked with unopened champagne bottles.

"Get down." Dominic grabbed Luke by the arm to pull him from the table. "This is our chance."

"But they're gonna die." Yanking his arm away, Luke looked at the people, his distraught eyes filling with tears.

"They think it's an act. Let it go at that."

"But they're gonna die!"

Not wanting a struggle, Dominic wrapped an arm around

Luke's legs and threw him over his shoulder. He pressed his way toward the door. "This is the best chance we'll have. We've got to get Clara and go."

With his head hanging upside down, Luke strained to lift it. "Tell 'em they're gonna die, Dom! Tell 'em!"

As they left the banquet hall, a mobster lifted his glass high in the air and shouted, "To the molls! The ladies of Hades! Don't go there without us, girls!"

"Clara! Clara!" Dominic shouted. "Where is she?"

Bolting through her room to search the closet and the bathroom, even dropping to his knees to look under the bed, Dominic regained his feet and turned wildly upon Luke.

"She was here when you left, wasn't she?"

"Yeah. Where'd she go?"

"You tell me," Dominic snapped. "You're the prophet."

A frown darkened Luke's face. "I only know what God tells me."

"Cut the comedy." Brushing him off with an impatient hand, Dominic leaned outside the door to search the hallway. "If you know where she is, tell me. If not, use your divine powers to find out. Clara!" He swore and glared over his shoulder at Luke. "Why couldn't you stay up here like I told you? And while I'm at it, what was that 'heir to the curse' nonsense you laid on me down there?"

Luke folded his arms across his chest. "It ain't nonsense!"

"On second thought, can it. I don't have the patience for one of your ambiguous answers."

"And I didn't wanna come downstairs! Mario made me!"

"I said, put a lid on it!" Shaking his head in frustration, Dominic grumbled, "I can't understand why everyone and their brother want to get their paws on you. One would think you were a golden Kewpie doll. All I want is a girl, and I'm thwarted at every turn."

Taking a step forward, Dominic paused as a horrible thought struck him.

"Oh, no. Don't tell me she went to the library." He groaned and rubbed his eyes hard with the palms of his hands. "I told her not to leave this room. I can't believe this. Nothing is going right. Why can't anyone do what I tell them?"

"How come she went to the library?"

"Because she's lost her mind. She might just lose her life." He stopped rubbing his eyes, now red with irritation, and glared at Luke. "Get downstairs. We have to find her before Papa does."

Clara's slender fingers trembled as they worked the dial of the safe. Terrified she would be caught, her eyes darted to the library door every few seconds while her ears concentrated on catching the intricate clicks of the combination.

Locating the wall safe had been simple; she had found it behind a heavy, beveled mirror that opened on hinges like a door. Discovering the combination, however, was not. She had rifled through the desk and flipped through the pages of several nearby books in the hope that someone had written it down for convenience—all to no avail. Now she had resorted to safecracking. After turning the dial and hearing a few clicks, she tried the handle. The safe remained stubbornly closed.

Time was running out. Her anxiety intensified the longer she remained. With her ear tuned for more clicks of the combination, she tried the handle a second time, but the safe remained secure. She gave up. Dominic would be furious to learn that she had risked her life to retrieve the photographs of Luke.

Worried that she may have jeopardized their escape for nothing, she grabbed the mirror to close it when the dial began to spin rapidly of its own accord. With a shriek of surprise, she took a quick step back. Amid a series of clicks, an invisible hand rotated it to the right, back to the left, and to the right once more before the handle came down and the safe door opened wide.

"Do you seek to rob me, *bella mia*?"

A terrified scream escaped her throat. She whirled around and pressed herself against the bookshelf. Standing directly before her was Papa Fratelli.

Thirty-Two

That dirty, rotten, no-good brat." Joe Fratelli sat amidst the dancing and gaiety of the party, the sole figure not in constant motion. He drooped in a chair in the center of the room, his legs spread open, his shirt undone, his bow tie lost amongst the confetti sprinkled across the floor. He drank bourbon straight from the bottle.

"Who does that kid think he is, feeding me that hooey? 'Your enemy will strike you six times.' Ah, forget about it. The kid's jingle-brained. Yeah, that's it. Jingle-brained."

The sound of feminine laughter brought his head up. Two women sashayed before him, almost skipping, their arms around each other's waists, shimmering in his double vision. He reached out for them, touching only their ghostly twins as they giggled and hurried away.

"Joe." Someone shook his arm. He did not bother to see which one of Papa Fratelli's boys it was. "There's some news hawks outside who want to take some pictures. Should I let 'em in?"

"Pictures of me? You mean Dominic. He's got the mug the dames can't get over." He wiped his mouth on his sleeve after taking another swig from the bottle. "He's also a first-class sap. I don't get his angle, muscling in on me over that brat."

"They want pictures for—get this, Joe—the *Society Page*."

Joe straightened in his seat. "Me? In the *Society Page*?" Running his fingers through his slicked-back hair, he stood, grabbing the chair to keep from tottering over. "That'd be first-rate. Send 'em in."

Facing the orchestra and rocking on his heels, he stopped the music with an exaggerated wave of his arm. "Close your yaps! The snoop hounds want a shot for the Society Page!"

The guests flocked happily to their tables, drawn from the entrance hall and other rooms. No one heeded the twenty young waiters who positioned themselves every few feet around the room behind their covered champagne carts. They stood quietly with their backs against the walls.

Two men in suits and bowlers entered the hall, carrying a large camera and tripod. Whistling at the grandeur of the mansion, one said to Joe, "Ritzy layout you got, Mr. Fratelli. Mind if we set up the camera in front of the band?"

Joe spun around. A hand caught his elbow, steadying him on his feet. He tried to focus on the man before him with two overlapping faces, both smiling wide, toothy grins.

"Anywhere. Just make sure you get me in the shot. I'll be here in front."

"We wouldn't dream of missing you, Mr. Fratelli. I don't see Papa or Dominic. Think they'd like to be included in the shot?"

"If you can find 'em, you can ask 'em."

"We'll hunt them down later."

Waiting patiently until most of the guests found their chairs or wobbled behind them, the photographer addressed the multitude. "Good evening! What a swell party! Papa Fratelli sure knows how to dole out the mazuma! And I see the bootleggers have kept your storehouses well-stocked!"

A cheer accompanied the ring of crystal striking crystal. The photographer peered into the camera, paused, then surveyed the scene.

"Let's have you all stand up. You'd make much better shots."

The partygoers complied. Some held their glasses in the air. Others kissed in lingering embraces. The photographer bent behind the camera once more.

"Nice, big smiles. That's right. Hold it. This one's for Don Pompliano. He wants something to remember you by."

Their smiles faltered.

With a flash of powder and a corresponding boom from the camera, the waiters reached into the carts. A split second after the picture was taken—when the flash had blinded the guests—the deafening sound of Thompson submachine guns blasted into the crowd. Few understood what was happening until the bodies, twisting and jerking in the throes of death, began to fall. Then the screaming started.

In murderous deliberation, the killers swept their tommy guns back and forth, their faces grimacing behind the yellow fire bursting from the barrels of their oscillating weapons. Dishes and food erupted into the air. Shattered mirrors and chandeliers exploded fine, razor-sharp daggers into the torrent of panicked guests. They collapsed like broken dolls in succession, dropping on each other as bullets pierced their flesh.

The tumult of screams and gunfire raged in Joe's ears. Stunned with disbelief, he gaped at the photographer, who was brandishing a pistol and shouting at him.

"Why'd you hit the Pompliano boys?"

"What?" Joe asked.

"You heard me! You popped the Pompliano boys! Why? Open your yap, or I'll fill your belly with metal!"

"We had nothing to do with it!"

"Wrong answer!"

The pistol exploded. Six bullets blasted point-blank into Joe's chest. He jerked violently with each hit, then pitched backward over the chair. He felt no immediate pain. Staring at the ceiling in shock, he heard a strange gurgling. It filled his ears, a smothering noise that filtered the screams to a dull pitch. Gasping, he managed to roll onto his stomach. Pink, frothy blood gushed from his mouth. He realized suddenly that the gurgling was coming from his throat.

Looking up, he watched helplessly as men and women stormed toward him in a deadly rush for escape. They trampled him until bullets ripped mortal holes in their bodies, and they crumpled on top of him in a mounting heap.

Only a few of the Fratelli mobsters were able to knock over tables and fire under cover. A wounded man, trying to crawl to the safety of one of these tables, dragged himself across the floor, pulling the lifeless body of a young woman behind him by the wrist. A killer noticed the movement. He rushed forward. Devoid of mercy, he placed his tommy gun at the base of the man's head and pulled the trigger.

In military fashion, the killers maneuvered through the array of bodies, kicking guns from limp hands, studying the fear-struck faces that stared at nothing, systematically shooting anyone who moved. Not until every member of the Fratelli family, the servants, and the orchestra lay upon each other, twitching in the grotesque agonies of death, did the shooting stop—not until the dead and dying lay together in one vast, crimson pool.

The barrage of gunfire brought Dominic to a halt. Standing in the middle of the hallway on the third floor, he pressed his back against the wall. With one hand, he grabbed Luke by the collar and yanked him back. With the other hand, he pulled out his revolver.

"Get behind me. Keep quiet."

He poised the gun beside his head. They crept down the hall and surveyed the staircase before descending it stealthily to the second-story landing. Once there, Luke crawled behind the landing wall. Dominic stayed just inside the hallway entrance. The shooting had diminished in its ferocity, permitting shrieks and groans to echo high into the rafters, carrying with them the caustic odor of gunpowder. Sporadic gunfire promptly ended the cries.

Luke peeked over the landing.

"Can you see anything?" Dominic whispered.

Luke's spine grew rigid. Repeating the question, Dominic watched Luke sink to the floor, his hand covering his mouth as though he might be sick. His eyes were enormous inside his ashen face.

"Why didn't they listen to me? God, why didn't they listen to You?"

A sickness rose in Dominic's stomach. "What did you see?"

"They're all shot up. Everybody."

"Don't kid me, Luke."

"I ain't. They're all dead. Some guys with big guns shot 'em."

"Even the women?"

"Yeah."

Dazed, Dominic braced himself against the wall. "It doesn't make sense. Who would do this? We're not at war. Who would butcher the entire family?" Looking at Luke, he asked hollowly, "Why didn't you warn me?"

Luke shook his bowed head. "I did. I warned everybody."

"Joey was in there." Dominic suddenly felt like a lost, frightened child. "Maybe Papa. Did I lose my entire family? What about Clara? Luke, *what about Clara*?"

"I don't know."

"I must know. We're not leaving until I know."

"Dom, look." Luke pointed down the staircase, where one of the killers was cautiously climbing. Creeping backward, Dominic shot a meaningful look at Luke. He slunk into the corner until Dominic shook his head, motioning him to come forward—to stand up, in fact.

Luke shook his head emphatically. Dominic nodded sternly. Luke mouthed the word *no*. Dominic mouthed the word *yes*. Clearly not wanting to withdraw from his hiding place, Luke reluctantly obeyed.

When the young killer arrived at the landing, he jumped slightly to see Luke standing there. Turning his body away from Dominic's, he lowered his weapon and his guard.

"Nobody said there'd be kids here," the killer said. "Who are you? Nix. The last thing I want bouncing around in my head is your name. What are you doing here?"

"I was goin' downstairs," Luke said.

The killer took a quick glance over the landing. "You picked a lousy night to go downstairs. Who else is hiding up here?"

"Dominic."

This put the man back on his guard. He raised his weapon. "Dominic Fratelli?"

"Yeah."

"Where?"

"Behind you."

The only sight of Dominic the gunman saw was the flash of his fist before it struck him squarely in the face. Dominic felt the bridge of the killer's nose give way beneath his knuckles. With blood marring his fist, he caught the killer and dragged him into the hallway.

"Grab the gun," he whispered.

Glancing down the staircase, Luke picked up the tommy gun and followed.

Dominic dragged the unconscious man into a dark bedroom, closing the door after Luke had hurried inside. The soft glow from the snowy acreage outside barely illuminated the room. "Drop the hardware, kid. I don't like the way it looks on you."

Luke laid the tommy gun on the floor. "What are you gonna do with him?"

Dominic drew his revolver. Revenge flashed in his eyes.

"No!" Luke cried in a hushed voice. He tried to pull Dominic's arm away. "You can't!"

Dominic shoved him against a piece of shadowed furniture. "Toughen up. I know this man. He's a Pompliano thug. He would've killed us without a second thought. What's more, he would've taken our thumbs as souvenirs."

Grabbing a pillow from the bed, he kneeled over the man, placed the gun against his heart, and smothered it with the pillow.

Luke jumped when the gun fired. Dominic stood, breathing a vengeful sigh. In the glow from the window, he found that Luke's doleful expression elicited more uneasiness than he wanted to feel. He preferred looking at the corpse.

"This is war, Luke. People die in wars. Wise up to it."

THIRTY-THREE

"You didn't touch it! How—how?" Clara cried, looking from Papa Fratelli to the safe and back again.

"I possess many skills." He approached her, his mouth curling into what was supposed to be a smile.

The distant sound of music still reverberated through the library walls; she had falsely trusted in the sound to measure her safety, believing that it would suddenly grow louder if the library door were opened. If it were to stop suddenly, then she would assume that something was amiss at the party. Either way, she had intended to run at its warning; yet there stood Papa Fratelli before her, and the music played on uninterrupted.

"What are you looking for?" he asked. "Money? I could give you more than you would ever want."

"I don't want anything from you! Get away from me!" Desperate for a weapon, she grabbed a slender crystal vase from the desk and smashed its bottom on the hardwood edge. A shower of glass sprayed across the floor. "Stay away from me!" she warned, extending the jagged shard toward him.

Amused, he lifted one thick eyebrow. "First you rob me, then you threaten me in my own house. Is this the behavior of a future daughter-in-law?"

"You tried to kill me!"

His dark, evil eyes fell on the suitcase she had carried down with her, her coat draped carelessly over it.

"My son wishes to marry you, and, as such, I have given him my blessing and you a reprieve. Do not give me reason to revoke it. Go back to your room. Put an end to this silly scheme."

She glanced at the door, knowing it would be useless to make a run for it. He would overcome her instantly. She prayed that Dominic would enter.

Papa Fratelli bowed his head so that his glowering eyes leered at her. "I will not waste my time trifling with a rebellious woman. Do you intend to obey me?"

She could still feel the grip of his hands upon her throat from the previous night, squeezing away her life. She tightened her hold on the shard, and the fragile end of a piece of crystal broke away. Her courage fell with it. She did not notice that the music had stopped playing.

"*Bella mia*, you are beautiful," he said, nodding with resolve. "You would give Dominic beautiful sons, but you are obstinate. You will not be an obedient wife. As I decided before, Dominic must find another bride."

He had barely stepped toward her, his hands stretched for her throat, when she raised her weapon and struck with a forward rush. He had no chance to recoil. With all her might, she threw herself against him, embedding the shard deep into his throat. She felt his flesh tear open against the force of that thrust. Withdrawing it with as much savagery, she stumbled back against the bookshelf, horrified at the sticky warmth that coated her hands and the weapon.

Tugging at the collar of his shirt, Papa Fratelli adjusted it as though it were too tight. He swallowed. A gush of blood poured from the mutilated hole, coursing a swift stream down his white shirt and tuxedo that puddled at his feet. His tongue flashed like a serpent's, licking the blood that ran from his lips. The taste seemed to awaken a dire craving. A devious red gleam flashed in his eyes.

"What are you?" Her fingernails raked across the volumes of books, stripping the leather from the bindings. "You're not human!"

He grinned a hellish, lustful grin. "No, *bella mia*, I am not." His powerful hands seized her body. He disarmed her in an instant, driving her to her knees with brutal force. Grabbing her hair and yanking her head back so her throat was exposed, he raised the shard above his head—and froze.

The blast of machine guns caught his ear.

With gasps of terror heaving in her chest, Clara watched him cock his head toward the screams of the dying. Blood still drained from his throat. Bafflement filled his bloodshot eyes. The hand that held her hair tightened its grip until she cried out. At that, he looked down as if he had forgotten her. He seemed uncertain about what to do.

The library door burst open. A young killer in a waiter's jacket stood in the entryway, his machine gun poised. Black hair fell in thick strands over his forehead.

"Jackpot!"

With a gleaming smile, he took several steps into the room. The door closed behind him. "Ol' Papa himself. You're gonna be a feather in my cap. Drop the frail and lose the shiv."

He aimed the tommy gun directly at Papa Fratelli's chest. To Clara's astonishment, Papa Fratelli dropped the crystal shard and released his hold on her hair. In a near faint, she collapsed onto the floor.

Motioning sideways with his gun, the young man ordered, "Back off. Into the chair, so there's no funny business."

Papa Fratelli submitted without argument. All strength seemed to have abandoned him. As he sank into the nearest chair, his whole frame convulsed in involuntary spasms, sending spurts of blood from his throat. When the seizure passed, he hung his head and closed his eyes. "This body has served its purpose," he wheezed. "Do as you wish."

The gunman looked hurt. "What? Ain't you curious why we done what we did? We wasted everybody! Don't you want to know why?"

Papa Fratelli lifted his head with great effort. When his eyes opened, only a vague lingering of life remained. The expression was feeble, but it was pure evil. "The prophet was right. Hell's greatness has increased this night...."

"We hit you! We hit you hard 'cause you fingered the Pompliano brothers! We weren't even at war, and you whacked 'em for no reason!"

"I never ordered the hit on the Pompliano brothers."

"You're lying!" Infuriated, the gunman perfected his aim, growling, "I oughtta pump metal into you real slow like."

One bloody hand brushed the air as though swatting away a bothersome gnat. "Believe what you wish," Papa Fratelli said slowly. "Do as you wish, for I grow weary of your voice."

"You talk tough for a man about to die. Maybe I'll just let you bleed to death instead."

Papa Fratelli closed his eyes for the last time with the faltering declaration on his bluish lips, "I would prefer you shot me. Let it not be said that a woman killed me."

The killer looked at Clara. "You done that? Swell job, sister. You just made a friend."

The tommy gun exploded in a hail of flame and smoke. Clara threw her hands over her ears as the gun blasted in the killer's hands. Bullets mercilessly thrashed Papa Fratelli's body, mutilating it in a jolting frenzy. He threw back his head. One horrible scream, an exalted shriek of torture and triumph, tore from his throat. The shooting stopped as Papa Fratelli's demoniacal cry faded into the air. The fiendish gleam of evil departed his open eyes, leaving his mouth gaping, his corpse outstretched in livid blood.

"Set your baby browns on him, sister. He caught fifty slugs if he caught one."

Still covering her ears, Clara barely heard the gunman. When he jabbed her shoulder with the gun's hot muzzle, she flinched and threw her head back with a sharp cry. The killer's face—swarthy, boyishly attractive, almost innocent-looking—now frowned at her.

"Stand up."

Her arm trembled in his hand as he brought her to her feet. She turned to see the mangled body of her oppressor slumped in the bullet-razed chair, his torso a butchered mass of bleeding pulp. A groan sounded in her throat. She snapped her head away from the ghastly sight.

"Look at me," the gunman said. "Why'd you plant the shiv in his apple?"

"He...he was going to kill me. I was trying to get away. Why did you...?" Numbness was creeping upon her. A lack of oxygen, the smell of blood, the gruesome corpse—it was becoming too much. She felt like she was going to faint.

"Revenge. Papa put the blast on the Pompliano family—*my* family. He killed the Don's three sons—his *only* sons. They weren't doing nothing. They was just having dinner and got plugged. Papa had 'em hit, so we hit back. We hit hard."

"No...more...Fratellis? Dom—Dominic?"

"Dead. Joe, too. Everybody. We mowed 'em down. The Fratelli family don't exist no more."

She did not realize she was swaying until his hand steadied her. "A little boy. Did you see...a little boy?"

"He's sleeping with the angels, sister. Everybody in this joint's been blown away. There's over a hundred stiffs in the banquet room alone. It'll take the coppers days to sift through them." He was quiet for a moment. "Say, you're a swell dish. You a torch singer? Seems I've seen you before. What's your name?"

"Clara Crawford."

His face brightened. "That's it! You was in the movies! The

silent ones. I always thought you was a tomato. How'd you get in this racket?"

A simple shrug was all she could manage.

"Look, doll, I gotta make this quick before the heat's on. There's no way I can get you out alive. Not supposed to be any witnesses. Get me?"

She nodded, biting her bottom lip to fight the oncoming tears.

"I ain't crazy about whacking a hot toddy like you, seeing as you tried to off Papa yourself, so here's the gist. Play a corpse or be one. After we blow, wait five minutes, then hightail it. You never saw us. You was never here. If somebody sings and I find you was the canary, you'll wish you'd died tonight, 'cause I'll track you down. It'll take a week for you to die. Get me?"

Scarcely believing he would spare her life, she searched his face to determine if he was merely trifling with her. His expression, though apprehensive, was serious. "I won't betray you," she said. "I promise."

"On your face, then. We gotta scram before the cops get wise. If my pals see you move a muscle, you won't be playacting."

As she started to bend down, he stopped her.

"Not here. Over by Papa. It's gotta look like I walked in on you. Move it."

Swallowing her repulsion, she forced herself to lie at Papa Fratelli's feet.

"Get on your side," the gunman said. "Turn your face from the door. Now, bring your knees up like I shot you in the stomach. Yeah, that's it. No matter what happens, don't move."

Closing her eyes and half believing he would change his mind and shoot her before he left, she heard him walk toward the door with the final words, "Play it straight by me, Clara Crawford. Cross me and you're dead."

THIRTY-FOUR

The oppressive darkness of the bedroom weighed heavily upon Dominic. Waiting helplessly while sporadic gunfire ended the lives of his friends worked his nerves like the pricking of needles. He could do nothing for them while protecting Luke, whom he had tucked securely under the bed. It took every bit of his endurance to linger in the gloom with the tommy gun aimed at the door instead of creeping through his home, systematically killing every murderous Pompliano he found there.

"Luke," he whispered as a thought occurred to him, "that angel of yours—is he around?"

"I ain't seen him," Luke said, his disembodied voice ringing clearly.

"Swell. I don't know if that means we're in trouble or we're *not* in trouble."

"I can—"

"Shhh! Listen. I heard a car door slam."

Emerging from the shadows, Dominic peeked out the window to see several Pompliano gangsters squeeze into five cars. They made little noise—no shouting, no exclamations of victory. They were as quiet and efficient as lions after disemboweling their kill, leaving quickly without looking for the man Dominic had murdered, whose body lay cooling inside the room. Without turning on the headlights, they drove from the estate in silence.

As he turned from the window, a movement caught his eye. A woman was running—or stumbling, rather—through the snow in high heels, balancing herself with a weighty suitcase. Dominic might have laughed at her clumsy efforts if she had not been running a desperate race for survival, shooting terrified glances in every direction.

"Clara." He smiled with relief. "She must think we're dead." He looked at Luke, who peeked out from under the bed. "Get out. We have to go."

It took less than a minute for them to run through the hallway, down the stairs, and out into the night. Motioning Luke to get into the Deusenberg, Dominic hurried to the corner of the mansion, stretching his neck out in the hope of seeing Clara.

"I see her!" he called over his shoulder. "She's outside the gate." He turned, took two steps, and stopped; his breath caught in his throat.

"What's the matter, Dom? In a sweat to go someplace?"

Blocking the car with his solid, obese frame stood Benny, his legs wide apart, a grin of triumph on his blanched face. In one hand, he held a gun, its barrel pressed against Luke's temple beside his astonished eyes. In the other, he held Luke firmly, his chubby hand tightly covering the boy's mouth.

"Didn't think you'd see me again, did you?"

Concealing his surprise with a sullen cock of his eyebrow, Dominic asked, "Why aren't you buried in an unmarked grave?"

"Because if you're an enemy of the Fratellis, you're a friend of the Pomplianos. They saw your boys dump me in the back of a car. Next thing I know, they pumped 'em and pulled me out. They even gave me this." Benny referenced the gun and shook his injured head with care. "It was wrong, you buffaloing me. I was just obeying Papa."

"Papa's dead."

"I know. Joe, too. How's it feel to be the new don?"

Startled by the obvious, Dominic paused, again trying to mask the shock of Benny's words. "Feels like a tailored suit. So, let's do some business. Unleash the kid."

"Can it. I never backed out on no hit, and I've been itching to waste this pup."

"Kill him and you'll have to kill me. You're a superstitious man. Don't you know it's bad luck to kill your don?"

"I'll take my chances. Anyway, nobody's left to settle the score."

"Then I'll settle it myself." Dominic raised the tommy gun.

"Funny guy. Shoot that thing and you'll blow him away, too."

"You're right." Tossing the tommy gun into the snow with his left hand, Dominic pulled his revolver from its holster with his right. "I'm more accurate with this."

Benny prodded Luke's head with the gun, forcing a wince from his muffled mouth. "Shed the heater, or I'll splatter his brains all over your fancy car."

Dominic did not move.

"You ain't fooling nobody, Dom. He's been your pet since day one. You ain't gonna watch me drill him. But there's something in what you said. I can't pop you here. Nobody'd trust me if they saw me whack my own don—even the Pomplianos. That *would* be bad luck."

"Spill it, already."

"I'll give you what you planned for me. Drop the rod and get behind the wheel. We're going for a ride."

Knowing Benny needed only a vague excuse to shoot Luke, Dominic reluctantly tossed the gun into the snow.

"Move, punk," Benny snarled, yanking Luke around and shoving him into the door.

Luke glared at him, wiping the filthy taste of Benny's

palm from his mouth with the back of his hand. With Benny's suspicious gaze fixed on Dominic, both entered the front seats from opposite sides of the car. Benny sat with his back against the door and his gun pointed at Dominic.

"Where's the cemetery?" Dominic asked.

"The South Platte."

"Water's low. We'll be bobbing by morning."

"I'll be booking it east by morning. Shove in the clutch."

Dominic started the engine, turned on the headlights, and shifted the car into first gear. As he drove from the estate, he saw here and there the grisly sight of Fratelli guards lying prone on the ground, the snow beneath them melting from the warmth of their blood.

Stopping at the gate, he glanced up and down the street, less to check traffic than to search for Clara. Nothing. She was gone. Part of him felt relieved. If Benny had seen her, it might be three graves, not two. Even so, Dominic had not made any plans to reunite in case of separation. It had never occurred to him. *How stupid.* He cursed himself.

He drove through the city toward the river, encountering sparse traffic on the cobblestone streets. He knew well the location that Benny intended. Dim streetlights could not entirely disclose the outlines of factories, unoccupied buildings, and blackened alleys. The white sky revealed nothing but the dancing of snowflakes.

Dominic breathed a toilsome sigh as they drove into the industrial end of lower downtown. He glanced over his shoulder into the engulfing darkness swallowing the street. In the midst of this blackness sat Luke in the backseat, motionless, his eyes going from the back of Dominic's head to Benny's profile to the road.

"Hope I ain't keeping you from nothing," Benny said. "Maybe you had a date with that wide-eyed dame." With his free hand, he reached into his crumpled suit pocket to extract a match and the last bent cigarette from a crushed pack. "Too bad you won't see her no more, but that's the breaks."

Pinching the cigarette between his lips, he lit it and took a long drag with cool regard. With eyes half closed, he tapped the cigarette ashes on the floor as noxious smoke curled upward.

"Maybe I'll pay her a visit, you know, offer my condolences. Can't you just see that bit of fluff crying on my shoulder?"

Dominic threw him a murderous glare. Benny erupted in laughter. Glancing into the backseat, he saw Luke's head bowed, his eyes closed, and his hands folded in silent prayer.

"Hey! None of that, you little—!" The last word was cut off when he stuck the cigarette in his mouth to free his hand, which he used to grasp Luke's shirt and gave him a brutal shake.

Dominic seized the opportunity to grab Benny's gun hand. Bracing himself, he slammed it into the dash as his feet pounced on the clutch and the brake. The car jerked to a violent stop. Luke flew into the back of Dominic's seat. Benny flew into the dash. Glass sprayed across the hood as his head burst through the windshield.

Before Benny could react, Dominic smashed his hand into the dash again. Shouting at the strike upon his knuckles, Benny almost lost the weapon. They grappled, Benny trying to aim the gun at Dominic and Dominic fighting to stop him. In the struggle, the weapon was lifted above their heads toward the backseat. Avoiding its aim, Luke slid to the floor. The gun exploded, blowing a hole in the backseat. Dominic lost his grip from the force of the shot. The sound deafened him; he sat momentarily stunned.

"You stinking rat! I'm bleeding again!" Blood poured from the deep gashes on Benny's head. Slivers of glass trickled down his face and onto his clothing. Spitting out the bent cigarette, he twisted his face in rage. "Out of the car!"

Fumbling with the passenger's door, he tumbled outside, never allowing Dominic to leave his sight. He lost interest in Luke.

Dominic promptly surveyed the area. The mouth of an unlit alley yawned a short distance away. Two tall brick buildings loomed on either side, increasing its obscurity. Now, to get Luke and himself into its shadows....

He looked at Luke. The midnight breeze mussed his hair. Dressed only in dark trousers with suspenders and a white cotton shirt, he shivered against the air's frigid bite, holding his arms closely to his chest. His lips had begun to turn blue.

"Into the street," Benny ordered with a jerk of his gun.

Complying, Dominic positioned himself between Benny and Luke, who walked ahead.

"I'm giving the kid my jacket, all right?" Dominic said.

"Why bother? The dead don't care if they're cold."

Nevertheless, Dominic removed the tuxedo tailcoat and handed it to Luke, who was swallowed in its immensity, dragging the coattails through the snow.

Keeping his front averted, Dominic felt for Benny's semi-automatic, which he had taken at the party, in the waist of his pants, bending both arms so its retrieval would not be obvious.

"Stop and turn around. I want to see your mugs when you die."

They had almost reached the alley. Both stopped, but only Luke turned around. He noticed the gun in Dominic's hand almost immediately. A gleam of hope flashed in his anxious eyes.

"I got no problem shooting you in the back," Benny said.

"I know," Dominic said over his shoulder. "It's your favorite target."

"Funny guy. The kid's got more guts than you. He looks

death in the face. Now, turn around. If you don't, I swear I'll make him suffer."

"How many kids have you made suffer, Benny? He can't be the first."

"I got no conscience to lean on, so face me or he gets a bellyful!"

"Didn't you plug an old lady once for a five-dollar bill?"

"Shut up, you stupid goon! Turn around!"

"Benny."

"What?" he screamed.

"Your pants are unzipped."

Benny looked down. The words had hardly passed Dominic's lips before he spun around. Dropping to his knee, his foot slipped in the snow as he fired three shots. With a shout, Benny reeled backward from three direct hits in his right shoulder. His feet soared into the air, landing him flat on his back.

Dominic uttered a curse; he had missed Benny's head. He came to his feet, signaling Luke to run into the alley, when Benny reared back up, yelled something unintelligible, and fired a scarcely aimed shot at Dominic.

An unseen force drove a fierce blow deep into Dominic's stomach. A staggering jolt of pain assaulted his spine. He doubled over, his legs folding beneath him. He fell hard on the cobblestone street.

"Dom!" Sliding to a halt, Luke turned and ran back. "Dom!"

Lifting his head, Dominic saw scarlet beads spattered across the snow. The sight of his own blood bewildered him. Clutching fistfuls of snow, he tried to pull himself up, to stand.

"Dom!" Luke cried. "Where'd he get you?"

"In...the stomach. I can't...move my legs."

"Stand up and take it!" Benny shouted, struggling to get up.

Seeing this, Luke grabbed Dominic by the arms and scampered backward toward the alley, pulling Dominic with all his might.

"No, Luke! Let me go! Get out...of here!"

Crouching in the snow, his primary arm useless, Benny fired wasted bullets with his unsteady left hand until Dominic and Luke vanished into the alley and he was out of ammunition.

"Stop! Stop! I...can't...take it!"

Dominic clenched his teeth to keep from screaming. The dragging of his body kindled a torturous, burning pain from his abdomen to his back. Though his legs were numb, his spine felt like it had been snapped in two.

"Hang on, Dom," Luke encouraged breathlessly, looking over his shoulder. "I wanna get you in this doorway so you'll be hid."

Inside the shelter of the alley, he carefully propped Dominic in a recessed doorway. Then he twisted the doorknob and shook the locked door, to no avail. Running across the alley to a similar door, he performed the same desperate act. Frantically, he searched up and down the alley for any glimmer of hope, finding none. In uncertainty, he collapsed on his knees beside Dominic.

"What do we do now, Dom?"

Lying crumpled in the corner of the doorway and struggling with his paralyzed lower half, Dominic hunted frantically for his gun, patting down his pockets, feeling the wet cobblestones for the security of the weapon.

"Where's my gun? What did you do...with my gun?"

"You must've dropped it in the street."

Looking at Luke for an intense moment, Dominic felt the blood drain from his face. Without a gun to defend them or legs to run with, he was useless, defunct, a cowering mass of bleeding flesh. He was dead.

Luke's trusting, earnest gaze waited with fear yet confidence, anticipating Dominic's instruction. Dominic shoved him with such force that Luke reeled onto his back.

"Scram, kid. Benny's...gunning for you."

Stunned by this sudden repulsion, Luke crawled back but remained out of reach. The injured confusion in his eyes made Dominic cringe.

"No, Dom. I ain't gonna."

"Don't you get it? I can't...protect you!"

"No!" Luke yelled back, angered with rapid comprehension. "You didn't leave me when I was hurt or sick! I ain't leavin' you!"

"Little...fool! He'll kill you!"

"I ain't leavin', so quit askin'!"

"I'm not asking...I'm telling!"

"Then quit tellin'!"

Without warning, a spray of blood shot from Dominic's mouth. His body convulsed in a fit of labored coughs. Wracked with pain, he fell to the side against the icy cobblestones and felt the flow of blood gush from his mouth.

"Dom!" Luke came forward, his ready hands touching Dominic's shoulders.

"I'm okay," Dominic managed to sputter, but he knew he wasn't. He was choking on his own blood. He lay there momentarily after the coughing had passed, watching the red stream course between the stones and encircle Luke's shoes. He felt his breathing become rapid, deep.

"Are you dyin'?" Luke asked.

With Luke's help, Dominic forced himself into a sitting position and avoided looking at Luke's eyes. With every ounce of fortitude, he tried to hide the excruciating pain.

"Are you dyin'?"

Unable to avoid Luke's gaze for long, Dominic stared hard at him, fighting with himself to remain strong, but the answer was too apparent. All hope withered in Luke's eyes. Then, falling victim to his emotions, he pulled Luke close to his chest. Luke wrapped his arms tightly around his neck and started to cry. In the softest of whispers, Dominic said, "Pray for me, Luke....Please."

Between choking sobs, Luke prayed with the words and faith of a child, imploring heaven for deliverance and Dominic's healing; but as Dominic became faint for lack of blood, as his arms weakened in the hug, as his breathing grew shallow, Luke prayed for the deliverance of his soul. When he finished, Dominic could barely keep his eyes open.

"Thanks. It doesn't hurt...so much...now."

Benny stumbled back to Dominic's car, barking a volley of curse words. His shoulder throbbed with the gunshot wounds. Throwing the car door open, he destroyed the interior in a reckless search for bullets or another gun. He found nothing.

He turned and stumbled toward the alley. It was then that he saw his own semiautomatic lying in the middle of the street.

THIRTY-FIVE

Dominic took Luke's hands in his as he struggled to keep his eyes from closing.

"Benny's coming....You can't help me....Go....I don't want you to die."

The pallor of death consumed his youthful hue, leaving his swarthy complexion an ashen shadow. It took no effort to release Luke's hands—a sign that freed him from all obligations—since little strength remained in his grip. Refuting this, Luke held firm.

"No, Dom. I—"

The protest on Luke's lips surrendered to silence when an unexpected presence filled him with dread. He smelled sulfur. His head shot up. Expecting Benny, he saw instead a remarkably tall figure shrouded in a blackened cloak at the far end of the alley. No illumination touched its impenetrable gloom, which revealed only the pretense of a deep purple luster. The figure paused, discerned them crouching in the shadows, and glided slowly toward them.

"Dom, are you ready to die?" Luke asked quickly.

Unable to swallow his fears, Dominic turned his head away. He spoke so softly that the word was barely audible. "No."

"You wanna accept Jesus as your Lord and Savior?"

"It's too late."

"No, it ain't."

"You don't understand." Unable to look Luke in the face, Dominic grew agitated. "I've hurt people. I've...killed people. Murderers don't make it to heaven."

"It ain't too late."

He clutched Luke's hands in restless worry. "I've killed...a lot of people."

"It ain't too late."

"Blast it! Don't you hear?" He squeezed Luke's hands until he winced. "I murdered...two men tonight! I've murdered more than thirty people...in the past seven years! It's too late!"

Luke glanced at the approaching figure. Its emanating evil sent numbness through his limbs, overwhelming his spirit with grief. He distinguished its ghastly countenance through the amethystine brilliance of its eyes. An immense chain writhed in its hands like a disturbed serpent twisting with perversity. Luke understood; death had come for Dominic.

"The Bible says that if you confess with your mouth that Jesus is Lord, and believe in your heart that God raised Him from the dead, then you'll be saved. That means God forgives you because you believe in His Son. There ain't much time. You wanna accept Jesus or not?"

In all his shame and frustration, Dominic cried out, "Yes!"—the figure faltered—"but what makes you think... He'll accept me? I'm not good...not like you."

"Being good's got nothin' to do with it. It's about faith, and God won't turn nobody away who believes. Wanna pray with me?"

"You'd better be right...about this." With a quivering breath, Dominic nodded.

Luke closed his eyes. "Dear Jesus, I believe You are the Son of God...."

"Dear Jesus," Dominic repeated, "I believe You are...the Son of God...."

A prolonged growl rumbled through the alley. Luke

opened his eyes to look at the demon, which drifted forward with sudden haste.

"I believe You died on the cross for my sins and rose from the dead...."

The wind arose abruptly. As Dominic repeated the sentence, snow billowed into their faces like a whirlwind, stinging their flesh and stealing their breath.

Luke held Dominic's hands firmly. He yelled above the chilling tumult, "Please forgive me of my sins—"

The demon surged forward at an alarming pace, raising the serpentine chain above its head. The wind conveyed its persistent growl in echoing tones of discontent.

"—and accept me into Your kingdom!"

When Dominic's mouth opened to speak, the demon threw the chain. It spiraled through the air, carried on an incorporeal maelstrom, its coils prepared to fetter him in eternal chains.

"Please forgive me...of my sins"—a brilliant stroke of lightning illuminated the alley—"and accept me...into Your kingdom."

At the utterance of these words, Luke saw the flash of a sword above his head, a dazzling glimpse of his angel hovering protectively above them, and the chain twisted around the sword as a pierced serpent. With the sweep of his wrist, the angel flung the chain back at the demon. It soared through the air, striking the demon in the face with full force, instantly dissipating both into nothingness.

The angel vanished. The alley grew dark. Snowflakes swirled around them in an eddy, tousling their hair.

"Thank you, God," Luke whispered breathlessly. "Amen."

Dominic's chest heaved with a strained motion after he spoke the last words. He closed his eyes and leaned his head against the wall with the calm patience of one accepting death. "Is that...all there is to it?"

"Did you mean what you said?" Luke asked.

"Yes."

"Then that's it."

"You sure He won't give me...the brush-off?"

"He ain't like that."

Luke's shoulders sank in bittersweet sadness. Dominic's bloody hands slipped away to rest at his side.

"It's hard to believe...He would forgive me so easily... Someone like you, yes...not me. Why would He?"

"How much do you love Miss Clara?" Luke asked.

"I'd take a bullet for her."

"That's how much Jesus loves us. He chose to die so that we could live in heaven."

"You kidding me?" Dominic's eyes opened, brimming with tears.

"I ain't kiddin'."

"He sounds like...a stand-up guy." Blinking several times to clear his vision, Dominic looked away. "What do I say... when I see Him?"

"Say, 'Thank You.'"

He tried to smile. "Will you be there...someday?"

Luke glanced at the alleyway where he expected Benny to appear. "I might be right behind you."

"Will Clara be there...someday?"

"Yeah. Someday."

"You know, I only kissed her once...only once—"

His eyes squeezed shut. Faint groans sounded from his throat as he tried to stifle the cries of pain by gritting his teeth.

"Dom?" Luke's voice broke. He placed one hand on Dominic's shoulder.

With great effort, Dominic opened his eyes, licking his lips with a blood-covered tongue. "Luke?"

"Yeah?" He pressed close.

"I'm sorry...I'm so sorry...."

"Don't be." Luke wiped his tears away with the back of his hand. "It ain't your fault."

With his succumbing breaths, Dominic tried to form his lips into words he could not speak. As his eyelids sank over his dark eyes, the gleam of his spirit departed. His head fell to the side. A faint breath escaped his parted lips, and he was silent.

"Dom?"

Luke's hand fell from Dominic's shoulder, but his eyes could not leave the pallid face. Death had not deformed his features. Despite the blood on his lips, the tranquil peace that rested on his brow made it seem as though the Lord Himself had gently closed his eyes.

"Don't worry, Dom." Luke removed the tuxedo tailcoat and draped it across Dominic's chest. "I won't leave you out here by yourself."

"Like I said, the dead don't care if they're cold."

The rash voice behind Luke acted like a saw upon his nerves. He jumped to his feet with a gasp, only to be seized by Benny's hand.

"Where do you think you're going, punk? Huh? I know where—facedown in the gutter after I pump you full of lead. I'm gonna get a real bang out of this. Ha! Get it? I'm gonna get a *bang* out of this."

He shoved Luke down on top of Dominic's body and pressed the muzzle of his gun against Luke's forehead. Somewhere in the distance, a church bell struck midnight.

"You want one in your ticker or right through your skull?"

Luke frowned. "You choose. I ain't afraid to die."

"Don't get cute. I'm in a giving mood. I'll give you a bullet, all right. If you're nice, I'll give you two."

"Give me ten if you want! I'll spit 'em back at you!"

"Brave words, Prophet. Will you challenge me, as well?"

A scream rose from Luke's throat. Dominic's body spoke

and moved beneath him; its arms wrapped around him. Screaming one terrified shriek after another through the rising sulfuric stench, Luke fought until he escaped. Staggering to his feet, he stumbled backward to watch Dominic's dead body bring itself to a standing position. The eyes were open, but they were not Dominic's. They were hot coals without pupils or irises.

"No, Dom," Luke moaned. "Not you. Please. Not you."

A smile of pure evil spread across Dominic's face. Stunned, Benny took two uneasy steps backward.

"The curse continues, Prophet. You robbed me of his soul, but I still have his body."

The demon reached for him. Luke dodged the grasp. Like a madman, he tore down the alley with slipping, uncertain feet. Before he had gone far, he heard Benny exclaim, "Hey, you're supposed to be dead."

A diabolical laugh followed, pursuing Luke with the fear that hell had opened behind him and set every devil on the loose. He ran the length of the alley and cast one last terrified glance over his shoulder as he turned the corner—just as something dark reached out for him. An arm wrapped tightly around his waist, squeezing him, lifting him from the ground. Luke screamed a shrill cry that echoed between the brick buildings.

"Lights out."

The man's voice sounded deep, cold. The words were hissed in his ear as a gloved hand pressed a handkerchief against his face to smother his screams. He tried to shake it off, crying out from the biting fumes that stung his nose and burned their way into his lungs. He threw his head back, struggling, kicking, until the warmth that clouded his head surrendered his senses to the dark.

Thirty-six

The startling ring of the telephone jarred Joshua from his sleep. He lay there unmoving, his nose bent against the pillow. The bedroom felt cold outside the blankets, and he did not want to stir, but he could take the unremitting shrill for only so long. Fumbling for the telephone on the nightstand, he brought it to his ear and mumbled an impolite, "Yes? What is it?"

"Josh?"

A woman's voice—soft, attractive, timorous. Forcing his eyes open, he blinked dismally at the alarm clock to determine the time. Seven o'clock.

"I'm sorry, Josh. Did I wake you?"

"Who is this?"

A short pause, then, "Please don't hang up. It's Clara Crawford."

It took a split second for the name to register in his mind and an instant for a volcanic fury to overcome him. His voice forsook him, and there was silence on the line.

"Are you still there?"

He bolted straight up. "What do *you* want?"

"I—I hoped I could talk to you—"

"You hoped *wrong*!"

He slammed the receiver down so hard in the cradle that the telephone seemed to jingle in pain. New Year's Eve rushed back into his thoughts, bringing with it every emotion—horror, betrayal, torment—that had besieged him and driven him to the edge of a nervous breakdown.

Fuming, he fought a short battle with the blankets to get out of bed. Storming back and forth in his pajamas, he kicked his shoes across the room, yelped against the pain, snatched the pillows from the bed, and kicked them instead.

The veins in his neck and face bulged with the fierce beating of his heart. After long minutes of pacing, sitting, standing, and pacing again, he composed himself sufficiently to wonder why she had called him. He dismissed the question with a curse.

"That tramp set me up. Because of *her*, I almost killed that boy. Because of *her*, I could've gone to prison. Now, I'm forced to let a murderer go free because *she* set me up. Now, *she* has the audacity to call me at home."

With slight variations, Joshua repeated these phrases while he bathed and dressed. Taunting his nervous stomach by nursing this resentment, he continued to quarrel with himself as he left his house and bent to retrieve the morning newspaper, which was lying half-hidden beneath a bush.

Before he could straighten, his attention was seized by the arrival of shapely feminine legs warily approaching him. He stood slowly, his gaze following the attractive legs upward to the silk dress, the fashionable coat, the gloved hands holding a large, brown envelope, the pretty face, the smart hat—the pretty face. Fascination no longer held his attention. He reeled back with astonishment.

"What are *you* doing here?"

He spit the words with such viciousness that Clara cringed. Instantaneous tears welled in her eyes. Struggling to hold them back, she dropped her gaze to the ground and lifted the envelope.

"I have something—"

"Have you no scruples, woman?" Taking one lurching step

back, he pointed his trembling forefinger directly in her face. "Stay away from me! You've brought me nothing but misery! Leave me alone!"

Tears overflowed her brown eyes as they flashed up at him. Ignoring her quivering lower lip, he stormed past her toward the garage, almost knocking her over. He lifted the garage door with a violent surge of energy, disappeared within, and started the car. Gunning the accelerator, he squealed the tires as he backed his brand-new dark blue Packard out into the street, glared at her, and drove away.

Gangland Slaughter of Fratelli Family

Last night, police discovered the gruesome annihilation of one of the most infamous crime families in Colorado: the Fratelli family. The largest Mafia hit in American history occurred last night when a rival criminal gang invaded the twenty-fifth birthday extravaganza for Dominic Fratelli, youngest son of notorious kingpin Antonio "Papa" Fratelli, at the Fratelli Estate and opened fire on unsuspecting victims with machine guns. Twelve people are known to have survived the massacre. Over one hundred others, men and women, were brutally murdered. Papa Fratelli and his two sons are believed to be among the dead. It is not known if Louie Fratelli, grandson of the crime lord and currently out of prison on bail for murder charges in the death of Rev. Fred MacDonald, was present.

Survivors are refusing to provide descriptions or identities of the gunmen, holding fast to the criminal's rule not to divulge information to the police.

> However, police suspect a long-standing conflict between the Fratelli family and the Pompliano gang, led by Giovanni Pompliano, may have led to the bloodshed. They are questioning suspects and racketeers gathered throughout the night to solve this heinous crime, but will not say whether they have uncovered any pertinent information. They suspect it will take several days to complete the gruesome task of identifying the bodies.

The article continued, but Joshua stopped reading. He laid the paper on his office desk, not knowing whether to be horrified or to rejoice. With the death of Papa Fratelli, the weight hanging from his neck since New Year's Eve seemed to dissolve like moist cotton candy. He felt ready to burst. He thought of calling Andy Ballantine, the one person who had shared his torment, but their last meeting had destroyed their personal and professional relationships. With a sharp intake of air, a thought occurred to him.

Oh, no! Clara!

Twice she had tried to contact him. Twice he had rejected her. He slapped himself on the forehead for his stupidity; she was trying to tell him something, trying to hand him something. Throwing his paperwork into his briefcase, he rushed out of the office. Although he knew she would not be standing where he had left her, he clung to the shred of hope that she might have left an address or telephone number where he could contact her.

When he reached home, Joshua parked the car and ran to the front porch. He did not see a note but, when he opened the screen door, his hopes rose. Concealed against the front door lay the large, brown envelope that she had tried to give him. He snatched it up. In the privacy of his living room, he spilled the contents onto the coffee table: a letter, a Bible, and—his breath caught in his throat—the negatives and photographs of the boy, the evidence Carpinelli had held over his head like the blade of a guillotine. He picked up the letter. Her delicate handwriting wavered in his trembling hands.

Dear Josh,

I wanted to explain the contents of this envelope, but I understand why you don't want to see me. By now, you must know of the murders at the Fratelli Estate. I was there when it happened. Everyone is dead. Papa, Dominic, and the little boy, Luke, are all dead.

I found the negatives and pictures Mr. Carpinelli had Dominic take the night of the accident. I believe they are the originals. I don't know if he made any copies, but, since Papa and Luke are dead, I don't know that it matters anymore.

I also wanted to give you this Bible. I hate to give it up, because it is the only thing I have to remember Luke by, but I think it might be more important to you. One of Papa's men, Benny Rosario, gave it to him. Inside the cover is a name you will recognize. I discovered it this morning.

I wish I could speak with you, but I won't bother you anymore. If you want to see me, I'll be at the Blake Street Café at 6:00 tonight. I'll wait for half an hour. If you decide not to come, I'll understand.

Josh, if I never see you again, I cannot express how sorry I am. I know I can never make up for what I've done to you. Please forgive me.

Clara

Joshua's eyes fell on the Bible. Opening the cover, he read:

This Holy Bible Presented to the Reverend Fred MacDonald, Ordained on this Ninth Day of May in the Year of Our Lord 1929, in the Service of Our Lord and Savior Jesus Christ

"Careful," Jack Novak said, gently laying Luke's unconscious form upon the unmade Murphy bed. "You're handling dynamite."

Novak looked warily around the tiny studio apartment; nothing appeared out of place, including the dust. He hurried to the only window in the apartment, a bay window that faced the bright blue roof of the neighboring hash house. With a brief glance through its streaked glass, he closed the blinds tightly, feeling confident that he had not been followed.

Returning to the bed, he regarded Luke, who lay limp on the mattress, his head turned to the side and his bluish lips slightly parted. Unbuttoning his bloodstained shirt, Novak looked for corresponding wounds across his stomach, chest, and arms, but found none. Satisfied that Luke was unhurt, he covered him to his chin with a blanket.

Novak pushed his hat to the back of his head and retrieved a half-empty bottle of scotch from behind the icebox. He poured the liquor into a sticky glass that sat alone in the kitchen sink. Grabbing the candlestick telephone off the end table below the window, he told the operator, "Give me Sunset 9525."

It rang. The rattling peal made him nervous. He started to pace. It seemed like a long time before a woman finally answered.

"Carpinelli residence. Maid speaking."

"Let me talk to your boss."

"Mr. Carpinelli isn't available."

"Look, sister, tell him if he doesn't get on this phone in a flash, this gumshoe will take a certain orphan and turn him into front-page news. Savvy?"

She hesitated, then said, "Just a minute."

He used the time to swallow a third of the Scotch in the glass. When the telephone was picked up again, he heard Carpinelli's noticeably shaken voice on the other end.

"Yes?"

"Morning, Angelo. I thought you'd be among the dead at the Fratelli Estate. How is it you're still alive?"

"Who is this?"

He smiled. "That hurts. It's Jack Novak. I heard the Fratellis had a bang-up party last night. Weren't you invited?"

Silence.

"I read that almost everyone died, which means Papa and his sons. So, you're out of a job. Right?"

Silence.

Novak continued, "Well, maybe it doesn't interest you, then, but a mouse squeaked out of the party last night when no one was looking."

"What?"

"A mouse named Erik Warner, going by the name 'Luke.' Does he still interest you?"

Hope lit Carpinelli's voice. "He's alive? Do you have him?"

"Yes, he's alive, and yes, I have him. I have a bare spot on my mantel that fits him nicely."

"Bring him to me at once."

"What's he worth?"

"What?"

"What's his value?" Novak asked. "How much mazuma will you fork over for him?"

"Don't play games with me. I can have you cemented in the foundation of a building by nightfall, Jack. Bring that boy to me now!"

"Who's going to plant me in concrete? You? I'd like to see you try. Your gang is dead, so get this: I'm selling him to the highest bidder. I have one or two others who might be interested in a bargain. Care to start the bidding?"

Silence.

"I'll make it simple for you, Angelo. Offer me ten Gs."

Silence.

"Okay, fifteen Gs. The longer you wait, the higher the price."

"I'll give you twelve thousand."

"I said fifteen. Question. You want the kid dead or alive?"

"Alive, you fool!"

"Just checking. Thought you might want him planted beside his dearly departed father and brothers. Papa paid me five grand to pop them. I have enough leverage now to demand my own price." Novak looked at Luke with a wry smirk. "How about I work him over? He bruises beautifully."

"Are you insane? No!"

"You sure? A bit of color will suit him. He's kind of pasty."

Carpinelli shouted something. Novak cut him off.

"Can it. I'm joking. I need to touch base with the other buyers to see if they'll bump your offer. You'll hear from me. So long, Angelo."

A volley of threats burst from the telephone until Novak disconnected the call. Throwing his head back to gulp the last of the scotch, he turned toward the Murphy bed. He approached it and leaned over to stare thoughtfully into Luke's senseless face. With a hand on his chest, he checked Luke's shallow breathing.

"You should be out for a while—long enough for me to visit an old friend."

The morning newspaper lay spread upon Carpinelli's kitchen table. The bold headline was saturated with tomato juice, which he had accidentally knocked across it when he read about the Fratelli massacre. The glass lay broken on the floor.

With his head bowed, his hands folded together tightly, and his knuckles pressed to his mouth below his swollen, broken nose—almost in a position of prayer—he propelled himself back and forth through the room, stopping occasionally to set his crazed eyes on the newspaper with an intensity close to hysteria.

Improbable thoughts of escape entered his mind. Though no longer blessed with the gift of prophecy, he nonetheless foresaw his doom; for his failure to kill Luke, he would forfeit his own life. Luke's surviving the massacre was another misfortune, yet, if he retrieved the boy, he might mollify the demon with a sacrifice and deliver his own neck from an early hell.

"If eternity is what you fear, give me one reason why I should not send you there."

The sound of the voice behind him pitched through his body like an electric shock. A scream burst from his mouth as his legs wilted beneath him. He sank to the floor in a heap. Looking up, he saw Dominic dressed in the blood-soaked tuxedo, the young man's tall form looming above him. Dominic's once genial face now revealed only the demonic evil residing within. His once brown eyes were like coals aflame.

"Dominic!" Carpinelli shouted in terror.

"You know my name, you traitorous old fool. Use it."

"Aeneas!"

The demon stepped closer, forcing Carpinelli to cower against the floor like a beaten dog. He trembled violently. His fingers clutched at the strings of the carpet. Saliva dribbled from his lips.

"Everything is lost," the demon bellowed. "Everything I built is gone. Everything except you, you unfaithful cur. Why should I not rid myself of your stench as well?"

"Aeneas!" Carpinelli cried, lifting his hands beseechingly. "Have mercy!"

"You implore *me* for mercy? I want nothing more than to separate your soul from your flesh and fling it into the depths of the earth. Why do I even hesitate?"

"The prophet! I can get him for you! I swear!"

An unbelieving growl from the demon's throat stiffened every one of Carpinelli's hairs. With the promise of an upraised hand, he swore, "I know where he is! I'll sacrifice him to you! I swear!"

The demon glowered, bringing its eyebrows low over the burning embers of its eyes.

"*Whosoever shall offend one of these little ones that believe in me, it is better for him that a millstone were hanged about his neck, and he were cast into the sea*," the demon said. "You dare to taunt God with this abomination?"

A cold shiver pierced Carpinelli's soul. He went pale. These words, a terrifying remembrance of Holy Scripture, overwhelmed him with horror.

"To destroy this child-prophet—even to harm him—will intensify your eternal torment." The demon's sneer evolved into a smile of fiendish revelry. "See that you do."

THIRTY-SEVEN

"Buck up, Andy. You look like you lost your last friend." Without attempting to hide his grin, Novak picked up the scattered pages of the newspaper off the front porch, noting the foremost headline: GANGLAND SLAUGHTER OF FRATELLI FAMILY.

Despite the chilly morning, sweat beaded on Andy's broad forehead above his protruding eyes. His hands shook with shuddering horror. Unshaven and dressed in plaid flannel pajamas under a dark blue robe, he had just picked up the newspaper from the front steps of his house and read the headline when Novak arrived. Stunned by the news, he had let the paper slip through his fingers and scatter about his feet.

Novak finished gathering the pages and led Andy into his own house, closing the door behind them.

"Sit down before you flop, old boy," Novak said, maneuvering Andy into a living room chair. He looked into Andy's bewildered blue eyes, snapping his fingers twice in front of his face. "Brother, I didn't think you'd take it this hard. Want some coffee? Some smelling salts? Maybe a piece of toast? No?"

Novak grinned at Andy's silence. He turned himself around, hands on his hips, a whistle of appreciation passing his lips as he took in the large, modernly furnished house. "Swell digs you got here. How come you never invited me over? We could've sat on the front porch. Played checkers."

Looking up into Novak's smirking face, Andy said, "You're responsible for this."

"Me?" Novak pointed to himself with disbelief. "How do you figure?"

With a sudden burst of hostility, Andy jumped to his feet. Blood rushed to his face, turning it bright red. "I told you to stir up a little dispute between the Pompliano and Fratelli families to get the pressure off my client! I never said to start an all-out war!"

"First off," Novak said, "there's no such thing as a *little* dispute between Mafia families. Second, how can you be certain the Pomplianos did this?"

"You know it, I know it, and soon the police will prove it. I told you to shoot *near* the Pompliano brothers that night at that restaurant, to scare them, to instigate a little animosity between the gangs—not to *kill* them! You murdered Don Pompliano's three sons, and, because of you, they murdered the entire Fratelli family!"

"Which is no great loss, I assure you."

"You'll hang for this, Jack."

The grin vanished from Novak's face. "If the police untangle my name, they'll find yours tied to it and your client's, too, whoever he is. I won't do the dance alone. Three necks can stretch as easily as one."

Andy pinched his eyes closed to rub them with his fingers. "Why did you kill them?"

Settling in the vacated chair, Novak pushed his hat to the back of his head. "You hired me to ransack Angelo's home and office for some photographs of Erik. Remember? So I checked his house. I found squat. I checked his office. There was nothing there, either, with the exception of *me* when Angelo strolled in with two of his goons. He waylaid me."

"You never told me this." Andy stopped rubbing his eyes and looked sharply at Novak, who shrugged.

"Angelo gave me a choice: squeal on my employer or die. I die for no one, so I sang like a songbird. Every note a gem. It's not hard to find the right key when there's a Luger stuck in your ear."

Andy's shoulders sagged. A deep sigh came from his chest. "That's why every attempt I made on this case was thwarted."

"Don't beat yourself up. The story's not finished. The night of the Pompliano hit, I demanded that Angelo pay me for my services. He said my pay was his decision to keep me alive, which he could change at any time. I got steamed, so I saved the little tidbit about the intended *near hit* you planned on the Pomplianos. I made good on the hit and made sure the Pomplianos believed the Fratellis did it. That would serve Angelo rather well, I thought—and I still think it."

"It served me, as well. What did you have against me? I paid you well."

"Yes, and I think you may pay me well again."

"Wait a minute." Andy inhaled sharply. "The day Angelo had Erik brought to the courthouse, I sent two men to that girl's apartment to grab him when he came back. Dominic murdered those men. You warned him they were inside, didn't you?"

Novak nodded admiringly. "Smart boy. I had to prove to Angelo I was worth keeping alive, which brings me to another subject—"

"Those men had wives! Children!"

"Want me to cry? Want me to send flowers? Look, there's only one child who concerns me: Erik Warner. He skipped out on the chopper squad last night."

Andy's eyebrows lifted into startled points. "He's alive? Where is he?"

"He's safe and sleeping like a baby."

"How did you find him?"

"You don't think I spend my nights washing my hair, do

you? I'm a PI. It's my job to be nosy, and I was nosy at the Fratelli Estate last night. I saw the bloody aftermath. What a mess. I also saw Dominic, Erik, and Benny Rosario beat it. I followed, and after Rosario killed Dominic, I snagged the kid. No doubt I saved his life."

Andy narrowed his gaze with understanding. "And how much do you want for him?"

"You catch on quick in your pajamas." Novak settled comfortably in the chair. "Twenty thousand dollars. Now, drop the dime to your client that I've got the kid on ice and I don't want him to melt."

Upon hearing these words, Andy hesitated.

"What's that look for?" Novak asked.

"What part did you play in the deaths of Neils Warner and his two sons?"

"I'm glad you're keeping up with me."

All at once, Andy seemed ill. Staggering to another chair, he collapsed into it. "I sent you to get a signature on a document and you murdered them instead?"

"I told Angelo I was going to get the farmer to relinquish the kid, and I did. I came back to town and got a call from Papa Fratelli himself offering me five grand to end all question of guardianship. So, I went back that same day. I took care of the farmer with his own gun. He was such a wreck that I probably did him a favor. The kids heard the shot and ran in. I didn't like it, but I took them outside. I made them kneel in the snow—"

"Shut up. I don't want to hear it."

"It was a nasty bump-off, but I did it, and I made it look like a murder-suicide."

"How can you live with yourself?" Andy shook his head with disgust. "How can you stand to look in the mirror knowing you murdered two young boys and their father?"

"I got five Gs for an hour's work. That's how I live with it. For twenty more, I'll give this kid the same send-off, or I can deliver him without a scratch. Your choice. But if you won't call your client, I'll give Deputy District Attorney Joshua Parnell a ring myself."

He watched with pride as Andy's eyes protruded again. "How—!"

"It's not hard to figure. He's your friend, and he's prosecuting Louie Fratelli. Who else would it be? Let's give the young man a jingle, shall we?"

"No," Andy whispered, shaking his head. "I'll give you the money. I owe him this."

"How considerate. Oh, did I mention that Angelo has an interest in the snatch racket, too? I wonder if he'd up his price. Mind if I use your phone?"

Andy closed his eyes. He leaned his head back while Novak grabbed the telephone off the table nearby.

After requesting the number from the operator, Novak said over his shoulder, "You know, that boy is a good-looking kid. If neither of you want him, he'll bring a nice price in the right market. It'd be a shame, though, because those kids don't last long. They're good for, oh, say, three to four years. Tops."

"Whatever Angelo offers you," Andy said, his voice hollow, distant, "I'll give you ten percent more."

"Now and again," Novak continued, "their bodies turn up in the foothills. Sometimes they're in one piece. Sometimes the animals find them first. Sometimes—"

"Dry up, already," Andy snapped. "I'll give you twenty percent."

Novak smiled. "Brother, this kid must be made of diamonds."

Thirty-Eight

"Hello, Clara."

Not having heard the door open in the hum of the bustling café, Clara looked up from the table at the sound of her name. Seeing Joshua, she tensed, startled by his arrival as though she truly hadn't believed he would come. An untouched cup of coffee sat before her on the white tablecloth. A heavy smell of grease hung in the air.

"Hello, Josh."

A fragile smile crossed her face—one that could be shattered easily by an unkind word. He noticed at once the brilliant bruises on her throat.

"May I?" he asked, indicating the vacant chair across from her.

"Of course. Coffee?"

"Yes, please." He removed his hat and tried to conceal his own anxiety.

She signaled the waitress for another cup.

A nerve-racking silence hung over them while they waited for the coffee to arrive. When it did, relieved for the distraction, Joshua poured the cream and sugar, stirred it, took a sip, returned the cup to its saucer, and gave Clara an embarrassed smile. His mind searched frantically for the apology he had prepared, rehearsed, and now forgotten. Her eyes were fixed staunchly on the cup before her, and he realized that she had not looked him straight in the eye since he had sat down.

"Thanks for coming," she began, biting her lip. "I won't keep you. I just wanted to say—"

"Clara," he blurted, "I'm sorry for what I said today. There's no excuse for my behavior." Again, he caught the startled look in her eyes as they flashed at him, then dropped once more.

She suffered a waning smile. "There's every excuse for your behavior."

"No, there's not. I'm ashamed of myself."

"You have no reason to be ashamed. I'm the one who wronged you. I'm so sorry."

It was his turn to be startled. Humility was something he had never expected from this wild party girl. As he considered her, his sight fell on her bruised throat.

"Who did this to you?"

"It's not important." Unsettled by the visibility of her bruises, she adjusted her coat collar to conceal them. "Did you get everything? The photos? Negatives? The Bible?"

Lowering his voice, he leaned into the table so that she could still hear him. "You don't know how grateful I am to get those photos and negatives. I burned them. You must have risked your life to get them."

"They were at the Fratelli Estate," she said, taking up her spoon. He watched the languid motion of her pale, thin hand as she stirred the coffee absently. "Last night, before Dominic, Luke, and I were going to run away, I—"

"Dominic Fratelli?" he asked with astonishment.

"Yes. He had decided to leave the mob. We were going to be married."

"Dominic Fratelli was leaving the mob? Papa's favorite son was leaving the mob?"

"For Luke and me, yes. He was willing to risk his life."

"Was he killed in the massacre? And the boy, too? Luke?"

Visibly choking back her tears, she nodded.

"I'm sorry," Joshua said. "It must have been awful to see them die."

Pulling a handkerchief from her purse to dab at her eyes, she said, "I didn't see them die."

"You saw their bodies, then?"

"No. I was told they were dead by...by someone who would know. I was in the library, trying to get the photos out of the safe. Papa caught me. He almost killed me, but—"

She stopped abruptly.

"But what?"

"A young man stopped him. He shot Papa to death."

"Who was this young man?"

She shook her head. "I can't tell you."

"Can't or won't?"

With a nervous glance, she looked at those nearest the table to see whether anyone was eavesdropping. "I won't. He saved my life."

"Was he one of the killers?"

"I've said too much," she whispered fearfully.

"Clara," he urged, "you must tell me who these murderers are so the police can arrest them. Do you realize how many people they slaughtered?"

"I realize all too well!" she shot back, her frightened eyes alive with sudden passion. "I was there, remember?"

"Shhhhh." He cautioned her with a downward motion of his hand. She understood and subdued her voice.

"I lost the only family I had last night. For some reason, God chose to spare my life through this man. The police will solve the case on their own. I came to tell you certain things. Nothing more."

"Fair enough," he conceded, not willing to lose her cooperation. "Just tell me what you can. How does the Bible fit into all this?"

She dabbed her eyes with the handkerchief again and took a shuddering breath. "This morning, I saw the name *Fred MacDonald* written inside it. I recognized it as the name of the preacher Louie murdered. I didn't realize its importance until I remembered the Bible was given to Luke by Benny Rosario, one of Papa's men."

"Benny Rosario. I know him." Joshua leaned away from the table. "The first time I faced Angelo Carpinelli in court, he was representing this foulmouthed, overweight racketeer on a felony charge. Why would he give Luke a Bible?"

"Luke asked for one. Angelo told Benny to get it."

"And somehow he got his hands on the victim's Bible. Did he say how it came into his possession?"

"Not to me," she said.

"Would anyone else know?"

"Dom might've known."

He took a sip of the cooling coffee, nodding absently while his mind processed all that she said. "Were Benny and Louie at the party?" he asked.

"I was upstairs most of the time. I don't know who was there."

"What about Angelo?"

"I don't know. I'm sorry."

"Don't worry about it. I'll visit the morgue on the way home. If Louie's dead, there'll be no trial Monday morning, and justice will have been served."

"If Louie's alive, he'll never be convicted of murdering that preacher." Clara spoke the words with such certainty that Joshua's nerves tightened.

"How do you know that?"

At first, she appeared to regret her words. She paused, then leaned forward and whispered, "Who is the judge presiding over the case?"

"I think you already know." He felt a sinking sensation in

the pit of his stomach, which was strangely offset by the fragrance of her perfume.

"Clarence Whitfield?"

With a sigh, he nodded.

"Did you know he and Papa often did favors for each other?" she asked.

"Such as?"

"Such as Whitfield promising Papa that Louie wouldn't spend a day in jail, that there would be a mistrial, or that he would be acquitted."

"How do you know this?" he asked.

"It gets worse. He knows all about you. He knows about the accident on New Year's Eve with Luke. He's prepared to use it against you, if necessary."

"Clara, how do you know this?"

"Because in return for his promise...Papa gave him...me."

The sinking sensation churned his stomach. He did not know what to think; he certainly did not know what to say. Words of consolation came to his lips. They seemed inappropriate, so he swallowed them and said nothing. He noticed her nails digging deeply into her palms as she stared at the table.

"Two nights ago," she said without looking up, "I was forced to spend the evening with Judge Whitfield. He took me to a speakeasy where he got drunk. He felt free to talk in front of me, and he told me everything. Afterward, when I wouldn't let him touch me, he was livid. I had to hit him over the head to get away. When Papa found me, he did this." Her trembling fingers touched her battered throat. Still, she did not look up.

"You didn't—" he stopped, feeling like an absolute idiot. "I'm sorry. I shouldn't—"

"I know what you think of me, Josh, but there are things you don't know about me. He didn't touch me. I wouldn't let him."

"I'm, uh," he stumbled over his tongue stupidly, "...glad."

"Anyway, I've no proof of what he said, no witnesses, nothing on paper. I've nothing except my word. Do with it what you will."

Another silence ensued. He watched her closely, hoping she would look at him. She looked everywhere else—at the table, the floor, the customers, her cold coffee, her hands—but never at him. His voice was gentle when he spoke.

"Thank you, Clara. I appreciate you telling me this. I'd like to ask you something else. What do you know about Tony Garda?"

"Tony?" Grateful that the attention had been taken from her, she finally looked up. "He was one of the boys. I didn't know him well. I heard that he betrayed the family somehow, so Papa took care of him."

"The police shot Tony. Could Papa have arranged it?"

"It's possible. That was one of his methods. He owned the police, and no one questions it when a cop kills a mobster."

"Was Tony with Louie the night he killed Fred MacDonald?" he asked.

"I don't know. No one talked about it."

"Do you think Papa killed him to keep his mouth shut?"

"It wouldn't surprise me. He's killed for less."

"So, Tony's knowledge outweighed his usefulness." He looked at her pensively. "You've, um, never heard any stories about...demons, dungeons, skeletons...things like that in the Fratelli mansion, have you?"

Her face went blank. "What?"

"Never mind. Tell me, what will you do now that you're free from the Fratellis?"

With a sigh, she gazed back at her hands. "I don't know. Dom had everything planned. Now he's dead and nothing is planned. I'll leave town. I know that." She made a frustrated movement with her hands. "I really don't know. I'll just have to depend on God."

Baffled by her choice of words, and baffled with his incessant attraction to her, he asked, "Can I buy you dinner?"

A sad smile crossed her face. "You're very kind, Josh. You don't have to be."

"Personally, I'm starved," he pressed. "I haven't eaten all day. Let's get a menu."

"You really don't have to. I should be going anyway."

"But I *want* to."

She looked up. That startled expression in her eyes returned when she found him staring eagerly into her face, obviously hoping she would say yes.

"Okay, Josh. Thank you."

"Great!" He grinned. With a wave of his arm, he caught the waitress's attention.

THIRTY-NINE

The last customers to leave the café, Joshua and Clara lingered outside the door while the lights inside were extinguished. Something in their abrupt dousing triggered a forlorn ache in his heart—a loneliness fueled by the midnight hour, the quiet gloom of the street, and their breaths dissipating into fine wisps of steam. He shoved his hands into his pockets, trying to conjure up a reason to detain her.

"I wish you'd eaten more," he said, frowning. "You're too thin."

"I don't have much of an appetite. Thank you for dinner, though," she said, wrapping her coat tightly around her against the winter night. With a parting smile, she took a step back. "I guess I'd better go."

"Let me drive you," he offered, taking an equal step forward. "I'd like to show you my new car."

"Thanks, but I'd rather no one know where I am staying. It's safer that way."

"What if I need to reach you?"

After a moment's thought and a sideways glance at the café, she said, "Leave a message with the manager here. I'll check with him occasionally—until I leave town, that is."

"When that will be?" he asked, not caring to hide his disappointment.

"When I'm feeling better. That's all I can say."

"Where will you go?"

"Far away." She took another step backward. "I really must go."

He took another step forward. "Do you need anything? Some cash to tide you over? Anything?"

"You're sweet." She tried to hold the remains of her smile. "Thanks, but I have some money tucked away."

He did not return the smile. "I'm not ashamed to say it, Clara. I wish you wouldn't go. I think if we tried, we could make a go of it, this time under the right circumstances."

Her eyes widened with genuine surprise. She paused, as if repeating his words in her mind to make certain she heard him correctly. "How can you say that after what I've done to you?"

"Because of what you've done *for* me and because you seem so different. You're nothing like you used to be—ah—" he fumbled mindlessly, "—and even though that didn't sound like a compliment, I meant it as one. I want to know more about you. I know so little."

"Josh," she said kindly, "when was the last time you saw your wife?"

Bowing his head, his nudged a small piece of ice across the sidewalk with his foot.

"Ex-wife. We're divorced. She left me for another man. Am I that transparent?"

"Only to me. I know you're lonely. So am I, but there's too much pain and too many memories here, and even though you've forgiven me, I haven't forgiven myself." Once more, she took a step backward, this time turning away. "Good-bye, Josh."

Even as his mouth opened in protest, the words that would entreat her to stay failed him, leaving him to watch her slender form fade into the darkness. His shoulders sagged. The diminishing sound of her steps made him want to follow her; he even took a step in that direction before dismissing the idea. It would be better to respect her wishes and go about his unhappy business—a trip to the city morgue.

Pandemonium. That word—and its infernal connotations of a fiery hell—came to Joshua's mind when he arrived at St. Joseph's Hospital and took the stairs to the basement morgue. Immediately, his stomach grew nauseated. He wished his handkerchief were mentholated as he pulled it from his pocket and opened the morgue door.

The removal of the bodies from the Fratelli Estate was complete, and the identification process was underway. Dozens of bodies shrouded with sheets lined the hallways, some on stretchers, some directly on the floor. Police and medical attendants, their hands and clothes soiled with blood, rushed from side to side, pulling the sheets from the corpses, subjecting Joshua to the frigid, blue-gray faces of the Fratelli dead. Pressing the handkerchief over his nose and mouth against the smell of decaying flesh, he tried to avoid stepping in the blood that seemed to be everywhere.

After questioning several people, he found the chief medical examiner, an overburdened older man in a white smock. Forgoing a handshake after eyeing the bloody gloves on his hands, Joshua introduced himself, explained his business, and followed the man into a chilled room overflowing with corpses.

A mounting list of the names of the dead was provided. He scanned it for Dominic Fratelli, Louie Fratelli, Angelo Carpinelli, and Benny Rosario. Nothing. When Joshua asked how he could verify whether those he sought were among the unknown dead, including a young boy, the medical examiner invited him to join in the search. As for a young boy, he knew of no children found among the dead. Joshua thanked him.

Declining the offer to inspect the corpses, he chose to leave his card with the names written on the back.

Afterward, he took the stairs up to the hospital, where a list of patients was provided. He found a name—Louie Fratelli, slightly injured, suffering from a flesh wound in his posterior, found cowering beneath the body of a dead woman in the banquet hall.

It figures, Joshua thought. *The one Fratelli who deserved to be shot survives by his own cowardice. I guess the trial continues.*

His eyes scanned the list further. They stopped on the name Benny Rosario—found in an alley, severely beaten, suffering from three bullet wounds.

With a smile, he thought, *The trial continues, but not without a subpoena for Benny Rosario as a witness for the state.*

The Windsor Hotel. Clara looked wearily at the number on her door as she inserted the key into the lock. Upon entering the room, she pressed in the light switch next to the door. Its tired yellow glow illuminated the small room and its menial furniture—a narrow bed, a dresser, a nightstand, and a single chair—yet did nothing to alleviate her sadness.

Seeing Joshua relieved the burden of guilt from her soul but, in turn, accentuated her loneliness. Dominic and Luke were dead, brutally murdered. She could not escape the guilt that she should have died with them. The pressure of tears built behind her eyes.

Tired and painfully cold, she locked the door and secured it with the chair beneath the knob before removing her coat and hat, kicking off her shoes, and crawling into bed in her clothes. To change into her nightgown would have taken too great an effort. It was almost too much to stretch forth her arm to turn on the lamp on the nightstand, but she needed the light. The glow of the anemic bulb above was not enough, and the darkness was unbearable.

As she had done the night before, she wrapped herself in the blankets, expecting to cry herself to sleep, and prayed. She perceived the lagging of time by her tears and the length of her prayer. Finally, as she teetered inside the breadth of sleep, she screamed a short, piercing shriek. Something had touched her face—the caress of a clammy hand.

Her eyes snapped open to find the room in blackness. A footstep sounded near the bed. It stopped with the creak of a floorboard. A dreadful chill seized her. She threw a fearful glance around the shadowed room. In a recessed corner, a looming movement caught her eye.

Sitting up, she fumbled for the lamp on the nightstand. The click of the switch sounded loudly in the darkness but accomplished nothing. The room remained black. Frantic and certain she heard someone breathing, she turned the lamp on and off three times. The series of clicks did nothing to provide light but did much to antagonize her already jangled nerves.

A ghostly sigh. She gasped. In a melancholy tone, the intruder spoke her name.

"Who is it?" Her voice shook. "What do you want?"

The sigh faded, leaving in its mournful wake the low, constant breathing.

She needed a weapon. Taking the lamp in her hand, she brought it toward her. There was no resistance. She felt for the cord, found it, and discovered it was not plugged into the wall. That determined it beyond all other reasoning; someone *was* in her room. Somehow, an intruder had unlocked the door and gotten through the barricade of the chair.

"Protect me, Lord," she whispered.

She maneuvered her feet to the floor while her eyes remained on the corner where the phantom lingered and breathed. With a start, she ran for the door, simultaneously throwing the lamp with all her strength into the haunted corner. It hit something and shattered.

The intruder rushed toward her. She heard his feet cross the floor. She sensed his outstretched arms. Groping desperately for the wall, she reached it, found the light switch, and pushed it in. The light came on. Anticipating the grasp of violent hands, she spun around with a shriek and threw her arms up in defense—to find no one there.

The room, bathed with light, was empty of everything except the furniture. The lamp lay broken on the floor. The chair leaned unmoved beneath the doorknob.

Hastily, she searched the room—under the bed, in the closet, in the bathroom, behind the doors. No one. She was alone. Her legs almost failed her as she stumbled toward the bed.

"I didn't imagine it." She brushed the hair back from her face. "I wasn't dreaming. Dear God, be with me."

She came to a sudden stop. Her hands flew to her mouth with a terrified cry. On her pillow lay the crystal shard she had thrust into Papa Fratelli's throat. It was still wet with his blood.

FORTY

The streetlight below his second-story window lit up only a fraction of the sidewalk and the street. In its final hours of life, the bulb blinked, sporadically alternating between burning brightly and flickering to a dim glow. Had Jack Novak been on surveillance, lurking in the night's shadows, he would have preferred this dusky, uncertain atmosphere; it added obscurity, which added protection. Tonight, however, it was *he* who felt watched, and this erratic, unreliable streetlight now denied him a clear view of the street. Anyone could approach his apartment building without being noticed; that person need only wait for the streetlight to dim.

A glance behind him ascertained the presence of his packed suitcase by the front door. A quick study of his studio apartment confirmed he left nothing behind that could not be replaced. A sporadic kick accompanied by a muffled scream of frustration verified that Luke—gagged, tied, and lying on the Murphy bed—had regained consciousness.

Novak looked back outside. He expected Andy to arrive at 8:00 p.m., bearing a ransom of thirty thousand dollars; it was now 7:55 p.m. He wished Andy would hurry, since he had promised to deliver Luke to Carpinelli at 8:30 p.m. After his business with Andy, there was no time to lose for Novak to hightail it out of town, yet a nagging feeling in his gut warned him that something was wrong—a detective's hunch that had seldom failed him.

Grabbing the scotch bottle from the windowsill, he unscrewed the lid and took a drink. A movement caught his eye. Turning, he saw Luke rolling across the bed, ready to fall off. Setting the bottle back on the sill, Novak rushed to him, catching him as he tumbled. With a plop, he tossed Luke back on the bed. Disheveled and tormented, Luke squinted against the brightness of the ungarnished lightbulb hanging from a cord directly overhead.

"Look, kid. I promised to deliver you without a scratch. Damaged merchandise reduces the price. So shut up and lie still."

In response, Luke thrashed around in rage, kicking the bed and bouncing on the mattress.

"Stop it, Erik!" Novak raised his hand. "You want me to dust one across your mouth?"

Luke stopped to glare through his tousled hair with furious green eyes.

"Keep it quiet, or I'll put you back to sleep."

Notwithstanding the gag, Luke garbled out a sentence.

"What?"

Luke mumbled the question again. Novak reached down to remove the gag.

"Who are you?" Luke demanded.

"The last person to see you alive if you keep acting up."

Luke looked around the room with quick, jerking movements of his head. "What am I doin' here, and how'd you know my name?"

"You're here because you're my ticket out of town. As for your name, your father told me. Any more lousy questions?"

For the first time, fear showed in Luke's eyes. "You takin' me to my Pa?"

"Only if you plan on living in the graveyard."

Luke eyed Novak with a vacant stare, a look that turned to puzzlement.

"You didn't know, did you? Well, that's the breaks. They're dead. Rattle my nerves again and you'll find yourself with them. Got it?"

A choking sound came from Luke's throat. "Pa...? Charlie...? Nate...?"

"Yeah, Pa, Charlie, and Nate. You aching for a family reunion?"

"You killed 'em?"

Novak turned away, preferring to look at the window.

"Why?" Luke asked with a sob. Tears glistened in his eyes. "Why? What'd they do to you?"

"They made me rich"—Novak replaced the gag—"and you're going to make me richer."

To his surprise, his hands shook. Withdrawing to the window, he took a swig of scotch, wiped it from his mouth with his sleeve, and waited for the burning liquor to compose his nerves. Unexpectedly, a single scream from the bed, a solitary cry of heartbreak, assaulted his nerves anew. It reverberated through the room, bounced off the window, and assailed him like a slap. He took another gulp of scotch.

Outside, the headlights of an oncoming car skimmed the building as it completed a turn. Squinting into the darkness, Novak thought he recognized it.

"Good. You're on time, Andy. I'm ready to lose this kid. He gives me the creeps."

But the car kept going. It slowed down at first, pausing as if the driver was contemplating whether to park, then sped up suddenly, continuing down the road. Novak pressed his forehead against the cold window, straining to see the car as it disappeared beyond his sight. He straightened his back. Maybe he was wrong.

He risked a glance at Luke. Quiet and no longer resisting his bonds, Luke lay on his side, curled into a ball. He quivered slightly, crying silent, anguished tears.

A car door slammed. Then another. With his attention on Luke, Novak had missed the approach of another car. He looked outside and saw no one in the dim glow of the streetlight. Another sound reached his ears: footsteps—two sets—ascending the staircase, each telltale step pronounced by the creaky, timeworn wood. Then, abruptly, they stopped. As his apartment stood at the top of the staircase, Novak knew that they had paused before his door. He looked at it; the skeleton key was in the keyhole, right where Novak had left it after bolting the door. The chain lock a few inches above it hung securely fastened in its plate.

A hand grabbed the door handle, turning it unsuccessfully. Novak extracted the gun from his holster as another car door slammed. Peering out the window, he saw the streetlight burning brightly. Andy was parked across the street, standing hesitantly beside his car, his gaze alternating between Novak's apartment window and the Phantom Rolls Royce parked directly under the streetlight.

Novak's heart jumped in his chest. Uttering a monosyllabic curse, he spun around to see the chain on his door slide to the left and swing from its mount, unfastened from its plate by an invisible hand. Next, the unseen hand turned the skeleton key to the right, moving the tumbler and throwing the bolt.

"That's not possible," Novak said, his wide eyes fixed on the door.

He lifted his gun. The door opened. He caught a glimpse of two men standing in the entry, one behind the other, just as the solitary light bulb in the room exploded, plunging him into darkness. The sound startled Novak. He fired his gun. The blast threw him back against the window, and, like the manifestation of a ghost, the dark silhouette of the foremost man stood immediately before him.

"You have something I want."

Novak recognized the voice, but before he could react, he was disarmed with the sweep of the man's hand while another hand grabbed him fiercely by his jacket, lifted him, and tossed him across the room like a useless rag. He collided painfully with the wall, his head and body denting it, and fell to the floor with a thud. Dusted with flakes of plaster, he uttered a feeble groan, rolled over once, and curled into a ball. Something was broken inside. He could feel it.

"Is he alive?"

"Yes, he's alive," said the other man, leaning over Luke.

"Take him to the car."

Novak recognized the voice of the second man as Carpinelli. Enfolding Luke in a blanket, Carpinelli lifted him, still bound by the twine, and left the apartment.

The other man turned back to Novak. Placing his foot on his side, he deftly rolled him onto his back. Novak bellowed in pain as the heavy foot pressed down on his chest. Grabbing the man's ankle, he peered up, identifying him from the glare of the window as Dominic. Novak knew then that he was dead.

"Set me straight," he said, gasping. "What's so great... about the kid? Is he...somebody?"

"Only the mouthpiece of God. Fool. Your greed blinded you to his true value. Think on that as you enter eternity."

A sneer twisted Dominic's mouth as he pointed a gun at Novak's head.

"Not in the face," he pleaded. "Give my mother...something to look at."

Dominic smiled derisively. He aimed the weapon between Novak's eyes and pulled the trigger.

Long after Dominic had driven Luke and Carpinelli away from the murder site, long after Novak's body lay motionless in the silence of his apartment, another set of headlights switched on from across the street. A car crept forward. In the driver's seat sat Andy, shaken and disconsolate that once more his attempts had been thwarted.

Forty-One

Please, have a seat," Joshua said. Having anticipated the meeting, Joshua had removed the files from the chairs in his office and even brought in a third chair so that Edmund and Edith Elliott and Joan MacDonald would each have a place to sit when they arrived. It felt good to be prepared; it did not happen often.

"Thanks for seeing me on such short notice," Joshua said, sitting in his own squeaky chair behind his desk.

"We're happy to do whatever we can for you," Edmund said, smiling kindly.

"Well, Reverend, I wanted to see you for two reasons. The first is to tell you that I spoke with the coroner, and Luke was not among the victims at the Fratelli Estate. So there's hope that he's still alive."

"Oh, praise God," Edith breathed, bringing a lace handkerchief to her eyes. "We haven't slept since we heard about it."

"Yes, praise God," Edmund repeated, gently patting his wife's arm. "The Lord takes care of His own."

"Ah...yes..." Joshua said. "Anyway, Dominic Fratelli also wasn't among the victims, so, chances are, Luke is with him. The second thing I wanted to discuss is the trial tomorrow morning. As you know, I wasn't encouraged by the proceedings last time we all spoke. Since then, however, I've received evidence that may place a Fratelli gang member at the scene of the shooting, if not Louie Fratelli himself."

Joshua turned to Joan. "Mrs. MacDonald, I recall during the testimony of Dr. Kelsall, the physician who attended to your husband, that Fred asked for his Bible before he died. Do you remember this?"

"Yes." She nodded, sitting up straight with anticipation. "Yes, I do."

"Did you give it to him?"

"No. I couldn't find it."

"Have you found it since?"

"No."

"Can you remember the last time you had it in your possession?"

"I've thought about that many times," Joan said. "We had it with us when we drove to my parents' house for Thanksgiving. That's the last I remember seeing it."

"Can you remember if you had it in the car at the time of the attack?"

"I think so. We didn't leave it at my parents' house, so I suppose we had it with us."

"At any time did the attackers enter your car or take anything from your car?"

"No. Never. Why?"

With that assurance, Joshua opened the center drawer of the desk, pulled out the Bible Clara had given him, and presented it to the young widow. "Mrs. MacDonald, is this Fred's Bible?"

Her blue eyes widened. With trembling fingers, she took the black leather book from him, opened it, and stroked its thin, almost translucent pages. "Yes." Tears shined in her eyes. "This was his. Where did you find it?"

"It was in the possession of one Benny Rosario, a racketeer known to be involved with the Fratelli family. Does that name mean anything to you?"

"I've never heard of him."

"Can you think of any reason why this man would have Fred's Bible? Joan?"

"I'm sorry." She was crying, clutching the Bible to her chest. Edith wrapped her arm around her daughter's shoulders. "I don't know why this man would have Fred's Bible. Do you?"

"Not yet," Joshua said, leaning back in his chair, "but I intend to find out."

"Mr. Rosario?"

Without knocking, Joshua opened the hospital room door and stepped inside. He found Benny propped up in bed by numerous pillows and scowling at him through two swollen black eyes in a face marred with bruises and lacerations. Bandages swathed his head in a turban-like headdress. A sling carefully cradled his right arm to his chest.

Joshua surveyed the room with a glance. It was small and chilly, its walls painted a pale turquoise. He crinkled his nose at the smell of turpentine and rubbing alcohol and thought it ironic that he was conducting the interview in the same hospital where Fred MacDonald had died a few months before.

"Mr. Rosario, I'm Deputy District Attorney Joshua Parnell. May I speak with you?"

"I know who you are, shyster," Benny snapped. "What do you want?"

"A few minutes of your time," Joshua said, approaching the bed. His footsteps sounded loudly on the linoleum floor. "How are you feeling?"

"Like a cement truck worked me over."

"Is there anything I can get for you?"

"Yeah, get yourself out of here." Benny waved his good

arm toward the door. "There some law says I have to listen to you yap?"

"No law, but it would behoove you to hear what I have to say." Joshua gestured toward Benny's wounds. "Who did this to you? Perhaps I can bring charges against them."

"Some cannons buzzed me, all right?"

"Excuse me?"

"Got a problem with your hearing? I said I was mugged, and don't bother asking who, 'cause I don't know."

"How many attackers were there?"

Suspicion narrowed Benny's eyes into a glare. "Three."

"Can you describe them?"

"No."

"What did they steal? Did they steal your wallet?"

Benny hesitated. Involuntarily, his eyes darted to the bedside tray.

Following the motion, Joshua said, "Or is *this* your wallet?"

"No, they didn't take my wallet," Benny unwillingly conceded.

"Or the money inside it, I see." Picking up the worn, brown wallet, Joshua thumbed through the numerous large bills inside. "They weren't industrious thieves."

"Hey! You got no right going through my stuff! Put it back!"

"Oh, sorry." Joshua returned the wallet to the tray. "They didn't take your gun, either, did they? A .45 semiautomatic. The police discovered it after the garbagemen found you facedown in the gutter." A snide smile crossed his face. "They're happy to keep it for you. Might even link it to some crimes they can't solve."

With his bloodshot eyes suddenly bulging, Benny shouted, "Look! What do you want from me?"

"Answers. You must have heard about Dominic's birthday party two nights ago. It's the talk of the town."

"Yeah, I saw it in the paper. What of it?"

"You mean you weren't there? Didn't they invite you?"

"I wasn't there," he grumbled, not meeting Joshua's eyes.

"Not at any time?"

"What are you driving at?"

"Well," Joshua stroked his jaw with dramatic flourish, "I've spoken to some of the survivors who claim you *were* there. They said you had a fight with Dominic. Isn't that right?"

"I wasn't nowhere near there. See?"

"So, you know nothing about the murders?"

"I don't know from nothing."

"Odd," Joshua said. "That's not the story I'm getting. I heard you pulled a gun on Dominic, so he knocked you over the head—"

With a sharp movement of his head, Benny looked away. "You don't know from nothing."

"—and told some of his boys to take you for a ride. Is it possible those bandages on your head are covering a gash made by the butt of Dominic's gun?"

"I told you, I was mugged."

Lowering his voice almost to a whisper, Joshua asked, "Why did Dominic order your death? Did he find out you were working for someone else? Who is it, Benny? Who's pulling your strings?"

"You trying to railroad me?"

"The murderers were disguised as waiters. The police think they had help from the inside—someone who got the hit men into the mansion. Is that someone you, Benny?"

"I want my lawyer."

"Let me guess: Mr. Carpinelli?" Joshua chuckled with satisfaction at Benny's perturbed frown. "Don't expect much help from him. Papa Fratelli's not pulling his strings any longer, so there's no reason why he should defend you. You realize that, don't you?"

Benny looked back and forth between Joshua's eyes.

"A conviction of first-degree murder in this state brings the death penalty," Joshua taunted. "Are you ready to swing for one hundred and nine murders? That's how many people died that night, Benny. Did you know that? One hundred and nine living, breathing souls. Some of the girls were as young as seventeen." He inched closer to the bed, whispering, "Know how easy it would be for me to prove you're guilty? They'll build a special gallows for you."

"You lousy, stinking—!"

A brisk knock on the door broke off Benny's affront. When it opened, two police officers stepped inside.

"Gentlemen," Joshua said with an outstretched arm. "I take it you're here to keep Mr. Rosario company and to see he receives no unwanted visitors. Good. Please close the door. I'll be with you in a moment."

The police closed the door and left them alone once more. Joshua eased himself onto the edge of the bed.

"Next time I see you, Benny, it will be behind bars with a public defender fresh out of law school, freckle faced and green, ready to defend you. Are you prepared for that?"

Benny squinted his raccoon-like eyes. "Which side of the bars you gonna be on, shyster? You think you got me, but you forget. I got something on you."

"Whatever do you mean?" Joshua asked with cool indifference.

"You forget about that kid you hit?" Benny jabbed his thumb at himself. "Well, I ain't forgot. I'm sure there's others who'd like to know what I have to say about him."

Joshua shook his head, crossing his arms in a relaxed fashion. "I don't know who you're talking about."

"Don't play dumb. That big-eyed brat you polished your

car with. I saw you in the dame's apartment." Benny's eyes brightened with sudden remembrance. "There's pictures. That's right. I got you now, and you thought you was setting me up." He pointed his thumb at himself again with pride.

Joshua leaned forward. "There's no evidence. I destroyed the pictures, but there were other witnesses, weren't there? Dominic, for one, if he's still alive—but he won't say anything, because it would make him an accessory to blackmail, among other unpleasant charges. What about his girl, Clara? She would remain silent for the same reason. And what of the boy? His body wasn't found with the victims. He's disappeared, and you don't even know his real name."

"Don't forget Mr. Carpinelli," Benny proclaimed. "He was there."

A pleased smile brightened Joshua's face. "I could never forget Mr. Carpinelli. Right now, he's trying to save his own neck. He'll never confess he had anything to do with the boy. He won't even acknowledge the boy's existence. If he did, he'd cut his own throat. Besides, he's busy trying to free Louie. You have convictions as long as my arm with dozens of misdemeanors and two felonies. One more and you're a three-time loser. It's a life sentence—that is, if they don't throw you a neck-stretching party."

Enjoying the myriad of expressions crossing Benny's face, Joshua waited until every word he'd spoken hit home in the gangster's brain. Suddenly, a dawning expression leaped into Benny's eyes.

"I'm on to you. You want me to make a deal. You want me to rat on Louie."

Joshua scooted closer. "You were there, weren't you? You saw Louie shoot Fred MacDonald. You're the unknown accomplice who grabbed his wife when she ran for help and threw her into your car."

"What if I am?"

"Did I mention that Joe Fratelli was murdered with a .45 semiautomatic exactly like yours? He was shot point-blank in the chest."

"All right." Benny leaned against the pillows with a sigh. "What are you offering?"

"A misdemeanor for reckless endangerment on the MacDonald murder. You'll serve six months. In exchange, you'll testify that you saw Louie murder MacDonald."

Scrutinizing Joshua's face, Benny asked, "What about the Fratelli murders?"

"I won't direct any suspicion at you."

"What about protection?"

"From whom? Everyone is dead."

Benny shook his head. "Dominic ain't dead. He did this piece of work to me. He can rub me out and nobody'd be wiser."

"I'll guarantee safe passage anywhere you want."

Benny's eyes glinted with cunning. "What about dough?"

"Two hundred dollars, *but*, if you go back on this, if you fail to speak the truth tomorrow at the trial, the deal's off. Understand?"

"Yeah, I got it."

"It is a deal?" Joshua asked.

"Deal."

"Fine. Now, tell me about Tony Garda."

Forty-two

Combating the fervent desire to see Clara proved futile. Joshua stationed himself at the Blake Street Café at a table facing the door, his eager eyes inspecting the women as they entered; so far, none of them had been she.

Clara had remained on his mind since the previous evening, and, sitting there waiting for her uncertain arrival, he realized that he was still enamored with her. Because of the drastic turn of events and the hatred he had recently felt toward her, this frightened him. He admonished himself for not standing up and leaving, but he stayed there nonetheless.

He looked down to stir his coffee and, when he looked back up, was surprised to find Andy standing before his table. Fidgeting with his fedora like a chastised child, Andy could not meet Joshua's eyes. He looked instead at Joshua's tie.

"May I sit down?"

Saying nothing, Joshua scooted out the opposite chair with his foot as an invitation.

"Thanks." Andy sat, adjusting his gaze to his hat. "I followed you from your office. I hope you don't mind."

"Proceed, counselor," Joshua said, with a blasé motion of his hand.

"I owe you an apology. When you asked for my help, I took into confidence a man I trusted, Jack Novak, a private detective. I hired him to retrieve the photographs of the boy. Angelo caught him searching his office. According to Jack, he forced him to conspire against us, and so he betrayed me and you. That's why everything I attempted on your case failed miserably."

Joshua opened his mouth to speak.

With an uplifted hand, Andy said, "Let me finish, because it gets worse. The boy, Erik, escaped the Fratelli Estate the night of the massacre."

"So, he *is* alive," Joshua interrupted.

"Yes, but that's not the bad part. Jack found him and held him up for bid between Angelo and me. I offered the highest dollar. We planned to exchange the money for Erik at his apartment. Angelo and Dominic disrupted these plans. Dominic murdered Jack and took Erik, probably back to the Fratelli Estate." Andy's chest heaved with a sigh as he eyed the blanched knuckles of his fists. "I almost had him, Josh. I was prepared to pay the ransom. I'm sorry. I'm so sorry."

When Andy, who could not bear to look Joshua in the face, did not receive a response, he risked a glance. He found Joshua deep in thought, holding his chin in the palm of his hand with his elbow resting on the table.

"Say something, will you?" Andy begged.

"I wonder what purpose Angelo and Dominic have in mind for Erik."

"That's it?" Andy asked, aghast. "I come to you on my knees and that's all you have to say? Well, it's obvious. They still want to blackmail you. Isn't that what this whole thing is about, or did I miss something?"

Joshua looked at him. "You missed something. Remember Clara? She stole the photographs from the Fratelli mansion and gave them to me. I destroyed them. The negatives, too. So, Angelo hasn't any evidence against me. Erik doesn't know who I am, so it's just Angelo's word against mine, and I hardly think he'd dare to bring it up. The Fratellis have enough problems without this, what's left of them. So, again I ask, why do they want Erik?"

"What *I* want to know is why you're trusting that vamp!" Andy shook his head with disbelief. "How do you know she didn't make copies of those negatives? How do you know she won't blackmail you herself?"

"She won't. She's changed."

"She's poison. She's a woman of easy virtue, and that's putting it nicely."

"Don't say that," Joshua admonished. "She's trying to do what's right. She didn't ask for anything in return. Let's get back to the subject at hand: Erik. What do we know about him? We know he was born and raised on a farm. We know his mother is dead. We know his father and brothers—"

"Ohhh...." Looking ill, Andy grabbed a napkin to wipe his flushed brow.

"Ohhh...what?"

"Neils Warner didn't kill his sons and himself. Jack murdered them. Papa Fratelli paid him five thousand dollars to do it."

"What?" Joshua sat back with surprise. "Why? What would that accomplish?"

"He wanted full guardianship over Erik. That wasn't possible with his father alive. You're right. Erik has some other value. Who else would know? The Elliotts?"

"Possibly. Andy..." Joshua scratched his ear awkwardly, "this may sound like a strange question, but...do you believe in God?"

Andy raised his eyebrows. "I'm Catholic."

"I'll take that as a yes. What about demons and prophets and things like that?"

"What are you talking about?"

"Never mind." Joshua's face cracked into a smile. "Maybe Clara knows more about Erik."

"You're taking an awful chance trusting her."

"Maybe I'm a sucker, but I'm telling you, she's changed."

"She's an actress, and she played you for a dope."

"Then I'm a dope, because I'm falling for her. Again."

Andy's mouth dropped. "Are you dense, man? That's how she hooked you the first time."

"Then I'm dense, because I'm waiting here and I don't even know if she's coming."

"Mind if I wait, too?" Andy asked with an incredulous nod. "I'd like to see this Mary Magdalene."

"Fine, but don't be offended if I tell you to beat it."

"Does this mean you accept my apology?"

Joshua smirked. "If you let me buy you dinner. If we're going to wait, we might as well be on full stomachs."

Joshua motioned for the waiter, but his hand froze in midair; a devious transformation overcame his face. His eyes dazzled with conniving strategy; the smile that turned his mouth into a scheming leer took Andy aback.

"What?" he asked doubtfully.

"How would you like to settle the score with Angelo?"

A smile crossed Andy's face. "I'd like it very much."

"Let's give him some of the grief he's given us. Legally."

Andy's smile increased. "I'm listening."

Clara ventured outside only once that day. It was dark when she entered the Blake Street Café ten minutes after Joshua and Andy departed. She asked if Joshua had left any message for her. The answer was no.

Picking at her meal, she scarcely ate a bite of the food placed before her. Afterward, she wandered the empty streets nearby, not wanting to return to the hotel. She had not slept the previous night after discovering the bloody shard on her pillow. With trembling hands, she had tossed it out the window, watching it shatter on the pavement below. Subsequently, she had requested another room. Now that she had finally left the hotel, she was afraid to return until exhaustion and the growing cold dictated that she must.

Back in the hotel room, she bolted the door, secured it with a chair beneath the knob, and prepared for bed. Fatigued and wanting nothing more than to curl up beneath the covers, she crawled into bed wearing her slip and stockings. She left the overhead light on.

She was not certain whether or not she had fallen asleep, but an urgent sense of dread forced her to lift her head and listen to the sounds of the night with uneasiness. She heard something that sent her heart into a palpitating flutter—a noise like the unlocking of rusty bolts. The sound stopped, then renewed faintly as if the hand creating the noise had hesitated. She fixed her eyes on the door. The knob began to turn. The door opened slowly.

Where's the chair? her mind screamed. It was not in front of the door where she had placed it. It was now in a corner of the room. A hand reached inside the room to press in the light switch. With a horrifying click, the room went dark.

Uttering a cry, she sat up in bed. Most of the room was lost in shadow. The furniture stood solidly black in the light that streamed through the window, casting a rectangular pattern on the floor.

Someone entered. She became dreadfully cold, freezing from her feet upward. In the darkness, she could not tell who it was. He seemed to glide through the obscurity. From the light of the window, certain remembrances seized her. She recognized his silhouette.

"Did you think you could leave me, bella mia?"

"Papa!" she screamed. Her hand flew to her mouth.

"You will never leave me."

He drew near. Terror seized her as Papa Fratelli's blood-soaked body moved through the light from the window, his throat torn open, the gaping wound bleeding freely. He reached for her.

"No! Papa!"

His iron fingers grabbed her shoulders, digging cruelly into her flesh. She saw his unblinking, bloodshot eyes come closer, his pallid face filling her vision before it blurred. In a dizzying whirl, her head fell back. His hands were upon her throat, his breath upon her face. She closed her eyes and fell into blackness.

FORTY-THREE

Joshua could not believe his eyes. Sitting at the prosecution table in the courtroom, he stared unabashed at Carpinelli, who slumped in the chair behind the defense table.

Carpinelli seemed to have aged twenty years overnight. His gray hair was now a shock of white, his gaunt face was yellow, cadaverous, and his nose was clearly broken. A black cane with a silver handle rested on the table. Others in the courtroom stared with the same astonishment, including Louie, who sat gingerly beside him on a plush pillow.

A movement caught Joshua's attention. He turned to see a uniformed deputy sheriff enter the courtroom, bypassing the newspapermen who lingered near the door. Joshua's eyes widened with delight as the young man made his way toward Carpinelli.

"Angelo Carpinelli?" the deputy sheriff asked.

Carpinelli looked up with uncertainty and surprise. "Yes?"

In response, the young man placed a white envelope in Carpinelli's skeletal hand.

"Consider yourself served," Joshua said under his breath.

As the young man left the courtroom, Carpinelli withdrew the document from the envelope to read its contents. With a start, his head jerked directly toward Joshua. In return, Joshua leaned back in his chair, his pleasure undisguised in a mollified smile.

"All rise," the bailiff announced. "Division Six of the Tenth District Court of the City and County of Denver is now in session, the Honorable Clarence Whitfield presiding. Please be seated and come to order. Criminal case 31-1887, the People versus Louie Fratelli."

Emerging from his chambers, Judge Whitfield maneuvered his large frame into his chair with the affectation of complete authority and apathy. Gazing somberly over the wire-framed glasses perched low on his nose, he said, "Prosecution, please proceed."

Joshua stood, holding several papers in his hand. He expected his nervous stomach to be queasy, demanding its medicinal bicarbonate of soda; instead, he felt stalwart, self-assured, composed—strange emotions for him. He set his shoulders back, declaring the unassuming words that would turn the case on its head.

"Your Honor, I'd like to file a motion for the admission of new evidence. I also want to add two names to the witness list."

"Your Honor," Carpinelli said, stuffing the folded document inside the pocket of his suit, "the defense knows nothing of this."

"Who are these witnesses?" Whitfield asked.

"One is an eyewitness to the crime whom I became aware of only yesterday," Joshua said as he distributed the papers to Carpinelli and Whitfield. "The other approached the state, claiming to have evidence of a high official obstructing justice in this case."

"Judge—"

Whitfield cut Carpinelli short with a flick of his thickset hand. Without the slightest emotion, he said, "Due to the sensitive nature of this claim, we'll discuss it in my chambers. Gentlemen?"

Joshua tried to keep himself from smiling as he followed

Whitfield and Carpinelli, who hobbled with the cane, into the chambers beyond the courtroom. Once inside, Joshua closed the door and found himself pinned between two unhappy Fratelli sympathizers.

"What do you think you're doing?" Whitfield demanded.

Joshua looked at him innocently. "The motion is valid to this case. What's more pertinent than an eyewitness? This is the first break the state has had."

"I'm talking about the official obstructing justice, and you know it. What nonsense is this?"

"The witness approached me—"

"Who?"

"Miss Clara Crawford." Joshua only partially suppressed a knowing smile. "Until recently, she worked for Papa Fratelli as, one might say, an envoy to prominent men of the city. She's eager to reveal matters that will greatly benefit the state in the case against Louie Fratelli."

Enjoying the torturous consequence of his words, Joshua watched the blood vanish from Whitfield's face, leaving the skin above his grizzled beard sweaty, blanched. He dangled the judge over the fire awhile longer and then, with the slightest of smiles, said, "Miss Crawford mentioned that she saw you, Judge. She said something about an argument and a head injury. She was concerned that you might be hurt. Shall I tell her you've recovered? Personally, I believe you have a valid case if you wish to press assault charges against her."

Understanding struck Whitfield like a blow between the eyes. He looked at Joshua with a baleful glare. His mouth barely moved as he uttered, "No. Please express to Miss Crawford that it was a simple misunderstanding. I hold no animosity. Regarding the alleged obstruction of justice, I'm not willing to embarrass this court or the suspected official. I see no reason to tie up the proceedings with an investigation I don't believe will affect the outcome of the trial. Later, if need be, the situation may be investigated. That notwithstanding, I expect you to do everything in your power to prevent Miss Crawford from discussing her allegations with anyone. Is that clear?"

"Very clear," Joshua said. His smile grew wider. "Regarding the eyewitness, I trust that he, Benny Rosario, will be allowed to testify, as I'm certain Your Honor desires a fair trial."

"I object," Carpinelli said with an emphatic shake of his white head.

"Overruled," Whitfield rejoined. "Anything further?"

"There most certainly is." Joshua pulled the document from his pocket.

Grabbing it from his hands, Whitfield read it. Without moving his head, he raised his eyes above his glasses to scowl at Joshua. "What's the meaning of this?"

"It has come to the state's attention," Joshua said, "that a young orphan named Erik Warner is in Mr. Carpinelli's custody. Evidence shows he assumed guardianship without bona fide authorization, which raises the concern that Erik is being held against his will. This subpoena is for Mr. Carpinelli to relinquish Erik to the custody of the court until the issue of legal guardianship is settled. There is a local couple who wants to adopt him. They are prepared to press charges if the boy isn't immediately presented as a ward of the court."

"This is outrageous!" Carpinelli yelled.

"Mr. Rosario," Joshua continued with a sideways glance, "is willing to testify that Erik resided at the Fratelli Estate prior to the massacre and that he survived the massacre. I also know that Erik was subsequently in the care of a private detective, Mr. Jack Novak, who was, shall we say, *encouraged* by Dominic Fratelli and Mr. Carpinelli to entrust Erik to their safekeeping. While Mr. Novak can't testify to this, I'm sure the police will find sufficient evidence to prove it once they're pointed in the right direction."

"That won't be necessary." Whitfield folded the document and tapped it with annoyance against his thigh. "Will all charges be dropped if this boy is transferred into the court's custody?"

"Yes, Your Honor."

"Then have the adoption papers on my desk tomorrow morning. I will ensure that they're processed quickly. Any arguments, Mr. Carpinelli?"

"Uh...ah..." Carpinelli uttered. "This isn't something I can easily—"

"Any arguments, Mr. Carpinelli?"

The knobby Adam's apple in Carpinelli's throat rose and fell as he swallowed. "I'll—I'll need at least a week to consider the state of this affair."

Whitfield glared at him. "I don't see that there's anything to be considered. The boy *will* be relinquished into the court's custody within twenty-four hours."

With his head bowed and his hands clenched together, Carpinelli looked as though he could not trust his voice. He simply closed his eyes and nodded.

Whitfield restored his rancorous glare to Joshua. "Any more surprises?"

Joshua did not attempt to hold back his grin. "No. I'm quite finished."

FORTY-FOUR

"The state calls Benny Rosario to the stand," Joshua announced.

All heads in the courtroom turned to watch as a policeman pushed Benny up the aisle in a wheelchair. Dressed in a wrinkled black suit, his right arm in a sling, the turban-like headdress still encasing his head, Benny regarded the crowd with a battered frown, his dark eyes searching their faces for anyone familiar. When he passed Joan, he winked. She met his gaze solidly and tightened her squeeze on Edmund and Edith's hands, who sat on either side of her.

While rolling by the defense table, Benny scrutinized Carpinelli, who did not bother to look up, keeping his attention on the paperwork before him. Louie scooted forward slightly on his pillow, enough to cast a warning glare at Benny, who accepted the threat with no emotion.

Joshua watched him approach with feelings of expectant victory. He risked a look at Judge Whitfield, perched high on his bench, and met his marbleized stare. Joshua quickly looked back at Benny.

Unable to take the stand, Benny was wheeled around and placed before it to face the crowd. The policeman who had maneuvered the wheelchair leaned against the wall as the bailiff led Benny through the oath. Meanwhile, Joshua stood. He paced methodically before the jury, both hands behind his back, the fingers of one tapping the palm of the other. He knew what questions to ask Benny, but he had to be wary about how he posed them to avoid Carpinelli's objections. He began with a simple one.

"Would you tell the court your name, please?"

Lifting his chin with pride, Benny announced loudly, "Benny Rosario."

"Mr. Rosario, explain your relationship with the defendant."

Joshua turned to see Louie's upper lip twitch. He lacked the swaggering assurance of previous trial days as he whispered a concern in Carpinelli's ear. Carpinelli shook his head in response. A sudden onslaught of unnerving twitches assailed Louie's lip.

"I worked for his grandfather, Papa Fratelli," Benny said. "Me and Louie sometimes did jobs together."

"By saying Papa Fratelli, do you mean Antonio Fratelli, the known kingpin of the Fratelli Mafia family?" Joshua asked.

"Yeah. Everybody called him Papa."

"What kind of jobs did you do together?"

"We'd rough people up, tighten the screws on them that owed Papa dough, things like that."

"Did a man named Tony Garda also work for Papa Fratelli?"

"I object," Carpinelli said. While his protest stopped the exchange of words, his movement to push himself to his feet was sluggish. "This line of questioning is irrelevant."

Joshua took one step toward the bench. "I will show the relevancy quickly."

Whitfield cast him a despondent look. "Objection overruled. The witness may answer."

"Yeah, Tony worked for Papa," Benny answered.

"And did you know him personally?"

"Yeah. Me and Tony was pals, till he meets up with this preacher and finds religion. I didn't go for the idea. We quit hanging together."

"Do you know who the preacher was?"

"Sure. The guy Louie got pinched for whacking."

Joshua frowned. "You mean Fred MacDonald?"

Benny shrugged indifferently. "Yeah. Sure."

Joshua's frown deepened. "Please answer yes or no."

"Yes."

"Mr. Rosario, what became of Tony Garda?"

"Ha!" Benny laughed, bounding slightly in the wheelchair. "What became of him? He became a stiff! That's what became of him!"

Nodding, grinning, Benny looked around the courtroom, expecting the crowd to join him in his joke. No one laughed. Joshua clenched his jaw to keep his anger down.

"Do you mean Tony died?"

"Yeah. The cops used him for target practice."

"I'll take that to mean the police shot him to death." Joshua rubbed the back of his neck with his hand, ruefully avoiding stares from Whitfield and Carpinelli. "Please explain the circumstances surrounding the shooting."

"Objection." Carpinelli rose slightly from his chair. "Unless the witness was at the scene of the shooting, he isn't qualified to answer the question."

"Objection sustained," Whitfield said, pinching his lips together with gratification.

Joshua ignored their slight triumph and continued. "Mr. Rosario, do you know whether Tony was trying to leave the Fratelli family?"

Benny nodded. "He wanted to be one of them Holy Rollers, but nobody dusts off the mob. I told him so."

"Is leaving the mob considered a betrayal? Something worthy of death?"

"Oh, yeah, that and he lifted something from Papa."

"What did he steal?" Joshua asked.

"A book. I saw it. It was old. I figured he could get a few bucks for it, but not enough to risk his neck over. I told him so."

"Is that what he intended—to sell the book for profit?"

"No. He went screwy over some stuff he says he found in the Fratelli mansion. He pocketed the book 'cause he could stash it easy. He wanted to show it to the preacher."

"Did he say why?"

"Yeah. Before Tony found religion, he was heavy in the occult. We both was. We'd go to séances and things like that together. It was a lark for me, but Tony was deep into it. When he found these things in the mansion, he spooked and beat it like he was on the lam, so I tracked him down and asked him what gave. He made me swear not to tell, then said he stole the book to give to the preacher." Benny gave a short laugh, shaking his head. "He thought something evil's going on in the Fratelli mansion, something like devil worship. I told him he's off his track, that he'd better put it back. He said no. Said he was gonna blow after he saw the preacher."

"And did he give it to the preacher?" Joshua asked.

"Far as I know."

"Do you remember when this was?"

"Last November, I think. I felt lousy about it, but I played the stoolie and told Papa. Tony's my pal, but I got ambitions, see? Papa was real interested. Gave me a stack of C notes. Told me to burn Tony and the preacher. What's more, he told Louie to do it with me."

A volley of gratifying gasps from the crowd contended with the nerve-racking screech of Carpinelli's chair as he pushed it back and strove to come to his feet.

"Objection!" he bellowed over the crowd's murmurings.

"For what reason?" Joshua demanded, turning to look at him.

Whitfield slammed the gavel down several times, his expression sour with impatience. When the room quieted, he glared at Carpinelli. "Unless you can offer one, I see no reason for the objection. Overruled."

Shaking his head, Carpinelli reached behind him to find the chair with a trembling hand. He sank into it as though he might drop.

"Thank you, Judge," Joshua said. "Please continue, Mr. Rosario."

Benny took a deep breath. "Anyway, Papa gave me the skinny. I was supposed to do the preacher and Louie was supposed to do Tony, but it didn't go that way. We lost track of Tony. He beat town. Wasn't till the preacher died that Papa tracked him down. Knowing Louie was gonna get marked for the preacher's murder, Papa set up a meeting between Louie and Tony at a restaurant to make Tony the fall guy."

"Objection. This testimony is outside the knowledge of the witness," Carpinelli said, not bothering to stand this time.

Joshua looked at Carpinelli again. "Unless you were there when Papa Fratelli gave the order, how do you know it's outside his knowledge?"

Whitfield frowned. "Point taken. Shall we continue with this objection?"

Carpinelli's face turned red hot. He shook his head. "I withdraw the objection."

"So, anyway," Benny continued, rolling his eyes at the interruption, "Papa told Louie to take Tony to the restaurant. The cops was waiting inside to pop him 'cause nobody questions it when cops kill a gangster. It was a walk in the park."

Joshua adjusted his suit jacket and straightened his spine. "Mr. Rosario," he said, "tell the court where you were on November 26, 1931."

"Me and Louie was at a party. I remember, 'cause it was Thanksgiving, and Papa gave the boys a swell dinner."

"Tell the court what happened that night."

Nodding, Benny settled himself in his wheelchair. "We was at this party, like I said. Plenty of skirts and booze. I didn't want to leave, but Louie struck out with a certain dame and wanted to breeze. We took my car."

Glancing at a piece of paper on the prosecution table, Joshua asked, "What is the make and model of your car?"

"It's a Studebaker. I bought it new in 1928."

Joshua smiled and glanced at Joan. "Let the record show that Mrs. MacDonald claimed the vehicle the perpetrators hit them with was a 1928 Studebaker."

Joan smiled slightly. Tears glistened in her eyes.

"Mr. Rosario," Joshua looked back at Benny, "what time did you leave the party?"

"Somewhere 'round midnight. We'd tipped a few and I was ossified. I wasn't driving so good, and I hit this car crossing the street."

"Where were you?"

"Downtown. I was hot about my car, so we crawled out to give this mug a thrashing. I went to grab the dame, but the door was locked."

Extending his arm by invitation into the crowd, Joshua asked, "Is that woman in the courtroom this morning?"

"Right there." Benny pointed at Joan, making her gaze widen with alarm. "The swell-looking blonde with the nice gams."

"What happened after that?" Joshua asked.

"Louie said he knew the guy behind the wheel, thought it was the preacher, the one Papa put the curse on."

"Reverend Fred MacDonald?"

"Yeah."

"Did you recognize him?"

Benny nodded. "Yeah. We knew who he was 'cause we planned to burn him. So, Louie wanted to see his driver's license, to make sure, I guess. When he got it, he went to the headlights to read it and the car started backing up. So, Louie jumped on it and threw his fist through the window. The car stopped and him and the preacher started fighting. Then the dame jumped out. I grabbed her, see, to shut her up 'cause she was screaming, and I threw her in the back of my car, but she got out on the other side. Next thing I knew, Louie'd shot the preacher. He always was a crack shot. After that, we beat it to the Fratelli Estate and laid low."

Joshua glanced at Louie and Carpinelli. Both sat motionless with blank expressions.

"What gun did Mr. Fratelli use to kill Reverend MacDonald?" he asked.

"He used my gun, a .45 semiauto. He took it off the front seat."

"Why didn't he use his own gun?"

Benny smirked and rolled his eyes. "He gave it to some pro skirt 'cause he forgot to bring dough to pay her with."

Turning back to the prosecution table, Joshua picked up the Bible and handed it to Benny. "I give you People's Exhibit 16. Do you recognize this Bible?"

Taking it in one hand, Benny looked the book over. "Yeah, I found it in my car."

"Where exactly in your car?"

"In the backseat."

"Please open the cover to the presentment page and read what it says."

Placing it on his lap, Benny opened it and began to read it to himself.

"Out loud, if you please," Joshua requested.

"This Holy Bible Pre...sented to the Rev...er...end Fred MacDonald, Or...Ord..."

"Ordained," Joshua suggested with the cock of his eyebrow.

"...Ordained on this Ninth Day of May in the Year of Our Lord Nineteen Hundred and Twenty-nine in the Service of Our Lord and Sav...ior Jesus Christ."

A low moan came from the crowd. Joan lowered her head on her mother's shoulder to cry. Louie leaned into the table to stare at the whitened knuckles of his folded hands.

"Mr. Rosario, how did this Bible get into the backseat of your car?" Joshua asked.

"The preacher's dame must've dropped it when I threw her in. That's the only thing I can think of. I never would've taken it."

"Thank you," Joshua said with a slight smile. Looking at Carpinelli, he said brazenly, "Your witness."

Carpinelli stood, pressing his weight on the cane. With his shoulders drooping forward, he already looked defeated. When he spoke, his voice cracked. He stopped, cleared his throat, and tried again.

"Mr. Rosario, are you currently employed?"

"No." Benny leaned back in the wheelchair and crossed his left ankle over his right knee. He looked bored. "My boss croaked three days ago."

"And what did you do for Papa Fratelli?"

"What are you, a chump?" He threw up his good hand in frustration, gesturing toward Joshua. "I went over that with him. I was one of Papa's boys, his muscle, his hired gun, whatever you want to call it."

"Did you ever lie for him?"

Benny leaned forward and pointed his finger at Carpinelli. "Yeah, but so have yo—"

"Just yes or no, Mr. Rosario. Just yes or no."

"Uh...yeah."

"Have you ever lied to the police?"

Adjusting himself uneasily, Benny said, "Why you asking this?"

"Have you ever lied to the police, Mr. Rosario?"

"I guess so."

"Have you ever been in trouble with the law?"

"Why?" Benny demanded defensively, leaning forward in the wheelchair.

"The witness will answer the question," Whitfield growled from the bench.

Benny looked up, saw Whitfield's hostile frown, sighed, and answered unhappily, "Yeah."

"Do you have a police record?" Carpinelli asked.

"Who doesn't in this town?"

"Never mind the rest of this town," Carpinelli said as he retrieved a paper from the defense table. "Shall I advise the court as to what is on yours? One count of aggravated assault and one count of extortion, both felonies, not to mention numerous misdemeanors. Were you convicted of those felony charges?"

A snarl twisted the corner of Benny's swollen lip. "You ought to know. You defended me."

This time the crowd laughed, including Joshua. It rippled through the courtroom, visibly jangling Carpinelli's nerves. Unable to suppress his apparent humiliation, he pulled a handkerchief from his pocket and dabbed his face while Whitfield used the gavel to bring order back.

"You've been convicted of two felonies," Carpinelli said at

length. "Do you know what the penalty is if you're convicted of a third?"

Joshua came to his feet. "Objection. The witness isn't an attorney. He isn't an expert in the law."

"Objection sustained," Whitfield said.

"I'll rephrase," Carpinelli said. "Are you being charged with another felony?"

Benny's eyes darted at Joshua. "I was gonna be. The DA said if I testified, he'd drop it."

Carpinelli uttered a short, disdainful grunt. "How opportune. You have two felonies. If you're convicted of a third, you'll spend the rest of your life in jail."

Joshua stood again, raising his hand in appeal. "Objection. Is there a question here?"

"Sustained," Whitfield said. "Mr. Carpinelli, kindly address the witness with questions."

"Yes, Your Honor." Carpinelli stared at Benny with his dark, stern eyes sheltered beneath his brooding eyebrows. "Are you testifying against my client so that Mr. Parnell will drop the third felony charge against you?"

Benny looked down at the sling on his arm.

"Answer the question."

"If you say so," Benny muttered.

"A yes or no will do."

"Yeah," Benny admitted unwillingly.

"Are you certain you're not saying what the state desires to hear to avoid a life sentence?"

"I ain't lying, if that's what you mean," Benny shot back.

"Of course. You never lie. Isn't that true?"

"Your Honor," Joshua demanded, "is the defense suggesting the state suborned this witness to commit perjury?"

"I withdraw the question." With a shake of his head, Carpinelli said, "You are indeed a lucky man, Mr. Rosario." He returned to his chair, almost falling into it from exhaustion.

Whitfield saw this. He looked at Joshua and asked, "Does the state have anything further?"

"No, Your Honor, the prosecution rests."

"Then we'll break for a short recess. I think it will do everyone good. The defense may commence when we return."

Whitfield lifted the gavel. Before he could bring it down, Carpinelli lifted one of his feeble, pale hands for notice.

"Your Honor, the defense rests, as well."

A heavy silence hung over the court while every stunned eye turned upon him. Whitfield laid the gavel down quietly.

"I hope I heard you incorrectly. Am I to understand you're not going to argue the defendant's case?"

"It is the defense's belief that the state has failed to support their case beyond a reasonable doubt," Carpinelli explained with a tired sigh. He blinked his eyes numerous times. "The state's witness openly admitted having lied to the police in the past. His willingness to testify to avoid prosecution solidifies this belief. If one were to discount Mr. Rosario's questionable testimony, one would find that the state falls short of establishing guilt beyond a reasonable doubt. As such, it isn't necessary to proceed with the defense's case."

Whitfield's face turned red. "This is America, Mr. Carpinelli. Every defendant has the right to a fair trial. I strongly suggest you produce your witnesses. You have thirty minutes."

Carpinelli stood, a task that took great effort. "Sidebar, Your Honor?"

Whitfield nodded as Carpinelli and Joshua approached the bench.

"You could give me thirty days and these witnesses would not appear," Carpinelli said softly so the jury would not hear him. "They were among the victims at the Fratelli massacre. They're dead. Though we lost the eyewitness testimony that

Mr. Fratelli was miles away from the murder scene, he steadfastly maintains that he is innocent."

"Produce something," Whitfield said with a sharp click of his tongue. "I won't allow a defendant on trial for murder to receive an inadequate defense."

"I'm giving my client the best defense he can receive. If you demand it, I request that the depositions and interrogatories of the witnesses be read into evidence."

"Motion denied."

"As a rule of law," Carpinelli said, "if a witness is unable to appear to testify, his statement can be read into record."

"Only when the statement was given under oath," Joshua interjected quickly, "and the state has had a chance to cross-examine him. That isn't the case here."

"That's why I denied the motion," Whitfield said.

"Then I move the court to declare a mistrial on the basis that Mr. Fratelli cannot receive a fair trial," Carpinelli said.

"Justice delayed," Joshua said quietly, "is justice denied."

A hush hung over the courtroom. Whitfield glanced at Joshua, who returned the look without flinching. The stillness lingered until the newspapermen began to murmur among themselves.

Quickly, as if he feared he might change his mind, Whitfield said, "I will not declare a mistrial. All opportunities were accorded the defendant, and justice will not be delayed."

Louder, so that all could hear, he announced, "Mr. Carpinelli, if you have nothing to add on the defendant's behalf, closing arguments will begin after a short break. The jury will then be sequestered until arriving at a decision. Court adjourned."

He picked up the gavel and slammed it down.

Immediately following the closing arguments, Joshua drove to the Blake Street Café, hoping to find Clara there. He felt elated and yearned to share the exciting turn of events with her. He waited two hours and finally ate alone. When he left, he asked the manager to give Clara a message to call him. He went home disappointed. He dreaded another night alone in his empty house.

FORTY-FIVE

"Where's that lousy nurse?" Benny grumbled. "I'm hungry."

Reclining in his hospital bed, Benny looked around for something he could throw at the closed door—something breakable that would attract attention. He had lain in bed for several hours without anyone coming to check on him. At first, he did not mind, because he was able to take a nap. Now, as the sun was setting behind the closed blinds, shadowing the room with the dusky gloom of evening, he minded. He wanted the light on. He wanted dinner. He looked down at the handcuff that secured his good arm to the bed rail and thought of the policemen stationed outside his door.

"Yo! Coppers! How about shedding some light on this joint!"

No one responded. He cursed and lay back against the pillows, uttering his annoyance with an exasperated grunt. Turning his head toward the door, he saw his wallet lying on the bedside tray, cash bulging beneath its worn stitching.

He was two hundred dollars richer—thanks to Joshua Parnell—and, for the first time in his life, he was better off than Dominic. The infamous Fratelli family was a memory. Louie would probably hang, leaving Dominic alone to gather the scrambled pieces of his life. Benny, however, saw light on the horizon. After a six-month stretch in jail, he would move to a new city, link up with another racket, maybe even track down the Pompliano gang.

He glared at the door again. After shouting angry threats at those he believed purposely ignored him, it occurred to him that he could not hear a sound beyond the door. No nurses or doctors walked the hallway. No visitors sought patients' rooms. The cops did not banter between themselves. The hospital was as silent as the morgue below.

He tried one last time. "Nurse! Where's my dinner?"

"A last meal? Is that what you want?"

Benny's heart leaped in his chest. His eyes darted from side to side. The voice came from somewhere in the shadows.

"Did you think it would be easy, Benny? That you could testify against a member of the family without paying the price? You vowed your loyalty to the Fratelli family. You have broken the *omertà*."

He discerned a dark silhouette in a corner of the room. He pulled himself up in bed.

"That you, Dom? How'd you get in here? Turn on the light so I can see you."

Dominic's eyes opened. The glow from the two bloodred pools was sufficient to cast a crimson radiance upon the room. Benny's mouth dropped. It was Dominic's body, handsome face, and tailored clothes; it was not his eyes.

"Wh-what's wrong with your eyes?" Benny sputtered. "That some kind of gag?"

Dominic approached the bed. He reached inside his suit, drawing his gun.

"No! Wait!"

Wrenching his arm from the sling with a shout of pain, Benny grabbed his wallet and threw it at Dominic. A plume of cash flew through the air.

"Here! Take it! It's yours!"

"I do not want your money," Dominic said, stepping on the bills that lay scattered on the floor.

He aimed the gun at Benny's head. Benny's eyes grew wild. He raised his arms in complete surrender.

"You got me all wrong, Dom! I didn't want to squeal on Louie! I didn't have no choice! The DA was gonna finger me for the massacre! Come on! I'm begging you here! What do you want from me?"

"Your soul," Dominic said. "You are unfinished business. You betrayed the family. You murdered your own don."

"Yeah!" Benny pointed a trembling finger at him. "I killed you! Why ain't you dead?"

"You murdered Dominic Fratelli." He jabbed the gun barrel between Benny's bulging eyes. "I am not Dominic Fratelli."

In disbelief, Benny watched Dominic's appearance change. His body increased in stature and width to that of a giant. His forehead dipped into a point above his eyebrows as his nostrils stretched gruesomely upward. His bloodred eyes became catlike slits, grimly illuminating his cadaverous gray flesh.

"What are you?" Benny shouted.

"Remember the prophet's vision?" the demon hissed. "He foresaw your doom. What you loathe most awaits you. Prepare to meet it."

To his horror, Benny watched an abyss open before him in the demon's glowing eyes. He saw eternity. He pinched his eyes shut. The gun exploded. The sound thundered through his head as through an endless cavern, echoing off solid walls of rock.

When Benny opened his eyes, he lay crumpled in a subterranean pit. Struggling against the narrow walls of the hole, he pushed himself first to his knees and then to his feet. Looking up through the darkness, he found that the mouth of the pit opened over an insurmountable distance of smooth stones. Beyond it, he saw nothing, yet he clearly heard the cries of the dead.

Tremendous heat radiated from fiery masses glowing on the walls. An evil stench made it impossible to breathe without choking. As he searched frantically for some method of escape, he heard an ominous hissing noise. He snapped his head back and threw up his arms. A waterfall of black shadows plummeted toward him. It was a frenzy of cats, their mouths open in ravenous fervor, their razor-sharp claws catching on his naked body.

Through the torrent, he seized them by their matted fur and ripped them off, but the level kept rising and the cats returned to sink their terrible claws and fangs into his bleeding body. In pain and in horror, he screamed until his cries became hollow winds of air escaping his throat through his wide-open mouth.

Near the mouth of the pit, a creeping mass of gnarled flesh dragged a heavy covering behind its withered form. It pulled the covering into place, securing Benny's personal hell in the midst of eternity.

"Josh? Can you hear me? It's me. Clara."

With the earpiece pressed to her ear, Clara stretched on tiptoe to reach the mouthpiece of the crank telephone bolted to the wall. She threw a nervous glance around the dismally lit hotel lobby. Not a soul lingered nearby—not even the manager—yet she sensed a myriad of eyes upon her, peering furtively from the garish paisley swirls in the wallpaper. The green velveteen sofa and chairs seemed crouched in readiness, their clawed feet poised to pounce. A brooding grandfather clock, stained black, stood guard by the front desk, its swinging pendulum marking the seconds of her life with solemnity.

"I'm so glad you called," Joshua said through the earpiece. "I've been worried about you."

She strained her neck to speak into the mouthpiece and to keep watch on the lobby at the same time, afraid that someone might sneak up from behind if she looked away.

"I have to see you, Josh. I have to see you now."

"What's wrong?" The relief in his voice turned abruptly into concern.

"Do you..." she hesitated, "do you believe in ghosts?"

"What? No. Of course not. What's this about?"

"If there's no such thing as ghosts...I think I'm going—Papa Fratelli came to my room last night. He was dead. He grabbed me. He said I could never leave him. Oh, Josh, it was awful. He was dead and he grabbed me."

There was silence on the line. A creaking of the hardwood floors made her shudder with an involuntary gasp. She threw a terrified glance over her shoulder.

"Josh? Are you there? Please be there."

"Clara," he said slowly, "tell me where you are and I'll pick you up. Okay?"

"Before he came, I blocked the door with a chair. When he came in, it wasn't there. That's when he grabbed me. I fainted. When I woke up, the chair was under the door again. I don't understand it. It doesn't make sense." She knew she was babbling. She ran her fingers through her hair in hopes of regaining control.

"It was just a bad dream. Where are you?"

"No!" she nearly screamed. "It wasn't a dream! He grabbed me! I have bruises where he grabbed me! And—and the night before, he was there, too. He—he—the glass I stabbed him with, it was in my room. He put it on my pillow. It was bloody."

Joshua was silent.

"Don't you understand? I stabbed him in the throat with a piece of glass, and he put it in my room!"

"Tell me where you are, Clara. Just tell me where you are."

"No, I can't wait. I've got to get out. Meet me at the Blake Street Café."

"No." His voice grew stern. "It's dark and I don't want you on the streets alone. Tell me where you are. I'll be right there."

"He's coming for me, Josh. I know it."

The grandfather clock struck the half hour in a deep, pealing tone. The resounding clang made her jump. It forced a shriek from her mouth.

"Clara!" Joshua yelled.

She spun around and ripped the earpiece from the telephone in one startled movement. No one was there. The hotel was quiet. No one stood at the front desk. No one entered the lobby. Feeling as though some concealed hand was prepared to grab her if she remained, she dropped the earpiece and ran upstairs to her room.

Hurriedly donning her hat and coat, she quickly glanced at the mirror. The harried, wild gleam of her reflection startled her. Shadows lined the hollows of her cheeks, enhancing the dark circles below her eyes. She lacked all color. The hands that buttoned her coat looked almost skeletal.

Turning from her image with dismay, she grabbed her packed suitcase and opened the door of her room. She glanced into the hallway. Empty. Not wishing to disturb the silence, she stepped out, closed the door, and walked quietly toward the staircase. The dusky yellow lights dangling above, swathed in dust, created shadows that unnerved her. She expected every door she passed to burst open, yet all remained staunchly closed. An eerie sensation crept up her neck.

Upon reaching the staircase, she took one step down and froze. A creak sounded from the foot of the staircase, an elongated groan of dry wood yielding to a weight. She stared down the empty staircase. Another creak, then another. The complaining squeaks grew closer, louder, like the footsteps of someone ascending. She squinted into the gloom. She saw no one. Returning the way she came, she walked quickly until she was almost running. The ghostly ascent continued. She heard it over the steps of her feet and the pounding of her heart.

When she reached the end of the hallway, the lights flickered. She stopped with the awful impression that she was not alone. Another stair creaked behind her. Slowly, she turned around. Near the top of the staircase, the faint silhouette of a man materialized, emerging from the menacing haze of shadows that stirred around him. She took an uncertain step back as he gained the top stair and moved into the dim light.

"Bella mia...I have come for you."

She cried out with a startled sob. The suitcase slipped from her fingers. Spinning around, she ran down the other hall. There was no sound of pursuing feet, yet she knew Papa Fratelli was behind her, gaining on her. Throwing a glance over her shoulder, she missed her aim and ran directly into the wall, pushed herself away from it, and stumbled forward.

"There is nowhere you can hide."

She heard a series of loud pops, followed by the shattering of thin glass. One by one, the light bulbs were bursting. In quick succession, they exploded in the lobby, up the staircase, and down the length of the hall after her. She screamed as they erupted above her, showering her with hot glass.

The hotel was plunged into darkness. Still she ran, her hands guiding her, feeling her way along the wall until it dropped into an opening. She hurried into it. With her arms outstretched, not knowing what was ahead, she careened straight into a wall. The force sent her reeling to the floor. It was a dead end. She was trapped.

Crawling to the wall, she crouched in the corner, shaking violently. With every passing second, she expected him to appear or to feel his lurid hands on her. She felt exposed, defenseless. More than once, she groped the space around her to see if he stood there, but she felt nothing. Her chest tightened with pain and she realized that she was holding her breath. Slowly, she exhaled.

A daunting amount of time passed. She could barely keep herself from screaming, from dashing back down the hall to end the ordeal, give up, and let him have her. Death was better than living this terror, and yet Papa Fratelli never appeared. Doubts haunted her mind. She wondered if it had been her imagination. Instead of relieving her, this thought tormented her even more. If it was all her imagination—the bloody shard, the moved chair, his vicious hands inflicting bruises on her body—then she was truly going insane.

Trembling, she came to her feet. With careful steps, she moved away from the wall, her hands out before her with the horrible expectation of touching him, and tiptoed forward until she felt the wall. Pressing her back against it, she edged toward the first hallway, flinching at the betraying sound of glass crunching beneath her feet.

Turning the corner at last, she saw a bluish glow illuminating the stairs at the end of the hallway. Papa Fratelli was not there. A tremulous sob of relief issued from her chest. She rushed toward the light, reached the staircase, and sprinted down the stairs. She was halfway down when fierce footsteps closed in behind her. She screamed as powerful hands lunged from the darkness. They caught her, brought her to a violent halt, and spun her harshly around.

The glow from the streetlights cast a blue haze through the lobby windows. In contrast, the crimson pools of Papa Fratelli's eyes lit the gore of his mutilated throat below his ghoulish face. He drew her ruthlessly against his chest, his lips drawn back over his teeth.

"I have chosen you, bella mia...."

"No! You're dead!" She hammered her fists against him in a frenzy of terror. "You're dead!"

His fingers gouged into her arms. He lifted her from the floor. *"You shall be my bride...."*

"No, no, no," she whimpered. His voice was hypnotic. She felt her body grow limp as her struggles subsided.

"You shall give me two sons...."

Her vision blurred. Unable to resist, she hung like a rag doll in his hands, her eyes gazing blankly into his mesmerizing pools of lava. Then his dead lips were upon hers, pressing her lips painfully against her teeth. A sickening curtain of blackness swept over her.

"Clara. Can you hear me?"

A gentle hand stroked the hair from her face. An embracing arm kept her limp body from tumbling down the stairs. When she opened her eyes, the face that filled her vision was not Papa Fratelli's.

"It's okay. I'm here."

Gazing into his warm, brown eyes, she dug her nails into his arms lest he disappear.

"Dominic!" She threw herself against his chest. "You're alive! You're alive!"

"I've looked everywhere for you," he whispered, his arms wrapping tenderly around her. "You shouldn't have left the Fratelli Estate."

"I thought you were dead! Oh, Dom! Get me out of here! Take me away!"

"Anything you want, baby."

He cradled her in his arms. She clung to his neck, weeping as he descended the staircase. Nestling her face into his shoulder, she inhaled the wonderful smell of his cologne.

"I'll take you home," he said, his voice gentle, soothing. "Nothing will separate us again."

Joshua waited at the Blake Street Café for one nerve-racking hour, tormenting himself with worry and torn between wanting to search for Clara and not wanting to leave in case she arrived. The scream she had uttered in his ear before the telephone went dead still rang in his memory.

Finally, tossing a dime on the table for the coffee he did not drink, he left a message with the manager for Clara to take a taxi to his house and wait there. Then, he hurried to his car. He searched every street within a six-block radius of the café. He never found her.

Forty-six

Justice delayed is justice denied. Joshua pondered these words while sitting behind the defense table, waiting for the jury to return to the courtroom.

After closing arguments the previous day, they had been sequestered, fed, and tucked warmly into their hotel rooms. The following morning, they had wasted no time deliberating Louie's fate: one hour—enough time to enjoy breakfast at the city's expense. Apparently, their minds had long been decided.

When did they decide? Joshua wondered. *Before Benny's testimony, or afterward? Were they bought off? Does Papa Fratelli still wield influence from the grave?*

He concealed his own guilt, but he secretly labored beneath the weight of his own culpability, which had caused such profound injustice to so many people—primarily Luke, whose death he had almost caused, whose life he had tossed into ruin. His actions and personal failings had delayed justice—almost denied justice—yet he knew that whatever the verdict, in the end, in the last fading seconds of the eleventh hour, he ultimately had done all he could do to give Fred MacDonald justice.

In that knowledge, he found a measure of...what? Not peace. He felt no peace; he was racked with guilt. Not freedom; he was chained to a secret that would destroy his career and put him in jail. Not even solace; he once thought himself a man of character but now found himself a coward.

Blessed is he whose transgression is forgiven, whose sin is covered.

The memory of those words unleashed a wave of gooseflesh on his arms. He had heard those words before. Where?

Turning slowly in his chair, he looked at Edmund Elliott, who sat in the bench directly behind him. Smiling cordially at Joan and Edith, Joshua beckoned Edmund forward with a wave of his fingers.

"Reverend," he whispered, "later, may I speak with you privately? You said something to me once that I would like to know more about."

"Of course," Edmund nodded, a slight but knowing smile crossing his face.

Joshua turned back around with the feeling that Edmund had already guessed the topic. *Am I that transparent?*

"Gentlemen of the jury, have you agreed upon a verdict?"

Joshua looked up with a start. He had been so lost in thought that he had missed the jury's entrance. He now followed Whitfield's somber gaze as the judge addressed the twelve men sitting in the jury box. The crowd followed suit, their heads turning as one, their eyes searching the jurors' faces for some inkling of the decision.

"We have, Your Honor."

All heads turned toward the foreman, a stout, balding businessman. He stood, cleared his throat, and straightened his brown suit—nervous reactions to the crowd's rapt attention. His trembling hand passed a slip of paper to the bailiff, who, in turn, handed it to Whitfield. Without emotion, Whitfield read it to himself, folded the paper, and regarded the defense.

"The defendant will rise."

Carpinelli helped Louie out of his cushioned chair. Neither showed any emotion. Joshua turned to give Joan an encouraging pat on the arm. She smiled timidly and squeezed the hands of her parents, who sat on either side of her. Several newspapermen hovered near the door, their pencils poised over their writing tablets, their feet ready to run.

"What say you?" Whitfield asked.

The crowd leaned forward in their seats. With a side-glance at Louie, the foreman cleared his throat again. His voice quavered.

"We, the jury, find the defendant, Louie Fratelli, *guilty* of murder in the first degree."

A roar of glad exclamations rose in the courtroom, sending a delighted ripple of gooseflesh down Joshua's arms. Smiling, he spun around to hug Joan, Edmund, and Edith, each thanking him and praising God, their eyes moist with tears. Joshua then looked at Carpinelli, who stared gravely at Whitfield. Louie's face was drawn and pale. He almost sank into the chair. Carpinelli stopped him with a hand on his arm.

"Gentlemen of the jury," Whitfield asked when the laudatory moment subsided, "what penalty do you affix?"

"Your Honor," the foreman proclaimed, his voice louder, his confidence boosted by the crowd's approval, "we affix the penalty of *death*."

The press dashed from the courtroom in a race to the telephones, causing such an uproar that Whitfield used the gavel to bring back order. At length, he looked at Louie and Carpinelli intermittently, a deep sigh resounding from his chest.

"Mr. Fratelli," he said regretfully, "the jury has determined you will pay with your life for the crime of willfully murdering Reverend Fred MacDonald. I, therefore, deliver you to the custody of the sheriff of the city and county of Denver. Within twenty-four hours, you will be delivered into the custody of the warden of the state penitentiary, who will keep you in solitary confinement until such day and hour when you will be taken to the place of execution. There you will hang by the neck until you are dead."

Louie wilted into his chair. Carpinelli crumpled beside him. Whitfield's solemn gaze fell on Joshua as he slammed down the gavel.

"Court dismissed."

Immediately following the trial, after the police had escorted Louie away, Carpinelli retreated to his office. He spoke to no one. Once there, he locked himself in without turning on the lights, pulled the window blinds down, and sat behind his paper-strewn mahogany desk. Unlocking it with a small skeleton key, he pulled opened the top drawer. There a revolver lay, waiting.

It felt cold and awkward in his hand. He turned it over gingerly, testing its weight, his finger lightly touching the trigger. The afternoon sun, leaking through the blinds, glinted off the black steel. This weapon, a gift from Papa Fratelli, had ushered many into the hereafter. Now it would escort him into eternity, but it would not escort him from judgment.

He was doomed. There was no way to elude judgment in this life—or in the next. He also knew the demon would not relinquish Luke to the custody of the court. He had promised to sacrifice the boy, but that was when the demon had threatened his life. Now, in the pensive quietude of his office, he thought it better to end his life before he was forced to commit the young prophet's murder. At least then, when he passed into eternity, the boy's blood would not be on his hands. He lifted the gun to his head. Its cold barrel had scarcely touched his temple when he heard a strange voice.

"Regions of sorrow, doleful shades, where peace and rest can never dwell, hope never comes that comes to all, but torture without end...."

Carpinelli's head jerked up with fear. In Dominic's body,

dressed in a tailored dark blue suit, the demon leaned nonchalantly against the wall, its hands in its pant pockets, a smug smile on its face.

"A fiery deluge, fed with ever-burning sulfur unconsumed. Such place Eternal Justice had prepared for those rebellious, here their prison ordained in utter darkness, and their portion set as far removed from God and light of heaven...."

"I wouldn't be so arrogant if I were you," Carpinelli said, laying the gun on his desk mournfully. "You're describing your own eternity."

"And yours. What stops you, prophet fallen from grace?" the demon prodded him. "Your judgment is decided. It can go no worse for you."

Carpinelli felt like a weight had fallen on his head. He bowed it feebly, saying nothing.

"Or do you have one last task to complete—a promise to keep? Tonight, you must spill the prophet's blood before my bride, and in no quick manner."

"You have her, then?"

"Yes, I have chosen Clara. I will take her, and she will be my wife. In nine months' time, she will give me a son. Within a year of that, my second son will be born to continue the curse."

"Then what?"

The demon approached the desk. Leaning toward Carpinelli, it flattened its hands on the papers.

"Then I shall have no more need of you."

"What?" Carpinelli implored, bringing his head up. "Won't his death appease you?"

The papers beneath the demon's hands began to smolder, to wrinkle from an unseen heat, creating a fine vapor of smoke that rose listlessly upward.

"I stand upon a mound of prophets' skulls, Angelo. Though I can destroy the boy's body"—its fingers wadded the papers into smoking balls—"I cannot have his soul. I must console myself with yours."

The papers burst into flame. Jumping to his feet, Carpinelli whipped off his jacket to beat out the fire. Taking a step back, the demon smiled.

"Have you forgotten?" Carpinelli panted, having successfully extinguished the fire. "Another prophet will arise. *You* can't kill him. *You* need me. You've lost sight of your limitations, Aeneas. You're only the *sixth* demon. You must write the seventh scroll in Christian blood for the curse to continue. You need me."

A thoughtful frown darkened the demon's face. "Who is to say I have not already written the seventh scroll?"

"Then *rewrite* it in the boy's blood," Carpinelli pressed. "You still need me."

His head snapped toward the door. Someone turned the doorknob without success, then knocked. A woman's voice—his secretary's—asked, "Mr. Carpinelli? Are you there?"

He glanced at the demon as a key was inserted into the lock. The tumblers turned and the door opened. Taking one step into the room, she froze with surprise to see him standing there in the near dark. When she turned on the light, he threw the gun into the drawer and slammed it shut.

"I'm sorry, sir," she said. "I thought you were out, but I heard voices."

Carpinelli turned to find that the demon had vanished. In his ear, he heard Dominic's disembodied voice, a voice deep with the inflection of satanic hatred, a voice that made his blood run cold.

"Be at the estate by eleven tonight. By midnight, I want him dead."

FORTY-SEVEN

Mommy!" Luke woke with a start. His eyes snapped open. He saw nothing but darkness.

"Mommy!" He felt the warmth of her embracing arms. She was stroking his hair, kissing his forehead, humming a familiar tune. The aroma of freshly baked bread was in her clothes as he rested his head on her shoulder.

"Mommy!" Groping desperately, he crawled to find her in the dark when the chains on his ankles caught him. Reality struck him like a blow; she was only a dream.

"...Mommy." He curled into a ball and buried his face in his arms. Never before had he felt more cold.

Shackled in fetid gloom in the bowels of the Fratelli mansion, he pulled against the chains that pinched his ankles and doomed him to languish in the circular structure of stones. His lungs ached for fresh air; the rot of mold induced a wheezing rattle in his chest. His bones jutting against his skin, cushioned only by his dampened clothing, made it impossible to be comfortable on the stone floor.

He wondered how long he must wait to die, how long it would take him to starve to death. Pangs of starvation seized the hollow of his stomach, telling him that he had been imprisoned for days. Time, otherwise, passed like an ambiguous dream, curtailing his memory to mere flashes of recollection. He remembered Carpinelli carrying him down into darkness through a trapdoor in the library floor of the Fratelli Estate, beyond a passage, through a room lit with candles, and into a stone chamber. Too weak to struggle, he begged Carpinelli for help but received only silence. Carpinelli would not even look him in the eye when he took away his socks and shoes and chained him to the floor, leaving the fetters to chafe his bare ankles. With horrifying finality, Carpinelli left him in this stone structure, cutting off all light as he slammed the door, removing all sound as he bolted the lock. Carpinelli had buried him alive.

Inspecting the boundaries of his prison, Luke groped as a blind man in an unfamiliar setting. His fingers first discovered a stone slab in the center of the room. When he touched it, something crawled on his hand and scurried up his arm. With a shudder of disgust, he shook it off and continued to touch the chilled, smooth surface of the slab.

His hands then fell on something strange: moldy sticks covered with a blanket of cobwebs and cloth. He found several sticks, some thicker than others, some longer, some with bulging ends. When he came upon the round cranium of a skull, felt the empty sockets of its eyes and the teeth protruding from its jaw, he screamed and threw it down.

He fumbled about in horror until he found the door, pounding on it and throwing his weight against it. He wrenched at its hinges and dug at its base until his fingers hurt, but no sound came from beyond. He was alone. Sliding to the floor, depression overwhelmed him. In the cold obscurity of that vault, with only a crumbling skeleton for empathy, he shivered and breathed one word: "Jesus."

He remembered little after that. The illusion of his mother's touch was most prevalent—that and the ache of his heart for his brothers, even for his father.

A sound reached his ears. He raised his head to listen, wondering whether he had imagined it. The door rattled. Someone drew the bolt with a sharp jerk. The door creaked open on its rusty hinges. A glowing light assaulted his eyes so severely that he winced and closed them. When he opened them again, he saw the door standing ajar. A tall candelabra stood on the floor, its yellow flames flickering from lack of oxygen.

Turning his head to see who had entered, he saw a pattern of cobwebs stretched across the ceiling where pale spiders tried to hide themselves from the light. Turning his head further, he found the trapezoidal hunk of granite in the center of the circular room where the headless skeleton lay. In the middle of its ribcage, a merciless spider tugged at an insect. Beside the skeleton stood Dominic, an expression of gratified scorn on his face revealing the demon dwelling within.

"*Precious in the sight of the Lord is the death of his saints*," the demon said. "How precious is your death, Prophet? Are the heavenly multitudes prepared to watch you die?"

Confused at first to see the countenance of his dead friend, Luke tried to swallow, to maneuver his parched tongue, which stuck to the roof of his mouth. A faint voice, cracked with dryness, strained from his throat, "Absent…from the body…present with…the Lord."

Disappointment weighed on the demon, frustrated to find no fear in Luke's face, only relief the end had come.

"You robbed me, Prophet. I claimed Dominic's soul the day I conceived him. Now I am left with only his shell. Instead of wallowing in torment, he sits in the heavenly places. How shall I fill this vacancy, Prophet? Whose life do I take to replace this loss? Tell me, as there is one greater than I to whom I must answer." He paused, then said, "What of Clara?"

Unable to hold his head up any longer, Luke laid it back on the floor. "She's bought…with the blood…of Jesus."

"She will give herself freely, for she sees me as Dominic. She will learn the truth too late. She will bear the curse."

This forced Luke to lift his head. "God…will…protect her."

An evil smile enlivened the demon's face. With one stroke of its arm, it swept the decayed skeleton off the slab, scattering the bones into a clattering confusion across the floor. Then, it seized Luke by his arms and yanked him off the ground so that their faces were inches apart. Luke's body dangled like a limp rag. His head lolled on his neck.

"Perhaps, Prophet, but will He protect you?"

Clara stirred herself awake. Comfortable and warm, she rolled over on the bed, stretched leisurely, and opened her eyes. The soft glow of a lamp illuminated the room she recognized as her own in the Fratelli Estate. She yawned, feeling light-headed and a bit drugged. She had slept longer than she expected to, and recalled the wine Dominic had persuaded her to drink.

Gasping suddenly, she said, "Oh, no. Josh."

Before she could sit up, she heard a knock on the door. It opened slowly. Dominic entered, moving quietly as if afraid to wake her.

"It's okay. I'm awake." She smiled and patted the mattress beside her.

"Don't get up." A handsome grin crossed his face. "I just came to check on you."

"You gave me something to help me sleep, didn't you?"

"A sedative. You needed the rest." Sitting beside her, he brought her hands to his lips, kissing each while his brown eyes sought hers in an unblinking stare.

"I was so sure you were dead," she said. Though she tried to retain her smile, she could not stop a tear from escaping her eye. "How did you find me?"

"I have my ways. Why are you crying? You're safe now."

"I know." She tightened her grip on his hands. "I'm so glad you're here. Where's Luke?"

Lowering his eyes, he bowed his head, fixing his gaze on their entwined hands. "He didn't make it, Clara. He was killed in the hit."

Her hand flew to her mouth. "Oh, Dom! No!"

An uncontrollable sob suddenly shook his whole frame. Tears dampened his eyes as he lifted his face toward the ceiling in an attempt to regain control. "There was nothing I could do. The lousy thugs shot him in the back. He died in my arms."

A pang of grief seized her heart. She sat up, throwing her arms around his neck, her happiness instantly swept away. His arms were quick to respond, bringing her body close to his.

"The poor baby," she whimpered. "Did he suffer?"

"Miserably."

He whispered the word in her ear. It forced an aggrieved cry from her throat. Hot tears streamed from her eyes. She squeezed him tighter and felt the heat of his breath on her neck, the quivering of his muscles as he braced himself against her.

"It's not right," he said softly. "He was so young."

"I know," she whispered, trying to be strong for him. "At least he's not suffering anymore. He's with Jesus."

"AAAHHHH!" He shoved her onto the bed as if she had burned him. A flash of red glinted in his eyes. He stood suddenly and twisted away.

"Wha-what's wrong?" she asked, sitting back up.

"Nothing. I...just....The image of Luke lying in his blood flashed in my mind. I can't get it out of my head. I keep thinking there's something I could've done. Something...."

"I'm so sorry." She came to her feet, her arms open to comfort him. "I wish I'd been there for you. Come here. Let me hold you."

He turned back to her, his arms enveloping her, his lips pressing against hers in ardent passion.

FORTY-EIGHT

"Quickly. Do it quickly." Carpinelli's footsteps echoed across the bloodstained marble floor, resounding against the solitude of the towering walls.

The butchered bodies of the Fratellis were gone; only the war zone—bullet holes, shattered glass, broken furniture, bullet casings, blood—remained. He dragged his feet through it with the help of his cane. With a brooding frown, he entered the library, hesitating before the trapdoor in the floor.

A rising draft gently lifted his white hair. For several minutes, he gazed down the stone stairs, muttering, "Quickly. Do it quickly."

He forced himself downward. The glow of candles in the passageway directed him into the secret chamber, where he found a crystal chalice, turned purple with age. Next to it stood a dagger, its point piercing the wooden table. He stopped to consider them with his lips pinched into a hard line, his perspiring hands clamped together. A deathly silence lay within the stone walls.

"Quickly. Do it quickly."

A feeble cough caught his ear. The flow of cold air on the back of his neck made him shiver. Placing his black cane, the silver handle foremost, on the table, he exchanged it for the chalice. Yanking the dagger from the wood with his other hand, he placed it in the pocket of his suit jacket. Overcome with dread and a burgeoning sense of doom, he stepped inside the ceremonial chamber.

The sight of Luke's thin body stretched upon the granite slab, illuminated by the candelabra, made him falter. Luke's face was turned away. Chains bound his wrists above his head to iron rings in the stone. His bare ankles were bound likewise. His shirt was torn open, exposing his emaciated ribs, sunken stomach, and the ghastly pallor of his flesh to the candlelight. Every gasp for breath caused his ribcage to rise against his almost translucent skin.

Carpinelli stepped forward. He set the chalice on the slab. With one hand on the matted shock of brown hair and the other on Luke's jaw, he gingerly turned Luke's head toward him. The sight of his ashen face made Carpinelli cringe. He could not meet the stare of those glazed, green eyes peering from the dark circles that encompassed them, nor look at the cheekbones that were hollow from starvation. His fortitude failed him. He felt sick. Seeing the defenseless boy before him and understanding the penalty he would pay for this crime robbed him of the determination he had mustered over the last several hours.

"I can't do this. I just can't."

Upon recognizing Carpinelli, Luke's eyes came alive with hope. One barely discernible word passed from his bluish lips.

"Please...."

"Are you in pain?"

"Please...."

Reaching into his pocket, his hand trembling against the dagger, Carpinelli extracted a silver flask. He unscrewed the lid and brought it to Luke's lips.

"Drink. It's water."

Luke tried to lift his head but could not. Moved to pity, Carpinelli helped him with a hand beneath his neck. He drank eagerly until the flask was empty. Gently laying Luke's head back down, Carpinelli returned the flask to his pocket and withdrew the dagger. The candlelight gleamed across the silver blade and the gold handle.

At that, their eyes met. He saw the hope die in Luke's face. Guilt-ridden, Carpinelli could not bear to look at Luke any longer. He looked at the dagger instead. It felt like a heavy piece of ice.

"I'm sorry, Luke. I have no choice, just as I had no choice but to chain you down here. I didn't want to. Aeneas forced me."

Luke's gaze turned to the chalice.

"It's for your blood. Aeneas will write the seventh scroll in your blood. It must be done for the scroll to be imperishable."

He stroked Luke's hair with a nervous hand. Luke stiffened at the touch.

"I wish there was another way. I don't want to hurt you, but it's you or me, and I know you'll go to heaven. I won't."

Feeling dread rise within him like a nauseating wave, he jerked Luke's head back and positioned the point of the dagger next to his jugular. Luke flinched. A faint cry escaped his throat. He swallowed against the dagger's pressure and closed his eyes.

"You won't suffer." Carpinelli gripped the dagger tightly. "I promise."

"How thoughtful of you."

The cynical voice behind him sent a bolt of panic through his heart. Before he could turn, something hard struck the back of his head. The ground turned black before it rushed up to meet him.

"That felt good," Joshua said. "That felt *really* good."

He stepped over Carpinelli's slumped body and breathed a relieved sigh. Pulling a handkerchief from his pocket, he dabbed the sweat from his face before wiping the smudge of blood from the butt of his pistol. Placing both into his suit pocket, he looked at Luke, whose eyes were closed, his lips moving in terrified prayer. Joshua's mouth dropped.

"My word. Erik? What have they done to you?"

Upon hearing his real name, Luke opened his eyes.

"Hold on, Erik. I'll get you out."

With his foot braced against the slab, Joshua pulled back on the chain, trying to pry it apart. He soon realized the futility of this. What he needed was the key; what he found, still clutched in Carpinelli's hand, was the dagger. He took it and worked at the bolts holding Luke's wrists. Plied with enough pressure, the rusted stem of the first bolt gave way. Luke's right hand was free.

FORTY-NINE

Please, don't. This isn't the time, Dom." Bracing her hands against Dominic's chest, Clara gently pushed him off, releasing herself from his arms and his impassioned kiss.

"It's the perfect time." Enticed by her refusal, he embraced her once more, his hands wandering, his lips fervently seeking hers.

"No, it's not." With more resolve, she shoved him away and took two steps back. "You just told me Luke was dead. Do you honestly think I could do this now? Besides, we're not married. I want to do one thing right in my life. Let's get married first."

"Clara," he groaned in agitation, his eyes tracing her figure, "I already view you as my wife."

"No, Dom. I want to get married first. We'll go to the justice of the peace tomorrow morning. Please. I'm not asking that much."

Approaching her carefully, he cupped her jaw in the palm of his hand. She pressed her cheek into its warmth with a mixture of sadness and affection.

"You're a beautiful woman, Clara. That's why I offer you this chance: to love me tonight and live, or deny me and die."

The words, spoken tenderly, soothingly, did not immediately strike her with their meaning. She looked at him with confusion. "What?"

"It must be tonight."

She turned away in disappointment. "Don't force me. I want it to be special. I want it to be right in God's eyes."

His fingers sank into her flesh as he grabbed her arm, yanking her around. She uttered a short cry before the blur of his hand struck her viciously across the face. The blow sent her to the floor, stunned.

"Woman!" he bellowed, his eyes alive with fury. "Do not try my patience! You will be my bride! If not, your corpse will rot with the prophet's! Do you hear me?"

Placing her hand on her burning check, she looked up at him in astonishment.

"Do you hear me?" He took a menacing step toward her.

In the cruelty of his eyes, she saw the ruthless malevolence of Papa Fratelli. She backed away in terror. "Why are you doing this? This isn't like you! I thought you loved me!"

"I love no one."

The door stood open behind his domineering form. She scrambled toward it. In two steps, he seized her. With one arm around her waist, the other hand on the nape of her neck, he pinned her close against his chest. She felt the hot caress of his lips on her throat.

"No! Let me go!"

Leaning as far back from him as she could, she slapped him hard across the face. Laughing, he shoved her onto the bed. She pushed herself up, brushing her hair from her eyes to see his grinning face marred with a red welt.

"I have been slapped many times, *bella mia*"—he stepped toward her—"and I have always begged for more."

Clara's high-pitched scream filtered down to the dungeon. Joshua, prying diligently at the bolt securing Luke's left wrist, stopped when the piercing sound reached his ears.

"Clara!" Swaying from one foot to the other, vacillating between freeing Luke and rescuing Clara, he ultimately slapped the handle of the dagger into Luke's free hand. "Here, kid. Work on this."

Scrambling from the chamber, Joshua stumbled up the stairs into the library. From there, he dashed out into the entrance hall, sliding to a stop to listen for Clara's screams. He did not wait long. The shrill of three short cries made him look up the banister of the grand staircase. He stormed the staircase three steps at a time to the second story. Rounding the landing, he took the second flight two stairs at a time. At the next landing, he trotted upward, single step, until he staggered, winded, into the third-story hallway.

"What are you?" Clara screamed. "You're not Dominic!"

Locating her room by the sounds of struggle within, Joshua stepped back and thrust his weight against the door. It did not move. Rubbing his shoulder ruefully, he turned the knob and threw the door open.

He found Dominic pinning Clara down on the bed, her hair disheveled, her dress torn, her mascara smeared with tears. He was toying with her, enjoying the fight as she wrestled against him, her fingers clawing at his face, her legs kicking furiously.

Joshua clenched his hands into fists. "Let her go!"

They stopped struggling and turned their heads toward him with surprise. Clara's face brightened with hope. She stretched her arm beseechingly toward him.

"Josh!"

With an animalistic growl, Dominic reared up to confront him with inhuman eyes—demonic eyes of burning coal, glaring without hindrance of sclera, iris, or pupil. Taken aback for an astonished instant, Joshua scrambled with his coat pocket to retrieve his pistol as Dominic moved toward him.

"Hold it!" Joshua shouted, ripping the pocket to pull the gun out. "One more step and I'll shoot you—you—what happened to your eyes?"

Dominic stopped. He smiled at the gun wobbling in Joshua's hand. "Have you ever used a gun?"

Joshua hesitated before answering. "No," he swallowed, "but I just might hit what I'm aiming at, and I'm aiming at the knot in your tie, so move away from her."

"If you intend to shoot me, you will want to place your finger on the trigger."

Risking a glance at the gun, Joshua felt the blood rush to his face. He fumbled for the trigger, then aimed the gun back at Dominic.

"A wise man would leave this place," Dominic said. "How wise are you?"

Joshua took a deep breath to steady his voice. He planted his feet solidly. "I'm not leaving without Clara and the kid."

"Kid? Luke?" Pushing herself up from the bed, Clara shot a look at Dominic. "He's alive? You said he was dead!"

"If he is alive," Dominic grumbled through his teeth, "it will not be for long."

"No!" She rushed toward him.

"Clara, get back!"

With a shriek, she threw herself at Dominic, her nails scratching at his face. His arm shot up and caught her by the throat. Her scream ended with a short gasp as he held her at arm's length, his hand squeezing.

"I am done with you, woman."

"Let her go!" Joshua stepped forward. Gripping the gun with both hands, he fired two bullets into Dominic's chest.

The impact propelled Dominic back a step. He glanced down, watching the blood flow from the holes in his chest, marring his white shirt with two growing stains. With Clara's writhing body still in his grasp, he looked at Joshua. "You are not a wise man." Dominic opened his hand, and Clara sagged to the floor.

Joshua stepped back in disbelief, watching as bloody foam gurgled from the bullet wounds. He pulled the trigger a third time before Dominic grabbed him by the collar, drew him up, and flung him across the room with a jerk of his arm. For an instant, Joshua was airborne, his arms and legs floundering wildly. Then he crashed into the wall. He fell full length on the floor. The impact knocked the air from his lungs. He dropped the gun.

Dominic drew near with deliberate steps. Striving to catch his breath, Joshua pushed himself to his hands and knees. He had barely lifted his head when Dominic's foot flashed before his eyes. The toe of Dominic's black shoe kicked him sharply in the face. Joshua's vision went black for a second, then returned with an explosion of pain. Finding his face deep in the carpet, he lifted his head again, groaning. Warm blood spilled down his cheek.

Dominic crouched beside him. Seizing a handful of his hair, he yanked Joshua up so that his terrified eyes were even with his own. Joshua felt the heat from his glowing eyes as they illuminated his bleeding face with a crimson glow.

"You cannot kill me. I am older than the foundations of the earth." With diabolical pleasure, Dominic smashed the back of Joshua's skull into the wall. A volley of lights burst in his sight before he crumpled to the floor.

Luke inspected the gleaming dagger in his hand. Uncertain of what to do with it, he brought it above his head and poked at the bolt shackling his left hand. After numerous jabs, his strength deserted him. With the dagger clasped in his hand, he prayed, *Please, Lord. Free me.*

A low rumbling assaulted the room, a quivering tremor that shook the dungeon. Dirt sifted from the walls and ceiling. The floor rippled beneath the bones, clattering them horridly with renewed life. With the grating sound of rock scraping rock, the granite slab sank a foot into the ground with a staggering jolt, jarring his body.

The quake ceased as abruptly as it had begun, settled into a rumble, then terminated completely. Luke moved his stiff legs and arms to find them free of the chains. Still, he lay there, destitute of strength. He tried to sit up but collapsed back onto the slab. *Please, Lord. Heal me.*

A wind rose through the room, billowing his clothes, stirring the bones, removing the rancid stench of mold and death with the circulation of warm, fresh air. Arching his back, he gasped large gulps of air. It permeated his oxygen-starved lungs and breathed energy into his muscles. The wheezing in his lungs cleared.

"Thanks, Lord," he breathed. He sat up, dangling his legs off the granite slab. Suddenly, a withered old hand reached up and grabbed his thigh. With a startled scream, Luke swung his legs around and jumped off the other side.

On his knees, clutching the slab for balance, Carpinelli tried to stand. Rubbing his head with his other hand, he dragged himself to his feet and looked up. When he saw that Luke was free, fear leaped into his eyes. He made a clumsy, headlong dive over the slab for the dagger. Luke backed away, the weapon clenched in his fist.

"Come here, child." Half sprawled across the slab, Carpinelli leaned upon it for support, stalking Luke with unstable steps. "I won't hurt you."

"Liar! You were gonna cut my throat!" Luke took stronger steps backward.

Carpinelli trudged forward, his arm outstretched. "You

don't understand. Aeneas won't show you any mercy. Trust me."

Luke's bare foot came down on one of the bones. The femur snapped like a dry stick. "Did *he* trust you?" he demanded, pointing at the disintegrating skeleton.

A tired sigh escaped Carpinelli's lips. "I had nothing to do with his death. He was a prophet who failed long before I came about. He was sacrificed when Papa Fratelli turned twenty-five and the curse was passed on. A sacrifice must be made, Luke. If it isn't you, it will be me."

With that, he flung himself forward, his arms extended. Luke dodged the grasp, but as Carpinelli landed on the floor, his hand caught Luke's ankle and yanked his foot out from beneath him. With a shout, Luke tumbled on his chest. Kicking desperately, he made full contact with Carpinelli's face several times. Still, Carpinelli clung tenaciously to the ankle, snatching eagerly for the other flailing foot.

Twisting his body around, Luke clambered for the door. His fingertips had barely scratched the frame when Carpinelli caught his other ankle and jerked him down. Without thinking, Luke spun around and slashed the dagger across Carpinelli's knuckles. His skin split open like slashed tissue paper. He cried out. Suddenly, Luke was free.

Luke scrambled from the room. Pressing all his weight against the heavy wooden door, he closed it and fumbled with the bolt, slipping it into place just as Carpinelli reached the door.

Carpinelli shook it wildly. "Luke! Open this door!"

With the bloody dagger still in his hand, Luke stumbled backward, resting against the table to catch his breath. The door that had bound him in darkness now held his would-be executioner securely.

FIFTY

"Luke! Unlock this door!" Carpinelli shouted, shaking the door vigorously.

Paper fluttered through the air onto the book-strewn floor as Luke tossed the volumes aside. Rummaging through the chamber, he grabbed the ancient books from the case, examined whatever loose sheets fell from their bindings, then pitched them apathetically over his head. He searched each book but found nothing. Frustrated, he flung the last one to the floor.

"Where is it, Lord? Where's the scroll?"

Whirling around, he realized there was nowhere else in the room to search. From the inadequate light of the candles, which formed sinister shadows in the corners and filled the air with the smell of hot wax, he saw the room held only the table, the chair, and the bookcase—*the bookcase.* He seized it, braced his foot against the wall, and toppled it onto the mound of books.

The crash reached Carpinelli's ears. He stopped pounding on the door. "You can't bring him down, Luke! It's useless!"

Behind the bookcase, tucked neatly into a sizable hollow cut into the wall, sat a bulky metal chest. Luke kicked the books out of the way and dragged the chest, covered with a tapestry of spider webs, out of the hole. He wiped them off, shook the clingy threads from his fingers, and crouched before the chest. A padlock the size of his fist held it resolutely closed.

"It's useless, Luke! Do you hear me?"

Grabbing Carpinelli's cane from the table, Luke slammed its silver handle against the padlock, disturbing a terrified spider that scurried from the keyhole.

"Lord," Luke said, "give me strength." Lifting his arms above his head, he brought the cane down again. Repeatedly, he struck the lock with relentless blows until his hands throbbed and the handle of the cane lost its form. The padlock remained secure.

"Okay, Lord." Throwing the cane aside with exasperation, he rubbed his sore hands. "*You* do it."

There was a slight movement of the lock, a click, and the padlock fell open.

Luke stared at it, blinked, and smiled. "I should've asked You first." Kneeling before the chest, he threw open the lid. His smile soon diminished. Dozens upon dozens of browning ancient scrolls lay inside, some disintegrating, some carefully rolled and tied, none conspicuous in its content.

"Which one, Lord?" He looked at the ceiling with bewilderment. "Which one?"

"Who are you?" Clara implored, rubbing her throat tenderly. Tears ran unchecked down her cheeks. "You're not Dominic. He would never hurt me or Luke. Are you...Papa?"

Dominic turned from Joshua's prone and beaten figure to face her. The sight of his glowing eyes and the blood oozing from his chest made her recoil. "Stand up," he said.

Too terrified not to obey, she came to her unsteady feet while he approached her, cringing as he placed his burning, sinewy hands on her arms.

He pulled her close to his face. "Will you submit?"

Wincing, she tore her sight from his mesmerizing eyes to look at Joshua's inert body. "Will you let him go?"

"Yes," Dominic answered easily.

"And Luke, too?"

"Yes."

Looking back at him, she narrowed her eyes. "You're lying."

He smiled. "Yes."

"Then I won't submit."

The smile faded. He seized her by the hair and yanked her head back. She cried out softly.

"Then you and the prophet will die together."

The candle flame flickered as Luke used it to set fire to the scrolls. He promptly moved back to witness the blaze escalate quickly into a small inferno. Sparks shot into the air with the roar of the fire, even as curling wisps of brown smoke ascended from the metal chest. He coughed and waved his arms to dissipate the smoke.

"Luke! What are you doing?" Carpinelli shouted. "What's burning?"

Fascinated, Luke watched the burning spectacle feed upon the parchments until they disintegrated into fragile sheets of ash, the smoldering fire succumbing to embers.

"What have you done?" Carpinelli shook the door furiously. "Answer me!"

Luke stirred the ashes in the chest with the battered cane, digging in anticipation of finding the two imperishable scrolls that he knew would survive the fire, just as they had survived every other attempt at destruction. Upon discovering them, he shook off the ash and spread them on the table, securing the curled ends with books. The scrolls were similar, both written in Latin and penned in reddish brown ink. He frowned. His eyes combed the foreign words without understanding.

"Give me wisdom, Lord."

"Let her go...Dominic."

Joshua regained his feet by holding tightly to a nearby chair, trying to ignore the hammering in his head and the acute pain in his jaw. The lower half of his face felt sticky with blood. Squinting to correct his blurred vision, he tried to locate the gun.

Dominic regarded him with an impassive glance over his shoulder. His hand still clutched Clara by the hair. "Fool. Do you still intend to stop me?"

"I intend to try." Leaning against the wall for support, Joshua forced his eyes open to keep himself from losing consciousness. His head felt heavy on his neck.

"Josh," Clara pleaded, straining against the hold on her hair, "get Luke and go."

"Luke is beyond saving," Dominic said. "He is dead by now. There is no hope for him and none for you. Move." With a jerk of his wrist, he pulled her toward the door by her hair.

Joshua staggered in front of them, grabbing a porcelain lamp off an adjacent table as he hurried past it. Raising it above his shoulder, he threatened, "For the last time, let her go."

Dominic shook his head. Seizing upon his distraction, Clara lifted her foot and gave him a forceful kick on the shin. With a rush of anger, he twisted her hair against his fist, making her scream.

Joshua swung the lamp like a baseball bat, pinching his eyes closed as it smashed across the side of Dominic's head. Shattered fragments of porcelain exploded in their faces.

Staggering from the swing, Joshua fell into the wall. When he opened his eyes, he saw blood coursing down Dominic's face.

Without any reaction of pain, Dominic threw Clara aside and lunged at Joshua, tackling him, dropping him flat on the floor in the hallway. The back of Joshua's head hit the floor, triggering another burst of fireworks before his eyes and an excruciating pounding through his skull.

FIFTY-ONE

Luke studied the scrolls with bewilderment. He chose one and strained his eyes to scrutinize the words.

"Et...ait...ei...tibi...dabo...potestatem—"

Every nerve in his body screamed, *WRONG SCROLL!* Flustered, he turned to the other.

"Et factum...est...proelium in caelo Michahel...et angeli... Aww!" he growled in frustration. "I can't read this, Lord!"

Before his eyes, the interpretation suddenly became evident. In a loud voice, he said, *"And there was war in heaven: Michael and his angels fought against the dragon; and the dragon fought and his angels, and prevailed not; neither was their place found any more in heaven. And the great dragon was cast out, that old serpent, called the Devil, and Satan, which deceiveth the whole world: he was cast out into the earth, and his angels were cast out with him."*

"No. It cannot be." The demon looked up in horror.

Filtering through the levels of the mansion, carried like a ghostly intonation, Luke's words rang solely in the demon's ears, even as it twisted Joshua's throat in its hands. Terror stiffened the hair on its neck. It faltered. Its grip loosened.

"Thou, Aeneas, once glorious, wert with them that fell. It is thee who slayeth the innocent, thee who deceiveth the godly, thee who murdereth the prophets of the Lord."

No longer interested in Joshua, the demon clambered over him to its feet. Freed, Joshua inhaled a desperate breath of air.

"Now, thy name is Eliakim, for the Lord shall judge thee. No more shall the living suffer thy tortures. No more shall the unwary fall into thy traps of death, for the living God has seen all. This day the pit shall house thy demonic being where thou wilt be reserved unto judgment."

Hauling himself up, Joshua fumbled after Dominic—

"I, the prophet of the Lord, through the power of the Blood of the Lord Jesus Christ, do bind thee in the weak mortality of the body thou has consumed..."

—and wrenched the demon back with a hold on its arm. Joshua threw his whole body into the punch and landed it firmly on the demon's jaw.

"...and in the feebleness thereof, rob thee of thy strength."

Without the demonic power to manipulate Dominic's body, the severed spine bucked, collapsing the demon on its back in the hallway. Surprised, Joshua looked down at his fist.

Groaning, the demon struggled with its paralyzed lower half to roll onto its stomach, to drag its useless legs through the hall. Joshua watched with astonishment and looked at his fist once more.

The demon grasped shreds of carpet one after another to pull along Dominic's bleeding, agonized body. When it reached the stairs and strove to grab the banister, the prophet's voice echoed in its ears.

"Thy power forsakes thee...."

It lost hold of the banister, tumbling headlong down the staircase to the second-story landing. Once more, it struggled to maneuver the next flight of stairs.

"Thy sight deceives thee...."

The floor seemed to open beneath it. The banister

disappeared, and again it rolled wildly down the staircase into the entrance hall below.

"No pleas shall reach thy demonic host, for thou shalt stand judgment alone...."

"Prophet!" it screamed. "If I am sent into the pit"—its body contracted in agony—"I will torment the souls of your father, your mother, your brothers! For eternity, they will be mine! Do you hear me, Prophet?"

"Ah...ah...No pleas shall reach thy demonic host—"

"Prophet!" Drawing itself toward the library, leaving streaks of blood to mark the trail of its paralyzed body, the demon shouted, "Prophet! They suffer in torment! As you speak, they burn! For eternity, I will torture them! For eternity, you will know this!"

"...de-demonic host for thou shalt s-stand judgment alone—"

The demon paused at the library door to regain the breath Dominic's body required. Then, with desperate snatches at the legs of the furniture, it pulled itself to the trapdoor, leaned forward, and plunged down the stone staircase.

Luke faltered. The words of the scroll died on his lips. A sickening despair gripped his stomach. Until then, he had failed to notice that Carpinelli was kicking the door with propelling thrusts of his foot. The rotting wood surrounding the bolt threatened to give. Luke forced his eyes back to the scroll.

"Hell from beneath is m-moved for thee to meet thee at thy coming! It stirreth up the d-dead for thee!"

Splinters of wood flew into the air as the bolt nearly succumbed to Carpinelli's force.

Luke heard a tumultuous clatter. He glanced fearfully toward the passageway to see a dark mound turn itself over and crawl toward the chamber with long stretches of its arms. Luke looked back at the scroll, searching frantically for the place where he had left off.

Carpinelli had almost kicked the door down when the demon's glowing eyes radiated from the shadows, drawing nearer with each extending arm, each grunt of pain. Luke looked furiously for the dagger. It was beside the scorched chest. He grabbed it and returned to the scroll.

"Prophet!"

The voice was so close that it startled him. He jumped to find the demon in the doorway, propped up by its arms. Its face—Dominic's face—was smeared with blood and sweat, contorted with hatred.

"Read quickly, Prophet, for I am here."

Carpinelli burst through the door. The broken bolt flew across the room. He looked at the demon first, then at Luke, then at the scroll, then back at the demon, trying to decide what to do.

"Kill him!" the demon yelled.

Luke pointed the dagger at Carpinelli. "Stay away!"

"Kill him, or I will pull you into hell with me!"

Carpinelli took a step forward and then a step backward as Luke slashed the knife threateningly at him. He stepped forward again, reaching for Luke's outstretched hand. Luke moved back, and he grabbed the blade instead. Luke yanked the dagger from him. Recoiling in pain, Carpinelli shouted, his scream echoing through the room. He glared at Luke and carefully opened the fingers of his clenched hand. Blood dripped from the sliced flesh to the stone floor. He squeezed his fist shut.

"Kill him!"

The dagger whistled as Luke sliced it through the air. Leaning back to avoid being cut, Carpinelli caught Luke's wrist with his bloody hand. His weapon useless, Luke threw his other fist at Carpinelli's face. He seized that arm in midair, too, and pressed Luke back into the wall.

The demon dragged itself forward, rage twisting its face. "I said kill him!"

Luke no longer needed the scroll. He glared at the demon.

"Thy judgment approaches!" he shouted, bracing his back against the wall. *"The earth opens her mouth to receive you alive into the pit of Sheol!"*

The ground rumbled. A vibration resounded through the rock, shaking the mansion for several seconds and coating them with a light layer of dirt from the stones shifting above their heads. Then, all was silent. They looked at each other and waited. Nothing happened. The pause was too long.

Sneering, the demon maneuvered itself into a sitting position. "Is that your best, Prophet?"

The rumbling returned at once, surrounding them from all directions, roaring in their ears with a deafening thunder. The floor swelled. Carpinelli released Luke, who reached for the wall to steady himself. Before his hand could touch it, it swayed away from him. He staggered sideways and fell. He lost the dagger.

The ground surged like ocean waves, breaking apart the stones, shoving them upward into askew barriers. Luke and Carpinelli's screams competed with the noise as the floor heaved, pitching them into the air. The candles fell, plunging them into utter darkness.

Luke hit the ground hard, then was tossed into the air again like a weightless object. Landing on his back, he felt blocks of stone crash beside him. The ceiling was caving in. He rolled over, scrambling across the unsteady floor to find protection under the table. When he fumbled across it, he found Carpinelli beneath it, clinging to a leg in stupefied horror. He kicked Luke with fierce jabs of his feet, forcing Luke to crawl away.

The rumbling grew louder in the intense darkness. Rubble shifted beside Luke as he groped to find a wall that might lead him to the doorway. His grasping hands felt nothing but air. Twice he was sprawled facedown on the floor, unable to keep his balance and coughing from the billowing dust. In desperation, he edged over the stones in his way, praying he was going in the right direction.

From nowhere, a hand seized his wrist. Bloodred eyes opened straight before him in the darkness, illuminating the room with the brightness of fire. Luke screamed. The hand drew him forward, raking his body over the rocks. He tore at the hand with his fingers, then sank his teeth into it.

Another hand gripped him by the back of the neck, dragging him forward until the demon, which lay facedown, its lower body crushed beneath the stones, could wrap its arms around Luke's body, pinning him against the floor. Its mouth pressed against Luke's ear, its breathing rapid, heavy.

"You will die with me, Prophet. The Lord God will have His judgment, but He will pay for it with your life."

Fifty-two

The shocking upheaval of the foundation flung Clara across the bed. Joshua reeled across the floor, swinging his arms frantically to keep his balance. From the depths of the mansion to the attics came the shattering of glass, the creaking of wood under immense strain, and the ominous rumbling of shifting concrete. The building shook violently. With a bounding motion, the settee leaped onto the dresser, smashing it in one deciding blow and spilling its contents. An armchair whirled across the floor, jamming itself in the door frame.

Clara lay on the bed, gripping the mattress with her eyes squeezed shut, while the frame bucked erratically, tossing her from side to side. Struggling to keep his footing on the crests of the floor, Joshua wove back and forth as on a ferocious sea. When he neared the bed, he jumped on it, throwing himself over her as pieces of the ceiling crumbled upon them, dusting them with white plaster.

"Are you okay?" he yelled over the demolishing roar.

"Yes! What's happening?"

"I don't know, but let's get out of here!"

He pulled her from the leaping bed, holding her close as they swayed across the dancing floor. At the door, he released her to wrestle with the armchair that had barricaded them in. After prying it out, he reached for her. Her hand stretched out for his at the instant the floor opened beneath her feet. She plunged through a jagged hole.

"Clara!"

She screamed. He dove toward her, grabbing her arms, her dress, anything he could seize. With more than half her body hanging through the floor, she grasped frantically at the unraveling carpet and broken floorboards, her flailing feet kicking wildly.

"Josh!"

"Hold on!"

With his heart racing and his muscles trembling, Joshua tried to keep his eyes from focusing on the aerial view of the mansion collapsing beneath Clara's dangling feet, a gaping maw of broken rafters and plummeting walls hungering for her fall.

Lying flat on his stomach, he had braced his feet against the wall for leverage when a movement caught his eye. The outside wall was moving—slightly at first, and then, like a flowing curtain freed from its rod, it folded upon itself, opening the room to a wintry blast of night air. He yanked Clara up through the hole with renewed determination. Impatient to escape, he threw her over his shoulder and staggered out the door through the debris.

When he reached the grand staircase, a falling wall of bricks deluged the stairs, stopping him short. He glanced up to see the roof caving in. Several chimneys had broken through the ceiling, showering bricks everywhere amid scattering clouds of dust. As though endeavoring to keep the mansion together, the rafters had resisted the pressure to spread apart until now. They broke with vociferous snaps, spiraling downward and impaling the floors below.

Joshua hurried down the staircase to the second floor, pressing tightly against the walls and climbing over rubble. There was nothing to hold on to; the rafters had knocked out the banister and parts of the staircase. He continued downward, reaching the entrance hall only to find the front door jammed shut by the displaced foundation. Setting Clara on her feet, he wrenched at the door with all his strength before it reluctantly scraped open wide enough for them to slip through.

"Go!" he shouted.

She darted through the opening, waited outside until he followed safely, then ran across the snow-covered lawn with Joshua holding her hand, pulling her along. She suddenly stopped and yanked her hand free. When he turned to look at her, her eyes were wide with horror.

"Luke!" She started to run back, slipping in the snow. He grabbed her wrist and held on tightly.

"It's too late!"

"No! Luke!" She fought him, slapping his hands off her arms.

Not wanting to hurt her, he wrapped her in a bear hug, pinning her arms, and lifted her off the ground as he ran from the mansion. He made it only a few feet before tripping, landing them both in the snow.

A horrendous rumbling from behind made them look back. The mansion veered to one side. With graceful suppleness, it rocked back, a vacillating motion produced by the waves rippling on the ground, breaking the mansion's foundation, toppling its towers and moldings, casting its windows from their ledges into nimble flight, all amid the sounds of breaking glass and splintering wood.

Stunned neighbors congregated in the street, gawking at the uncanny force of the quake that affected only the Fratelli Estate. Screams of surprise competed with the rumbling thunder of groaning masonry as fiery currents from the ground coursed through the mansion like the spindly caress of orange fingers. Many ran from the area, cowering, their curiosity overcome by terror as the convulsing bolts engulfed the mansion in an array of flowing light, its brilliance prevailing over the darkness.

"Aeneas!" Carpinelli screamed, cowering under the table. "Help me!"

Stones battered the table in heavy procession until it succumbed and broke in two, crumbling directly onto Carpinelli's back. Laid flat and pinned against the floor, he fluttered his eyelids as he strove to retain consciousness. Blood ran down his face in a crooked stream.

"Aeneas…help…."

Walls crashed around them, missing Luke and the demon by inches. Luke felt riveted to the ground, held there by the demon's tenacious arm. With the acceptance of his fate, he threw his arms over his head and braced himself to die. Inaudible over the thunderous noise, he prayed, "Jesus… Jesus…Jesus…."

The contracting tremors magnified, culminating into one great, tectonic quake as one wall of earth slipped in one direction and the other in the opposite way, splitting the ground open like an angry wound before them, separating Carpinelli from Luke and the demon.

From the jagged chasm rose columns of vaporous steam. Tremendous heat and sulfur blistered the air. Cracks in the chasm walls spewed swollen fountains of lava down the precipice into a cauldron of fiery magma. Explosions hurled rocks, red-hot scoria, and debris up to the horrid mouth of the concavity.

From where Luke lay, held fast, he heard Carpinelli's muffled cries of sorrow. His arms and legs writhing in pain, Carpinelli's attempts to free himself from the crushing mass on his back only agitated the weak ground beneath him. As

Luke watched, the earth gave way in a succession of crumbling rock, plunging Carpinelli headfirst into the chasm. The heat set him aflame before his screams were cut short by his plunge into the boiling rock.

The two scrolls wavered briefly on the edge of the pit before spiraling down toward the hellfire, flitting from the roar of the heat, then bursting into flames.

"Take courage, Prophet," the demon said derisively in Luke's ear. "You will never grow old. You will never fight a war. You will never bury a wife. Behold, Prophet," the demon made a flourishing gesture with its hand toward the chasm, "your martyrdom awaits."

Almost immediately, the ground beneath them sagged. It broke, whirling them downward with sickening speed. Luke cried out with one short scream. The demon clung to him in the headlong plunge before a powerful hand from nowhere caught Luke's arm. Two brilliant streaks of lightning flashed instantaneously, one on each side of him. He was suddenly free and flying upward.

Below him, the demon tumbled into the yawning chasm, uttering a blasphemous roar, plummeting head over heels into the lava churning below, its severed arms following.

Outside the mansion, the rising subterranean pressure buckled the earth. The force threw everyone standing on the Fratelli Estate to the ground. Cars pitched into the air. Sidewalks and driveways broke open. Giant water pipes bowed and snapped, twisting upward like grotesque snakes, shooting geysers several feet into the air.

Unable to withstand the upheaval, the front of the mansion crumpled across the snow. Tottering momentarily, the remaining building collapsed upon itself in a disintegrating shudder. Then the shaking stopped. The deep thunder of rupturing earth grew abruptly silent, leaving only the sound of rushing water.

People stared in shock at the smoldering destruction. A deathly quiet pervaded the night until the sound of sirens broke the air. The noise awakened the crowd; they moved forward slowly, coming through the gate for a better look.

Clara hid her face in her hands, weeping bitterly. "Luke! No! We should've gone back! No, no, no!"

Joshua wrapped his arm around her shoulders and rocked her gently, condemning himself for not having done something. Anything. He should have freed Luke first and not left him to be crushed under tons of brick.

"Dead!" she cried. "Luke! Dominic! I'm all alone!"

"You're not alone, Clara. I'm here."

She drew close to him and buried her face in his chest, sobbing. He removed his suit jacket and placed it around her shoulders, encircling her tenderly with his arms.

The sirens grew closer. Soon, the area teemed with firemen and policemen. Ambulances bounced over the jumbled roads. Newspaper reporters dashed back and forth among witnesses, jotting down quick quotes on small pads of paper. Firefighters rushed forward as police pushed everyone back, leaving Joshua and Clara to soberly watch their silhouettes as they fought to extinguish the orange flames rising from the sunken ruins.

"Josh," Clara asked, her voice trembling, "how did you know...I was here?"

"Where else could you have been?" He smiled gently, offering her a handkerchief from his suit pocket. "Are you okay?"

"I don't know. I don't know anything anymore." She breathed a shuddering sigh, wiping her tears with the handkerchief, then pulled back from him, looking at him searchingly with wide eyes. "Did you hear that?"

"Yes." He took a quick glance around, his heart beating against his chest. "It sounded like a laugh—like a kid laughing."

He stood and helped her to her feet, at the same time looking behind her, then over both of his shoulders. No one stood near.

"Wishful thinking," he said, wrapping his arm around her once more. "I'm sorry, Clara."

As they turned to leave, they bumped into a man standing directly behind them—a fireman with strands of red hair sticking out from under his helmet and soot streaked across his sweating face. His sudden materialization startled them both, especially as he appeared to have been standing there for some time, watching them and listening to their conversation.

"Miss Crawford, you are not alone. The Lord has not forgotten you nor forsaken you. He has delivered you, and His grace will sustain you."

Fresh tears poured down her cheeks. She dabbed at them with the handkerchief as the fireman placed a reassuring hand on her forearm.

"Be comforted," he continued. "Dominic is with the Lord. One day, many years from now, you will see him again."

"If...if he's with the Lord," she said, a well of emotion rising within her, "then how could he...why did he...?"

"Dominic was not responsible for what happened in there. Perhaps," he smiled kindly, "there is one who can explain it to you." He reached behind him and pulled out a ragged boy, smeared with dirt, who grinned at Clara and giggled as one confiding a secret.

"Luke!" With ecstatic amazement, she threw her arms around him, squeezing him relentlessly and kissing his dirty face.

"Oh, thank God," Joshua said with a rush of relief. Those

words, and his sincerity in saying them, surprised him. He covered his mouth with his hand to hold back his emotions, blinking away the tears that threatened to spill out.

"Yes, Mr. Parnell," the fireman said with a knowing nod, "you should thank God. '*Blessed is he whose transgression is forgiven, whose sin is covered.*'"

Joshua's eyes opened wide.

"You're alive!" Clara brushed Luke's tangled hair back from his eyes and coddled his face in her hands. "Oh, Luke! How? How did you get out?"

"My angel saved me," he said innocently, his green eyes bright with delight.

"Your angel? What do you mean?"

Luke wiggled happily from her grasp and pointed at the fireman—who was no longer there.

Epilogue

May, 1936
Loveland, Colorado

Fratelli Killers Executed

This morning, at one minute after midnight, the thirteen men found guilty of the Fratelli massacre were hanged together in a mass execution. All were members of the Pompliano crime family.

Four years ago, they slaughtered one hundred and nine people with machine guns in a merciless bloodbath, the nation's largest gangland slaying. The killers infiltrated the birthday gathering for Dominic Fratelli and opened fire on the guests, many of whom were young women. Police believe the slaughter was in retaliation for the deaths of Giovanni Pompliano's three sons, whose murders were allegedly credited to the Fratelli family. It was never proven the Fratellis were responsible for the murders.

The killers were indicted by the testimony of several survivors. In the well-publicized trial, they provided police with the identities of—

"That's last Sunday's paper. Would you like to look at today's?"

Startled, Clara looked up from the newspaper to see Edith Elliott place a dish of fresh bread before her on the kitchen table. She set the paper aside in exchange for a slice, busying herself with a jar of canned preserves in the hope of blinking away tears before her hostess noticed them. The bread was warm and inviting, but she had no appetite.

"I'm so sorry." Edith glanced at the paper, cringing at the headline. "I didn't mean to leave this out. Edmund is behind in his reading. Are you all right, dear?"

Clara laid the bread down to dab at her eyes with a handkerchief. Edith sat beside her, patting Clara's hand with her own soft, wrinkled one.

"It's taken a long time to get over that night, and the trial brought it all back. It was like reliving a nightmare. But Josh has been wonderful and patient. Tell me, how has Luke dealt with it?"

"The first year was hard on him, poor child. His heart was broken. He had so many people to mourn, but Christ has been with him at every moment. Now he has friends and is doing well in school, but there are times when he's quiet, when his mind is far away. There's an intensity to his eyes, and I can see that the Lord is teaching him, preparing him."

"I've missed him," Clara said. "It's been so long since I've seen him. He was such a cute little boy."

"Oh, he's not little anymore." Edith's faded blue eyes twinkled. "He grows out of his clothes almost as fast as I can make them. He's as tall as Edmund, and he's not finished growing. We had some pictures taken of him when he turned sixteen. Let me get one for you."

Leaving the kitchen, Edith returned with a framed black-and-white photo that she handed to Clara. The young face had lost some of its childish qualities, but these were admirably replaced with the first signs of manhood. His hair was darker, his jaw stronger, and the gaunt lines of starvation were gone.

The shadows beneath his eyes had disappeared, leaving them bright and intelligent. Clara smiled at the picture; his grin was still boyish.

"He's handsome. Has he broken many hearts?"

"Oh my, yes. Every girl in town knows who Luke Elliott is. Here they are, dear."

The squeak of the back door announced Edmund and Joshua's entrance. Upon seeing Clara, Joshua's face widened into a grin. He took her hands into his own and kissed her on the cheek.

"Everything is set, honey. Are you ready to be a bride?"

"Yes, darling, but Luke isn't here. I want him to be here."

"I told him to be back by three," Edmund said, glancing at the clock on the wall.

"He will be, then," Edith said with assurance.

A mile from the parsonage, Luke walked barefoot along the dirt road that followed the river into town. Holding a homemade fishing rod over one lean shoulder, he took care not to drag the rainbow trout dangling from a string in his other hand. Shirtless under his overalls, he squinted up at the sun, enjoying the light wind that stirred the line of trees along the river. The breeze felt good against the hot rays that burned his shoulders and tanned his skin to a light brown.

The sound of a car behind him made him turn around. Waving at a pesky gnat that hovered near his eyes, he discerned a convertible approaching. Dust billowed behind its wheels. He stepped aside for it to pass, but it slowed to a stop beside him.

"Hello there."

Luke looked more at the navy blue Sports Roadster than at the driver.

"That's a swell car, mister."

"Thanks. Did you catch those fish in the lake back there?"

"Yes, sir." Luke lifted up the four speckled fish for approval.

"Nice catch. Hey," the driver shrugged sheepishly, "can you direct me to Loveland? I took a wrong turn somewhere, and I'm late for a wedding."

"Straight ahead." Luke motioned with his head to his right, his attention absorbed with the white-rimmed tires with red-spoked wheels, the chrome grill and bulbous headlights sitting inches above two horns.

"Are you going that way? I could give you a lift."

Luke's eyes lit up. He looked at the driver for the first time, a broad-faced man dressed in a casual beige suit with no tie. The open air had barely mussed his short blond hair.

"Swell. Thanks."

The man stretched to open the passenger door and helped Luke situate his fishing pole between them. Slipping inside and shutting the door, Luke placed the stout fish directly on his lap, careful to keep them from touching the dark gray interior.

"Andy Ballantine." The driver released one hand from the steering wheel to shake Luke's hand.

"Luke Elliott."

"*You're* Luke Elliott?" Andy studied him with interest. "You're taller than I expected."

"You know me?"

"Yes, through Joshua Parnell. I'm his best man. What a coincidence I should run into you. We can go to the church together."

With boyish wonder, Luke's curious gaze inspected the gauges on the dashboard, his hands yearning to touch them. The warm breeze sifted his bangs, exposing the slight white scar on his forehead as Andy placed the car in gear and drove forward.

"I know everything about you, son. I even know who gave you that scar. Josh ran you down with his car. Did you know that?"

"Yeah, I know, but I forgave him."

"How noble. By all rights, you should be dead, yet here you are…alive."

Luke looked sharply at Andy, who kept his concentration on the road ahead as it curved slightly and ascended a hill.

"Such a beautiful day," he continued. "Feels like years since I've tasted freedom—the freedom of a day off, that is. To be young like you, without responsibility, without worry. That's the way it should be. Your life must feel ideal right now."

"I…I guess so."

"For being so young, you've had it pretty rough. The bright side is that you've already faced your worst days, what with Papa Fratelli trying to kill you and the brutal murders of your father and brothers. Oh, and not to mention Dominic dying in your arms. Those days are in the past, right? Now there is only hope for the future."

The Roadster hit a bump. The fish bounced from Luke's lap with renewed life, each one straining against the string. He caught them once more, suppressing their attempts to be free and feeling their dead black eyes and tiny teeth on his palms.

"The couple who adopted you—they are all you have left in the world. It must trouble you to see them grow old, to watch them fade a little every day. What will you do when they are gone?"

Luke swallowed hard to mask his inward gasp. His fingers dug deep into the trout, restraining the dead things from any chance of movement.

With a sideways glance, Andy searched his face. "What happened to your hope for the future, son? It shined in your eyes moments ago. Now there is only fear." Almost imperceptibly, he pressed his foot on the accelerator, pressing Luke backward into the seat. "Fear not. I will sustain them for you. I ask only one thing in return...*Prophet*."

With a shout of surprise, Luke pressed his back against the door. Andy turned his head toward him, his eyes red, enlivened coals that melted the flesh from his face into streams of tissue and steaming blood. Sulfuric haze exhaled from his mouth as he spoke.

"You did not know that Aeneas wrote the last scroll, did you, Prophet?"

The car jerked as he swung it into a field dense with grass. Luke grabbed the door handle to hang on. The car turned, left the field, and retook the road in the opposite direction, speeding alongside the river. Luke looked over the door at the sharp drop below him where rocks cushioned the riverbed. Understanding his intent, the demon grabbed his arm with a burning hand. Smashing the fish directly in the demon's face, Luke wrenched himself away and leaped over the door.

For a second, he felt suspended in midair, the ground blurring beneath him. Then, he landed hard on his bare feet, crumpled from the impact, and toppled down the rough slope. Sky and ground melted together. Cruel rocks sliced into him as he bore down upon them. His hands flailed for anything to break his fall, but he did not stop until he landed facedown with a splash in the river.

Pain roared through his skull. Pushing himself up from the frigid water with a gasp, he rolled, stunned, onto the bank. The earth spun with a sickening movement. He tried to lift his head to focus on the road above for the demon, which he expected would soon descend, but the nauseating rise in his stomach forced him to close his eyes.

Hard breaths rose from his chest, his lungs fighting for space against his pounding heart. He felt broken, beaten, but after a short while, he dragged his legs beneath him. Lolling slightly, he crawled up toward the road against the dirt and rocks that slipped beneath his bleeding feet. There was no sign of the demon or the Roadster—no sound but insects enjoying spring.

He had to get home; no one else could protect his family. He pushed himself over the sloping plain, taking shortcuts and climbing grassy hills to stumble down the other side with the rush of his momentum, plunging through brush and thickets, not caring that his feet took the brunt of every twig and root that waited in concealment. At the top of the hill that overlooked Loveland, he collapsed on his hands and knees, panting, searching the streets in vain for the convertible Roadster.

"God, give me strength," he breathed and forced himself down the hill.

Knowing the demon was probably at his house, he continued to run block after painful block, his sweat mixing with the river water. As he approached the parsonage, fatigue slowed him to a stumbling jog until he fell on his knees before a window. Clutching its sill, he saw Edmund, Edith, Joshua, and Clara talking comfortably on the couch inside the living room. The demon was not there.

Luke slipped to the ground, leaving bloody smears on the windowsill. He closed his eyes, feeling the cool grass beneath him while the breeze caressed his broken skin. When his breath returned, he opened his eyes.

"Your head is bleeding."

Luke drew in a sharp gasp. The demon stood over him, the eyes having returned to a natural blue, the face unmarred.

"Some months ago, the court appointed Andrew Ballantine as substitute executor over the Fratelli Estate—what little was left. He ordered that the debris be sifted through and everything salvageable set aside. The fire destroyed almost everything...almost."

Kneeling, the demon wiped the blood from Luke's forehead

with its thumb to rub against its fingers, analyzing its slick texture.

"I have heard of nothing else except you the past four years. Oh, and before I forget, Angelo Carpinelli sends you his greetings. He misses you. He wishes you were there."

The demon pressed its lips tightly together, a smirk of reveling pride.

"I am Therion, the seventh demon of The Order of the Scrolls. Aeneas implored me to end your life, but I will not start my reign with the wrath of God on my head."

The demon placed its hot hand gently over Luke's eyes, closing them. Luke's panting quickened as a surge of terror rushed through him.

"Do not come after me, Prophet. Enjoy your youth. Enjoy a long life. Do not come after me."

The hand dissolved from Luke's face and he snapped his eyes open. The demon was gone.

About the Author

Born and raised in Colorado, award-winning author Nancy Wentz graduated *cum laude* from the University of Colorado. Two of her short stories, "Henry Cushing" and "Babi Yar," have won awards in the National Writers Association Short Story Contest. She has also written plays for the youth group to perform at her church and has freelanced articles for her current employer. Nancy has a great love for history and English literature and, in their pursuit, has found her creative outlet by incorporating aspects of both into her writing. Her voice is unique in that it reflects a classic nuance not typically seen in modern writing.

Nancy became a Christian in her childhood and has prayed consistently for God's will in her life. Through trials of brokenness and faith, God has shown her that He uses the most insignificant and defeated things to bring about His will and glory. This theme has been the inspiration behind much of her writing: that God chooses the foolish things of the world to confound the wise. Nancy is married and has a beautiful young son. She and her family are active members of their church.

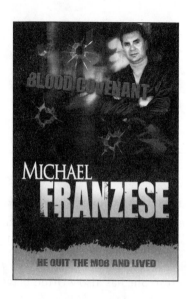

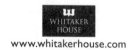

The Molech Prophecy
Thomas Phillips

Former gang member Tommy Cucinelle thought he had left his old life behind when he became a Christian. That's why he's surprised when his pastor asks him to use his discarded "skill"—finding people who don't want to be found—to locate the church secretary after she mysteriously disappears and the church is vandalized. Tommy's investigation brings him face-to-face with unpleasant memories from the past that threaten his new identity, but inner turmoil is soon the least of his worries….

ISBN: 978-1-60374-055-5 • Trade • 336 pages

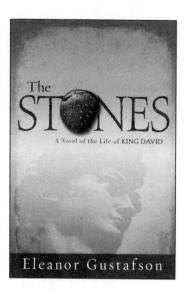

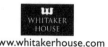